The Shore

D0976301

MORE HOT READS FROM SIMON PULSE:

Invincible Summer

Hannah Moskowitz

Kiss It

Erin Downing

Endless Summer

Jennifer Echols

Shirt and Shoes Not Required

Todd Strasser

LB (Laguna Beach)

Nola Thacker

SIMON PULSE
NEW YORK LONDON TORONTO SYDNEY

This book is a work of fiction. Any references to historical events, real people, or real locales are used fictitiously. Other names, characters, places, and incidents are the product of the author's imagination, and any resemblance to actual events or locales or persons, living or dead, is entirely coincidental.

SIMON PULSE
An imprint of Simon & Schuster Children's Publishing Division
1230 Avenue of the Americas, New York, NY 10020
This Simon Pulse paperback edition April 2011

For information about special discounts for bulk purchases, please contact Simon & Schuster Special Sales at 1-866-506-1949 or business@simonandschuster.com.
The Simon & Schuster Speakers Bureau can bring authors to your live event. For more information or to book an event contact the Simon & Schuster Speakers Bureau at 1-866-248-3049 or visit our website at www.simonspeakers.com.
Designed by Cara Petrus and Karina Granda
The text of this book was set in Caslon.
Manufactured in the United States of America
2 4 6 8 10 9 7 5 3 1
Library of Congress Control Number 2010929850
ISBN 978-1-4424-1970-4
These titles were previously published individually.

TABLE OF CONTENTS

Shirt and Shoes Not Required

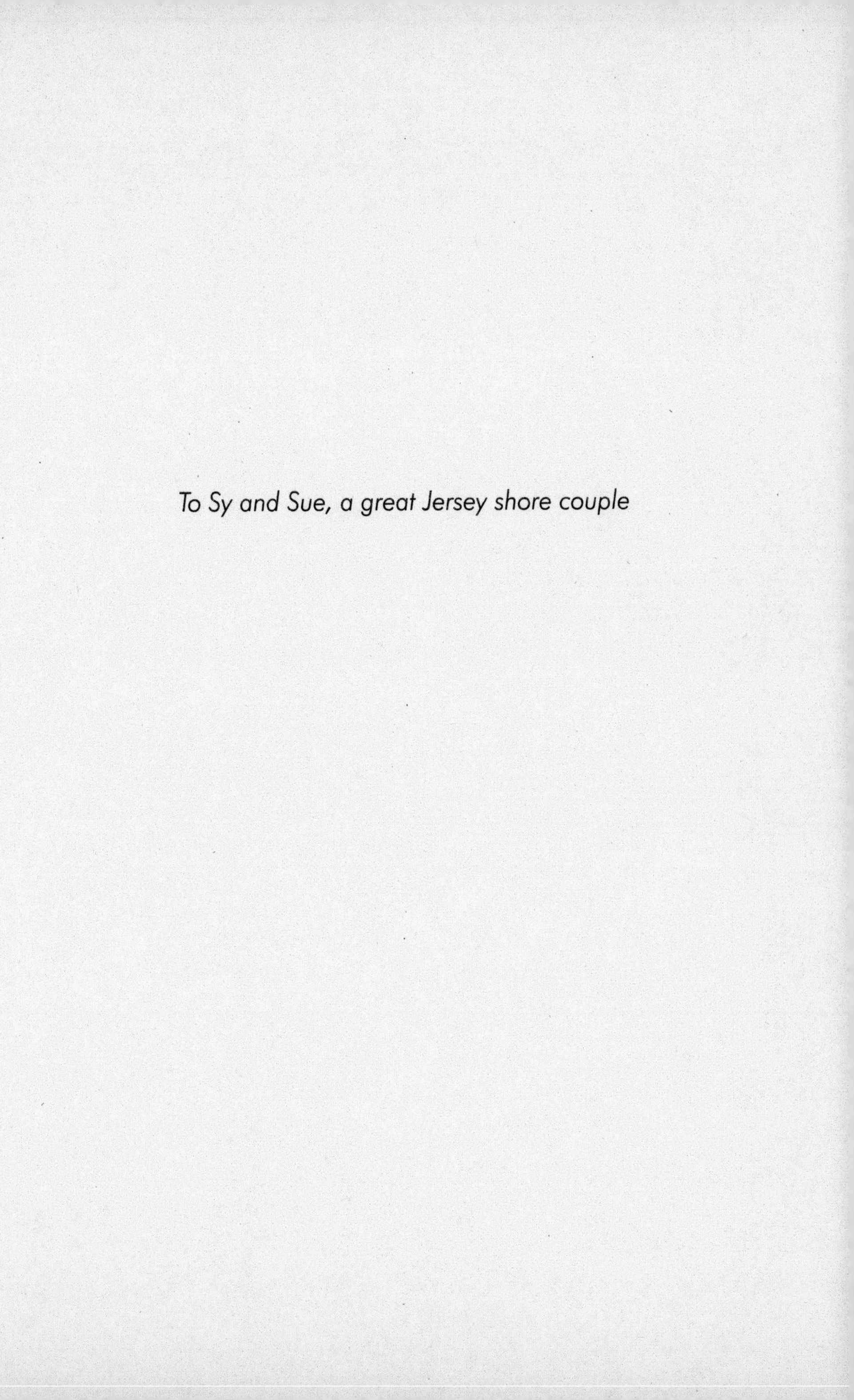

To Sy and Sue, a great Jersey shore couple

One

"School's out for . . . ever!"

Okay, so maybe it was one of the lamest songs ever to come out of the 1980s, but Avery James had to admit that thumping out of the radio in her pickup, it sounded dead-on. Driving with the windows down and the warm June breeze whipping her light brown hair, she turned the music up a little louder.

Summer, there was nothing like it. And this year, she was going to make the most of it. It was June 23, and the rest of her life stretched before her, beginning with two months of sun, sand, all-night parties—and no one checking IDs too close—to celebrate her release from the minimum-security prison known as high school.

Cruising down the road toward Wildwood, New Jersey, the salty smell of the ocean filled her nostrils and a thrill ran up her spine. *This is it!* Ever since she was a kid she had heard about the beachside community that was the summer hangout for thousands of high school and college students. Now she was finally going to see for herself.

She drove over the causeway—the breeze adding a ripple to the green water below—and into town, passing the blocks of rental houses and condos, motels, gas stations, and liquor stores that serviced vacationers. Her first impression was that every other car was a brand-new convertible or a tricked-out import complete with spoiler and rims. Compared with them, her rusty, dented red truck was almost an eyesore. But that was okay; she liked being different. A girl driving an old pickup stood out in the crowd. It didn't matter that the real reason she drove the pickup was that it was free. The truck was a hand-me-down from her uncle.

The sky was blue and cloudless, the sun big and yellow. Its rays warmed her arm in the open window. Avery tucked a strand of hair behind her ear and double-checked the addresses for the house she would be sharing. She was looking for number 15. As she drove toward the beach the numbers got lower. 93 . . . 87 . . . 81. The houses were mostly two stories and larger than she had expected. Some were freshly painted with neatly trimmed green lawns. Others were victims of the salt air and harsh winter weather—paint flaking, battered shutters hanging askew. Houses like that anywhere else might have been considered dilapidated, but here they seemed charming and rustic.

She passed number 19 and slowed the pickup, but her heart

sped up in anticipation. Seven people would be sharing the house, including her boyfriend, Curt. No parents, no rules, nothing to hold them back from having a great time. Daytime, nighttime, all the time. That was, *if* they could stand one another. She wondered what her housemates would be like. Maybe it wouldn't be important. Her cousin had once shared a house at Wildwood with three other girls and swore she never saw two of them more than five times the entire summer.

A brisk ocean breeze swept in the open window, and Avery tasted the salt in the air. She couldn't wait to get into her bathing suit. The scent of suntan lotion and ocean water mixed with the aroma of funnel cake and popcorn. *Ah, bliss!*

Her thoughts turned to Curt. He should have arrived two days ago with his band. Almost instantly the muscles in the back of her neck began to tighten with nervous tension. They'd had a fight the last time they'd seen each other because she didn't want to live in the house the other band members had rented for the summer. Curt hadn't called her cell to let her know he'd arrived, so she was pretty sure he was still annoyed. But she knew she'd made the right decision. He was so involved with that band, it was hard to get him alone. She wanted time with him this summer. It wasn't that she didn't enjoy hanging out with the other musicians; she just wanted something different, something special. As she pulled up to number 15, her new summer home, she hoped that she had found it.

Avery parked the pickup on the street outside the house.

Like most of the other houses on the street, it was two stories tall. The dull gray paint and black trim were weather-beaten but not yet flaking. What lawn there was had been recently cut, but already a few gnarly looking weeds poked up through the grass.

She pulled her cell phone out of her pocket, pressed the 2 on the speed dial, and got Curt's voice mail. His clipped message, "You know what to do," was followed by the requisite beep. "I'm here and it looks great," Avery said. She hung up and breathed in the warm air for a moment, had another thought, and hit redial. "I can't wait for you to see our place if you haven't already. . . ." She paused and found herself unwilling to hang up. The memory of their argument was fresh in her thoughts, and she didn't want their summer together to begin on a bad note. "I really think you're going to love it. We'll get to have time together and it'll be fun. I can't wait."

She got out of the truck and looked around. The street ended two houses down, and beyond that was the beach and then the vast blue green ocean stretching out to the horizon. White-tipped waves crashed on the velvety golden sand, and sprays of water looked like millions of diamonds glittering in the sunlight.

"What a dump," someone behind her muttered. Startled, Avery turned to see a girl with expertly highlighted honey blond hair, tan skin, and stormy blue eyes climbing out of a cab. She was wearing a tight pink baby doll tee with a light blue terry cloth miniskirt. While neither was see-through, they might just as well have been, given what they revealed about her drop-dead figure. She was carrying a brown Louis Vuitton overnight bag. The cabdriver opened the trunk and placed two large matching suitcases on the curb.

"Ahem." He cleared his throat and held out his hand.

The blonde gave him a perplexed look.

"I don't drive for free, sweetcakes," said the cabbie.

Where Avery would have apologized like mad for the oversight, the blonde merely looked annoyed as she opened her bag and paid him.

"Ahem." The driver cleared his throat again.

The blonde gave him an exasperated "Now what?" look.

"You ever heard of a tip?" he asked.

Rolling her eyes dramatically and acting as if he'd just asked her for one of her kidneys, she opened her purse and pulled out a hundred-dollar bill. "Got change?"

The driver frowned. "That's all you got?"

"Sorry." The blonde stuck the bill back in her purse.

Muttering to himself, the cabbie got into the cab. Avery couldn't help but feel a bit shocked that the blonde had stiffed the guy. From the looks of things, she could have easily afforded the tip.

"Excuse me." Leaving the matching luggage on the sidewalk, the blonde pushed past Avery. *Pretentious blue blood,* Avery thought. *The kind who spends a thousand dollars on designer clothes tailor-made to give the wearer a casual, just-thrown-together look. What is she doing renting a room in this place? Mommy and Daddy can probably afford to buy her a beach house of her own.*

The blonde rang the doorbell. Almost instantly it was opened by a guy who looked about twenty years old. It seemed to Avery that he must have been waiting for the knock. His straight brown hair fell down his forehead, almost into his eyes, and he was wearing a white T-shirt, and green plaid shorts that revealed pale, bony arms and legs. The black socks and shoes did little to enhance the look. Behind his thick, black-rimmed glasses his eyes sparkled with excitement.

The blonde wrinkled her nose. "You're . . . not one of my new roommates, are you?"

"No, I'm Fred, your landlord," he said, extending his hand.

"Oh! The landlord! So nice to meet you!" The blonde's frown turned into a smile, and her voice became sweet. "Sabrina Morganthal," she said, taking his hand in hers instead of shaking it. "Would you be a dear and help me with my bags? They're too heavy for me, but I'm sure they'd be no problem for you."

It was Avery's turn to roll her eyes. *She has to be kidding. Fred may look a little dense, but he has to see that she's playing him!*

All Fred seemed to see was Sabrina's hand holding his, and the bare arm, and amazing body behind it. He smiled wide. "My pleasure."

Sabrina batted her eyes. "Oh, thank you. I really appreciate it." She sailed past him and into the house.

It was hard to believe how quickly Sabrina had gone from being rude to the cabdriver to sugary sweet with Fred. The poor guy practically tripped over himself in his rush to get her bags. He didn't even notice Avery on the walk as he dashed past her and tried to pick up both bags at once.

"Uhhh!" He grunted and struggled to drag them up the walk. Meanwhile, Avery went inside the house. Sabrina was standing in the middle of the living room with her back toward her and her hands on her hips, surveying the place. Avery immediately liked the way the light streamed through the windows. The walls were painted a pale seafoam green, and the carpet was the color of sand. The living room had two sofas, three comfortable chairs, and a television set.

"Decorated it myself," Fred announced proudly once he made it inside and let go of the bags. "Well, with a little help from my mom. The entertainment center has a wide-screen TV, DVD/VCR with Surround Sound. The CD player holds twelve disks. *And* we've got Wi-Fi. Nice, huh?"

"Fabulous," Sabrina said with feigned enthusiasm. Avery wasn't particularly interested in the entertainment center. Instead, she focused on the staircase that led up to a second-floor landing. She could see several doors, no doubt bedrooms.

"And over here is the kitchen." Fred was still giving Sabrina the guided tour.

"You don't say," Sabrina replied. "I never would have guessed."

Avery bit her lip to keep from laughing. Fred couldn't be more than a year or two older than her. This must have been his first venture into real estate, and he was too eager to please.

Sabrina flipped her hair in that way that seemed to come naturally to beautiful girls. People had told Avery she was beautiful, but she'd never quite believed it. Maybe that was why she wasn't blessed with awesome hair flippage.

Meanwhile, Sabrina was getting impatient with Fred's house tour. "Can we get to the bedroom already?"

An astonished look spread over Fred's face. It suddenly occurred to Avery that he might have misunderstood the statement, especially if one believed all those stories about how wild "summer girls" could be. She clapped a hand over her mouth to keep from laughing while Fred moved toward Sabrina, almost as if he was going to embrace her, clearly misreading her intentions.

Before he could get too close, Sabrina raised a hand to stop him. "Isn't there something you should take care of first?"

Fred scowled, raising one eyebrow, then the other, clearly wracking his brain to figure out what she meant. Meanwhile, Sabrina laid a hand gently on Fred's arm. "I meant, my bags, Freddy. Someone has to get them upstairs."

"Oh . . . uh, right. Right!" Fred hurried for the bags while Sabrina, with the air of a queen, went up the stairs.

Avery's cell phone rang. "Hello?"

"Hey, baby." It was Curt, and he sounded like he was in a

good mood. She felt a tingle of relief. "Got your message. You seen our room yet?"

"Not yet. The landlord's got his hands full with one of the other renters," she said ruefully.

"Okay, I'll be there in ten."

"I love you," she said.

He'd already hung up. Well, at least he'd sounded happy. She closed her phone and slid it back into her pocket. Fred came past with Sabrina's bags.

"Excuse me," Avery said. "I'm Avery James."

"Be right with you." Fred lugged one bag up to the second-floor landing, then turned and hurried back down for the second.

"I'm also renting here this summer," Avery said.

"In a minute," Fred gasped under the strain of the heavy bag, his forehead beginning to glisten with sweat as he headed back up the stairs.

Annoyed, Avery seated herself on the couch and listened to the sound of footsteps and doors opening and closing as Sabrina inspected the upstairs bedrooms and Fred tagged along. It was only when she heard footsteps coming back down the stairs that she looked up.

"—and that's why I need the big bedroom, sugar," Sabrina purred to him as he followed Sabrina down the steps.

The big bedroom? Avery felt a jolt, then stood up and cleared her throat. "Excuse me? Fred? I thought my boyfriend and I are supposed to have the large bedroom."

Fred stopped and looked flustered and confused. "Oh, gee. I'm sorry, she . . ." He gestured toward Sabrina but then trailed off, like he wasn't sure what to say.

"We paid for that room in advance," Avery stated, trying to sound forceful but fearing that she sounded wimpy.

Fred bit his lip and glanced over at Sabrina, who gave him a coy smile and batted her eyes. He turned back to Avery. "I'm really sorry, but she was here first. If it's the money you're worried about, I'll refund the difference."

Now Avery was pissed. "Actually, I was here first. But she pushed past me. And my boyfriend has been in town for two days, but you told us we couldn't check in until today, so he waited."

Again Fred's eyes slid to Sabrina. Avery realized that he was under her spell and there was probably nothing she could say that would make a difference. She took a deep breath and calmed herself. She was here to have a good time this summer, not make enemies on the very first day. Besides there had to be another decent bedroom. If Curt didn't like it, she'd let him work it out with Fred.

"I get to pick the next bedroom," Avery said. "No matter who shows up next."

"I promise," Fred replied. Having put out that fire, he sidled over to Sabrina. "So, uh, I was wondering if you had any plans. . . ."

Sabrina gave him puppy dog eyes. "Oh, Freddy, I just

remembered I promised a friend that I'd meet her on the beach."

Disappointment spread over Fred's face, but he quickly caught himself. "Yeah, okay, maybe later?"

"You're a sweetheart." Sabrina gave him a peck on the cheek and ran back upstairs to her room. *Which had been my room,* Avery reminded herself bitterly, then sighed. *Oh, come on, get over it. It's not worth ruining your first day for.* She went outside to get her bags out of the truck. The sun was strong, and she liked the feeling of heat on her head and arms. *This is going to be a great summer.*

Then she heard the voice that she hoped was going to make it so great. "Hey, baby." It was Curt, strolling toward her on the sidewalk. Tall and lanky, he took his time, with that slightly disheveled look that made it seem like he'd just woken up. His black hair was tousled, and he wore baggy jeans and a black long-sleeved Metalhead T-shirt that was so wrinkled, it looked slept in. He had a bag slung over his shoulder and a couple day's growth of dark stubble on his jaw. Comparisons to Colin Farrell were not out of the question.

She threw her arms around him, and he dropped his eyes down to hers. They were dark like his hair and smoldered with an inner fire. "Miss me?" he half asked, half growled in the voice that always made her heart pound. He wrapped his arms around her and kissed her. In the heat in his kiss she tasted something unexpected and pulled back. "Drinking already?"

Here we go, Curt thought, annoyed. They'd hardly been together a minute and Avery was already upset about something. What was the big deal, anyway? He'd only had a beer. So what if it was the middle of the day? She probably thought he was just goofing off, and didn't understand how hard he'd been working to get his band, Stranger Than Fiction, or STF, ready for a summer of shoreline gigs. The afternoon beer was just a way to relax a little, cut through the tension and stress of trying to get the guys in STF to rehearse. Especially when they were so close to the beach, beautiful water, and lots of babes in bikinis. Avery would understand soon enough. In the meantime, he wanted to check out the house where she'd insisted they stay this summer instead of with the band. He had to admit that from the outside, at least, the place looked nice, nicer than the dump his bandmates were renting.

"They're a corrupting influence," Avery said, referring to the other members of STF. She was only half teasing.

"That's what they say about you," he replied, also only half teasing. He slid his fingers through her soft brown hair. He liked the way her eyes sparkled when she gazed up at him. *Like I'm the only guy in the world.*

She let go of him and moved to the back of the pickup and began unhooking the tarp. He got on the other side to help her. "You bring the rest of my stuff?" he asked.

"Of course." She paused. "Where's Lucille?"

Lucille was not a person, it was a cherry red 1975 Fender

Stratocaster guitar and, Avery sometimes suspected, the closest "woman" to Curt's heart.

"I'm going to keep her at the other house," Curt answered. "It's easier than hauling her back and forth."

"Oh." Avery averted her eyes and busied herself with the bags, but Curt knew she was disappointed. It was some dumb symbolic thing to her, like if he left his guitar with the band, then he wasn't entirely there with her.

A nerdy-looking guy with brown hair and black-framed glasses came out of the rental house. He was wearing plaid shorts with black socks and shoes. "You two moving in?"

"Fred, this is my boyfriend, Curt," Avery said. "Curt, this is Fred. He's our landlord."

Curt was surprised. While nerds often had an ageless quality, this Fred guy didn't look much older than he was. Kind of young to own properties.

"How did you know my name?" Fred asked Avery.

She looked stunned. "I'm Avery, remember? We just met. You know, inside, when that other girl stole our room?"

"Someone else got our room?" Curt asked with a frown.

"Oh, uh, I'm really sorry about that," Fred said sheepishly. "Like I said, I'll refund the difference in rent to you, and I'll be glad to show you the other rooms right now."

Curt bristled. Half the reason he'd agreed to stay here instead of with the band was that Avery had told him she'd found a really nice room for them. "You mean someone else snagged our room and you didn't do anything about it?"

"I tried," Avery mumbled.

Curt knew Avery wasn't real big about asserting herself, but given what a wimp this Fred nerd was, he thought he could take advantage of the situation. Curt narrowed his eyes menacingly at the landlord. "We paid for that room in advance. You had no right to give it away."

"Look, I said I'm sorry and I'll refund the difference," Fred answered uncomfortably. "I'll let you have the next best room."

"I think you'll have to do better than that," Curt said with just a hint of a threat in his voice.

"I . . . I don't understand what you mean . . . ," Fred stammered.

"Think about it," Curt said.

"Oh, well, I guess I could give you a discount on the other room," Fred said.

Curt smiled. "There you go."

"Let me show you what I've got." Fred turned and led them into the house. Curt grabbed a couple of bags from the back of the pickup, and he and Avery followed.

"I still think we should bag this whole thing and stay with the band," Curt muttered to Avery as they entered the house.

"I want us to have more privacy," Avery replied.

"Privacy?" Curt scoffed. "In a house full of strangers, that's a good one."

She turned scarlet but didn't say anything. Curt sighed. The whole situation was lame.

Inside they followed Fred up the staircase to the second-floor landing. Suddenly a hot-looking blonde came out of the room at the end of the hall, wearing a pink bikini top and pastel green shorts. Curt felt his eyes bulge. She was gorgeous and had a killer bod, top and bottom. If she was one of his roommates, he suddenly had a whole new reason for staying here. The blonde smiled warmly at Fred, then flounced past them on her way to the stairs. When she passed Curt, he caught a whiff of perfume that had to be expensive. Even better, she brushed against him in a way that let him know she had done it on purpose. As she passed, he couldn't help imagining what she'd look like with less clothing.

"Was that the big bedroom she came out of?" Curt asked after the blonde had passed.

"Yes," Fred said, sounding miserable.

"I want to see it," Curt said.

"Why?" Fred asked.

"So I know I'm really getting a discount on the piece of crap room we wind up with."

Fred's shoulders sagged. "Uh, sure."

Curt smiled. He was gonna talk this wimp down until they got a room almost for free. But when they reached the door of the big bedroom, they discovered that it was locked.

"You've got a spare key, right?" Curt said.

"Uh, no, I don't," Fred said, shrugging and looking embarrassed.

Curt rolled his eyes. What kind of landlord didn't keep spare keys? This guy Fred was a joke.

"Here, this room is the next largest," Fred said, hastening to open another door on the landing. This room wasn't much larger than Curt's bedroom at home, with only a double bed and a small dresser. The walls were drab, and the carpet was worn in spots. On the other hand, it was clean and it smelled okay, which was a major improvement over the rooms in the house where the other members of STF were staying.

"How much is it?" Curt asked.

"Eighteen hundred for the summer," Fred said.

Curt narrowed his eyes. "So what are you gonna do for us?"

Fred started to squirm, and a line of sweat formed on his upper lip. "I . . . I could give it to you for, say, fourteen hundred."

"That's not good enough," Curt said. "You broke your promise, remember?"

Fred swallowed. "Twelve hundred?"

Curt shook his head. It almost wasn't about the money. It was about making this guy pay for not upholding his half of the deal. Now it was a challenge to watch this guy squirm and see how low he would go.

"A thousand?" Fred asked.

"Still not good enough," Curt growled even though inside he was laughing. At this rate they would get the room for nothing.

"No," Avery interrupted. "A thousand is fine. That's a very fair price, and we appreciate it."

Fred sighed with relief, but Curt was annoyed with Avery.

"Well, good, I'm glad we settled that," Fred said, handing them a key to the room. "Just promise me you won't tell any of the other renters, okay? This is our secret."

Curt and Avery went back downstairs and out to the pickup to bring in the rest of their gear.

"Why'd you do that?" Curt asked. "I probably could have gotten him down to nothing."

"It wasn't fair," Avery said. "He's trying to run a business, not a charity."

"Well, it wasn't fair of him to give away our room," Curt argued.

"He made a mistake," Avery said. "That doesn't mean you have to crucify him. Let's have a good summer, Curt, please? It's about having fun, not winning every battle."

Typical Avery, Curt thought. Always running from a fight. Never standing up for what she deserved. "You can't let people step all over you," he shot back.

"What are you talking about?" Avery asked. "He didn't step all over me. We got that other room for a bargain, and you know it."

With the last of the gear, Curt followed her into the house and up the stairs. In their new room, he dumped the stuff on their bed. "You'll put everything away?" he asked.

Avery looked up, surprised. "What?"

Curt broke into a smile. "Just kidding." He slid his hands around her waist and pulled her close. Her breasts pressed against his chest, and he breathed in her sweet scent. "I figured if you let Fred take advantage of you, you'd let me, too." It had been nearly a week since he'd held her this close and he could feel the growing desire mute any lingering annoyance he felt toward her for letting the blonde get their room.

Avery kissed him, but when his hands began to wander, she pulled back. "You can take advantage of me later," she whispered. "In ways that Fred will never know. But for now, help me unpack."

They started opening bags and putting things away. Even though he'd just as soon live out of a suitcase for the summer, Curt knew Avery enjoyed doing stuff like this. To him it was a little like playing house, but if she got a bang out of it, he was glad to oblige . . . up to a point. After a while other concerns began to nag him. The band wasn't ready. Their songs weren't ready. Shouldn't he be spending his time and energy on that?

"I better get back over there, Ave," he said. "The band's still got a long way to go and we should be rehearsing."

"Oh, okay." Avery hung her head, clearly disappointed.

"Hey, I'll be back later." Curt took her in his arms. "And if you're a good girl, I might just let you take advantage of me."

She smiled. "You should be so lucky."

"No, *you* should be so lucky." He kissed her hard and held her tightly, knowing she liked it when he lingered.

Soon enough, he left the room and headed back down the

stairs. He was just going out the front door when a girl came up pulling a heavy black suitcase on wheels. She had reddish, neatly bobbed hair and was wearing a baggy pink polo shirt with pleated khaki shorts. She looked like the kind of preppy girl who'd be class secretary.

"Excuse me," she panted. "You wouldn't know if the bathrooms are working, would you?"

"What?" Curt said, taken by surprise.

"I was warned that plumbing on this street can be kind of a problem. My cousin said she once rented a room in number twelve and they had to use a Porta Potti for half the summer."

"No kidding?" Curt said.

"So, can you tell me if they're working," the preppy girl said. "And if they're not, when they might be?"

"How should I know?" he asked, trying to figure out what was up with her.

"Aren't you"—she gave him a once-over, taking in his clothes—"like, a workman or . . . something?"

Now Curt understood. "No, I happen to be moving in here," he answered indignantly.

The girl raised her hand to her mouth. "Oh, my gosh, I'm so sorry. I didn't realize . . . wait, *you're* living here this summer?"

"Yeah, and your point is?" Curt replied. She was starting to annoy him.

"It's just that, so am I," she said, her brown eyes wide. "We're roomies!"

"Well, hey, that's just fabulous," he said, with feigned excitement. Unlike the hot blonde, this one was nothing to get excited about.

"Yeah, hi!" she answered even more excitedly. "Listen, I'm Polly." She offered her hand.

"And I'm Curt." He shook it.

"Look, I'm really sorry about what I said before," Polly gushed. "I just . . . well . . . the truth is, I have this way of putting my foot in my mouth."

No kidding, Curt thought.

"I mean, I do it all the time," Polly went on. "It's really best not to pay any attention to me."

Can't say I was planning to, Curt thought.

"Just ignore me and I'll go away," Polly said. "Also, another thing is, when I get nervous, I talk too much, you know?"

"I'm kind of figuring that out," Curt said. It was not unusual for girls to become nervous around him. And while this one definitely had the potential to be annoying, he couldn't help enjoying the idea that he had the looks that provoked it.

"Well . . ." Polly bit her lip, "I guess I'll go inside and see if the toilet's working, you know? So, uh, see you around, *roomie*."

He went past her and out to the street. *Roomie?* He was pretty certain no one had ever called him that before. Could he really spend an entire summer sharing a house with someone like that? She'd probably have them all singing "Kumbaya" around the campfire if she had her way.

He started for the band's house, but found his thoughts drifting back to number 15 and that hot blond babe who'd brushed against him. The good news was that he'd probably be seeing plenty of her around the house. And *that* was something to look forward to.

Polly brushed off the encounter with the moody but great-looking guy. It bothered her when she got nervous and began to blather, but this was the first day of summer and she wasn't about to let him or anyone else spoil it. She was frightened and excited the way someone feels just before they do something wonderful and unexpected, and scary. That's what this whole summer was going to be. She had never lived away from home before. Even after her freshman year of college she'd still commuted from her parents' house nearby. This summer that was going to change. She had made up her mind. She was going to do something on her own, and it was going to be wild and crazy. She entered the house. There were three doors off the living room, and the closest one to the stairs was a bathroom.

Polly went in and checked it out. The walls were painted white to match the tile. On the far wall there was a white shower curtain pulled across a combination shower-tub. Most importantly, the toilet flushed! Delighted that the plumbing worked, Polly was checking her hair and lipstick in the mirror when she heard voices. She came out to find a nerdy-looking guy with thick black glasses coming down the stairs. He was dressed in a white V-necked T-shirt, and green plaid shorts, with black socks and shoes. *Oh, please don't be one of my roommates,* Polly thought. All she wanted was one cute guy in the house. The tall, handsome guy had been too good-looking (a girl had to be realistic, she told herself), and this one seemed too far on the other end of the spectrum. *What are the chances of meeting Mr. Perfect?* Her summer plans involved a guy, but not just any guy; it had to be the right guy.

"Uh, hi." The nerdy guy seemed puzzled to find her coming out of the bathroom.

"Hi, I'm Polly Prentice," she introduced herself. "I'm renting a room here this summer?"

"Oh, yes," the guy said. "I've been expecting you. I'm Fred, your landlord."

"Oh, that's . . . er . . . very nice," Polly said, relieved that he wasn't one of her new roommates.

"Let me show you your room," Fred said. "It's down here."

Polly had one of the two downstairs bedrooms with entrances off the living room. The good news was that it was right next to the bathroom. She paused on the threshold of her room and took it in. It wasn't huge but it wasn't a cracker box either. The important thing was that it was all hers. There was a nice double bed with a white comforter and fluffy-looking pillows. A window looked out right onto the next street over. Not exactly ocean view, but, hey, at least the ocean was nearby.

She smiled. It was a perfect blank slate, and she was going to have a great time making it hers.

"So what do you think?" Fred asked behind her.

"Could I do a little decorating?" she asked. "Like maybe some shells from the beach? I could use the bigger ones to hold things like my jewelry and makeup. And stick the smaller shells around my mirror—"

"No glue on the walls!" Fred interrupted, sounding aghast.

"Oh, of course not," Polly quickly agreed. "I'll stick them with putty. By the way, was that a Wi-Fi router I saw by the cable box?"

Suddenly Fred brightened. "You bet. I just installed it," he announced proudly.

"Great!" Polly gushed. "I brought my laptop. This is going to be so much fun!"

They smiled at each other. But then the silence became awkward. Polly had the oddest feeling. Fred might not have been the best-looking guy around, but they shared some sort of connection. "Uh-oh. I'm going to start babbling," Polly warned him. "When I'm nervous, I tend to talk too much. Everything that's inside comes tumbling out. Some people say I overshare, but I just think I communicate well."

"Hey, I'm all ears," Fred said eagerly. "Babble away."

She glanced at Fred under her eyelashes and tried to make her next question sound casual. "So, how many guys will be living here this summer?"

"Three. And four girls, including you."

"Are . . . you going to be living here?" she asked.

"No," he said, then added, "but I'll probably be around a lot. You know, fixing stuff."

Polly quickly did the math. There were still two male roommates left. *Always good to keep your options open,* she thought as she went outside to retrieve her luggage from her car. A little while later, back in her room, she began to unpack, hanging up a few sundresses and putting everything else into drawers. She wondered for a moment what to do with her toiletries. Given that her bathroom was downstairs and liable to be used by everybody, she decided it was safer to leave her little bag in her room.

Satisfied, she left the room, hoping to meet some of her other roommates. A pretty girl with long brown hair was coming down the stairs. Polly admired the way the other girl's hair just seemed to float about her when she moved, and wished that she could get her own red hair to do something as nice. "Hi! I'm Polly," she said. "Are you one of the summer renters?"

"Yes." The other girl smiled and offered her hand. "Avery," she said. "Nice to meet you."

Polly was relieved by the other girl's friendly warmth. "So have you met any of the others?"

"Well, sort of," Avery answered. "Just first impressions, you know?"

"Oh, do I." Polly dropped her voice conspiratorially. "I just met this guy outside, dressed all in black. Good-looking, but kind of moody. And weird—I mean, who wears a long-sleeved black T-shirt at the beach?"

The girl named Avery smiled painfully. "That would be my boyfriend, Curt."

Polly lost her breath. *Oh, no! Foot in mouth again!* "I am *so* sorry!" she gasped. "Sometimes I just don't know what I'm saying. Like you said, first impressions, right? Of course I'm sure he's a wonderful guy. And since you two just got here, he wouldn't have had time to change into his beach clothes."

"Actually those are his beach clothes," Avery said, still smiling.

"All right, then just shoot me." Polly felt a wave of humiliation wash through her.

To her relief, Avery laughed. "Believe me, you're not the first person to notice that Curt is a little dark. He takes a while with strangers, but once you get to know him, he'll lighten up. After all, we're all just here to have fun, right?"

Polly smiled back. "Definitely. So you haven't seen any of the other guys who will be living here, have you?"

"Not yet."

"I hope they're nice," Polly confided. "And tall and strong and gorgeous. Of course, also sweet and gentlemanly."

"So, uh, let me guess," Avery teased good-naturedly, "you'd like to meet someone?"

Before Polly could answer, they were interrupted by

knocking on the front door. Polly went to open it. Outside was a good-looking, bare-chested guy with long, bleached-blond dreadlocks, a bright red surfboard under one arm, and a very large bong under the other.

"Hey." He had an easy smile. "This the rental house?"

"Yes," Polly said, staring incredulously at the bong.

"Looks pretty good." The blond guy gazed over her head into the house.

"You're . . . renting here too?" Polly asked.

"Sure am," he said. "I'm Lucas Haubenstock."

"Polly Prentice," Polly replied, thinking, *Two down, one to go.* The prospects were dimming quickly. He might have been good-looking in a laid-back California kind of way, but the dreadlocks and bong were definitely not her thing.

"Think I could come in?" Lucas asked. "This stuff's getting heavy."

"Oh, sorry." Polly moved out of the way. Lucas stepped in. As he did, the skeg of his surfboard bumped Polly, and she jumped back in surprise.

"Sorry, didn't mean to clip you," he said.

"That's okay" Polly said, giving him a closer look. He was wearing board shorts and Tevas. His bare chest was bronzed and thin, but muscular. She found herself starting to look where she shouldn't have, then swallowed and forced herself to look away. On second thought, she might not be crazy about the hair and bong, but the rest of him wasn't bad at all.

Once inside, Lucas put the board and bong down and looked around. Avery came out of the kitchen, and Polly introduced them.

"Nice house," Lucas said. "Would either of you know where the owner is?"

"Right here."

They turned to find Fred coming in carrying an armload of pillows. He dropped them on the couch and offered his hand to Lucas. "I'm Fred."

"Lucas Haubenstock."

"Right. From Princeton." Fred glanced at the board and bong and frowned. Then he looked back at Lucas. "Isn't there some economist up there with that name? I think I read his book in college."

"People have asked me about that before," Lucas said. "He might be some kind of distant relative or something."

Polly listened to the exchange with interest. Not only was Lucas good-looking, but he seemed easygoing and nice and had an unusual aura of confidence that she found appealing. Like Avery said, you couldn't always trust first impressions. Maybe Lucas was worth taking a second look at. She'd just have to see.

Fred took Lucas to see his room, and Polly turned to Avery. "Thirsty?"

"Yeah, actually," Avery said. She and Polly went into the kitchen. It was apricot colored and cheerful. An island in the center provided extra counter space. On the refrigerator were a few colorful magnets holding menus from places that delivered. One showed a slice of pizza with legs and arms dancing with a can of soda and proudly proclaimed: “Even the pizzas are partying at Pop’s!” Avery had a feeling she would definitely be dialing that phone number.

Since her mom had died Avery had spent a lot of time in kitchens and she moved through this one easily. There were six cabinets, and she opened all of them before she found the glasses. She handed one to Polly and grabbed one for herself. They filled them up with tap water and raised them toward each other in a toast.

“To a great summer,” Avery said.

“The best ever.”

They both drank, then made faces.

“Not the best tap water I ever tasted,” Polly said.

“We better add bottled water to the shopping list,” Avery agreed.

“Think I could have a bedroom downstairs?” they heard Lucas ask Fred.

“How come?” Fred said.

“I’d rather not have to carry my board up and down the stairs,” Lucas explained. “And there’ll be less chance of dinging your walls.”

Considerate, Avery thought. She sometimes wished Curt would be more like that.

"Okay, you can take the second room on the ground floor," they heard Fred tell Lucas.

"Sweet," was Lucas's answer.

In the kitchen, Avery leaned close to Polly. "How long until Fred asks Lucas about the bong?" she whispered.

Polly grinned.

A moment later, as if Fred had heard her, they heard him ask nervously, "You're . . . um . . . not planning on using that thing in the house, are you?"

"The bong? It's just for show. Artwork, you know?" they heard Lucas reply.

"Somehow I doubt that," Avery said under her breath.

Polly looked at her with eyes wide. "You think!?"

In that moment, Avery realized that Polly was even more naive than she looked.

"Didn't look like any artwork I've ever seen," Avery whispered.

But from the sound of things, Fred was satisfied with the answer because he and Lucas moved on to other subjects.

"He seems awfully nice for a stoner," Polly said in a low voice, not that she'd known many stoners in her life.

Avery nodded. "You never know."

The front door opened, and a girl walked in carrying a large blue backpack and a guitar case. She had long, straight black hair framing a pale face, and a silver nose stud. Her eyes were heavily mascaraed, and she wore a tight-fitting black shirt, high black lace-up boots, and striped leggings under a black skirt cropped to reveal a belly button piercing.

"It's Morticia from the Addams Family," Polly whispered, and Avery giggled.

The new girl had not yet noticed Polly and Avery in the kitchen. Inside the front door she put down the guitar case and unslung the backpack. "Hello? Anyone here?"

Avery watched as Fred left Lucas in his room, dashed across the living room, and greeted the new girl. "Hi, I'm Fred, the landlord," he said.

"April," the new girl said, and offered her hand.

"Here, let me help you." Fred reached for her backpack. "Whoa!" It must have been heavier than he'd expected because he nearly fell over backward trying to pull it on.

"Tell you what," April said, taking the backpack from him. "You carry the guitar."

Avery and Polly watched as Fred escorted her upstairs.

"Only one roommate left," Avery mused out loud.

"I thought there were two more," Polly said. "I counted three girls and two guys."

"You missed Sabrina. She left before you got here."

"What's she like?" Polly asked.

Avery had some ideas, but wasn't willing to go public just yet. "Uh, she's got really pretty clothes."

"And?" Polly asked with a frown.

"And she's pretty," Avery said awkwardly.

Before Polly could press her any further, Fred came back downstairs.

"Well, it looks like a great group of people," he said, his voice sounding strained. "I've gotta go. Now, remember, if there are any problems with the house—*any* problems—just give me a call. My number's on the fridge."

Fred excused himself and exited the front door. Avery and Polly were just finishing their water when the front door swung open and Curt strolled in carrying a six-pack of beer in his left hand and a half-empty bottle in a brown paper bag in his right.

Avery narrowed her eyes. *What is this new deal about drinking in the middle of the afternoon? And what happened to the rehearsal?* Still, she was determined not to say anything that would get him mad. Not now, at the beginning of their summer together. Curt came into the kitchen, gave Polly a look, then pecked Avery on the cheek and deposited the six-pack in the fridge.

"How'd the rehearsal go?" Avery asked.

"Eh." Curt shrugged. "Guys took off for the beach. We're never gonna get anywhere if they don't get serious."

"Well, it's the beach and it's new," Avery said. "Maybe in another week it'll be easier to get them to stay outside."

"Excuse me," Polly said. "I'm just curious. Was that beer yours, or for everyone?"

"Mine," Curt answered with a scowl. "Oh, you want one?"

"No, thanks," said Polly. "I was just wondering how it's going to work."

"How what's going to work?" Avery asked curiously.

"Well, like whose stuff is whose and what's what," Polly explained.

Curt frowned at Avery as if he didn't know what Polly was talking about.

Avery had to admit that she wasn't certain either.

"Maybe we should set up regular roommate meetings," Polly continued, "starting tonight so that we can all get to know one another and set some house rules. Most of us are here right now. We could get Lucas and April down here and discuss it."

"Lucas and April?" Curt repeated.

"Two of our new roommates," Avery explained.

Curt rolled his eyes and put down his empty beer. Then he opened the refrigerator, grabbed a new bottle, and twisted the cap off. He tossed the bottle cap onto the counter and took a long swig. Avery watched uncomfortably and didn't say anything. Meanwhile Polly stared at the bottle cap and the empty bottle and then back at Curt.

It was obvious to Avery that Polly wanted Curt to clean up his garbage. Frankly, it seemed a little anal that she expected him to do it right away. And, anyway, Curt didn't appear to notice. Polly let out a big sigh, grabbed the bottle cap, and tossed it in the trash. Then she picked up the empty bottle with two fingers and rinsed it out in the sink before setting it aside, presumably for recycling.

Curt smiled ruefully, and Avery felt embarrassed. "So, uh, what exactly do you propose discussing?" he asked.

Avery knew he was being sarcastic, but Polly mistook it for genuine interest.

"Recycling, for one," she said. "We should ask Fred where the recycling bins are."

Curt glanced at Avery and smirked. Avery braced herself. Sometimes when he drank he could get a little mean. Especially when he was frustrated with the band.

"And we need to discuss care and upkeep of the house," Polly continued. "Divide up chores. We need to all pitch in to keep the place neat and clean as a courtesy to others. We should also establish rules for the kitchen and food sharing. I figure we can each get half a shelf in the fridge for our own stuff, and community stuff can go in the door."

Curt opened the refrigerator and gestured toward the six-pack sitting in the middle of the top shelf. "Me and Ave'll take the top shelf."

Avery winced. He was starting to sound a little drunk. What a great way to kick off their summer.

"Okay, good," Polly said. "I'll take the left side of the middle shelf."

"Wonderful," Curt said with feigned enthusiasm. "I'm so glad we got that out of the way."

A door closed, and they turned to see Lucas come out of his room. He'd put on a bright yellow T-shirt with a picture of a surfboard on it. He saw Curt in the kitchen and came over to shake his hand. "Lucas Haubenstock," he said.

"Curt Wilson."

"I'm glad you're here, Lucas," Polly said. "We're just having a roommate discussion."

"I'd really like to stay, but I have to get over to the surf shop," Lucas answered. "My shift starts in ten minutes. Maybe someone could fill me in later?"

"Gnarly, dude," Curt said facetiously.

Lucas scowled at him, then waved good-bye. "Catch you guys later."

Polly looked disappointed, and Avery felt sorry for her. She was trying to do something good for all of them, but not getting very far.

"Go on. What else?" Avery said, giving Polly some encouragement and ignoring the dirty look that Curt fired her way.

"I think we should also discuss parties, noise levels, quiet hours, that sort of thing." Polly had to raise her voice because of some sort of commotion outside—shouting and laughing. It sounded to Avery like a group of rowdy guys out on the street—maybe getting an early start on their partying. They didn't pass by, though. Instead, they got louder as if approaching the front door.

The front door swung open, and in walked a guy wearing a white Abercrombie polo shirt with the collar turned up and khaki cargo pants. He had dark brown hair, a beer in one hand, and seemed to be leading the group, gesturing grandly and waving his arms around as the others filed in behind him. Suddenly there were a dozen people in the living room all talking and laughing.

"These your new digs?" someone asked him.

"Is right," he answered as he surveyed the living room.

"Hey, nice," said someone else.

"Where's the stereo?" asked a third.

"There a CD player anywhere?"

Polly, Avery, and Curt watched from the kitchen.

"You know any of these people?" Polly asked Avery and Curt, who shook their heads.

A husky, broad-shouldered, football player type with a diamond stud in his ear came into the kitchen and looked in the fridge "Got any ice?"

"Who are you?" Polly asked.

"Martin, who are you?"

"I'm Polly and I live here, do you?"

"In this dump? No way."

"Can I ask what you're doing here?" Polly said.

Martin gave her a strange look, then gestured at the crowd. "What's it look like?"

Just then two guys came in the front door carrying a half keg of beer.

"Hey, where's the keg go?" one yelled.

"Ask Owen." The guy named Martin pointed at polo shirt guy.

"This is ridiculous!" Polly declared. Avery watched with surprise as she marched up to the guy named Owen. "Are these your friends?"

"Who wants to know?" Owen asked with an amused look.

"I do."

"And you are?"

"Polly, and I live here."

"Hey, roomie!" Owen grinned and raised his hand for a high five. "I'm Owen, and guess what? I live here too!"

Polly didn't high-five his hand. "So these are your friends?"

Owen squinted at the crowd. "Well, let's see. Some of them are . . . I think. Some of them I never saw before in my life."

"Don't you think it's a bit . . . rude . . . to bring them all here without asking?"

Way to go, Polly, Avery thought, impressed.

"Rude?" Owen scowled at her. "Who are you, my mother? Whoa, loosen up, honey, you need a drink."

"But I don't—" Polly's protest was cut short by loud catcalls. All around the room the festivities momentarily paused while heads turned toward the front door. Sabrina Morganthal had just entered the house.

Two

It was morning. Lying in bed, Sabrina realized that she had a headache at the same moment that she realized the sun must be up. She opened her left eye a slit and confirmed that the sun was indeed shining on her. The brightness seemed to make her head throb more. She tried to remember the events of the previous night. All that came back to her, though, was being in her new summer rental house and a party going full blast. Hadn't there been some cute guy . . . ?

She opened her eyes wider and momentarily stiffened as she realized she didn't recognize the room. But then she relaxed. Oh, of course, she was in the new house. She wasn't used to the room yet. She winced, the thoughts buzzing inside her brain only making her head pound more loudly.

Her mouth tasted like a gutter, and her stomach felt rocky. *Hangovers suck,* she thought.

An unexpected groan startled her. Sabrina turned her head to find a short mop of unruly brown hair. *A guy? In my bed?*

Horrified, Sabrina instantly inched all the way to the edge of the mattress. *What is he doing in my—? No, wait!* She looked around. This wasn't her new room! This room was much smaller than hers and had a yellow comforter instead of the dark blue one she'd brought from home. She slid out of bed, only to realize that she was naked. She yanked the yellow comforter off the bed and wrapped it around herself.

The guy slept through it all, his face partly covered by the pillow, and shoulders bare, but the rest of him tangled in a sheet. *Thank God! Who in the world? What did I do? Think,* she wracked her brain. *Think.* But her head throbbed, and thinking hurt.

She couldn't remember. Oh, this was awful. Completely humiliating. She had to find her clothes and get out of there! But first she had to know who he was. Gingerly, she leaned forward and carefully lifted the pillow off his face. She saw dark, tousled hair, and a strong jaw covered with a little stubble.

Owen? Oh, no! Not Owen! She remembered a little more of the previous night now. *No! I didn't! I couldn't have! Not with him! Not with one of my roommates!*

Just then Owen rolled over lazily and yawned. He opened his eyes slightly and caught sight of her as she was wrapping the blanket around herself more tightly. He grinned. *"Hey, wuzzup? What a night, huh?"*

What a night? Sabrina thought. *Doesn't he mean, what a nightmare!?*

She wished she could remember what had happened. She took another look at him. He wasn't bad-looking with his dark hair and hazel eyes—she must have found them attractive the night before. This morning, though, the sight of him was unbearable.

She clutched the blanket tighter. Her head throbbed, but she had to figure a way out of this. She just had to! If she didn't, it would be all over the house in no time. Everyone would be talking. Oh, crap, this was so NOT the way she wanted the summer to start!

Then she had an idea. "What am I doing here?" she asked, pretending to be genuinely puzzled.

"You don't know?" Owen grinned.

"Do you?"

Owen stopped grinning and appeared as puzzled as she was pretending to be. "What are you talking about?"

"Well, I just can't remember anything," she said. "So I'm asking you, what am I doing here? What happened? How did I get here?"

He frowned. And in that frown she saw a glimmer of salvation. A possible way out of this mess.

"Well . . . I . . ." He started fumbling for words. "I mean, you're here, aren't you? And you're not wearing any clothes. And neither am I. So it's got to be obvious, doesn't it?"

"I just don't know," she said, putting on one of her greatest acts ever. "I can't remember. You don't remember either.

So maybe nothing happened. In fact, I'm pretty sure nothing happened. We were both so drunk, how could anything have happened?"

Owen's eyebrows dipped, and a look of consternation crossed his face. "Hey, what's the big deal? What if something did happen? What's wrong with that?"

Sabrina forced a sympathetic smile onto her face. "I'm so sorry, but what's wrong with it is that one, you're my housemate, and two, I don't do things like that. And even if I ever did, a housemate would be the last person I'd do it with. It's nothing personal. You understand, don't you?"

Owen's face grew harder, and then softer again. He smiled back as if he knew something she didn't know. Sabrina felt herself stiffen with anticipation.

"Well, now that I think of it," Owen said, "I do seem to recall that you came on to me. Not that you're my type, but I thought, Hey, I wouldn't throw this one out of bed."

Sabrina went cold. Her con job wasn't working. He was calling her bluff, and that filled her with fury. "Liar," she shot back.

But he only smiled. "Hey, how do you know? After all, you just said you don't remember anything."

"I'll tell you what I know," she said sharply. "I know . . . myself." But even as she said it, she could feel the doubt creeping in. She didn't know about last night—at least, not for certain. Maybe she had come on to him. Maybe there was a reason they'd woken up together, and naked. The thought made her shudder.

The uneasy feeling of uncertainty flooded into her. She had to get out of this room, now. "Where are my clothes?" she asked, looking around the room.

He shrugged. "Don't ask me."

She felt herself blush with humiliation and panic and she hated him for it. And hated herself for having given him that power. Clutching the comforter, she left the room, slamming the door behind her.

The second-floor landing was littered with plastic cups, empty bottles, and beer cans. Toilet paper streamers hung from the railing. Sabrina searched for her things. There was a plate with a half-eaten chili dog on the floor, but no clothes.

Where could they be? she wondered. Horrible thoughts came to mind. Were they . . . downstairs? Had she performed some kind of strip? The thought made her feel so ill, she could have barfed right then and there.

She heard a doorknob turn and a door squeak open. Downstairs, a guy with long, blond dreadlocks started to cross the living room. He was wearing a short black wet suit and carrying a red surfboard.

On the second-floor landing Sabrina froze, hoping he wouldn't notice her. She'd never seen him before. But had he seen her last night? How humiliating was this?

Suddenly, as if he could feel her presence, he stopped and looked up at her. Their eyes met, and Sabrina braced herself.

"Surfs up," he said, then continued on his way.

• • •

Avery sighed as she stared at the kitchen. The place was a wreck, every flat surface littered with empty glasses, cans, bottles, and anything else anyone could find to drink out of. The night before she had spent all but about half an hour of the party upstairs in her room, and now, looking at the aftermath, she was glad she had. She had come down once late in the night to get away from the loud groans coming from Owen's room. *I hope Curt and I don't sound like that,* she'd thought.

The moment she'd come downstairs and joined the party, guys had started hitting on her. Martin, the husky football player friend of Owen's, was particularly annoying. He had made a suggestion about using one of the bedrooms for something "better than dancing." What he didn't know was that Curt was sitting on the couch, watching and listening. Curt, being fairly drunk by then, had freaked out and several people had had to pull him away from Martin. Avery was glad, since Martin looked like he could have taken Curt apart with a single blow. Avery had convinced Curt to go back upstairs, where listening to the noise from Owen's room might have been annoying but was certainly safer than staying downstairs.

Now in the kitchen with sunlight streaming in, Avery put on the coffee, pulled a trash bag from under the counter, and started to clean. After a while she heard one of the upstairs doors open and Curt staggering bleary-eyed down the stairs. He took a seat at one of the barstools on the far side of the kitchen counter, pointed to the coffeepot, and grunted, "Fresh?"

Avery nodded. She'd already started it, anticipating that there would be a lot of hungover people in need. She found a clean mug in a cupboard and filled it with steaming java, adding just a touch of cream the way he liked.

Curt accepted the mug without a word and took a sip. He then pulled a pack of cigarettes out of his pocket and lit one up. Smoke curled around his head.

"Breakfast?" she asked.

He gestured at the coffee cup with the cigarette, as though saying that was all the breakfast he needed. Avery turned away, determined not to say anything and be accused of mothering him.

"You like being pawed at?" he asked, suddenly behind her.

"Excuse me?"

"That jerk Martin last night."

She had been through his jealous interrogations before and she was in no mood for it. "You *know* I didn't like it."

"Then why'd you talk to him?"

"He seemed harmless. At least at first."

"Guys are never harmless around a hot girl."

She smiled. He rarely complimented her outright, just made generalities like that and assumed she would know that he thought she was pretty. It was usually enough, though.

"I'm worried about money," he said, changing the subject. "I know it sucks, but I'm gonna have to find a job."

"What about the band?" Avery asked.

"We'll rehearse when I'm not working."

She froze. *The whole point of this summer was to spend more time with each other. Between the band and a job, I'll never see him.* "I have a better idea. Why don't I get a job? I'm sure I can make enough for both of us. That way you can practice with the band while I'm working and we'll have the rest of the time to spend together."

"You're sure?" he asked.

"Absolutely. It will be fine."

"You're the best, Ave," he said.

Before she could say anything more, Polly came out of her downstairs bedroom wearing a big T-shirt with a palm tree on it and matching palm tree shorts. Her red hair was slightly disheveled, and she looked pale and bleary-eyed. Avery understood. Being in one of the downstairs bedrooms, Polly had been at ground zero for the party last night. It looked like she hadn't managed to get much sleep.

Polly went into the downstairs bathroom, then came back out quickly and ran up the stairs to the second floor. Avery watched her. "I wonder what that's about?" she whispered to Curt.

Curt shrugged as if he didn't care and downed the rest of his coffee and held the mug out for more. Avery refilled his mug and handed it back to him. A few moments later, Polly came back down the stairs and entered the kitchen.

"We'd better call Fred," she said, coughing and looking pointedly at Curt's cigarette.

"Something wrong?" Avery asked.

Polly nodded, coughing some more. "The downstairs bathroom."

Curt gave Polly a wicked grin. "Well, ma'am, not much can be done about that. You know the plumbing round here's no darn good."

Polly blushed. Avery stared at the two of them, feeling bewildered. Clearly there was some inside joke she was not aware of.

"Is it the sink?" Avery asked.

"No, the toilet."

"There's a plunger upstairs. I can go get it," Avery offered.

Polly winced. "I think this goes beyond anything that we can fix, or would want to."

"I don't know, I'm usually pretty good at fixing stuff," Avery said.

"Not like this. Someone did . . . something . . . to the toilet. I wouldn't go in there, if I were you."

"Better call Fred, then, and confirm his worst nightmares," Curt advised. "Tell him we burned down his house. When he figures out it's not true, he'll be so grateful, he won't care what we do the rest of the summer."

"I can't do that," Polly said, looking horrified.

"Then give me the number and I'll do it," Curt said,

reaching for his cell phone while putting out the cigarette.

"No! I've got it," Polly said. She looked at the piece of paper tacked to the refrigerator that had Fred's phone number on it before picking up the phone and dialing. "Um, hi, Fred. This is Polly, one of your renters. Oh, I'm glad you remember me. Listen, there seems to be a problem with the downstairs bathroom. Yeah. No, I think it's going to take a plumber, or maybe a team of them. Thanks. Bye." She hung up and turned to Avery and Curt. "So, we really should try to get everyone together this morning to talk about the rules."

"Let me guess," Curt said. "Rules on how to go to the bathroom?"

Avery shot him a look that said, "Behave yourself."

"Rules on being considerate and not making a mess," Polly said.

"That mess could have been made by someone who doesn't even live here," Curt said.

"Then we need rules about that, too," Polly said in an exasperated voice.

Another second-floor door opened, and they looked up to see April emerging from her room. This morning she had traded the tight, black skirt and shirt for black jeans and a black tank top.

"Look who came out of her coffin," Curt mumbled.

April walked down the stairs slowly. The house stank of cigarette smoke. Totally gross first thing in the morning.

Several of her new roommates were standing in the kitchen staring at her. Their eyes were probing. She recognized the pretty, brown-haired girl and the preppy redhead from the day before. The good-looking, hungover guy with the messy black hair was new to her.

Being shy, she wasn't looking forward to meeting them. Some people thought she was antisocial. But for her it was easier to let people stare than to have to talk to them. She knew she sometimes came off as remote, but her privacy was worth it. The only reason she was in this rental house was because she didn't want to be with her mom, helping to take care of her grandmother and living three generations in a tiny vacation condo barely larger than her bedroom. She'd figured in a big house with lots of strangers she could slip unnoticed through the cracks. It might have sounded strange, but it was easier to be alone in a big group than a small one.

As she stared at the group in the kitchen, she thought about just heading out the front door, but she was dying for some coffee and decided to brave the kitchen and her new roomies. After all, it was inevitable that there was going to be *some* contact.

"Hi, I'm Polly," the red-haired girl said as April approached.

"April."

"Yes, we got that much yesterday," the brown-haired girl said with an easy smile. "I'm Avery. This is my boyfriend, Curt."

The good-looking guy nodded, taking April in from head to

toe. He might have been Avery's boyfriend, but his eyes implied that at least part of him was still on the prowl.

"Want some coffee?" Avery asked.

"Love some," April replied. Avery handed her a mug, and she sipped the steaming brew cautiously. "Thanks."

April sensed that the red-headed girl, Polly, seemed agitated. She kept staring toward one of the rooms off the living room.

"Problem?" April asked cautiously.

Polly nodded vigorously. "Just thought you should know. Don't go near the downstairs bathroom. Something exploded in there . . . I think."

April grimaced. "Thanks for the warning."

Curt lit a new cigarette. April stared at the butt smoldering in an ashtray, its dying smoke drifting upward to join with the smoke of its replacement. *Have you never heard of lung cancer?* she thought. A cloud of smoke hung motionless in the kitchen. April set the mug down abruptly and began to cough. *Or the hazards of secondhand smoke?*

"Can we talk about smoking in the house?" Polly asked, also coughing.

"Do you really have to smoke in here?" April wheezed.

Curt sighed loudly.

"I mean, it can't come as a surprise," Polly said. "It's practically banned everywhere."

"I agree. No spreading carcinogens in the house," April said.

"Big word." Curt smirked.

April glanced at Avery, wondering how she felt about her boyfriend being so obnoxious. Caught in the middle, Avery stepped back as if to avoid taking sides. At the same time, April had a sudden vivid memory of watching her grandfather in the hospital, dying of lung cancer, and still begging the nurses for a smoke. "You don't like big words, how about this: I don't want to get lung cancer because of you," she said.

Curt turned abruptly, heading for the door.

"Where are you going?" Avery called.

"To be with friends. Like I should have been all along." He slammed the door. The sound reverberated through the house. Suddenly feeling terrible, April glanced at Avery, whose shoulders were slumped when her boyfriend stormed out.

"Sorry," she muttered to Avery.

Avery looked distressed but forced a smile, anyway. "It's not your fault. You have a right not to have smoke in your house. Curt just woke up on the wrong side of the bed this morning. He's under a lot of stress right now."

"Why?" Polly asked.

"It's his band," Avery explained. "He's trying to get them ready for some gigs."

Avery seemed nice, and April couldn't quite understand why she'd want to be with such a jerk, unless this was indeed out of the norm. Maybe, like her, he had a hard time meeting new people for the first time. And, he certainly was hot-looking, so maybe April could get why Avery was with him. *If you don't mind cigarette breath.*

The swells had been great that morning, and Lucas felt quite pleased as he walked toward his summer abode, damp wet suit peeled down to his waist and his surfboard under his arm. As the house came into sight, the angry-looking guy, Curt—he thought that was his name—came out the front door. Lucas gave him a wide berth. Curt looked none too happy, and Lucas didn't need anything to spoil his rush.

Lucas walked in the front door and caught the smell of cigarette smoke. It came as a shock after the crisp, fresh air outside. Three girls were standing in the kitchen. Two he recognized from the day before. The one he didn't know was dressed in black.

"Where's the fire?" he asked, waving his hand in front of him as if to disperse the cigarette smoke.

"I think it just left," the new girl said.

Lucas was well aware that she was eyeing his bare chest. His own eyes fell on the ashtray on the counter. In it was a smoldering cigarette butt. A pack of cigarettes and a silver lighter lay nearby. Polly, the redhead, picked up the ashtray and doused it in the sink. Avery, the pretty girl with the light brown hair, was opening the kitchen window to let in some fresh air.

"Nicely done," Lucas said. He turned to the girl in black and offered his free hand, the one that wasn't holding a surfboard at the moment. "Sorry, I don't think we met yesterday. I'm Lucas."

"April," the girl in black said, tentatively shaking his hand.

"Pleasure to make your acquaintance," Lucas said, a bit too formally, before he caught himself. He winced, but no one seemed to catch his slipup.

"You didn't meet last night?" Polly asked.

"Are you serious?" April said. "I hid in my room."

"So, I guess this makes seven of us?" Lucas said.

"Yes," Avery answered, pouring herself a cup of coffee. "Want some? It's fresh," she asked, holding up the pot.

Lucas shook his head. "Not today, thanks." He basically lived a substance-free life, including caffeine, but again, this wasn't something he felt like broadcasting.

Polly was staring at his bare feet. He glanced down and wiggled his toes. "Something wrong?"

The red-headed girl jumped as though she had been caught doing something she shouldn't. "Sorry, it's just, well, you're tracking in sand."

Lucas grinned. "So I am. Since you haven't been to the beach yet, I brought some back for you."

Avery smiled at the clever remark. When Polly saw Avery smile, she tried to force a smile onto her lips as well, but it looked painful. Clearly the red-headed girl liked everything neat and orderly. The party the previous night must have been a nightmare for her.

"How was the surf this morning?" Avery asked.

"Really good," Lucas said.

"Why were you out so early?"

Lucas propped his board against the wall. "That's when you get the best waves," he explained. "Before the onshore thermals start to blow and the water gets filled with gremmies."

"Gremmies?" April repeated, puzzled.

"You know, beginners, dilettantes, poseurs. The usual riffraff."

The front door opened, and Curt trudged back in, looking sullen. He walked to the counter and picked up the pack of cigarettes and the lighter and stuffed them in his pockets.

"I always wanted to learn how to surf," Avery said, after glancing at Curt. "But it looks really hard."

"It's not. I could teach you, if you want," Lucas offered.

Curt glared at him, and Lucas stiffened. *Uh-oh. Male territorial behavior.* Lucas had merely been acting friendly. He gave Curt an easy smile. "Offer goes for anyone."

A door on the second floor opened and closed, and they all glanced toward the second-floor landing. A very attractive blonde, wearing tight jeans and a black wraparound shirt, started down the stairs, eyes squinting and hand pressed to her left temple. *Seriously hung over,* Lucas thought, suppressing a smile. *She is the one I ran into early this morning wrapped in a blanket in the hallway.* Without a word to the others, she entered the kitchen and poured herself some coffee.

She took several long sips before she acknowledged the rest of them. "Don't let me interrupt."

Lucas could see that despite the hangover she carried herself with poise and self-assuredness. The airs of a good upbringing. She was from money, and she had no intention of letting any of the rest of them forget it. He'd been surrounded by girls like her all his life; had even dated a few at boarding school. He sighed to himself. If he followed the path his parents were insisting on, he'd be surrounded by them for the next four years.

Despite three Advils and the two cups of coffee, Sabrina's head was still pounding like a drum. She was glad Owen wasn't up yet. She had peeked out of her door to make sure before she came downstairs. She wasn't ready to face him, certainly not when her head hurt and her stomach was lurching at random intervals.

"Has everyone met Sabrina?" Avery asked.

"We have now," said a girl dressed in black with heavily mascaraed eyes.

"And you are?" Sabrina asked her.

"April."

"I'm Polly," the red-haired girl with the lame clothes said, a little too cheerfully.

"Delighted," Sabrina replied drolly.

"And I'm Curt," said the good-looking guy with the wild black hair. "I'm the one you snaked the big bedroom from."

"I didn't snake a bedroom from anyone," Sabrina replied. "I

saw one I liked and asked Fred if I could have it. If you have a problem with that, you should take it up with him."

"That's all been settled," Avery said. "Come on, Curt, you know what I'm talking about."

Curt made a face, but said nothing more. Sabrina was used to men undressing her with their eyes, but this one took it to a whole new level. If he tried any harder, he'd be seeing straight through her. And it wasn't like she was looking her best this morning either.

"Um, Sabrina, if I could talk to you later in private . . . ," Polly started, and then drifted off.

"Why?" Sabrina asked.

"It's about some clothes," Polly said.

Oh . . . Sabrina smiled to herself. *Fashion advice. I should have guessed.*

"Burn everything you own, starting with that." In her hungover state, Sabrina didn't realize she had actually spoken her thoughts out loud until everyone started staring at her.

Polly's face hardened a little. "It's not about *my* clothes. It's about *yours.*"

"Mine?" Sabrina didn't follow.

"From last night," Polly explained. "I have them."

Sabrina's stomach suddenly heaved, and for a moment she thought she might throw up. She could see the others turning away or covering their mouths with their hands, all except Curt, who openly grinned at her. *They're all laughing at me!*

"How?" Sabrina asked, instantly flushing.

"They were all over the stairs," Polly said. "I thought you'd appreciate it if I picked them up."

Sabrina felt her heart plummet. It was all over. Everyone must have known about her and Owen. It was her worst nightmare. Not only being with Owen, but not even being subtle about it. *My clothes all over the stairs?* The image made her cringe.

"I can get them . . ." Polly trailed off, clearly unsure what else to say. Lucas and Avery had averted their eyes. April and Curt were still smirking.

Sabrina glared at them. "Just forget it, okay? It's not what you think."

"Then what is it?" Curt asked archly.

Sabrina wanted to kill him. Amazingly, Polly came to the rescue. "Hey! Now that we're all here, wouldn't this be the perfect time to discuss house rules?"

"We're not *all* here," Curt said dryly, casting a knowing leer at Sabrina, who felt her face color.

"Six out of seven is almost everyone," Polly said, and turned to Sabrina. "You could fill Owen in later."

Sabrina wasn't sure if she wanted to scream, or strangle someone. Not only had last night been a huge mistake, but now they all assumed she and Owen were a couple. She felt like shouting that there was no way she was talking to Owen later about anything, ever.

Polly continued: "Some of us have already worked out a plan

for the refrigerator. Everyone gets half a shelf for personal food, and communal food goes in the door."

"Avery and I have the top shelf," Curt announced.

"I think we need a schedule for chores," Polly continued. "How we're going to shop for communal food and supplies, party etiquette, and noise levels."

Did she really just say "etiquette"? Sabrina thought.

Curt lit up a cigarette, and April shot him a look that seemed to say, "Don't you ever stop?"

"He usually doesn't smoke this much," Avery said. Sabrina could tell she was the perceptive type.

"I think there should be a no smoking in the house policy," said April.

"Good," Polly said. "I agree with that."

"Yawn. Don't care," Sabrina said. It wasn't like she planned to spend much time in this house, anyway.

"I'd have to vote for smoking outside too," Lucas added.

"But what about . . . ?" Polly trailed off.

"What about what?" Lucas asked.

"Well . . . the bong," Polly said, her face coloring slightly.

"Oh, you see, it's an outdoor bong," Lucas said. Sabrina smiled. *So this one has a sense of humor.* The others looked puzzled, except Avery, who also smiled. Sabrina paid careful attention when Lucas winked at Avery.

They were suddenly interrupted by a loud, cheerful voice. "Whoa! Democracy in action!"

Everyone jumped. Owen, smiling, hair glistening from a shower, had caught them all by surprise. Everyone turned to him so quickly, it was like a spotlight had just come on. "Whoa, peeps, eyes back in your heads, please. Well, except for those who really want to stare," he said, paying particular attention to Sabrina.

The eyes now left Owen and focused on Sabrina, who groaned inwardly. If she was going to have to spend the rest of the summer associated with this idiot, she'd pack her bags and leave right now.

There was nothing Owen enjoyed more than a big entrance with all eyes on him. Even better, he could tell from their reactions that word of his previous night's conquest had already spread near and far. While the Avery chick was definitely pretty, there was no doubt in his mind that hot-body Sabrina was the prize catch of the house. And he'd succeeded on his very first night. Life couldn't get better than this.

"So what are we voting on?" Owen asked.

"Whether or not to allow smoking in the house," Polly answered. "We're up to Avery."

All eyes turned toward Avery. Owen had been there last night when Curt and Martin almost went at it, so he knew Curt was Avery's boyfriend. This vote meant that she was basically being asked to vote for or against her boyfriend.

"For the sake of the others in the house, I say keep it outside," Avery said.

"Gee, thanks," Curt grumbled.

"I'm not saying you can't smoke," Avery said. "Just not in the house."

In the meantime, Owen found himself sneaking a peak at Sabrina. Despite the humiliation she was facing, she held her head high and proud and he couldn't help admiring her for that. *No wait, what am I thinking? After the way she acted this morning, I can't believe I'd admire her for anything!*

To get his thoughts away from Sabrina, Owen looked at the one girl in the room he hadn't met. The one dressed in black. "Hey, where you been hiding?" he asked.

April held her hand up to him, palm facing his direction, as if saying, "Don't even try to go there," and didn't utter a word. Owen took the rebuff and was annoyed to see Sabrina looking so smug.

"So, Owen, what do you think about smoking?" Polly asked him.

A lot of Owen's friends smoked, and he had no problem with it. Actually, the idea of setting up nonsmoking rules in the house seemed like a bummer. Who wanted to party when you couldn't smoke? And if he agreed to ban smoking, who knew what else they'd decide to ban?

"I don't know, what do you think, Sabrina?" he asked. Maybe if he voted with her it would be like a peace offering or something.

She gazed up at the ceiling and said nothing. "She abstained," Polly said after a minute.

It was on the tip of his tongue to say that he had it on good authority that she didn't abstain. Owen knew it would get a laugh. Normally he'd just blurt it out, but this morning something made him choke the comment back. Sabrina would not appreciate sexual barbs aimed at her.

Owen said, "I'll abstain too." He glanced at Sabrina out of the corner of his eye. She seemed not to care. Even hungover and moody, she looked hot.

"It's official, then," Polly said brightly. "This is a nonsmoking house. Now we can talk about parties. I think we shouldn't throw one without everyone agreeing."

Owen winced. "Whoa! Wait a minute! This is getting out of hand. All we need is one person to always say no and there'll never be another party."

"So?" April asked.

Owen knew it. "You'll be the one, right?"

"Maybe," April replied.

Owen turned to the others, almost pleadingly. "Come on, guys, what do you want from me? If I knew I was going to need permission to throw parties, I would have stayed with my grandparents this summer."

"All in favor of getting permission for parties, raise your hand," Polly said. She and April raised their hands. "All against getting permission, raise your hand." Owen raised his hand quickly and was gratified that Curt and Sabrina did the same. Even with Lucas and Avery abstaining, those against asking permission succeeded.

"Okay, so I guess that didn't work." Undaunted, Polly continued. "Let's move on to chores. We have to divide up the work. There's trash to be taken out, vacuuming to be done, scrubbing of bathrooms and kitchens, and shopping for food."

Owen may not have had a headache before, but he was starting to get one now. This was summer vacation. Who wanted to think about all this crap? Luckily, he was not alone.

"Get real," Sabrina said, displaying her hands. "You're looking at a fifty-dollar manicure. These hands don't scrub toilets."

"Look, we all have to pitch in," Polly said.

"I'm sorry, but who put you in charge?" Sabrina asked haughtily. It was clear to Owen that she'd had enough. Again, he found himself feeling a grudging admiration. Sabrina certainly had no trouble voicing her opinions. He watched as she hopped down from the perch she had made for herself on the kitchen counter and went back upstairs.

"I'm just trying to help," Polly said in a small voice.

"Yeah, well, no thanks," Curt said. "I'm outta here too. Come on, Avery."

Avery started toward the door after Curt, then hesitated and patted Polly's arm. "I appreciate the effort. It'll be okay. Everyone's just tired from the party. Maybe we can try again when everyone's gotten a chance to know one another better."

Polly looked disappointed, and Owen was surprised to find himself feeling bad for her. After all, she was trying, and maybe in a way she was right. He might love to party, but he also liked a refrigerator with food in it and a bathroom you could use without worrying about catching some infectious disease. The others started to drift away, and Polly looked crushed, her shoulders slumped and her eyes cast down at the floor. Owen had an idea and instantly hated it, but at least it might make her feel better.

"Hey, you know what might bring everyone together?" he said after the others had left and he and Polly were alone in the kitchen. "Maybe we should have a clambake or something."

Polly instantly perked up. "That would be great! Just fantastic! Oh, Owen, I knew you were a good guy."

Owen groaned to himself. Now he almost wished he hadn't made the suggestion. Good guy? *There goes my image,* he thought. *A second ago I was top stud, now I'm Mr. Sensitive Fix Your Problems!*

"One thing?" he quickly added. "Let's pretend it was your idea, not mine."

"Why?" Polly asked.

"Just do it, okay?" Owen said. "It's no biggie."

Before Polly could press further, Lucas returned to the kitchen in shorts and a T-shirt, having ditched the wet suit.

"Clambake tonight at six thirty?" Polly asked.

"Great, I'll be here," Lucas said. "But right now, I've got to book."

Owen needed to leave too, to get to work. Today was his first day on the parasailing boat and he had to get checked out on the equipment. He and Lucas left the house at the same time. Personally, Owen didn't get the dreadlock thing on blond white guys. But Lucas gave off an aura of confident self-assurance that Owen inwardly wished he possessed.

They went through the front door together, into the morning sunlight. "Need a ride?" Owen asked.

"No, thanks," Lucas said. "I can walk."

"What? I've got cooties?" Owen joked.

Lucas grinned. "Okay."

The sun was already hot and heating the air. Owen squinted in the brightness and felt a stab of pain in his skull—a sign of the hangover he'd been trying to avoid all morning. He put his hand up to shield his eyes.

"You all right?" Lucas asked.

"The sun, it hurts us," Owen said in his best Golem impression.

Lucas chuckled. Owen smiled back. The smell of the surf was in the air. There were other scents as well, most of them sweet and sugary and sure to be coming from the boardwalk.

Owen could hear laughter and playful screaming from the direction of the beach. He pictured some girl squealing as a guy splashed her with water. His thoughts slipped back to Sabrina. Why did she have to be so bitchy that morning? It didn't make sense. Usually he was the one who woke up disgusted, not the girl. There was something about her that was different, though. He had woken up half a dozen times before she did and just lain there and stared at her. Her beautiful blond hair fanning out around her face on the pillow. He'd wanted to reach out and—

"Uh, Owen, your car?" Lucas asked, interrupting his thoughts.

Owen shook himself out of the daydream and pointed down the street to a red Mustang convertible. A minute later they were in the car and Owen relaxed into the familiar black leather seats. "So, where do you work?" he asked Lucas as he put the car in gear.

"Surf shop," Lucas said.

"Down on Main Street?" Owen started to steer in that direction.

"Yeah, but I'm not going there now. If you could drop me downtown I'd appreciate it."

"Sure, anyplace in particular?" Owen asked.

"Nah, anywhere'll be fine," Lucas said. "So what are you doing this summer?" It was a subtle change of subject, but Owen wasn't going to push it. If Lucas didn't feel like telling him why he wanted to go downtown, that was his business.

"The parasailing boat," Owen said.

"Never tried it," Lucas said. "Is it fun?"

"The chicks are," Owen said. "It's a great way to meet them. You meet a lot of chicks at the surf shop?"

"A few," Lucas replied noncommittally. "You can drop me here."

Owen pulled the car over to the curb. They were on a block with a bunch of storefronts—a deli, a check-cashing place, a nail salon—not exactly high rent. *Why here?* he wondered.

"Thanks for the ride," Lucas said, and got out.

Three

Later that afternoon as he left his and Avery's room on the second floor, Curt heard a guitar being strummed and a girl singing softly. For a moment he thought it was a radio, but then he realized it was coming from one of the rooms down the hall. He paused for a moment. It wasn't coming from Sabrina's room. Polly's room was downstairs. That left April.

He could relate to April's preference for black clothes, but didn't go for the excessive eye makeup. He just didn't get why she'd want to look like some character from a Tim Burton movie. He stepped closer to her door, trying to make out the words she was singing. She had a surprisingly good voice, kind of low and throaty. Her playing wasn't half bad, either, even if it was sort of minimalistic. But it was some moody folk ballad. He hated that kind of crap, so he surprised himself when, after another minute, he knocked on her door.

The singing ceased abruptly, and there was a moment's silence before April asked, "Who is it?"

"Curt."

"What do you want?" she asked.

Good question. He wasn't exactly sure himself, so he made up the first thing that came to his mind. "I want to apologize for being a dick about the smoking thing."

Another moment of silence passed. Then he heard bed-springs, as if she was getting up. Next the door opened a crack, and one of her heavily mascaraed eyes peeked out.

"Seriously?" she asked.

"Yeah, it was uncool. You've got a right to breathe."

He thought he almost detected a smile, but wasn't quite sure. "Thank you, apology accepted," she said, and started to close the door.

"Wait," he said.

She stopped and frowned.

"Can I come in?" he asked.

"Why?"

"I don't know. Talk. One musician to another. I heard you playing. You sounded . . . good." It wasn't entirely a lie. He might not have liked the style, but her playing and voice weren't bad.

She stared at him for a minute before stepping back and opening the door. He walked in and was instantly struck by how small and dark her room was. The bed was wedged against one wall, and clothes were hung on a pole that ran the length of the room. It took him a minute to realize that there were no windows. It wasn't even a room, just a big closet. An old Yamaha acoustic was propped in the corner. Piece of junk.

"Cozy," he said.

She bristled suspiciously. "I thought you wanted to talk about music?"

"Sorry," he muttered.

April shrugged and sat on her bed, picking up one of her pillows and clutching it to her stomach. The neck of her T-shirt opened out, and Curt caught a glimpse of her milky-white cleavage.

"At least it's mine," she said.

"I get that," Curt said. "I had to share a room with my brother till he went to college."

"Bites."

"Tell me about it," he said. "Made it worse when he would sneak girls in and kick me out. I'd spend the night in his car so Dad didn't catch me sleeping on the couch. Freeze my butt off."

"Doubly bites," she noted.

Curt dropped his eyes and studied his hands for a minute. "I don't know why I just told you that," he admitted. "I've never told anyone, not even Avery."

"Sometimes it's easier to tell painful things to a stranger than to someone you care about."

"It's not that painful," he protested.

"Yes, it is," she said. "It's written all over your face."

"What are you, a mind reader?" he asked with a grin.

She didn't smile back. "So, you want to talk music?"

Curt wasn't sure what he wanted to talk about. He was intrigued. There was something deep about her that he connected to. *It's like she gets it,* he thought. *Weird to know someone just a few minutes and to feel like we have a connection. Maybe it was the music.*

"I heard you singing."

She gave him an impatient look. "Yeah, I know. You said that."

In a weird way he liked that she was suspicious and reluctant. It made her sort of challenging. And then there was her enticingly pale, smooth skin.

"You sounded pretty good. Played pretty good too, I guess, if you like that sort of music."

"I take it you don't?" she said, only the twitch in her left eye revealing that the criticism bothered her at all.

"Well, personally, I wouldn't be caught dead listening to that stuff. It's all rock for me."

"Who do you like?"

"Who don't I like?" he asked.

She lifted an eyebrow.

"Okay, if I have to choose, I like classic rock the best," Curt said. "And Green Day, the White Stripes, Red Hot Chili Peppers, Nirvana." He hesitated. "You consider that classic rock?"

"Doesn't matter," April answered. "Kurt Cobain wrote great songs. You know some of the same people who write songs for rock bands also write songs for folk artists and ballads for country singers?"

"No way," Curt said.

"Way."

"I guess it's all in the interpretation," he said.

"That's all musical styles are, anyway," April said. "Different people's interpretations of the same themes, the same feelings, even the same songs."

"So, you're saying we're all just singing the same thing?"

"Essentially," she said, smiling again.

"I guess that's kind of cool," he said, even though he wasn't completely sure he agreed.

"I think so," she said.

"So, the song you were singing, who wrote it?"

Instead of answering, she pulled her knees up against her chest and seemed to withdraw.

"What's the problem?" Curt asked.

"I didn't think anyone was here," April said. "I guess I'm a little freaked that someone was listening and I didn't know it."

"Hey, it was just me," Curt said.

A crooked grin appeared on April's lips. "Maybe I'm just paranoid. I just work so hard on these songs, and they're also really private."

"Don't you want them to be heard?" Curt asked.

"Sure," said April. "Someday, when I'm ready."

"You write all your own songs?" he asked, honestly impressed.

April nodded.

"Songwriting isn't one of my talents," he said. "No one else in the band can write worth a crap either."

She was looking at him strangely, like she was studying him.

"What?" he asked at last.

"I'm still wondering what you're doing here," she said. "I mean, in my room. I'm pretty sure you're not here trolling for a girl or a band member, and it's hard to imagine you being into the stupid ritual bonding thing. So, what's the deal?"

He shrugged. "I'm not really sure, to be honest. I heard you singing and I guess I just wanted to talk. I wish I was living in the house with my band, but Avery wanted us to have some separate time. She doesn't get what the band means to me. She doesn't understand that it's who I am. There is no 'separate' between me and music. I don't know. Maybe I thought you might understand."

"Shouldn't you be telling this to Avery, not me?" April asked.

"Probably," he admitted, then decided to change the subject. "So, is it hard to write your own stuff?"

"Believe it. For every good one I write, I probably chuck ten bad ones."

"You come here for inspiration or something like that?" he guessed.

"As if," April muttered. "My mom brought my grandmother here for her health. She can't work full-time, though. This," she said, waving her hand around the cramped room, "is my compromise. I work and help pay for some of their expenses and I get to have my own place instead of sharing a one-bedroom apartment with them."

"Excellent compromise," he noted.

"I kind of thought so too. So, when I'm not working, yeah, I spend time on my music. You too, right?"

He shrugged, then nodded. "We're trying to get some gigs around here for the summer. I guess you could say we came here to be heard."

"Then I'm sure you will be."

"Thanks."

"That's cool," she said, waving it off. "What's the name of the band?"

"Stranger Than Fiction," he said with pride. The name had been his idea, and he considered it one of his finest contributions.

"Killer. So, are you?"

"What?"

"Stranger than fiction?"

"Sometimes," he said, shooting her a sly smile. He dropped eye contact with her, thinking about the band and everything they'd been through. They had started out rotating through all their garages until the parents freaked at the noise. After that, they'd practiced in one guy's barn. It sucked during the winter because it didn't have any heat. The second year they were together, the lead singer had overdosed and nearly died. The guy's parents had freaked and shipped him off to boot camp and the band had to find someone to take his place. They were trying to get money for better equipment and saving up for a recording session. Before that could happen, though, they needed better songs. It had been rough, but he knew STF could make it if they stuck together. They'd come a long way, and Curt wouldn't let anyone stop them now.

His eyes fell on a beat-up black notebook on April's bed. He picked it up and flipped it open.

"Hey!" April protested. 'That's private!"

Curt closed the notebook and put it back down. "These your songs?" he asked.

"Yes." She picked up the notebook and hugged it to her chest. Curt noticed she liked to do that with the things she treasured. He wondered what it would take for him to become something she treasured, and to receive the same treatment.

"Can you play one for me?" he asked.

"No."

"Come on." Curt smiled and turned the charm on. "I swear I won't tell anyone."

"I told you, I don't play my stuff for other people."

"Then what's the point? Besides, I'm not other people. I'm a musician, just like you," he said, mustering his most intense and alluring gaze.

April gazed back at him uncertainly.

"Swear I won't tell a soul," Curt said.

She slowly put the notebook down. Curt had a feeling he'd won her over.

"Oh, okay, just one." She heaved a sigh, picked up her guitar, strummed a few chords, and then started singing. "Our bodies went down . . . the moon went up. Slipping . . . sliding . . . the mating dance has just begun. It's the moon and not the sun. Yeah. It's the moon and not the sun."

Curt listened as she sang. The song was good. So good that he could almost hear it being sung by someone else.

Polly and Avery were up to their elbows in clams. They were at an outdoor fish market, surrounded by stalls selling fish, clams, crabs and all manner of saltwater crustaceans. As Polly dumped another handful of clams into a plastic bag she took a moment to look at Avery, who looked perplexed as she pawed through the slimy shells.

"First clambake?" Polly asked.

Avery nodded. "Is it that obvious?"

"Kind of. So, what's your story?" Polly blurted out.

"Excuse me?" Avery asked, looking puzzled.

"Sorry, I was just trying to make conversation," Polly said. "It's just if we don't talk about you, then I'm going to start babbling about me, and that's never pretty. Unless it's pretty boring."

Avery laughed. "Okay, if it will save you from boredom, what do you want to know?"

"What brought you here for the summer?"

"The chance to spend some time alone with Curt."

Polly felt a little confused. "Alone? In a house full of people?"

"People, yes. Parents, and other members of his band, no," Avery explained.

"How long have you been together?"

"Three years, ever since my mom died."

"Oh, I'm sorry."

Avery put her hand on Polly's arm. "No need to be sorry. It's okay. She was sick for a long time, and it's been a while now and I'm okay with it."

"I don't think I'd ever be okay with it," Polly said.

Avery shook her head. "You don't know what you can live through until you do."

Neither of them said anything else for a few minutes. They finished with the clams, then walked to a vegetable vendor. Polly picked the lettuce and tomatoes while Avery selected several fat, white mushrooms.

"Probably not the kind of 'shrooms Lucas likes, but he'll have to make do," Avery joked.

"Do you really think he smokes that bong?" Polly asked.

"Why would he have it?" Avery asked.

"I don't know," Polly said. "Somehow, it just doesn't seem to fit. It's like the dreadlocks. I'm just not sure they go with the person, you know?"

Avery moved toward the avocados. "I know what you're

saying. It's like we only see part of him or something, like he's some sort of shadow."

"Exactly!" Polly said, glad to have someone help her put her feelings into words. "Well, I guess we've got all summer to figure him out."

"If he lets us," Avery said while paying for the vegetables.

They left the market, Polly carrying the bag of clams and Avery carrying the vegetables. There was still about a half hour before they were supposed to meet everyone back at the house. The day had been really hot. Polly wiped the sweat off her brow and looked at her watch. "We should be getting back pretty soon."

"We have to pick up the drinks first," Avery said, nodding toward a convenience store. The window was covered with signs advertising Corona, Bud Lite, Heineken, and all sorts of other drinks. "What do you want to get?" Avery asked.

"I like Coke," Polly said.

"We have to get some alcohol, don't you think?" Avery asked as she pulled her hair up into a bun on top of her head. "Our housemates are going to get bent out of shape if we don't. What do you think, beer or wine coolers for a clambake?"

"Uh, uh, the wine coolers, I guess."

Avery gave her a funny look. "Have you had beer?"

"No," Polly admitted, and felt her face grow warm.

"You're not missing out on much," Avery said, wrinkling her nose. "We'll go with wine coolers."

Polly glanced at the store and the large sign that said, ABSOLUTELY NO ALCOHOL WILL BE SOLD TO ANYONE UNDER 21. She scowled. "How? We can't buy alcohol. We're both underage."

Avery smiled. "Leave it to me. You get the soda; I'll get the other stuff. When we're in that store, act like you don't know me."

Polly felt her stomach start to flip-flop. *There's no way we're going to get away with this,* she thought. All her life she'd been terrified of doing anything wrong, anything that might result in getting caught. Right now she wanted to run away as fast as she could.

But Avery went in and, after a minute, Polly followed and headed straight for the refrigerated cases of soda. She managed to get the bag of vegetables into her left arm and clutched two two-liter bottles of Coke to her chest with her right before turning around precariously.

When Polly saw Avery, her heart leaped into her throat. Avery was approaching the counter carrying two packs of wine coolers, walking calmly and slowly as though she bought alcohol all the time. She put the wine coolers on the counter. Just as the guy behind the counter was about to ask for her driver's license, she said, "Do you carry diapers? I had to leave the kids with my new boyfriend and I don't want to drive all the way to the grocery store. I don't trust him alone with them that long."

"Uh, sure," the guy said, pointing down an aisle.

"Great, thanks, be right back." Avery turned and went to the diaper section, looked for a moment, and then selected a package and brought it back to the man. "It's not the brand I normally use, but I guess it'll work."

The man started ringing up her items. "My wife used those for our kids and they seemed fine, never once had a leak."

"Really? Thanks, I feel better." Avery glanced at her watch. "If only my boyfriend were that dependable."

"Yeah." The man chuckled as he rang up and bagged the wine coolers and diapers. "That's twenty-one even."

Avery paid him and left the store. Polly's heart was pounding; she put the soda bottles on the counter and paid for them without saying a word to the man. She grabbed the bag and rushed out of the store, nearly colliding with Avery, who was standing on the sidewalk several feet away.

"Come on, let's get out of here!" Polly gasped, in full-flight mode.

"Take a breath and relax, Polly. We're fine," Avery said.

"I can't believe you did that," Polly said. "Oh, my gosh, I thought you were going to get caught and then—"

Polly realized Avery wasn't listening. She was staring across the street at some storefronts and old buildings that were being renovated. She saw a HABITAT FOR HUMANITY sign above the building, but nothing else stood out.

"What are you looking at?" Polly asked.

"Oh, uh, nothing," Avery said, turning back. "Hold on a second." She walked up to a woman approaching with a child in a stroller.

"Excuse me, ma'am? I bought the wrong type of diapers for my sister and I don't have time to return them. Could you use them?"

The woman frowned suspiciously as Avery produced the package of diapers. "Well, I guess," the woman said. "But I don't have any cash on me."

"Oh no, no, I just want to give them to someone who can use them. Does your baby wear this size?"

"Actually, yes," the woman answered.

"Then here you go. Happy early Fourth of July."

Avery headed back to Polly. Behind her, the woman called, "Thank you." Avery turned and waved.

"Come on, we better head back," Avery said to Polly.

They began walking. After a minute, Polly said, "Where'd you learn to do that?"

"One day I had to go to the store for some pads and Curt asked me to try to buy him some beer. I was so nervous that instead of grabbing stuff for me, I grabbed the first thing that came to my hands and it was a package of diapers. By the time I realized it, I was approaching the counter. I figured I would look suspicious if I turned back, so I just put them on the counter with the beer."

"That's so funny!" Polly gasped. "So the first time, it was totally by accident!"

"Right," Avery said. "People never want to think that someone with a baby is in high school. The cashier let me buy the stuff and never carded me. Curt's had me buy beer for him ever since. I always try to find someone I can give the diapers to."

"That's got to get expensive," Polly said.

"Yeah. I'm going to need to get a job pretty soon, anyway," Avery said.

"What do you think you'll do?" Polly asked.

Avery shrugged. "Don't know."

"I'm a waitress at a restaurant on the pier," Polly said. "Last I heard, they were still trying to fill a few positions. Maybe you could get a job there."

"You think?" Avery asked.

"Have any experience?" Polly asked.

"McDonald's?"

"Well, you could try," Polly said.

"That would be great, thanks."

"I start there tomorrow," Polly said. "You want to go with me in the morning?"

"Perfect."

It *was* perfect, as far as Polly was concerned. Avery was definitely the nicest girl in the house, although to be fair, Polly still didn't know much about April. Still, being Avery's friend could only help. Avery was the kind of girl guys just naturally flocked to. Maybe when they found out she had a boyfriend, a few of them might give Polly a look.

When they reached the house, April was already in the kitchen, pulling a steaming loaf of bread out of the oven. Polly looked at her in surprise. It never occurred to her that April might like to cook. Avery was quicker to respond.

"Smells great!" she said enthusiastically.

April beamed. "I do one thing well in the kitchen, and one thing only. I bake. So, I figured I could handle the bread."

Polly was envious of Avery for being so quick on her feet and knowing the right thing to say. And she was glad that April seemed to be getting into the spirit of the party. Avery dumped the clams into the sink.

"Slimy," April noted.

"You should have tried pawing through them," Avery said with a laugh.

"I'll leave that part to you guys," April said. "I have no idea what to do with clams. I've never been to a clambake."

"Neither has Avery. You two have something in common," Polly said.

April and Avery looked at each other, and Polly instantly felt like an idiot. It was a dumb thing to say. Like Avery and April were going to bond over the idea of never having been to a clambake before. If Avery always knew the right thing to say, Polly was the exact opposite. She could always count on herself to say the wrong thing.

"Well, well," someone said, "look at all the cooks in the kitchen."

It was Sabrina, in a cream skirt and a pink top with a draped neck that, of course, revealed enough to get her arrested in most

Muslim countries. Polly felt the muscles in her shoulders begin to tense. “We’re getting ready for the clambake. Want to help?”

“Oh, uh . . .” Sabrina appeared stymied. “I really don’t cook.”

“You left that to your mom?” Polly guessed.

“Not really. We’ve always had cooks.”

“You’ve got to be kidding,” April said, rolling her eyes.

Even Avery, the model of decorum, looked surprised. They hit an awkward silence. Polly was pretty sure none of them had ever met anyone like Sabrina before. What in the world was she doing sharing a summer house on the Jersey Shore with them? It sounded like she would be more comfortable on the French Riviera.

“You want to learn?” Avery finally asked.

Polly thought for sure that Sabrina was going to make some sort of sarcastic remark. Like cooking was for commoners. Instead, she was surprised when the girl said, “Well, okay, I’ll try anything once.”

The remark about trying anything once reminded Polly of finding Sabrina’s clothes on the stairs the night before. *No, no, that’s not nice,* she told herself, and tried to clear it from her brain.

“We’ll start you with something easy,” Avery said.

“How about you tear up the lettuce for the salad? Rip pieces up and dump them in the bowl.”

“Don’t you just chop it with a knife?” Sabrina asked.

“You could, but we’re not eating right away, and if you tear it instead of cut it, the lettuce stays fresh longer,” Avery answered.

Polly hadn't known that, and from the look on her face, neither had April. Then Polly realized why: *Avery has probably had to do all the cooking for her family since her mother died.*

"So, where are the guys hiding?" Sabrina asked as she tore the lettuce.

"Curt's rehearsing with his band," Avery said.

Polly noticed that April seemed rather flushed, as though the heat from the oven was making her overly warm. But that seemed odd now that she'd taken the bread out.

"And the . . . other guys?" Sabrina asked.

Suddenly Polly had a feeling she knew why Sabrina had agreed to help them prepare the meal.

"Lucas and Owen said they were going to the beach to get the fire started," April offered.

"I guess that must have been some party last night," Sabrina said, in what sounded like a complete non sequitur.

"You *really* don't remember?" Polly asked.

Sabrina shook her head. "I think I must have been really tired from moving here and everything. And I hardly had anything to eat. It's just a blank. I mean . . . was it that bad?"

Avery and April smiled at each other, but Polly felt bad for Sabrina. She would have felt sorry for anyone in that position. "No, not really," she said. "And you know what? I think Owen's a lot nicer than you might think. I know he acted like a jerk last night at the party. But he's got a sensitive side too."

"Would you agree?" April asked Sabrina.

"How do we cook the clams?" Sabrina asked, avoiding the question.

"We'll steam them by the fire," said Polly.

"Wait," said Avery. "Before we totally change the subject. I think that's something Curt and Owen have in common. I mean, they can both come off gruff, but there's another side to them as well."

"I'll take the clams outside and see how the fire's coming," April suddenly volunteered, scooping the clams out of the sink and into a bucket and hurrying out to the beach.

Polly watched her go. Neither Avery nor Sabrina appeared to think there was anything odd about April's behavior. But Polly definitely did.

Lugging the clams down to the beach, April was glad to get away from the other girls. She wasn't sure why she'd made the bread, except that she knew she could. She also didn't know why she'd played that song for Curt. But there was something magnetic about him.

Don't get sucked in, she warned herself. *You're not here to try to steal your roommate's boyfriend.*

But she could see that Curt had liked her music. She wondered if Avery appreciated music the way she and Curt did.

The bucket of clams was getting heavy. She glanced around, looking for the fire that the guys were supposed to have built. All she saw were people here and there who'd stayed late on the beach. Once again, her thoughts went to Curt and she imagined finding him on the beach, strumming a guitar.

Stop! she told herself. *Stop thinking about someone else's boyfriend. And where are those other guys, anyway?* she thought, getting annoyed. Typical. You do all the work and give the guys one simple job and they can't do it.

Finally she spotted a guy sitting on the sand next to what looked like a pile of driftwood. Sure enough, it was Owen. Polly might have insisted that he had a sensitive side, but from the little April had heard, his only clear goal for the summer seemed to involve sleeping with every girl in their house and then moving on to the girls in the neighboring rentals. April sighed and trudged over, lugging the bucket of clams. At least he'd distract her from thinking about Curt.

Owen sat on the sand, a beer in his hand, and stared at the ocean. The waves weren't as high as they'd been earlier in the day, but they were still impressive, rearing up as they got close to shore and breaking with a roaring crash that sent white foam billowing into the air. There was something both awesome and soothing about the power of the surf as it crashed into the sand.

"Hey," someone said. He turned and found the girl in black standing by the wood that he'd collected for the fire. A bucket sat on the sand near her feet.

"What's up?" Owen said.

"Where's the fire?" she asked.

"Couldn't get it started. Turns out I'm no Boy Scout." It was meant to sound funny or flippant but came out self-critical. He sighed and took a gulp of the beer. Why was he always so critical of himself? *How come I can't even start a lousy fire? Lots of guys' dads teach them that kind of stuff. Why couldn't mine?*

"What about Lucas?" she asked.

Owen pointed out at a figure on a surfboard out in the waves. "Surfer boy? I don't think he's that interested in fire, just water."

He took another gulp of beer, aware that the girl was staring at the stacked wood. They'd never actually been formally introduced, but he sensed that she was a strange chick, and he wasn't sure what to make of the dark makeup and black clothes. Definitely not like the party types he usually hung with.

The next thing he knew, she kneeled down beside the pile of driftwood and began to arrange it. "Here, help me start the fire," she said.

"I don't start fires with women unless I know their names first," he said.

"April," she said. "And you're Owen. Now how about a little help. There's not going to be a clambake without a fire."

Her tone of voice was about as unfriendly as you could be while remaining civil.

And, just like that, the quiet, contemplative Owen was gone and he was back to his usual, competitive, sex-driven self. The more a female resisted, the more he perceived her as a challenge. He stood up and took a piece of wood from her, intentionally brushing her fingers with his own.

"Hey, forget the stupid fire. Why don't we go have some fun?" he asked.

"Fun?" April repeated with a smirk. "We've barely been here twenty-four hours and you've already been on top of one girl in the house. I think you've met your quota."

"Not from where I'm standing," he said, hating himself for saying it. But at the same time, unable to stop himself.

"Grow up." She shoved a stick at him and it banged against his fingers. He bit his lip to keep from swearing.

"Okay, just what are we trying to do here?" he asked.

"With the fire, or are you determined to be an ass?" April asked.

Owen found himself grinning. "I like a girl with spunk."

"You don't quit, do you?" April shot back.

"No, I mean it." Owen raised his hands. "This is hands off. If you insist, I promise I won't put the moves on you for the whole summer. But I still like your attitude."

She gazed at him and just for a moment he thought he saw the slightest smile pass across her lips. As if she believed him.

"Fine," she said. "Here's some more of my attitude. Stand the wood up. We want to shape it like a pyramid. Put the smaller stuff in the center of the base."

"Yes, ma'am," Owen replied, jesting. "So, uh, how did you learn to do this?"

"My dad used to take me camping," she said.

"Lucky you," he said.

She frowned at him, probably thinking he was mocking her. "Yeah, matter of fact I was pretty lucky."

For a moment he was tempted to explain that he wasn't making fun. He was serious, and envious of anyone who'd managed to have a normal relationship with his or her father. But what was the point? Why would she care about his past? So instead, he helped her pile the firewood.

When they had finished, she straightened up. "You got matches?"

"You mean you're not going to rub two sticks together?" he kidded her.

She held out her hand, palm up.

He pulled some matches out of his pocket. "Can I do it?" he asked.

"Light the small stuff in the center," she said.

He struck a match and touched it to the end of one of the twigs. But before the kindling caught on fire, an ocean breeze snuffed out the flame. He dropped the match and lit another one. It went out as well. *So typical I can't do anything right.*

"Shield the flame with your hands," April said over his shoulder.

He did as she told him and was gratified to see the small

flame lick at the wood before taking hold. A thin column of white smoke began to rise, growing thicker as the flames rose and crackled. Owen backed away, and they stood together watching the flames rise. It was kind of nice, sharing this moment with a girl and not feeling the need to try to hook up with her.

Avery and Polly were coming down to the beach with bread, salad, and drinks when the fire went up with a roar. April and Owen were standing near it. Avery found herself wondering where Lucas was.

"Good fire," she said, putting the food down and looking around.

"If you're looking for surfer boy, he's out in the waves," Owen said as if he'd read her mind. "But that's okay. Turns out nature girl and I didn't need his help."

Avery's first impulse was to protest that she hadn't been looking for Lucas. But that wasn't true, and she knew that protesting would only draw more attention to the issue. As the others started to steam the clams and spread out the blankets, she turned and stared out at the waves. She could see a surfer close by, but with the sun going down and the light fading, she couldn't tell if it was Lucas. Whoever it was, he looked good, zigzagging across the faces of the waves.

"What you looking at, Ave?"

The sound of Curt's voice caught her by surprise. She jumped when he placed a hand around her waist. She thought he was still rehearsing with his band.

"The ocean," she said, a little too quickly, but if Curt noticed, he didn't show it. Avery turned and glanced at the others. Owen was sitting on a blanket, drinking a beer. Avery could see that out of the corner of his eye he was watching Sabrina, on the other side of the fire. Polly was checking on the clams, and April had finished spreading out the other food and had grabbed a wine cooler for herself.

"So how was rehearsal?" Avery asked Curt.

"Didn't get as much practice time as I wanted," he said, the frustration in his voice palpable. "It's hard to keep the guys focused. They still have that summer vacation mentality. To them, every day's a party day."

"That's too bad," Avery said.

"I'll try again later. Right now it's just good to be here," he said, wrapping his arms around her waist and kissing her neck.

Avery felt herself stiffen involuntarily. *What's that about?* she wondered as she forced herself to relax. She should have been happy. Here they were at the beach and she was in Curt's arms. *This is what we came here for,* she thought.

"How about a walk before dinner?" he suggested.

That sounded great. "Hey, Polly?" Avery called.

Polly looked up.

"How long until the clams are ready?" Avery asked.

"About fifteen minutes."

"Curt and I are going to take a walk."

"Have fun," Polly said.

She grabbed a wine cooler and they strolled down the beach hand-in-hand as the orange sun slipped below the horizon and the sky began to fade to dark. As they got closer to the boardwalk there were so many twinkling lights in every color imaginable that a person could spend hours counting them. Curt took her in his arms and pressed his lips against hers. As they kissed, the sounds of laughter and screams and whirring machinery reached their ears.

"Let's go on some rides tomorrow, okay?" she asked.

"Uh, okay, if that's what you want, sure," he said, sounding less than excited.

Suddenly she remembered her conversation with Polly earlier that day. "Oh, wait, I can't. I'm going with Polly to see if I can get a job waitressing."

"Oh, yeah?" Curt suddenly brightened. "That's great. Really good."

Avery couldn't help noticing that news of her possible job excited him far more than spending time with her tomorrow.

"But we'll still go on the rides, right?" she asked. "Maybe even tomorrow night?"

"Yeah, sure. Let's see how it goes." The answer was definitely noncommittal.

Avery decided not to push it. Besides, she could smell hot dogs and funnel cake coming from the boardwalk, and her stomach growled. "We should probably head back," she said.

They walked back slowly, the sounds of laughter fading in the background. Beside the fire Polly was putting clams out on plates. It was almost dark by now, and Avery and Curt sat on one of the blankets. Avery loaded up her plate with salad. Lucas trotted up with his dripping surfboard, his hair sticking to his head and his wet suit glimmering with seawater.

"Thanks for all your help with the fire, buddy," Owen said sarcastically.

"I'll make it up to you," Lucas said. "The waves were just too good to resist." He grabbed a piece of bread and took a bite. "Hey, this is great," he said. "Tastes homemade."

"That's 'cause it is," April answered.

"I made the salad," Sabrina piped up, clearly eager to receive her share of the attention.

"Wow, that's amazing. How did you do that?" Owen asked with a straight face.

Sabrina gave him a dirty look but didn't say anything.

Avery surveyed the group, their faces aglow in the light of the flickering fire. Everyone seemed fairly happy, everyone except Polly, whose expression went beyond happiness to ecstasy, as if this clambake was a dream come true. Their eyes met, and Polly grinned.

"This is so great!" she squealed. "We're all together and the food is great and the beach is great and the fire is just . . . just . . ."

"Great?" Curt asked, a bit snidely.

"Yes!" Polly said.

"Yeah, it really worked out," Avery said, wishing Curt hadn't felt the need to be so mean.

"It's pretty nice," April agreed, and the others nodded.

"Reminds me of clambakes we had at my grandparents' place in Maine when I was little," Sabrina said. "Of course we didn't have to do any of the work, but the food tastes almost as good."

Avery figured that in Sabrina's haughty way, that was supposed to be a compliment. April twisted around to look at Sabrina.

"How did someone like you end up renting a place with us?" she asked. "Doesn't your family, like, own a small country or something?"

Avery sucked in her breath, shocked by April's bluntness. Sabrina seemed not to mind the question, though.

"We've always summered in Europe, but this year they decided it was time for me to go solo," Sabrina answered. "They said I had to 'learn about real life' and all that crap. So, here I am, and starting tomorrow I'll be working as a nanny for a couple of brats to pay my way."

"Sounds like torture," Owen quipped.

Sabrina wrinkled her nose and made a face at him.

Avery tensed, worried that an argument was about to break out.

"Hey, everyone," someone said, strolling up out of the dark.

He was wearing black-rimmed glasses and plaid shorts.

"Oh hi, Fred!" Polly was the first to recognize and greet him.

In the firelight Sabrina rolled her eyes and Curt muttered something under his breath. Obviously some of them weren't happy to see the landlord; Avery found herself feeling a little sorry for him. Just because he was nerdy, they didn't have to be mean.

"So what brings you out on this balmy night?" Owen asked.

"Just wanted to check up on the house," Fred replied. Was it Avery's imagination, or was he gazing longingly at the food. "Bathroom all fixed? Everything okay?"

"Isn't that something you'd usually check on *during the day*?" Sabrina asked, stressing the last three words.

"Everything's fine, Fred, why don't you join us?" Polly asked, instantly prompting groans from some of the others. Polly looked around, a surprised expression on her face. Avery was quick to give her a reassuring nod, as if to let her know she'd done the right thing.

Fred sat down so eagerly that it was clear he'd been hoping for an invite. Polly piled a plate with food for him.

"I gotta go get some practice time in with the band," Curt said, getting up.

"Now?" Avery asked, disappointed.

"Yeah. I told you we didn't get enough rehearsal time before. I said I'd try again later," he said, pecking her cheek. "Well, now's later."

Avery felt sad as she watched him go. *I hope it isn't going to be like this all summer. Just when we start to relax and have fun, he rushes off.*

The group ate dinner and chatted. Most of them ignored Fred. Avery was sorry to see that even Polly tried to avoid him, as if she was worried about what the others would think. After a while, Avery stood up and wandered away from the fire. A light breeze was coming off the ocean. It ruffled her hair, and she tasted the salt on her lips. She walked along the edge of the water plunging her bare feet into the cool wet sand. The night sky was awash with stars. She liked it here, but it would have been nicer with Curt by her side.

By the time she returned, the fire had burned down to a small heap of glowing red ashes. Without the flames, it was hard to see. People were just dark silhouettes. Familiar voices drifted her way, and out of the corner of her eye she recognized Owen and Sabrina sitting several yards down the beach. Numerous empty beer bottles were stuck in the sand around Owen.

"I just don't want to end up like my father," he was saying in a slurred voice.

"Why are you telling me this?" Sabrina asked a little impatiently.

"I'm just trying to tell you . . . I like you." Owen sounded vulnerable . . . and drunk.

"Oh, come on, why bother?" Sabrina asked. "There are three

other girls in the house and a few thousand more staying up and down the beach. I really don't care what you're trying to prove. I'm not going to be your test subject, or girlfriend or whatever. Got it?" Sabrina said, her tone harsh.

Avery found herself wincing for Owen's sake.

"Oh yeah, loud and clear," Owen said.

They both stood up and moved off in opposite directions, Owen staggering back toward the remains of the fire and digging around for another beer.

"Hey!" a girl yelled. It sounded like April.

"Back off!" Owen growled.

"You'll burn yourself!"

Suddenly Owen was out of control, stumbling and careening around the fire. April and Lucas had hold of his arms and were trying to keep him from falling headfirst into the red-hot coals. Fred and Polly watched with wary expressions.

"Calm down," Lucas was saying. "You're a little out of it, man."

"What do you know?" he grunted. "You don't know anything about me!"

In the midst of the struggle, the sounds of voices and laughter came from up the beach. The smell of cigarette smoke was suddenly in the air. Avery turned and saw silhouettes and the red embers of cigarettes glowing in the night. A group of guys was approaching. The leader wore a white shirt unbuttoned at the collar and a yellow polo shirt underneath. It was Martin, the football player who'd hit on her the night before.

"Yo, Owen!" Martin said. "Whassup?"

Owen stopped staggering. "Martin, dude! Take me away."

"Away we go."

Owen staggered toward his friends. They clapped him on the back and welcomed him into the group, then headed off in the dark.

"I hate those kinds of guys," April muttered.

But the good news was that Polly and Fred had drawn near each other. Fred whispered something to Polly that made her laugh. Avery smiled, glad that someone was still having a good time.

"Guess it's time to clean up," Lucas said, and started to shake out the beach blankets. Avery started picking up plates, and April, Fred, and Polly joined in. Sabrina followed, carrying some forks. They were all a little smashed—not as bad as Owen, but enough that no one could quite make the trip back to the house in a straight line.

A few moments later, in the kitchen, they dumped the stuff on the counter. Fred started to roll up his sleeves.

"You don't have to help," said Sabrina, who leaned against the counter and watched while the others started to clean up.

"I want to," said Fred.

"You're our landlord," she said. "Remember?"

For a second it almost appeared that Fred had forgotten. Now he straightened up. "Yes, of course. Well, thanks for dinner."

He left. Avery glanced at Polly and saw the corners of her mouth turn down.

"I really don't get that guy," Sabrina said. "I mean, you almost get the feeling he's a landlord because it's the only way he can find friends. What a loser."

No one else commented. They neither agreed, nor dared to disagree. Lucas positioned himself in front of the sink and started to wash the dishes.

"There's no dishwasher?" April asked, surprised.

Avery hadn't looked before; she just assumed there was one. Didn't every house have a dishwasher these days?

"I'm too tired to clean up." Sabrina yawned.

Avery didn't believe her, and from the expressions of the others, she was pretty sure that no one else did either. But she wasn't in the mood to deal with Sabrina's attitude. Instead she said, "That's okay, we've got it *this time*," making sure to place emphasis on the last two words. Next to her, April snickered slightly, but no one said anything more.

Even with all four of them washing, it seemed to take a long time to clean up. Maybe because they were all a little unsteady. Avery was glad that Lucas was pitching in. She really didn't want to think of him as a slacker. "We should get paper plates if we're going to do this again," she said.

"Or at least have Polly talk Fred into buying a dishwasher for this place," April added.

"Why me?" Polly asked.

"Because Fred's got a thing for you," April said. Lucas's eyes met Avery's and he smiled.

"No, he doesn't," Polly protested, but Avery thought she detected just the slightest hint of pleasure on the girl's face.

"Does so," April said.

Polly gave Lucas and Avery a quizzical look.

"She could be right," Lucas said.

"It's a compliment," Avery said. "After all, before you showed up, he had his eye on Sabrina."

Polly looked somewhat dismayed. "Oh, great, the guy who everyone else thinks is a dork."

Avery knew right away that Polly was fishing for a protest. "He's not a dork, and, anyway it doesn't matter what anyone else thinks."

"Up to a point," said April, who probably didn't realize how Polly felt.

"I'd be nicer if I were you," Lucas teased April. "Otherwise, no dishwasher."

"You're right!" April pretended to gasp. "It'll be paper plates for the rest of the summer."

"I'll write them on the list," Avery offered with a wink.

After that they grew quiet and concentrated on the dishes. Avery wished that Curt hadn't left. She'd had such high hopes for this summer, but they were mostly based on Curt not running off to be with the band all the time. Besides, despite all the tensions from earlier in the evening, the wine coolers had left her feeling kind of warm and fuzzy and in the mood for something physical.

Finally, the dishes were done. Lucas turned off the water after handing the last plate to April to dry.

"It's a good thing this is the last dish," April said. "I'm tired. I'm going upstairs."

"Sleep tight." Avery waved.

"Nice doing dishes with you," Lucas joked.

"I'm going to bed too," Polly said with a yawn. "See you in the morning."

A minute later Avery and Lucas were alone in the kitchen. She hopped up on one of the counters, not feeling at all tired. "That seemed to go well. I mean, except for Owen."

"Yeah." Lucas leaned against the opposite countertop.

He'd changed into a white T-shirt and khaki shorts. "I'm glad we got together."

They exchanged smiles. Avery had a fleeting image of Curt rehearsing with his band. Should she have gone with him, to be supportive? The truth was, she'd rather be here. She glanced again at Lucas. The dreadlocks were a shock the first time you saw them, but it didn't take long to get used to them. And there was something sexy about the contrast of his light-colored shirt and shorts against his tan.

"Just graduate high school?" Lucas asked.

Avery blinked and realized she'd been drifting. "Yes," she answered. "You?"

He nodded.

"College in the fall?" she asked.

"I . . . guess." Lucas seemed to hesitate.

"Where?"

"Not sure yet. How about you?"

"I'll be going to a JC," she said. "There aren't any four-year schools close enough that I can commute to. If I start out at a JC, I can still be close to Curt."

"You two been together long?"

"A couple of years."

"The two of you could go away to college together."

"Curt go to college?" She laughed, and in so doing, leaned back and hit her head hard on the edge of the cabinets. "Ouch!" she said, her hand flying to her head.

Lucas stepped toward her. "Here, let me take a look," he said.

"No, I'm fine. I just bumped it," she said.

"Some bump," he said. "You hit the cabinet so hard, I'm surprised the whole thing didn't fall down. I better take a look. Besides, I used to be a lifeguard. I'm trained to look for dangerous bumps and bruises."

And just like that, his hands were on her head, gently parting her hair. Their faces were only inches apart. Avery's heart suddenly began to pound, and she licked her dry lips. She imagined him taking her in his arms and kissing her. It was just an idle thought, but she wanted him to do it.

"So you're not sure if you're going to college, or is it where?" she asked, trying to focus on something else. His touch was almost a caress. This wasn't supposed to be happening, but at the same time, she didn't want him to stop.

"Depends on who decides," Lucas said. "If my parents have any say in it, the if and where are already a done deal."

His hands found the place where she had hit her head, and she winced. "You don't sound too excited."

"Let's just say I'd rather forge my own path, and I'm not sure college fits into my plans right now."

"And working for Habitat for Humanity does?" she said.

Lucas's eyebrows rose. His eyes met hers. Clearly Avery had caught him off guard. "How do you know about that?"

"I saw you while I was shopping with Polly," Avery said. "Don't get me wrong. I think it's cool that you're trying to help out."

"Thanks." Once again he moved his fingers softly through her hair as if reluctant to let go. "Everything looks okay here. The skin isn't broken or anything."

He started to pull his hand away, but she didn't want him to. As if it had a will of its own, her hand reached up and grabbed his wrist, holding him close. They stared into each other's eyes, then Lucas's lips began to move toward hers.

Before either of them could move or say anything more, the front door opened and Curt entered.

• • •

Lucas was fully aware that he'd kept his fingers in Avery's hair longer than necessary. He was aware that if Curt hadn't come in just then, he would have kissed her. He'd wanted to touch her since he'd first seen her the day before. The words "soft" and "pretty" described both the girl and her hair, and he had to remind himself that he already had enough on his mind this summer without having the headache of messing with another guy's girlfriend.

And yet . . . there was something about her.

Almost irresistible.

At the sound of the door opening, Lucas backed quickly away from Avery. Avery slid off the counter and went to greet her boyfriend. Lucas wasn't sure what Curt had seen, and now he saw a suspicious look in Curt's eye and braced himself. But Curt's attention went to his girlfriend, and Lucas felt a strange mixture of relief and jealousy as the handsome scraggly rocker took Avery in his arms and gave her a hug.

"So what's up?" Curt asked.

"Just talking," Avery said brightly, as if she too was relieved that he hadn't noticed how close she and Lucas had come. "Did you have a good rehearsal?"

Curt's eyes lit up. "Great news. Darek got us a gig. One of those sunset concerts in the park. It's free, but it's the kind of exposure we need."

"Curt, that's awesome," she said, flinging her arms around his neck. Lucas turned away, thinking back to what she'd said about Habitat for Humanity. So she'd seen him while shopping.

"When's the show?" Avery was asking Curt.

"Two weeks."

"See, I knew good things would happen here," she said.

Lucas knew it was time to leave them alone. "That's awesome, bro," he said, offering Curt his hand. As Curt shook it, his eyes hardened slightly. "Thanks."

Lucas crossed the living room and headed for his room. He'd made a mistake, but fortunately it was a small one. Just the same, he wouldn't make it again.

Four

Polly checked her watch while she waited for Avery at the bottom of the stairs. It had been two weeks since she'd helped get Avery a job at The Seashell Restaurant. And every morning it was the same thing: Polly always up early and waiting. She knew she wasn't waking early because she was so eager to go to work. It was Avery she was eager to see. Avery, who was the nicest and sweetest friend she'd ever had.

I'll give her another five minutes, then I'll knock on her door, she thought, just as she did every morning. The minutes ticked by. Just as she was about to start up the stairs, Avery's door opened and she came out, closing it behind her.

Polly breathed a sigh of relief. She didn't want to be responsible for waking up Curt. That was definitely not her idea of fun.

"Am I late?" Avery said.

"No," Polly answered.

They smiled at each other. It had become a routine, a private joke they shared. As Avery came quietly down the stairs she glanced over at one of the sofas and saw something that was not routine. "He been there all night?"

Polly turned. Owen was sprawled on a couch. She hadn't noticed him before. Then again, she hadn't seen much of him recently. He was out partying every night and, she suspected, not always home in the morning. His clothes were badly wrinkled and stained in a few places. He was unshaven and a mess, *and* had drooled onto the couch. Polly winced. "Do you think we should wake him?"

Avery shook her head as she headed for the front door. "Best to just let him sleep it off."

"We've lived in the same house for two weeks and I'm not sure I've ever seen him sober after three in the afternoon," Polly said as she and Avery left the house and stepped out into the morning sunlight. "You think he's an alcoholic?"

"I hope not," Avery said.

A minute later they were walking down the beach, their shoes tucked into their tote bags. The sand squished between Polly's toes in a pleasing way. It was just after ten, and the beach was starting to fill up with families under the brightly colored umbrellas.

As usual when they walked to work, Polly dropped her eyes to the sand, searching for shells. She had only found one really good one, so far—it was the size of a baseball and black with gold streaks—and she kept it in a place of honor on her dresser in between a picture of her parents and another one of her grandparents.

"You're quiet today," Avery said, interrupting her thoughts.

Polly looked up quickly. "Sorry."

"No, it's cool, you're just usually more talkative. Everything okay?"

"Fine," Polly lied. In reality, things were far from fine. Every day all around her it seemed like everyone else was partying, hooking up, and even getting into relationships. *Why can't I just meet a nice guy?*

"How's the man-hunt going?" Avery asked with a grin.

Polly blushed, surprised that Avery had seemed to read her mind. "Not as well as I'd like," she admitted.

"What about Fred? He likes you."

"But nobody likes him," said Polly.

"That's not true," Avery said. "Just a few big mouths in our house."

"Yeah, but I have to live with them," Polly said. And, anyway, she didn't want to talk about it, and the best way was to change the subject. "What about you?"

"Me?" Avery asked, caught by surprise. "I'm with Curt."

"You never wonder about other guys?" Polly asked.

"Who?" Avery asked.

"Anthony?"

"Our manager Anthony?" Avery asked bewildered. He was the manager of The Seashell and therefore her boss.

"Yeah, he's gorgeous, and I think he likes you."

Avery laughed. "No way."

"Come on, even I'm not that naive," Polly said. "He's so obviously into you. Why else would he tell you that you were too pretty to be a waitress and make you the hostess?"

"Uh, maybe because he saw immediately that I'd make a terrible waitress and he couldn't think of anything else for me to do?" Avery said.

"Nice try, Ave," Polly scoffed. "*You're* not that naive either. Now don't make a big deal about it. It's not your fault you're beautiful and men fawn over you."

"That's not true."

"Which part?" Polly asked. "That you're beautiful, or that men can't help fawning over you?"

"Uh, both?"

"Sorry, even Lucas stares at you sometimes."

"He does?" Avery asked, sounding surprised.

Polly shook her head. It was ridiculous that Avery didn't know this. "They *all* do, Avery. Even the ones who pretend not to."

"I guess I just don't notice," Avery admitted.

"Well, do me a favor and from now on, notice a little. It's frustrating that you don't even enjoy it. I would kill to get a tenth of the attention you get."

"I'm sorry," Avery said.

"Don't be sorry, just don't pretend it's not happening," Polly said, surprised at her own bluntness.

"Okay, but seriously, I *am* sorry about the hostessing thing," Avery said.

"Well, at least as a waitress I get tips," Polly said, trying to make Avery feel better. "And don't forget, if there's a party of six, I automatically get fifteen percent."

"Right," Avery said, grinning. "Would it help if I steered the larger groups to your tables?"

"As long as the other waitresses don't notice, that would be great. Thanks!" Polly said, thinking, *I may not have met a guy but at least I've made a friend. Things could be worse.*

"I don't think I ever thanked you properly for getting me the job," Avery said.

"You're welcome," Polly said.

"No, I owe you. Suppose I make it my mission to help find you a guy."

"Serious?" Polly asked, excitement running through her.

"Dead serious. If I can't find a guy in this town who would want to be with a sweet and pretty girl like you, then there is no justice in this world."

Polly hugged Avery. "That would be the best present ever."

Avery patted her shoulder. "You deserve it."

A few minutes later they arrived at the restaurant. The exterior was made up of dark wood and brass, and a sign declared in delicate pink letters THE SEASHELL RESTAURANT. Large, round windows rimmed in brass faced the beach and the surrounding pier. There was an indoor seating area and an outdoor one. The tables and chairs outside stood on a deck that ran halfway around the restaurant.

Next door was the Surfin' Spot, a bar with live music where a lot of people, including Owen and his friends, often hung out. The bar was always loud and rowdy with people crammed inside and out. Anthony managed both places.

Polly slipped on her white Keds and Avery a pair of white strappy sandals. They climbed the steps that led up to the pier and to the entrance to The Seashell. Inside, the air was cool and the lighting muted. The nautical theme carried on with starfish, large shells, and red plastic lobsters scattered among fishnets hanging from the ceiling. Three other waitresses were already seated at a table, all wearing the same pale pink skirt and midriff shirt that Polly had on. Being a redhead, Polly had always avoided wearing pink and she knew that the outfit didn't look that great on her. As hostess, Avery wore a simple, strapless, white cotton dress that offset her smooth shoulders. Polly would gladly have changed places with her.

Anthony, the manager, came out of the kitchen and ran an eye over all of them. He was just over six feet tall and had the sandy blond hair and tan that would have made him look like a beach bum were it not for the pleated linen white pants and a white long-sleeved shirt with the sleeves rolled up to his elbows. As Polly had said, he was gorgeous.

"Okay, ladies," Anthony said, addressing them all. "We open in twenty minutes. Susie, Sandy, and Sarah will work the dining room for lunch. Polly, you work the deck, and if Terry ever shows up, she'll be out there with you."

Polly sighed, frustrated. She hated working the deck alone, and she was pretty sure she was stuck because Terry was a flake and often missed work. The other three, or the Triple S Threat, as they were called, couldn't be counted on to help. Susie, Sandy, and Sarah were triplets and they hated one another. They did, however, work well together in some sort of freaky super-connected way. Bottom line was that guests inside would be well taken care of. Polly and the guests outside would be miserable. *It's going to be one of those days.*

It's one of those days, Curt thought as he stared in frustration at his bandmates. Bobby, the bass player and songwriter, was sitting sullenly in a corner, his hand bandaged. The idiot had cut himself on a broken beer bottle. Austin, the lead singer, hadn't hit a single note all morning. Darek sat by his drums, his long brown hair flopping into his eyes, and glared out from beneath his locks.

"All right, guys, come on," Curt urged them. "Tonight's the night. We came here for the chance to play, and we've got to take advantage of it."

"I don't think we're in a position to take advantage of anything," Darek said quietly.

"Except maybe some hotties after the show," Austin said with a grin.

"If I were you, I'd be more worried about hitting notes than hitting on chicks," Bobby said.

"Maybe if you wrote notes and lyrics that actually flowed and made sense, my job would be a little easier," Austin flared.

"Maybe if you actually took care of your voice, you would actually be able to sing the music," Bobby said.

"Fine talk from a guy who messed up his hand right before the gig. How did you do that again?" Austin asked, his voice dripping sarcasm.

"Cut the crap, both of you," Curt said. "Arguing isn't going to get us anywhere."

"Neither is practicing, at this point," Darek spoke up.

Curt turned to look at Darek, feeling his temper start to get out of hand. The last thing he needed was for the drummer to start in with BS like that. They might have a long way to go as a band, but they had come so far already and he wasn't about to stop now. "I'm not giving up," Curt hissed finally.

"You miss my meaning, dude," Darek said. "Look, the night before a play opens, the actors take a break. They relax and don't rehearse."

"We're not actors," Bobby said.

"But we are performers," Darek shot back. "It's as much about the attitude as the playing. We should take a page from the actors. I don't think we should rehearse right before the gig. We should knock off, get some rest, relax, whatever, so we're fresh for tonight."

Curt figured it couldn't hurt. Anything had to be better than what they'd been doing for the last two hours. He nodded slowly. "Okay, maybe you're right. Sounds like a plan to me."

"Cool," Austin said, almost visibly relaxing.

"Just one thing," Curt added. "Austin, maybe you could gargle some lemon water or something. Bobby, see what can be done for your hand. Darek, get some sleep. We'll meet at the pier at seven to set up. Agreed?"

They all nodded. Curt put Lucille back in her case and started for the front door.

"And what are you going to be doing?" Bobby asked.

"Looking for a little inspiration," Curt said.

The band's house was one block over and five houses up from the one he and Avery were staying at. As Curt trudged slowly back toward the house he thought about Avery. They hadn't seen each other much in the past two weeks. She'd been putting in long hours at the restaurant, and he had been rehearsing with the band. It wasn't that he didn't want to spend time with her, it was just difficult to find the time to spend. He knew she wanted to go to the amusement parks on the boardwalk, but he just really wasn't into that. Sooner or later he'd take her, though.

He was worried about the gig. The recent rehearsals had been disastrous. Maybe Darek was right, maybe they just needed to kick back and relax until seven. The house came into sight and he headed for it. Avery would be at work with Polly. The only one who might be home was April. Her job at the video store came with crazy, random hours, usually in the evening. They'd talked several times about music since that first day when she'd played for him. He thought she was pretty cool, even if she was into that emo bleeding-heart music.

He entered the house and climbed the stairs. When he got to his and Avery's room, some impulse took hold and he headed past it and straight for April's door. He knocked and she opened it without even asking who was there. *Guess I'm the only person who visits her.*

"Hey, come in," she said, smiling. Today she was wearing a tight black T-shirt and tight jeans, which showed off the shapely figure she often hid under baggier clothes.

He forced himself to smile in return. "Still playing that emo junk?" he asked, kidding her.

She grinned and fired one back. "Still playing so loud that no one can hear what you're singing, or tell that you suck?"

"Fair enough," he said. "Of course, you've never heard me play, so that's just a guess on your part. But it just so happens that we're playing a sunset concert tonight. You want to come?"

She glanced at him out of the corners of her eyes. "What would Avery say?"

"Why would she care? I'm just talking to a roommate and fellow musician. Besides, you should come, you might learn something."

"And that would be that I was right all along and your band sucks?"

He actually laughed. "No, the band is good, especially if we're playing covers. It's our original songs that don't make it."

"Really?" she said, sitting on her bed and wrapping her arms around her knees.

"Yeah," he admitted, sitting down next to her. "We need better material, original stuff, to actually go anywhere. But the songs Bobby writes suck. Unfortunately, none of the rest of us writes any better."

"Sing me one," she urged.

"You serious?" he asked, gazing at her slowly, letting his eyes run briefly down her body.

"Of course, I am. Come on, I sang one of mine for you," she said. "And like you just said, we're all musicians here."

Curt nodded and picked up her old Yamaha acoustic. "Don't say I didn't warn you."

He began to sing "Love in a Strange World." He knew he had an okay voice and he played fine, but even he winced as he heard the words: "Love in a strange world, where I'm a boy and you're a girl. We buy a ticket for the lottery just like love we hope we'll soon see."

"Stop!" April held up her hand. "Please, stop." She picked up a pillow off her bed and buried her face in it.

"I told you," he said, putting down her guitar. Her shoulders were shaking. "What is it?" he asked.

The only reply was the sound of muffled laughter. Impulsively, he lunged forward and ripped the pillow away. Lying on her side on the bed, she looked up at him with eyes wide and dancing. Her lips were parted with laughter, and a strange sensation came over him. *What would it be like to kiss her?*

April didn't think she'd be able to stop laughing. The song Curt had sung was awful. Absolutely terrible. When he snatched the pillow from her, though, she suddenly felt something completely different. She was no longer thinking about the song. Now she was staring up at his handsome face. His eyes were intense, and his lips were curled into an alluring smile. She reached up and pulled his lips down to hers.

He kissed her gently. First her lips, then her neck. When his lips returned to her lips, she parted them. Meanwhile his hand slid over her T-shirt, and April began to feel herself flood with desire. She kissed him harder and threw her arm around his neck. His left hand slid under her T-shirt, and she let the rough tips of his calloused fingers slip up her stomach. She arched her back, inviting him to undo her bra. He started to fumble with it, tugging, pulling . . .

Then yanking . . .

She started to giggle. Maybe it was nerves, but she just couldn't help herself.

"You think it's so funny? You do it," he grumbled, and sat up.

She pulled her T-shirt down and stared at him. He might have been handsome and sexy, but he was seriously lacking a sense of humor. "Come on," she said.

Now he got it, and sort of smirked. "Believe me, I've never

had that problem before. At least, not in a long time."

"I believe you," she said, feeling both disappointment and relief. *I'm not sure what it is, but there is definitely something between us,* she thought. But whatever it was had passed . . . for now.

"So if I agree to come tonight, do you promise to play some covers? And absolutely, under no circumstances, play the song you just sang?" she asked, propping herself up on her elbow.

"I swear that if you come hear the band tonight, I won't play that song. On the other hand," he said, a mischievous twinkle returning to his eye, "if you don't come, I'll play it two doors down from you every night for the rest of the summer."

"I cave!" she shrieked. "Anything but that!"

"So, it's a deal?" he asked.

"Deal," she said, "now get out of here."

He left, and she closed and locked the door behind him. Her heart was beating hard from the excitement she'd felt. She'd liked kissing him. Was that what she wanted? What about Avery? After a minute she sat down on her bed and pulled out her cell phone. She hadn't spoken to her mom in several days, and wanted to do it before she went out. "Hi, Mom?"

"April, honey, how are you?" her mom asked on the other end.

"Good, how are you?"

"Oh, fine. Just fine."

April frowned. *Mom sounds really tired. I guess that's what happens when you're working two jobs and caring for an elderly mother,* she thought. She felt a twinge of guilt. *I should be there, helping.*

She swallowed hard. "Did Grandma give you the money I dropped by yesterday?"

"Yes, thank you so much."

"So guess what?" April decided to cheer her up. "I'm going out tonight, to a concert. And I was looking for some advice on clothes."

It seemed cheesy to be asking her mom for clothing advice, but if there was one thing her mom knew, it was guys. Her mom had never had a problem attracting men. Unfortunately, she did have problems keeping them from dying. After her father and a stepfather died, April had given up on thinking that any kind of relationship was permanent.

"Do you have a date?" her mom asked, excitement filling her voice.

"Well, maybe, I don't really know." She thought about what had just happened with Curt, and his insistence that she go to the concert. "It's complicated."

"It's always complicated, dear. But don't let that stop you from trying."

"Thanks," April said.

"So, how can I help?"

"You know that red coral necklace?"

"You want to wear it tonight? That's fine. Just come by and I'll give it to you."

"Thanks, Mom."

"And hon, one other thing? I know you love it, and it's you, but ditch the nose stud. Trust me on this one."

April smiled. *Some things never change.* "Sure, Mom."

Lucas turned the page of the thick old, dog-eared paperback. He had almost lost himself completely in the story when the bell on the surf shop door jingled. He stuck a flyer for the Stranger Than Fiction concert into the book to mark its place and then put it down on the counter.

He glanced up and watched in surprise as Sabrina entered the surf shop with two young boys. Sabrina was wearing the skimpiest bikini top—the sort of revealing scrap of clothing you could get away with at the beach, but was surprising to see around town. The boys couldn't have been much older than four and six, and immediately started running wild, touching everything they could get their hands on.

Sabrina did nothing to stop them. Instead, she gave Lucas a coy smile. "Hey, surfer boy."

"Hey, Sabrina," Lucas answered while keeping a wary eye on the two boys. "What's up?"

"Gotta buy the brats some body boards."

The boys had already discovered the body boards and were falling all over themselves trying to pull them out of the racks. *Crash!* They knocked over a display stand nearby. Sabrina continued to ignore them and tried on a pair of sunglasses.

Lucas left the counter and moved toward the boys. By now they'd both taken hold of a bright green body board and were having a tug-of-war.

"I want this one!"

"No, I saw it first!"

"Okay, guys, let go," Lucas said calmly. "Before you get boards you have to help clean up the mess you made."

"I don't have to do nothing." The older boy crossed his arms.

"Me neither." His younger brother imitated him.

Lucas glanced at Sabrina, hoping she might lend a hand, but she was too busy looking at herself in the mirror.

Lucas sighed and took the bright green body board away. "I just remembered. This one isn't for sale."

It only took a minute to find other body boards the right size for each of them. Lucas glanced carefully, though, at the four-year-old. "You sure you swim?" he asked.

"Like a fish," Sabrina answered from the counter where she'd picked up the book Lucas had been reading. "*War and Peace*? Are you kidding me?" she asked. "Why are you reading that?"

Lucas's mind jumped into overdrive. "Uh, I lost a bet."

"That's some bet," she said, eyeing him curiously. "I'm surprised you could even get a copy of something like this around here." She narrowed her eyes suspiciously. "Where'd you find it, anyway?"

"The used-book store," Lucas answered, and busied himself

carrying the boys' boards to the register. He placed them on the counter and turned around to see that they had followed him every step of the way.

"Did you know there's buried treasure at the beach?" the four-year-old asked him, wide-eyed.

"Jamie, shh, don't tell him," the older one warned.

"Why not, Tim?"

"He'll dig it up himself," said Tim.

Jamie turned to Lucas, and his little forehead furrowed with worry. "You won't, will you?"

"No way, little dude. It's against the pirate's code."

"See?" Jamie turned to his big brother. "He won't tell."

"Is it true?" Tim asked, staring at him intently.

Lucas dropped his voice to a whisper. "I've heard some things."

Tim eyed him suspiciously for a moment and then seemed to make a decision. "We heard it's under the pier."

"Really?" Lucas pretended to be surprised, "Just where did you get your information?"

"The old guy who sells cotton candy on the boardwalk," Sabrina explained, rolling her eyes.

"He used to be a pirate!" Jamie exclaimed, wide-eyed.

"He did not, and you're not going under that pier. It's dangerous. Now, just stop talking about it!" Sabrina ordered.

"Sorry guys, looks like you'll have to play Treasure Island some other time," Lucas told them sympathetically.

Sabrina leaned over the counter, giving him an even better look at what was threatening to spill out of her bikini top. Lucas averted his gaze.

"Funny thing about treasure," she said. "Sometimes it's right in front of your eyes and you don't even see it."

"I tend to prefer a more nuanced approach," he replied.

Sabrina quickly straightened up. "Sounds like you have classic literature on the brain," she said. Lucas shrugged. She tried to hold his gaze, but he wouldn't let her. Obviously she could be pretty observant when she wanted to be, but that didn't mean he had to answer questions about things he preferred to keep private. Finally she gave up.

"So, we'll take the body boards and these," she said, laying a pair of $200 Gucci sunglasses on the counter. Lucas had always considered the glasses a joke. He never thought anyone would ever buy them. Two hundred dollars was the price of a good wet suit. Of course, Sabrina had already let everyone in the house know she was rich, so he wasn't that surprised that she could afford them.

"Put it on this," she said, handing him a gold card.

He read the name on the card. "Victoria Summers."

"Their mom," Sabrina said, nodding at Tim and Jamie.

Lucas stared from Sabrina to the sunglasses to the card. He could understand charging the boards to their mother, but he was a little uncertain about the $200 glasses. "You want to give her a call and make sure it's okay?" he asked.

"No, she's working and she doesn't like to be disturbed.

Don't worry, it's fine. It's the card she's been having me use all summer," Sabrina reassured him.

Lucas decided to keep his misgivings to himself. He had no reason not to trust Sabrina. He swiped the card.

"Curt got you pimping for his band?" she teased, indicating the stack of flyers for STF on the counter.

"Least I can do for a roommate," Lucas replied with a smile.

Sabrina signed Victoria Summers on the credit card slip. "Then you're going to the concert tonight?"

"Probably. You?"

She shrugged. "Maybe. If there's nothing better to do."

Lucas almost had the feeling she was trolling for something, but decided to ignore it. There was a crash as the kids knocked over a surfboard in the back of the store.

Tim came running. "Jamie did it! I saw him!"

"No, I didn't!" Jamie cried, chasing his older brother.

Sabrina rolled her eyes at Lucas, who went around the counter to check on the damage. Luckily, the board was one of those cheap, factory-made things that were almost impossible to ding. When he returned to the front of the store, Sabrina was once again studying herself in the mirror. The boys had grabbed their new body boards.

"Dudes, you got to promise me you'll be extra careful when you're using those things," Lucas said. "There's always got to be a grown-up watching."

He was speaking more to Sabrina than the kids, but she didn't seem to notice.

"We'll be careful," Tim said earnestly.

They headed for the door. Sabrina turned and waved. "See you later, maybe."

Lucas watched them go. Sabrina was definitely not nanny material. He felt sorry for the mother who'd been blind enough to hire her. The boys were okay; they just needed someone to pay attention to them.

Avery popped into his mind. She would've been a good nanny. A good girlfriend, too. He shook his head and once again warned himself not to go there.

Curt chewed nervously on a thumbnail. The band would be performing in forty minutes, and he was worried. Darek, the drummer, was the only one ready and healthy. Austin, their singer, was still complaining about a sore throat, and Bobby the bass player's finger was still wrapped in a bandage. While Bobby insisted he was fine, Curt suspected otherwise.

They'd just finished the sound check when Avery climbed up on the stage and came over to him. She looked great in a lavender tank top, white peasant skirt, and wedge sandals.

"How're you doing? You okay?" she asked him, taking his hands, clearly concerned and hopeful that this would be the break Stranger Than Fiction had been waiting for.

"I'm okay," Curt lied. "We're going to really shake things up tonight."

"I know you are," she said, giving him a kiss.

"Can I get some of that?" Austin asked as he walked by.

"Knock it off, Austin," Curt said with a smile.

"How come Austin can make comments like that and you smile, but if anyone else does, you get mad?" Avery asked teasingly.

"Because I know he doesn't mean it," Curt said. He gestured out at the empty space in front of the band shell that would soon be filled, he hoped, with an audience. "Where are you going to stand?"

"Where do I always stand?" she asked.

"Front and center," he said with a smile.

"Then that's where I'll be, as soon as I get something to eat."

"Okay, then I'll see you in a little while."

"Okay," she said, giving him one last kiss before heading off.

"Curt!" Bobby called.

"Yeah?"

"We opening with 'Love in a Strange World?"

Curt winced inwardly. That was the song he'd sung to April, the one she'd made him promise he wouldn't sing tonight. And yet it was one of Bobby's favorites. "Uh, lemme think about it," he said.

"Hey, rock star!" he heard someone call. April was in front of the stage, wearing a low-cut sheer black top with a red necklace that hung provocatively down her chest. Standing above her on the stage, Curt had an unusually good view. Her tight black skirt hugged her hips. She was wearing only a touch of makeup and a simple pair of earrings.

Wow! he thought. "Hey, you look great."

"Thanks," April said, blushing slightly. "So, you amped?"

Curt nodded despite his worries. "Can't wait."

Darek joined Curt at the edge of the stage, his eyes wide. "Hey, introduce me to your friend," he said, his voice sounding husky.

"April, this is our drummer, Darek. Darek, this is April."

Darek reached down and shook April's hand, lingering over it for a second.

"Who are you?"

"One of my roommates," Curt said. "The one who writes songs. I told you about her."

"Oh yeah, the girl who writes like Dylan," Darek said.

Curt felt his face grow red. That had been a private comment he'd made for Darek's ears only. "Shut up, dude."

But it was too late. April realized where the compliment must have come from. "I've never been compared to Dylan before."

"Where are you going to be during the concert?" Darek asked.

"Front and center, with Avery," Curt answered for her.

"Okay, I guess that's where I'll be," April said. "I should go. See you guys after the concert?"

"Definitely," Darek said.

As soon as she was out of sight, Darek turned to Curt.

"What a hottie. Tell me she doesn't have a boyfriend, dude."

"Forget it, Darek, she's not your type," Curt told him. "Besides, she's got a boyfriend back home."

"Too bad," Darek said.

"Yeah," Curt agreed.

Five

The outdoor concert had started, and Sabrina was bored. Curt's band wasn't very good. Not that she was totally surprised. The strangest part was that when they played covers, they sounded bearable. People danced and seemed to have a good time. But each time STF started to play and original song, people stopped dancing and just stood around with their brains dribbling out of their ears.

Sabrina gazed around the crowd. Most of her housemates wore pained expressions as if they really wanted to go, but Curt had already managed to make eye contact with everybody and would be pissed if they took off.

The one person who seemed to be enjoying herself was Avery. Some good-looking guy, who Polly said was her boss at the restaurant, was dancing with her. Meanwhile, up on the stage, Curt had a serious frown, but Sabrina couldn't tell if it was because he was jealous or just concentrating on the music.

Curious, Sabrina moved close enough to hear what Avery

and the restaurant manager were talking about while they danced.

"You really should book the band for the Surfin' Spot," Avery urged.

"I just might," the handsome manager replied, although Sabrina wasn't sure how sincere he was. "I'll have to wait until the band that's playing there now finishes their contract. But then I'll consider it."

Sabrina rolled her eyes. She was certain he was just trying to play her. Especially the bit about STF. *This band couldn't get a gig to play a funeral, let alone a club.*

Sabrina glanced at the stage. Curt was watching Avery, and he looked pissed. Sabrina was pretty sure that was a look of jealousy, not concentration.

The song ended, and the crowd began to mill around.

"Hey, roomies," Lucas said, leading a new girl by the hand. She was blond and built, wearing a bikini top with spangles on it and a blue sarong. "This is Tara."

"Uh, hey," Avery said. Her voice sounded strained, and Sabrina looked at her more closely. Avery was studying the girl in a way that made Sabrina wonder. *Uh-huh, looks like Curt's not the only one who is jealous,* she thought. *Maybe Avery has a thing for surfer boy.*

Sabrina glanced around, curious to see what the rest of her roomies were up to. April was standing by herself, looking good, but scaring off any guy who got close. Owen and his idiot friends were drinking and chatting up some girls with too much make-up and low-cut tank tops.

Owen looked up and glanced at her. Sabrina rolled her eyes toward the night sky. *If you think I'm going to be jealous of those hags, you've got another think coming.*

Polly was hanging around them too, and that did make Sabrina curious. *She is so not the type.* Sabrina drifted closer to the group, keeping her ears open.

Polly was wearing a blue and green top, with red capris. As Sabrina moved closer, she heard one of Owen's buddies lean toward a friend and whisper, "She looks like a parrot."

"And talks like one too," the other guy whispered back.

Oblivious to what was being said about her, Polly tried to talk to them. "Hey, guys," she said in a forced and decidedly uncool way. Sabrina tensed as the guys started to smile meanly.

"Go fly away and find yourself a different perch," one of them said.

"Yeah, Polly Parrot," the other said. "Get lost."

Polly took off fast, but not before Sabrina saw the shocked look and tears in her eyes. Well, served her right, Sabrina thought. Parrots were definitely not supposed to share the pool with sharks. Now Owen came over with a look that said he'd witnessed the whole thing.

"Silly girl," Owen commented.

"Tell me about it." Sabrina snorted. "I can't believe she thinks that you or any of your friends would be remotely interested."

"Hey, with beer goggles on, she might not look so bad." Owen laughed. "Besides," he added, slightly more seriously, "it's not like I'm not getting much action anywhere else."

Sabrina couldn't believe it. "Nice try, but you should know by now that my role in life isn't to provide you with 'action.' You might think about being more selective instead of trying to jump every girl who walks by."

"I am selective," he said, his voice low and intense.

"So selective that it takes you thirty seconds to make a decision," she said sarcastically.

"You don't see it, but I'm a pretty good judge of character," Owen said, insisting on being serious.

"Really?" Sabrina asked, indicating the girls with the low-cut tank tops and too much mascara. "'Cause I haven't seen much evidence of that."

"I picked you, didn't I?" he asked sharply.

"There's always an exception," Sabrina shot back, gearing up for some nasty repartee.

But instead of a wisecrack, Owen took a deep breath and moved closer to her. "Look, Sabrina, seriously. I know that I don't come off like a prince. But I'm trying. If you knew what my life is like, what kind of crap I had growing up, you might cut me some slack. That first night I got with you because I was into you. I'm still into you. And if you want to know the truth, I haven't slept with anyone else since."

Sabrina felt the icy defenses inside her start to melt a little. She wanted to believe him. He looked so earnest while he gave his speech. But the beer in his hand and the cheap girls standing behind him making moon eyes at his friends did little to persuade her. "Why should I believe you?" she asked finally.

She was hoping he'd try to convince her. She was ready to be convinced. But, instead, his face hardened. "You know what? Bite me." He turned and stalked off.

Disappointment ran through her. Why didn't he stay and talk? *If he really wanted me, he would.*

Avery tapped her on the shoulder. "What's wrong with Polly? I saw her run off."

"She tried to mix with the wrong crowd," Sabrina said.

Avery's face fell. "Why do they have to be so mean?"

Because they're all so afraid of being hurt, Sabrina thought.

Up onstage, the band kicked into "Joy to the World (Jeremiah Was a Bullfrog)." Sabrina noticed that Martin, Owen's rowdy football-player friend, was headed her way with that stupid determined look drunk guys often get. It reminded her again of how much she wished Owen had hung around instead of getting all mad and storming off.

"Hi," Martin said.

"Good-bye," Sabrina replied, and turned away. As far as she was concerned, this was the perfect time to disappear.

• • •

The concert had finally ended, much to Avery's relief. She'd managed to see Curt for only a second afterward, but he'd seemed preoccupied and said he'd catch her later at the house. The whole evening felt like a bust to her. The band hadn't played well, and she wasn't sure she'd made much progress in trying to get Anthony to hire Stranger Than Fiction to play at the Surfin' Spot. Additionally, she felt sorry for Polly and hoped that she wasn't taking the insults too seriously. *Although I can't see how she wouldn't.*

She had trudged home alone. Lucas and his new "friend" Tara walked behind her. The sounds of them talking and laughing hadn't helped her mood. She felt like it had been a long time since she and Curt had laughed like that, and she couldn't help imagining herself walking with Lucas instead of Tara. After a while, Lucas and Tara veered off on a different path. Avery was somewhat relieved, but also jealous.

You have to stop thinking about Lucas, she told herself. *Curt's your boyfriend and just because he's going through a rough time doesn't mean you should think about another guy. After all, Curt was there for you in rough times.*

At the house, Avery climbed the stairs to her bedroom and changed clothes. Then she sat on the bed for a minute and looked at a picture of Curt and the band that she had in a frame on her nightstand. *I wish they'd played better tonight,* she thought. *I'll just have to try to stay upbeat for Curt. It's gotta be a blow to him.*

Maybe this would be a good night to take him out for a drink. She stood up and pulled opened her underwear drawer. Fishing underneath a stack of panties, her hands closed on an envelope. She pulled it out and opened it.

Something was wrong. The wad of bills inside was thinner than the day before. She quickly counted through it, trying to remember how much should be there, but she couldn't remember. She only knew the stack had been thicker. Taking out forty dollars, she carefully put the envelope back where she had gotten it.

Shoving the money in her shorts pocket, Avery headed downstairs. Everyone was hanging out in the living room, drinking beers or wine coolers. Curt had made it home and was in the kitchen, getting a beer. *I didn't expect him for at least another hour. I hope everything's okay.*

She joined him in the kitchen. "Hey."

"Hey." He glanced at her out of the corner of his eye and didn't look happy. He reached back into the fridge and offered her a beer.

"Listen, why don't we go out and have a drink?" she suggested hopefully.

"No, thanks," Curt replied.

"You sure?" she asked, disappointed.

"Yeah. Not in the mood."

Since there was no getting him out of his funk, she figured she might as well accept the beer and voice her other concern: "Honey, did you borrow some of my money?" she asked quietly as she cracked the can.

Curt turned and scowled at her. "No, why?"

"Nothing, I just thought I was a little short, but you didn't take any?"

"I said I didn't."

Avery immediately realized she'd made a mistake. Talking about the money only darkened his mood. "Forget about it. Maybe I was just too tired to count straight," she said quickly. "Do you have any Advil? I've got a headache."

"Because the band sucked?" he asked.

"No! I thought you were great," she lied.

"Then you must have been listening to some other band, because we sucked," he said.

She could tell that he was plummeting, and she knew from experience that there was no way to talk him out of it. Sometimes the best thing she could do was leave him alone and not antagonize him.

She walked into the living room. Everyone seemed to be there except for Polly and Lucas. "Anyone have any Advil?"

"I do," April said, getting up. "I'll get it for you."

"Thanks," Avery said, sitting down on the couch. She noticed Owen and Sabrina were sitting off to the side, near Polly's room, one on either side of Polly's door. They seemed to be getting along surprisingly well.

She was also surprised when Curt followed her out of

the kitchen. "Hey, Owen, Sabrina, what did you think of the band?" he asked.

"It was fine, you guys looked good," Sabrina said, avoiding his eyes.

"Your covers rocked!" Owen said with feigned, drunken enthusiasm.

"Thanks, but our original material bites," Curt said, sinking into a chair and taking a slug of brew. "We've got to do something before the Battle of the Bands."

Avery's ears perked up excitedly. Curt hadn't said anything about a battle of the bands before, but it was good news. Any chance the band had to be heard was good.

"You're going to be in that?" Owen asked, not doing a very good job of hiding his astonishment.

"We just found out tonight," Curt said.

"Before or after you played?" Avery heard Sabrina mutter under her breath.

"That's awesome, honey," Avery said quickly, hoping Curt hadn't heard Sabrina. "And don't worry about tonight. I know I enjoyed the concert."

"You sure you had time to pay attention?" Curt asked. "Looked to me like you were pretty busy doing other things."

Avery's head was beginning to really pound. "You mean Anthony? I was trying to get him to hire STF for the Surfin' Spot. He mentioned that this other band, Naked Mole Rats, is playing tomorrow night. Maybe we should go see them."

"Oh, Anthony mentioned that, huh?" Curt said, his voice heavy with sarcasm. "Well, if Anthony says so, then we should all just jump to it."

The words stung. Avery had only been trying to help. "What is that supposed to mean?" she asked, too tired to play games with him.

"It means it seems like you'll do anything Anthony says. I don't like how you're acting about this guy."

Avery glanced uncomfortably at Owen and Sabrina. She hated public confrontations, but her head hurt too much to move. "You can't be jealous of my boss. That's pathetic."

"You wanna know what's pathetic?" Curt asked aggressively. "A girl who has a guy who loves her and all she can think about is messing around with some smug jerk who she works for."

"Curt, you're just angry about tonight," Avery said. "There was nothing going on. You should know me better than that. He's not even my type."

"That's right, he's not, and you should remember that."

"I can't believe we're fighting over this," Avery groaned.

"So stop," Owen interjected.

Curt and Avery scowled at him.

"All of you, pipe down. Polly's got some guy in her room," Sabrina hissed.

"Yeah, we're trying to listen," Owen added, pointing.

Suddenly Avery realized why Owen and Sabrina had

positioned themselves near Polly's door. They were both trying to get as close to the door as possible to listen.

"Polly's got a guy in there?" Avery asked, pressing her hands to her temples.

"Yeah," Owen said, slurring his words. "Came home with him a little while ago. His hands were all over her. Go, Polly, go!"

"We want to see if she's got the guts to go all the way," Sabrina added.

"Oh, yeah," Owen said, raising his hand to give her a high five, but Sabrina pointedly refused.

"You guys are gross," Avery said, completely repulsed. "What kind of people are you that you're making a sport out of eavesdropping?"

"A sport, I like that," Owen said. "I'll get the *score*cards."

"It's her business—you should keep your noses out of it," April said, coming down the stairs and handing Avery two Advils. She quickly washed them down with her beer. Meanwhile, Curt got up and walked unsteadily toward the kitchen.

"Come on, don't act all high and mighty," Sabrina said.

"Yeah, admit it, your curiosity is killing you," Owen chimed in.

Curt returned from the kitchen with another beer. For the first time all evening, his mood appeared to lift. To Avery's chagrin, he joined Owen and Sabrina close to Polly's room. Sometimes she really had to wonder about him.

• • •

April couldn't believe how nasty Owen and Sabrina were, trying to listen in on Polly. "You guys are completely disgusting," she said.

Owen took a gulp of beer and brought a quavering finger to his lips. "Hush, little girl, this is important."

"Owen, you're drunk," April said.

"Am not," he protested, despite the empty bottles in front of him on the coffee table.

"And you're not an attractive drunk."

"Really? That's not what I hear—just ask Sabrina," he said.

Sabrina rolled her eyes and shook her head as if she wanted nothing to do with him.

Suddenly they heard a shout, and Polly let out a short, sharp shriek. Everyone got very quiet and still. Inside the room, the unpleasant noises continued. Outside the room, everyone began to look agitated.

"You little tease!" the guy inside Polly's room grunted.

"Ow! Stop!" they heard Polly cry.

"We can't let him hurt her," April said desperately to the others.

For a second, no one else moved. Then they heard a slap, and Polly cried out again.

"Curt! You have to stop him," Avery begged.

"Naw," he said, and took a long pull on his beer. "Cool it. Maybe it's not what you think."

But April knew that was bull. Curt had turned pale. He was scared. "It is too what we think," she said.

Sabrina turned to Owen. "How about you, hero? Man enough to take care of it?"

"Damn right." Owen staggered to his feet and stood for a moment, wobbling back and forth. "No one does that to a woman under my roof," he said, slurring his words. He took two steps, tripped on the leg of the coffee table, and crashed to the floor with a loud thud. It almost would have been funny had Polly not been crying in her room.

Sabrina bent over Owen and felt his face. "He's out cold."

"Ow! You're hurting me!" Polly cried from inside her room again.

Shaking with anger, April took three quick steps toward Polly's room and tried the doorknob. It was locked. Panic began to rise in her, and she pounded on the door. "Stop it!" she shouted.

The sounds coming from inside the room suddenly stopped. A second later the door swung open and a guy about three inches taller than April stared at her. His shirt was open, and he looked startled that so many people were in the living room. "What the—" he began to say.

Thunk! April grabbed him by the hair and slammed his skull into the doorjamb with a sharp crack. Then she yanked his head down so that it was eye level with hers. "Get out," she growled.

Blood started trickling down the side of the guy's face

from a cut on his scalp. April let go and stood back, and he fled through the living room and out the front door, slamming it behind him.

Polly came out of her room, her eyes red with tears and her clothes disheveled. April hugged her. "Are you okay?"

"I . . . I think so," Polly replied.

"Should we call the police?" Avery asked. "Do you need to go to the hospital?"

"Oh no, nothing like that," Polly quickly answered.

"Come on." April led her over to the couch and sat down. It seemed like more people were staring at her than at Polly.

"Wow, you're like Wonder Woman or something," Sabrina said, looking impressed.

"Men like that are pigs," April said, her shoulders still trembling as she tried to calm her breathing.

•

Avery stared at Owen, where he lay on the living room floor. He'd started snoring. But at least he'd made an effort to stop what was happening in Polly's room. Why hadn't Curt done something? Avery sat next to Polly and held her hand. She felt awful for the girl. Polly had wanted to meet a guy so badly and when she finally had, this had happened. *It's so unfair!* "Not all guys are like that," she said.

"Yeah," Sabrina chimed in, actually looking sympathetic. "Most of them don't hit."

"I'm sorry I've caused so much trouble," Polly said at last.

"Not at all," Avery tried to soothe her.

"It wasn't you who caused the trouble," April said.

"It was a good thing April knew how to deal with that guy," Sabrina said, shuddering slightly.

Yes, April knew what to do, Avery thought, trying not to glance at Curt. "I'm so glad you were here, April," she said.

Before the other girl could respond, they heard the front doorknob turn. Avery stiffened, wondering if the creep had come back.

The door opened, and Lucas came in with Tara, the girl from the concert. Avery felt herself tense.

As soon as he entered the living room, Lucas stopped. Avery watched him take Tara's hand and squeeze it as if to warn her that something was wrong. "What's going on? What happened?"

"A guy got rough with Polly," Sabrina said.

"Where?" Lucas asked.

"In her room," Avery answered.

"What was he doing in her . . . ?" Lucas trailed off. Avery could see that he'd just noticed Owen passed out on the floor. "Not Owen."

"No, someone else," Sabrina said. "You should have seen it. April kicked his butt out of here."

Lucas's eyes went wide with concern. "You okay, Polly?" he asked, compassion in his voice.

Polly nodded, but didn't say anything. Avery found herself wishing that Curt could have shown compassion or courage or anything rather than just sit there. *Owen wanted to help. Everyone did. Everyone except Curt.* She still couldn't bring herself to look at her boyfriend. Her eyes drifted instead to Tara, and the knots in her stomach tightened. *You have to stop comparing Lucas to Curt. This is so not good.* Her head began to throb even harder.

Six

Avery stood at the water's edge, staring out at the ocean as the waves lapped at her toes. She wore a red-and-white batik sarong around her hips covering the bottom half of her sky blue French-cut bikini. It was the fourteenth of July, almost a week since Polly had been pawed by that jerky guy.

The wind whipped her hair into her eyes, but Avery didn't care. She was too wrapped up in thoughts to notice wind and sand and surf. She had made her way to the beach just as the sun was rising, shooting brilliant hues of orange and scarlet across the dark sky.

Now as she stared across the crashing waves she was watching an internal slide show, trying to remember moments with her mother. How she had looked when she was still alive, trying to forget how she had looked lying in her coffin. Tears began to slide down her cheeks.

"You okay?" a quiet voice asked, interrupting her thoughts.

She turned her head toward the speaker without bothering

to wipe away her tears. It was Lucas in his wet suit, the morning sun glinting off the red surfboard under his arm.

She shook her head.

He put the surfboard down. "What's wrong?"

"Everything," she croaked. It wasn't like her to be so honest about feeling bad. Normally she would have forced a smile and told him nothing was wrong, and that she was perfectly fine. She wasn't sure if it was the concern in his eyes, or the roar of the ocean or the depth of her emotion that made her blurt out the truth, but she was relieved that she had.

He reached out and put a hand on her shoulder. "I've got time," he said quietly.

She nearly began to sob at that, but held herself back. Curt never seemed to have the time. She wanted to talk, not just cry incoherently. "I'm still upset about what happened to Polly," she said for starters. It wasn't what was bothering her the most, but it seemed like a safe place to start.

"So am I," Lucas said. "I wish I'd been there earlier. Maybe I could have done something to stop it."

Avery nodded. She tried to stop what she said next, but it came pouring out of her in a rush. "I can't believe that Curt just sat there and did nothing. Why? I mean, how could he just sit there?"

Lucas looked grim. "I don't know. Maybe he wasn't sure what to do. Maybe he just couldn't deal."

Could that really be what happened? she wondered. It seemed hard to believe, but Lucas looked so earnest, and being a guy, he would have better insight into the male psyche than she did. Maybe she should give him the benefit of the doubt. Still, a thought troubled her. "You wouldn't have let fear or some kind of crazy denial stop you from doing something, would you?" she asked.

His jaw set, and she saw a fierce look in his eyes. "No," he said quietly. "But that's me."

"That's you," she said. Curt had always seemed strong to her, but she was beginning to think that a lot of it was bluff and bravado. Looking at Lucas, she saw a different kind of strength. Lucas would never pick a fight or need to prove anything. He would most certainly end a fight, though, if he was in one.

She took a step backward and tried to control her breathing, which suddenly seemed out of control. She turned and stared out to the ocean. The early morning air was crisp and clear, and she could see all the way to the clear blue horizon.

"What is it?" Lucas asked gently.

Avery felt it rush out of her. "Today's the anniversary of my mom's death."

The next thing she knew, he reached out and pulled her to him with strong arms. She clung to him for a moment, allowing the grief to wash over her before finally moving away.

"Thanks. It's just hard, you know? I couldn't sleep and so I got up early to come out here to try to remember her."

"She must have been a wonderful woman to have raised a daughter like you," Lucas said.

"I'm not so sure," Avery protested.

"Come on," he said. "You survived something most people couldn't and managed to keep your sense of humor and decency."

"Thanks," she said, comforted by his words. "Every year I feel her slipping farther away from me. I'm even starting to have trouble remembering what she looked like."

Lucas put his arm around her and rubbed her back. She closed her eyes and tried again to fix her mother's face in her mind.

"You know what I do remember, though?" she asked, smiling through the pain. "My mom was crazy about anything French. My grandfather was, like, a quarter French and so she just grabbed on to that. It was the closest thing to an ethnic identity that she had."

The memory made Avery feel warm inside, connected to her mom, somehow. "I guess it was kind of fitting she died on July fourteenth."

"Bastille Day," Lucas muttered. "That's why you're wearing the colors of the French flag."

"Dumb, huh?"

"No, sweet."

"So how did you know?" she asked.

"About?"

"Bastille Day."

He grinned. "It's French Independence Day. Like our Fourth of July. Everyone knows about it."

"No, they really don't. You're the first person I've met aside from my mother who knew," Avery said.

He dropped his eyes. "I probably heard something about it on the Discovery Channel."

Avery nodded. The sun began to warm her skin. It was going to be a beautiful day and she was at the beach and she should have been happy. If only Curt had been the type of person who came to the defense of women, and knew what Bastille Day was.

Polly felt desperate. She'd come to Wildwood to have a great summer and meet a guy, and all she'd managed to do on her own is get assaulted by some creep. She couldn't believe she'd been so stupid. Forget about letting a guy in her bedroom again. She never wanted to get close to another guy for as long as she lived. Once again, she'd made a mess of things. It seemed to be the only thing in life she was really good at.

She sighed and flipped over onto her back on her beach blanket and spread some more sunscreen on her shoulders before closing her eyes. The sun felt good as it pounded down on her skin, but she knew how quickly it could become an enemy. *Just like the guy who hit me,* she thought. She shook her head angrily. She had done everything she could to get that jerk out of her mind, and kept trying to remind herself that not all guys were like that. But right now it felt like they were.

"Don't often see you this time of day," a voice interrupted her thoughts.

She opened her eyes and squinted as Lucas sat down next to her on the sand, putting his board down gently. He pulled a bar of surf wax out of one of his pockets.

"It's my day off," Polly said, propping herself up on one elbow to look at him.

"Nice," he said.

She watched while he applied wax to his surfboard in long strokes. His muscles rippled under his tan skin. He always seemed like a nice guy, polite. *A guy like him wouldn't hurt a girl. He's so sweet, and I don't think he even smokes pot. I haven't seen that bong since the day we moved in. Maybe it really is art, or an image thing, or something.*

She studied Lucas more closely, and then his surfboard. The nice thing was, she didn't have to worry about him hitting on her. Well, if she wasn't going to meet a guy that summer, maybe she could accomplish something else. "Is it hard to learn to surf?"

Lucas gave her a friendly smile. "Not really."

"Would you give me a surfing lesson someday?" she asked.

"Absolutely," he said. "It seems to be my calling lately. Two days ago I started teaching a couple of kids. If I can teach them, I can definitely teach you. What about right now?"

"Now?" Polly repeated uncertainly.

"Yeah, why not?" Lucas asked.

She could have come up with a million reasons. She'd just put on sunscreen. She wasn't wearing the right bathing suit. Didn't want to get her hair wet. But that was what she always did, wasn't it? So why not just go ahead?

"Okay, sure."

"Hey guys, what's up?" Avery asked as she walked over wearing a light blue bikini.

"Lucas is going to teach me how to surf," Polly said excitedly.

"Wow, that's awesome!" Avery said.

"I'll teach you, too, if you like," Lucas offered.

Avery glanced at Polly. "You asked first."

"Oh, it's okay," Polly said. It wasn't like she was trying to seduce him or anything.

"That would be great, thanks," Avery said.

"Well, all right, ladies," Lucas said as he stood and picked up his board. "Follow me."

Polly jumped up and followed him into the ocean with Avery right beside her. The water had a slight chill to it, but it wasn't enough to stop her. She kept her eyes on Lucas's tanned and muscled back and waded out behind him. Once they'd gone out a dozen yards, Lucas stopped and aimed the surfboard back toward shore. "Okay, who's first?" he asked.

"Am I going to get hurt?" Polly asked.

"You shouldn't," he answered. He pushed his hair out of his eyes and then looked from her to Avery. "Come on, don't be shy. Who wants to go first?"

"I will," Avery spoke up, and Polly was relieved. This way, she could watch and see what Avery was doing first.

Lucas patted the board in front of him. "Hop on."

Once Avery was lying on the board in front of him, Lucas put his hands on her waist to center her. Avery turned to look at him, and Polly noticed that her eyes were sparkling and her lips parted with excitement.

She's into Lucas, Polly realized. She felt her spirits plunge. From the way Lucas was looking back at Avery, it was clear he was into her, too. Things were happening all around her. Relationships, attractions, romance, excitement. But somehow she could never be part of it.

Out loud, Polly said, "'Water, water, every where, /And all the boards did shrink; Water, water, every where, /Nor any drop to drink.'"

Lucas flashed her a smile. "'The very deep did rot: O Christ! /That ever this should be! Yea, slimy things did crawl with legs /Upon the slimy sea.'"

Polly felt her jaw grow slack, and it came to her with a sudden surety that she and all the others had underestimated him. Avery stared, puzzled, from her to Lucas. "What's that?" she finally asked.

"*The Rime of the Ancient Mariner*," Polly answered.

"And what's *that*?" Avery asked.

"An epic poem by Samuel Taylor Coleridge. It's about an old man who's cursed as a young sailor. He alone of all his shipmates survives and he goes on to find redemption and to warn other people. He tells his story to a groom right before he's to get married," Polly said, staring hard at Lucas.

"How do you know it?" Avery asked Lucas.

He leaned toward her and gestured for Polly to come close. Then he dropped his voice. "If I tell you, you have to swear to keep it a secret, okay?"

Both girls nodded eagerly.

"I . . . ," Lucas began, "had to memorize it for English class."

The girls grinned. "Very funny." Polly smirked. She noticed that he was gazing over her shoulder. Turning, she saw a line of dark gray storm clouds on the horizon. Polly turned back to him.

"Wait a minute," she said. "Maybe I'm overgeneralizing here, but it seems to me that most people who walk around with a bong wouldn't be able to recite Coleridge."

Lucas grinned sheepishly. Polly noticed that Avery was gazing at him intently, as if she, too, expected an answer.

"It wasn't mine," he said. "It belongs to this guy who works at the surf shop. His parents were coming to visit for the weekend and he asked me if I'd hold on to it until they left. . . . And talk about leaving, that's what we ought to do."

He pointed toward the horizon. Polly turned to look and saw that the line of dark clouds was larger now. *They're coming fast. We should get inside,* she thought. As if on cue, the wind picked up and the water grew choppy with whitecaps forming on the waves.

"Ladies, I fear we're going to have to continue this surf lesson another time," Lucas said, as though reading her mind.

Polly waded toward shore, with Avery right behind her. The wind began to whip around her, and she grabbed her towel just as the wind began to lift it into the air. She snatched her bottle of sunscreen from the sand and began shivering as the wind felt like it was going right through her. Avery shouted, and Polly looked up just in time to see a beach umbrella tumbling toward her end-over-end. She jumped out of the way, and it blew down the beach, picking up speed.

"Back to the house!" Lucas shouted, the wind seeming to tear the words from his mouth. Flying sand stung their skin. Lucas was struggling to keep the surfboard from blowing out of his hands.

They had only taken half a dozen steps when the heavens let loose and cold rain poured down on them. Shrieking, they ran toward the house, half blinded and shivering.

Lucas was the last into the house, and Polly slammed the door behind him. The three of them stood shivering and dripping rain and seawater onto the floor. Polly's normally uncontrollable hair hung in wet, red clumps around her ears and down her back, little rivulets of water rolling off it onto her already soaked skin. Goose bumps stood up all over her skin. The chill made certain other parts of her anatomy stand out as well.

She glanced down at the floor. Pools of water were forming

beneath each of them, and they had tracked wet sand all over the entryway. *Great, something else to clean up,* she thought.

"Well, that was unexpected," Lucas said at last.

"I can't believe how fast that storm came up," Avery added.

"I vote for staying in tonight," Polly said, struggling to catch her breath and keep her teeth from chattering.

"I've got the perfect idea!" Avery said, heading for the kitchen.

Polly rubbed her cold arms and stared as Avery pulled something off the refrigerator.

"Pop's Pizza!" Avery said triumphantly, displaying a little magnet. "Let's order in."

Polly glanced out the window and saw sheets of rain coming down almost horizontally as they were being driven by the rain. "That sounds good. Owen was working the boat, so he should be home pretty soon. April's shift is over in half an hour. I'm not sure about Sabrina and Curt, but I don't imagine anyone will be going out in this weather, so we should probably order for everyone."

"Check how much community cash we have," Avery said.

Polly joined her in the kitchen and reached up to the top of the refrigerator for a clam-shaped cookie jar. She pulled it down and placed it on the counter. She looked inside and gasped.

"What is it?" Lucas asked, moving closer.

Polly slowly pulled out a crumpled ten and five ones. "There should be at least a hundred and twenty in here. Where's the rest of the money?" she stammered. "We're supposed to pay the electric bill on Friday."

Avery grabbed the cookie jar and inspected it. "Are you sure there was supposed to be that much in here?"

"Positive. Last night I put my tips in after work. There was no reason for anyone to take it."

A sad, almost nauseating sensation flooded through Polly. This wasn't the summer she'd imagined. One thing after another had gone wrong. And they really didn't need a thief among them as well.

The next morning was cool and misty. The house was darker inside than usual because there was no sunlight to stream through the windows. It made Owen restless and edgy. Or maybe it was Polly that made him restless and edgy.

Polly had called a group meeting in the living room to discuss something about missing money. Owen didn't actually care. Sabrina was at the meeting too, though, and he did care about her. Disturbingly so. She was perched on the arm of the sofa, legs swinging slowly back and forth, looking extremely bored and at the same time gorgeous in white capris and a light blue tank top.

Owen was regretting his decision to sit in one of the chairs. If he'd sat on the end of the couch, he could have been closer to Sabrina. He hadn't wanted to sit next to April, though, who had taken the middle of the couch. Lucas had the far end of the sofa and had his bare feet propped up on the coffee table.

Owen continued to stare at Sabrina, wishing he were closer to her. He could smell her perfume, and it was driving him wild with memories of their night together. *She might like to pretend that she doesn't remember, but I do.* For a moment he imagined brushing her honey hair back from her face, touching her golden arm, caressing her soft skin.

"Where's Curt? He's the only one not here," Polly said, interrupting Owen's thoughts as she paced in front of them like some kind of schoolteacher.

"Practicing for the Battle of the Bands," Avery said, perched on the edge of one of the other chairs, looking intent.

He's going to need a lot of practice, Owen thought.

Polly frowned. "He should be here. This is important."

"It may not matter," Avery said. "We're missing money from our room, too."

"So am I," Sabrina said.

"Is it possible someone outside the house has been coming in?" Polly mused.

"Like Fred?" April asked.

"I really don't think Fred could have done this," Polly said.

"Why not?" Sabrina asked. "After all, he does have access to everything."

"He just doesn't strike me as the type who would steal," Polly said.

"Why else would he always be hanging around?" April asked.

"Maybe because he owns the place," Lucas suggested.

"And he's paranoid," Owen added.

"And he's hitting on us, well, at least on me," Sabrina said, rolling her eyes.

Owen smiled at the thought of a nerd like Fred hitting on a hottie like Sabrina. He wished he'd been there to see that one.

"I think if Fred really wanted our money, he could have had it some other way, like charging us more for the rooms," Avery said.

"Okay, let's say for the moment that it's not Fred," Polly said. "We don't know who's taking the money, but we have to keep it safe."

"What do you suggest?" Lucas asked.

Polly sighed. "I don't know, maybe we should all move our money to different places. Also, we can put the common money somewhere safer."

"Stick it in the freezer," Owen suggested. "Burglars don't look there."

Sabrina rolled her eyes. "But none of this helps if one of us is the thief."

"Then we'll know them by their cold hands," Owen said, belatedly realizing that everyone else seemed to be reacting badly to Sabrina's statement, casting doubtful looks at one another.

"You really think one of us is stealing the money?" Avery asked quietly.

"I guess we have to consider the possibility," Polly said, her freckles standing out against her pale skin.

"There are other people who come and go around here," April said.

Owen narrowed his eyes, wondering if she was referring to his friends. Lucas also looked distinctly uncomfortable, and Owen remembered he had seen a girl in the house a couple of times with him.

"Well, we can each hide our own money and hopefully keep it safe. If we move the community cash into the back of the freezer, away from the ice cubes, then I guess we'll know if it's one of us who is stealing," Polly said slowly.

"Works for me," Lucas said.

"Everyone's also going to have to chip in extra money so we can pay the electric bill on Friday," Avery said, looking pained.

"I'm not going to be able to chip in until next Friday," April said.

Everyone gave her curious looks.

"A box of new DVDs was stolen from the video store," she explained. "The owner says it's my fault because it happened on my watch. He's taking it out of this week's pay."

"He can't do that," Sabrina said. "That's totally unfair. I'd never let someone do that to me."

"Easier said than done," April groaned. "I need this job, and I don't have time to go looking for another. Besides, by this point in the summer, most of the jobs are taken."

Owen had an idea. He had some extra cash and maybe he

could do something that would help April and score a few points with Sabrina. "I don't want to drink hot beer," he said, "so I'll cover April's share of the electric bill for Friday and she can pay it back later." He glanced at Sabrina hopefully, but she wasn't even looking at him. She was too busy inspecting her nails.

"Wow, I really appreciate that," April said. "I'll pay you back as soon as I can."

"Thank you, Owen," Polly said. "That's very generous."

The meeting ended with the agreement that everyone would be careful about their money and the community funds would be hidden deep in the recesses of the freezer.

Owen headed to the beach. The odds that anyone was going to want to go parasailing before the mist burned off were slim, but work was work. When he had finished prepping the boat, he got a hard lemonade out of the shack and settled himself down to a seat on the sand.

He'd only been sitting a little while when Sabrina appeared through the haze, towing her two young charges behind. Owen tensed, but she smiled at him. He never knew what to expect from her.

"Does anyone actually parasail on a day like today?" she asked, all honey and sweetness.

"Most likely not. I'll just keep the boat anchored there and wait."

"So, you're pretty much hanging out?"

"Yeah," he said, hope stirring in him. Maybe the offer to

help cover April's bill had made a difference after all. "Feel like joining me?"

"Sure," she said. "I just have to do a couple things first."

"Well, hurry up," he said, grinning at her.

"It would take less time if I could go by myself," she said, nodding at the kids.

Now Owen understood. She'd come by to dump the kids on him. He was tempted to tell her to drop dead, but caught himself. That wouldn't do him any good as far as she was concerned. He'd be better off taking the kids and scoring brownie points. "Sure thing," he said, forcing a smile. "They're welcome to share all the excitement."

The kids had plopped themselves down on the sand and got busy digging and making a sand castle with their shovels. Watching them didn't seem like a big deal.

"So you'll keep an eye on them?" she asked.

"No sweat."

"Thanks!" she said brightly. "I'll be right back."

She took off up the beach. Owen felt a mixture of excitement and nervousness. Okay, this was it. His second chance. And this time he'd better not blow it. He got up and went into the shack for another hard lemonade. He just wanted to calm his nerves.

April was relieved that Owen had come to her rescue by offering to pay her share of the electric bill. She wouldn't have expected that from him. On the other hand, she was bummed by the implication that someone in their house might be taking money. That really sucked.

She got to the video store and took a deep breath before going inside. She loved movies, but had grown to hate this job. Leonard, the owner, was an unpredictable tyrant who seemed to enjoy taking out his frustrations on his employees.

When she walked inside, she was surprised to find Sabrina there arguing with Leonard. The video store owner was a short, squat man with a balding head and bulging eyes. At that moment, his face was red and there were sweat stains under the arms of his blue Hawaiian shirt. He was waving his arms and spitting his words out along with a spray of saliva. "What about my missing DVDs!? Someone's gotta pay for them, and it's sure not going to be me. I wasn't even in the store when they disappeared."

"It's not going to be April, either," Sabrina said, her voice stern and strong and her eyes glittering like diamonds. "You have no proof that the DVDs were taken while she was working here. Besides, she doesn't make enough for you to take more money out of her salary. I know you can afford it. You're paying your employees dirt, and it would be a shame if the IRS found out you're also paying them cash off the books."

If anything, Leonard's eyes bulged out even farther. "But the DVDs—"

"Get a better security system and stop complaining,"

Sabrina snapped. "And don't forget, you can take the loss as a tax write-off."

April stared at Sabrina in amazement. She couldn't believe what she was witnessing. Sabrina glanced over and winked at her, then turned back to Leonard. "And another thing. April has been so traumatized by this whole experience that you'd better give her the day off."

"Now that's total bull!" Leonard argued.

Instead of yelling back, Sabrina smiled. "Can I use your phone? I need to call the IRS."

"Oh, go take a day off." Leonard waved at April.

April turned right around and headed out the door. A moment later, Sabrina joined her. They took off up the street, laughing.

"I can't believe you did that!" April said when they were out of earshot of the store. "How can I thank you?"

Sabrina shrugged. "It was no biggie. I didn't like the idea of some jerk taking his own security issues out on my roommate . . . and her paycheck."

"Well, thanks a bunch," April said, feeling an unexpected rush of warmth toward Sabrina. "You completely saved my butt."

"Guess I'm not as bad as everyone thinks, huh?" Sabrina said.

Guess not, April thought, *but it sure is a strange thing to say.*

Lucas was discovering the joys of teaching. His parents had talked about the rewards endlessly when he was growing up, and then they'd gone on to greater glory in the world of education, but until now, he'd never experienced it firsthand. Of course, teaching three kids to surf wasn't exactly the same as a full professorship at Princeton University, where not one, but both his parents taught. Nor had he written one of the great textbooks in his field the way his father had. But still, he found himself basking in admiration of his little class, who clearly drank in every word he said.

The two girls and one boy stood around him on the damp sand, clutching foam surfboards. He smiled at them all. "You're going to make great surfers. Just remember, what is the key?"

"Safety first," they chimed back.

"Excellent."

"And why'd we have to stop surfing today?" Lucas asked.

"It's getting too foggy," one of the kids answered.

"Right."

Someone behind him chuckled. Lucas turned to find Avery, smiling.

"Class dismissed," Lucas told the kids, who headed back to their parents, who were waiting nearby.

"Looked like you were having fun," Avery said.

"You mean the kids?" Lucas said.

"Them, but mostly you." Avery nodded down the beach. "A lot more fun than he's having today."

Lucas looked down the beach. Owen was propped up in a

beach chair with a bunch of empty hard lemonade bottles scattered around him. The guy's eyes were closed.

"Tough job," Lucas quipped.

"I don't think he's happy," said Avery.

Lucas looked up and saw Sabrina marching toward them with her lips pursed and her gaze fixed on Owen. April was following her.

"I have a feeling he's about to become even more unhappy," Lucas said.

Sabrina stopped next to them. "Owen?"

He didn't answer. His head had lulled back, and his eyes were still closed. Sabrina nudged him with her foot, and Owen opened his eyes. "Huh?"

"Where are they?" Sabrina asked.

"Who?"

"The brats, the kids," Sabrina said, becoming agitated. "You were supposed to be keeping an eye on them."

Lucas felt a chill. Those boys were young. Six and four. Too young to be left on their own on a foggy beach.

"Wha?" Owen seemed more awake now.

Sabrina stood over him and shouted, "Where are the kids? You were supposed to be watching them!"

Everyone began swiveling their heads, looking around.

"They've got to be around here somewhere," April said.

But Lucas didn't see them.

"What if they drowned!?" Sabrina shrieked.

"That's not going to help," Lucas said.

Meanwhile, Owen staggered to his feet. "They were right here. I don't understand."

"You don't understand?" Sabrina shouted. "Maybe you will if you have another drink, you idiot!"

"Yelling won't change anything," Lucas said, and turned to Owen, trying to ignore the stench of alcohol on his breath. "Where's the last place you remember seeing the kids?"

"I don't know. At the edge of the water, maybe?"

Sabrina screamed in fear. "They drowned!"

"Hold on," Lucas said. "There are lifeguards here, remember? Even on a day like today. And there are a few people in the water. Someone would've noticed two little kids in the water without supervision. They've probably just wandered off somewhere."

"Okay, great," Sabrina snapped furiously. "They're not drowned, just kidnapped!"

"Let's split up and search for them," Lucas said, seeing that someone needed to take charge. "April, you and Sabrina check down the beach that direction." He pointed away from the piers. "Avery and I will check in this direction. Owen, ask around and see if you can find anyone who saw them. Okay?"

Everyone started off. Lucas began striding quickly down the beach, his head turning left and right. A few steps behind him, Avery had to hurry to keep up. It was still too misty for most beach goers, and aside from a few surfers and some sand castle builders, he didn't see anyone, and certainly no kids. "Do you think we'll find them?" she asked.

"We've got to," Lucas said, his jaw set.

Who knew he could be so intense? Avery thought as she, too, scanned the beach and the water for any sign of the boys. *What would Curt be like in this situation? Would he even bother to look for the kids, or just say it wasn't his problem?*

"Shouldn't there be footprints or something?" she asked. She cast her eyes downward but couldn't make out any distinct prints on the sand except the ones they were leaving.

"If they were walking close to the water, we won't find any," Lucas said. "The waves would have washed them away. I figure they may have headed to the boardwalk. Maybe someone there has seen them."

Avery was forced into a jog to keep up. "You don't think they could have drowned, do you?"

Lucas stopped and looked at her. "You want to know the truth? Two kids that young, unsupervised, on a misty day like today? Absolutely. But I'm betting they headed for the boardwalk instead."

Avery suddenly felt chilled to the bone. She didn't want to imagine them struggling in the water, sucked out by a riptide. *Don't picture them dead. Picture them alive and happy and having fun,* she told herself.

They reached the boardwalk without seeing any sign of the boys.

"Okay, I'll take the right side and you'll take the left side," Lucas said. "That way, there's less chance that we'll miss them if they're here. I'll meet you at the other end. Ask everybody you see if they've seen a couple of small boys, light hair and green eyes."

"But the boardwalk's long," she protested. "Plus, all the piers."

"Then we better stop talking and get going," he said.

Her heart was really starting to pound from the adrenaline and the fear. Lucas looked at her with a forceful, determined gaze. "We have to find them," he said.

She nodded, touched his hand briefly, and set off down the left side of the boardwalk. The first place she stopped was a yellow and orange stand featuring foot-long chili dogs. The vendor was an older man with gray hair. "Excuse me? Have you seen two little boys come through here in the last hour?" Avery asked.

"Alone?" The guy's wrinkled forehead wrinkled even more. "Can't say that I have. I'll keep my eyes open, though."

"Thanks," she told him, and moved on, stopping everyone she could. No one, though, remembered seeing two little boys by themselves. The time flew, and she was even more frightened and frustrated when she arrived in front of the Spencer Avenue Pier. The pier was one of the amusement parks and boasted a massive wooden roller coaster called the Great White. Even at this time of the day the screams of the thrill riders pierced the air and the sounds of tinny music floated by.

A brief thought flashed through her mind. It was ironic that she'd finally made it to the Spencer Avenue Pier, and she wasn't going to get to go in. Despite his promise, Curt still hadn't taken her to the amusement park. *Maybe I'll just have to go by myself,* she thought. *Or maybe with Lucas.* Guilt started to rush through her, but before it could take complete hold, she felt someone come up behind her.

"Nothing," Lucas said abruptly. She looked at him and noticed that he suddenly looked older, his forehead creased with worry and dotted with beads of sweat.

"What do we do now?" Avery asked.

Lucas looked around, deep in thought. He stared at a booth that sold seashells, starfish, and sand dollars. A sign proclaimed, TREASURES FROM THE SEA. Next to it, an older woman sold cotton candy.

"That's it!" Lucas gasped. He grabbed her hand.

"Come on, let's go." He started running back toward the beach, dragging her with him.

"Where?" Avery asked, strangely thrilled that her hand was in his again.

"Under the pier. The boys wanted to look for buried treasure. They said the cotton candy guy told them about it."

Back on the beach they turned around and ran under the pier. It was dark and shadowy, and the crashing waves echoed in and out of dark brown pilings as thick as tree trunks.

"Jamie, Tim, you here?" Lucas shouted, his voice a hollow echo.

No answer.

With her hand still in his, Avery and Lucas walked underneath the pier and looked toward the water. There was no sign of the two little boys, and Avery felt her spirits plunge. The tide was coming in, and water swirled around her ankles.

"Go away!" a tiny voice called suddenly.

She and Lucas spun around. There, back in the shadows, were two small figures with bright yellow and red toy shovels.

"Jamie, Tim!" Lucas rushed forward.

"Go away!" the smaller boy yelled. "You said pirate's code!"

Avery felt a wave of relief wash through her. The smaller boy had tears in his eyes. "You said!"

"I know." Lucas kneeled down and patted the boy's head. "And I promise any treasure you find you can keep, okay?"

Now the older boy approached. He looked suspiciously at Avery and then said to Lucas, "What about her?"

"She knows the pirate's code too," Lucas assured him. "But listen, everyone's looking for you. So we have to go back now. Otherwise, they'll know where to look for the treasure."

"Do we have to?" the smaller boy asked, sticking out his lower lip.

"Yes. And if you promise never to wander off again, then I'll bring you back here in a few days and we can dig for treasure together," Lucas said.

The boys' eyes opened wide.

"Promise?" the older one asked.

"Absolutely," Lucas said "Do we have a deal?"

"Deal," the older one said.

"Deal," echoed his brother.

Lucas swept them up, one in each arm. "People were seriously worried about you, little dudes," he confided.

They started back down the beach and were about a hundred yards from the parasail boat when Sabrina saw them and started to run. "Oh, my God! Oh, my God! Where did you find them?"

In a way, Avery was relieved to see how frantic she looked. So she wasn't really a total ice queen after all.

Lucas explained what had happened. Sabrina had tears in her eyes. She even hugged the boys and scolded them fondly. April and Owen looked equally relieved.

"I've got to get both of you home," Sabrina said, grabbing the boys' hands and hurrying off with them.

"What a relief," April said.

"Yeah," Owen agreed, hanging his head. "I can't believe what an idiot I was."

Avery looked at him, then down at the empty bottles in the sand.

"Hey, don't worry," Owen said, reading her thoughts. "I'll never let that happen again. I swear."

Avery gazed at him for a minute. She had a feeling he wouldn't have to worry because there was no way he'd ever get the opportunity. The good news was, he seemed to have sobered up.

"Man, you think by now I would've learned," he muttered.

"You've done this before?" April asked.

"Not me," Owen said, dipping into a funk. "My old man. He spent his whole life drinking and chasing women and ignoring the people he was supposed to be taking care of. I keep swearing I don't want to be like him, and then I keep doing the same thing."

"But maybe not anymore, right?" April said.

"Hey, are you kidding? Those two little kids were supposed to be my responsibility," Owen said with a shiver. "If something bad happened to them, that would be the end. I wouldn't be able to live with myself."

The crisis averted, Lucas and Avery started back up the beach toward the house.

"I think everyone owes you a big thanks," Avery said.

"Hey," Lucas said with a shrug. "I just did what any guy would do."

"Actually, no, not any guy," Avery said.

"You don't know that for a fact," Lucas said, as if it was obvious who they were talking about. "Maybe he would have."

"Thanks, but you don't have to stick up for him," Avery muttered bitterly.

Lucas didn't answer. Avery knew she had to stop comparing Lucas to Curt.

And now she knew why she had to stop.

Because Lucas always came out ahead.

Seven

That evening Polly felt restless and she suspected several of the others felt the same way. The people next door were having a party, and the streets seemed filled with young people heading out to bars. Polly wished her roommates were in a better mood. She'd heard about the kids getting lost and how Avery and Lucas had found them. Tensions still seemed to be running high, though. Sabrina was walking around with a cloud over her head. Owen had tried to talk to her twice, and both times she'd given him the iciest looks imaginable. While Polly couldn't blame Sabrina for being pissed, she did think it was interesting that she was finally letting her feelings show. It was obvious that Sabrina was capable of getting really upset about something. It was also interesting to watch Owen try so hard to apologize. Finally he'd given up and left with Martin and his pals.

Avery and Curt had gone off somewhere with his band, and Lucas was out with that girl, Tara. Polly wished she had somewhere to go, but instead she'd ended up in the living room with Sabrina and April. Sabrina was flipping through a copy of *Vogue* almost as fast as April was flipping through channels on the television. Polly was working a particularly hard crossword puzzle and trying to block out the sound of the *Gilligan's Island* theme song when Sabrina ruined her train of thought.

"Polly, stop moping," Sabrina said, "it's depressing."

"Sorry," Polly said, sounding startled. "I didn't realize I was."

"Why aren't you out somewhere?" Sabrina asked.

"Why aren't you?" Polly asked back.

"After what happened today, I need a quiet night in," Sabrina said. "But you should be out chatting up eligible bachelors."

"Easier for you than me," Polly said glumly.

Sabrina sighed. "You know, you could get a guy if you just tried a little harder."

Polly didn't understand. "Believe me, I'm trying."

"I'm not talking about bar time," Sabrina said. "I'm talking about presentation."

Polly wrinkled her forehead.

April came to the rescue. "She's talking about your appearance. Although I do think she could be a little less insulting about it."

Sabrina scrunched up her nose and stuck out her tongue at April.

"If you really wanted to be helpful instead of critical, you could show her what to do," April said to Sabrina.

Sabrina gazed at the ceiling as if she was considering the idea. Finally she looked back at Polly. "It's not like I have anything better to do. All right, time for your makeover."

"Makeover?" Polly tried to sound surprised, but of course, she knew exactly what Sabrina meant. That girl may have been a snob, but she had an uncanny way of knowing what was on other people's minds. After checking out other girls around town, Polly had been thinking that her look could use some improvement.

Sabrina tossed her magazine onto the coffee table and got up. "I'll go grab my stuff from upstairs."

A minute later she was back with an assortment of makeup kits, flat irons, and a few other things Polly couldn't even identify. They went into the downstairs bathroom, and Sabrina started straightening Polly's hair.

"If it's straight, isn't it just going to look limp?" Polly asked nervously.

"Not when I'm finished with it," Sabrina said confidently, and glanced back into the living room. "Come on, April, I could use some help."

"I'm busy," April said from the couch.

Sabrina smirked. "Watching TV isn't busy. It's an excuse for not doing something interesting. You're the reason I'm doing this, and I know you know about makeup, so get in here."

April appeared in the bathroom doorway looking sullen.

Meanwhile, Sabrina stared at Polly in the mirror until Polly began to fidget. "What?" she said.

Instead of answering, Sabrina turned to April. "The eyebrows?"

April nodded.

"But I keep them plucked," Polly protested weakly, trying not to listen to the sizzle as the flat iron smoothed her hair.

"Please," Sabrina groaned. "Making sure they don't grow together in the middle of your forehead isn't enough. You need to actually shape them."

Polly knew she was right, but she winced just the same. As much as she wanted to change her look, she was afraid.

"Don't worry," Sabrina said, picking up a pair of tweezers. "I'll do them for you. Then you'll just have to maintain."

"Ouch!" Polly yelped as Sabrina yanked out the first few hairs.

"Always hurts more if someone else has to do it," April said. "Just remember, beauty is pain."

"I never hear Sabrina yelping," Polly said.

Sabrina laughed, and for once there wasn't a trace of sarcasm in it. "That's because most of what you've seen is natural. Back home I do plenty of screaming."

"Roughing it for the summer and you still look like a movie star. How very Ginger," April said.

"Ginger?" Sabrina said.

April jerked her head toward the living room, where the

television was still on and an episode of *Gilligan's Island* was playing.

Sabrina pouted. "And here I thought I was the millionaire's wife."

"That would mean you'd be married to Owen. He's definitely the millionaire," Polly said.

"Eww, please. Not in a million years would I marry Owen. Besides, it's the twenty-first century—why can't *I* be the millionaire?" Sabrina said.

"And be married to some woman? That's also very twenty-first century," April teased.

"I'd have a kept man."

"You can only have a kept man if you can *keep* a man," Polly joked.

"Listen, sweetheart, I could keep a man if I found one I wanted," Sabrina said, half seriously.

"But not Owen?" April asked.

"Please. He's not the millionaire. He's Gilligan. You can count on him to always screw things up."

At least they don't think I'm Gilligan, Polly thought, relieved.

"You know, on second thought, why support some stupid husband while he does nothing?" Sabrina said. "I'm not even sure I'll ever want to get married. My mother used to quote some famous dead woman who said that marriage means exchanging the affection of many men for the contempt of one. No, thank you. If Ginger really is a movie star, I'll bet she has more money than the millionaire, anyway."

"Told you you were Ginger," April said with a smug grin.

"Then who's the millionaire?" Polly asked.

"That would definitely be Avery," April said.

"Because she has to support that loser Curt," Sabrina muttered.

April and Sabrina switched places so that April could start work on Polly's right eyebrow while Sabrina moved the flat iron to the left side of her head. As April wielded the tweezers, Polly tried hard not to focus on the pain.

"So, am I Mary Ann?" she asked hopefully.

"No!" Sabrina and April chorused together.

Polly felt deflated. "Then who am I?"

In the mirror, Polly saw April and Sabrina exchange a glance. "You're the skipper," April said at last.

For a moment, Polly thought she might cry. *The skipper lost control of the boat and got them all stranded. All their problems were really his fault.*

"Oh, please," Sabrina grumbled. "Spare us the self-pity. The skipper was the one who tried his best to keep everyone safe. He was the responsible one."

That caught Polly by surprise. Sabrina actually understood what she tried to do. Rules and responsibility created order and safety. That was how she had always seen it. They didn't mean you couldn't have fun. Polly loved to have fun. Just not at the expense of others.

"Stop twitching," April ordered.

Polly laughed gently. "So, the skipper it is. Who does that make Mary Ann?"

"One moment," April said. She put down the tweezers, grabbed a towel and some makeup remover, turned on the water, and bent over the sink.

"What are you doing?" Sabrina asked, but April didn't answer. After a moment, she turned off the water and rubbed the towel over her face. When she turned around, she had no makeup left on and the change was dramatic.

Not only was April very pretty, she was also wholesome looking. But, most surprising, when she pulled her black hair back from her face, she looked just like Mary Ann.

"Oh, my gosh!" Polly gasped.

"So, that's what you really look like," Sabrina said, sounding impressed.

"Yup, that's what I've been hiding." April smirked. "I'm actually Mary Ann."

"You shouldn't hide under all that makeup," Polly said.

"So my mom tells me," said April.

"Okay, we've got Gilligan, the skipper, the millionaire and her wife, the movie star, and Mary Ann," said Sabrina. "That just leaves the professor."

"That's easy," said April. "Lucas."

"Yeah. What's up with him? He seems kind of smart for a surf slacker," Polly said.

"Believe it," Sabrina agreed. "I saw him reading *War and Peace*. He said it was a dare, but I don't buy it."

"Remember what Fred said about those famous professors at Princeton having the same last name as his?" Polly said, wincing with pain as Sabrina pulled a lock of her hair. "Lucas said he didn't know them, but you have to wonder."

"Know what's interesting about the guys in this house?" April asked. "None of them are what they appear to be. Scratch the surface and there's someone different underneath."

"Like Curt not quite being the man we thought he was?" Sabrina said.

"And Owen," April said.

"Oh, give me a break," Sabrina said dismissively.

"Are you saying he's *not* an alcoholic?" Polly asked.

"I think a big part of his problem are those creeps he hangs out with," April suggested. "Especially that guy Martin. Owen just might be a pretty decent guy if you got him away from the others."

"Easier said than done," Sabrina said. "Hey, here's a thought: Maybe we should all go out to dinner one of these nights. Show off the new Polly."

Polly stared at the stranger in the mirror. There was no denying it: Freckles smoothed out with foundation, eyes big and bright with mascara, eyebrows expertly trimmed, red hair gleaming and perfectly framing her face. That couldn't be her.

Just then, a sound came from outside the bathroom.

"What was that?" Polly whispered. "I thought I heard something."

Sabrina tiptoed over to the bathroom door and pushed it open. Outside stood Fred, a look of guilt all over his quickly reddening face.

"You weren't spying on us, were you, Fred?" Sabrina asked silkily.

"No, I, uh, just came to check out the upstairs plumbing." He seemed sort of dazed and wasn't even looking at Sabrina. Instead, he was staring past her at Polly.

"Hi, Fred." Polly smiled.

"Polly?" Fred stammered.

"Who'd you think it was?" April asked, teasing.

"I . . . I . . ." He still hadn't taken his eyes off her. "You look great!"

Now Polly felt her own face turn red . . . with delight and pleasure.

"So, are you here for Polly or the plumbing?" Sabrina asked.

"Uh . . ." From the way Fred hesitated, it was clearly obvious which he was more interested in. But being shy and uncertain of himself, he finally blurted, "The plumbing."

"Then why don't you go fix the pipes and leave us alone?"

He turned and beat a hasty retreat. Sabrina turned to Polly and April. They all shared a smile.

"He is so into you," April whispered.

"Men," Sabrina said, shaking her head and rolling her eyes.

All three of them laughed.

"We suck," Darek moaned from behind the drums. "We're never going to be ready for the Battle of the Bands."

They were in the living room in the band's house, which was jammed with instruments and speakers. Curt sat on his amp, cradling his guitar. They'd been rehearsing for days, but still hadn't found the groove. It was just after 10 p.m. and they'd been rehearsing since noon.

"We've just got to keep going," Curt said. "This is why we came here this summer, isn't it?"

He was met with groans of frustration.

"We can't quit now, not when we've come so far," Curt said, feeling more than a little frustrated himself.

"Yeah, but we've come as far as we're going to unless we do something about our songs. They suck," Austin, the lead singer, complained.

"They do not!" Bobby, the bass player and lyricist protested.

"They do, Bobby. Everyone knows it but you," Curt said tiredly.

"Yeah, well, I don't see anybody else in this band writing any songs," Bobby snapped.

"You're right about that, bro," Austin admitted.

"What are we going to do?" Darek asked. "If we sound like this at the Battle of the Bands, we'll be laughed off the stage.

There are bands coming from hundreds of miles away."

There was one idea Curt had been avoiding. It was dishonest and sneaky and would probably guarantee him an enemy for life. But if he didn't do it, the band was probably finished.

"I'll tell you what we're going to do," he said, getting up and laying his guitar against the amp. "Bobby, you're going to practice that bass fifteen hours a day. Austin, you're going to take care of those pipes. Darek, you're just going to keep on doing what you do best, buddy. And I'm going to come up with something."

"Like what?" Austin asked.

"A way to make us the best band there."

"How're you going to do that?" Bobby asked.

"Trust me on this," Curt said as he headed for the door. "I'll catch you guys tomorrow."

When Curt reached the house, he stepped inside. "Avery!" he shouted. "Ave!"

"She's still at the restaurant," Polly said from the kitchen.

"But it's ten. She should have been off an hour ago," Curt said, confused.

"Private party, she had to stay late."

"Then why aren't you there with her?" he asked.

"Because two of the other waitresses volunteered to stay and I didn't have to," Polly said. "Don't worry, she should be getting off soon."

I'll just go and see, Curt thought, and headed for the restaurant.

With the dark waves lapping at the shore, he marched down the beach. Curt didn't like the idea of Avery staying late at work. He didn't trust her manager, Anthony. The guy was a snake. The memory of him dancing with Avery at the outdoor concert was still fresh in his mind. Maybe Avery had been dancing with him because she'd wanted to get STF a gig at the Surfin' Spot, but that sure wasn't what Anthony had had in mind.

Besides, Avery had been acting a little weird lately. A little too clingy. It felt good to be needed, but something about it felt forced. As if she was forcing herself to be with him. And then there was all this crap about going out. For the last two days she had been going on and on about the frickin' pier. What did he care about rides and overpriced hot dogs? He had a band to whip into shape before the battle.

He could feel himself getting worked up as suspicions crossed his mind. *Staying late for a private party? What kind of party? If the restaurant was closed, then it didn't need a hostess, and Avery never waits tables. Could this private party be her and Anthony?*

By the time he reached the restaurant, his imagination was so far into overdrive that he practically collided with a couple who were leaving. He glanced through a brightly lit window and saw people seated at a long table. So there was a party after all. But the waitresses were clearing away the coffee cups and dessert plates, and the partyers were getting up and leaving. Then Curt spied Avery in a far corner of the room, talking and laughing with Anthony.

Curt bristled. The party was over. Why was she still hanging around with that guy? Great, with all the headaches he had with the band, he sure didn't need this. He yanked open the restaurant door and went inside.

It was an effort for Avery to stand there with Anthony chatting and laughing when she was only doing it for Curt's sake, still trying to get STF a slot at the Surfin' Spot. So Avery almost couldn't believe her eyes when Curt strolled into the private party room. "Curt! What are you doing here?"

"Walking you home," he said, smiling as broadly as he could. But Avery had seen this act before and she knew it was completely forced. "Curt, this is Anthony," she said.

Curt shook the restaurant manager's hand, Avery noticed that he seemed to be making sure to squeeze extra tight.

"I've heard a lot about you," Anthony said. "How's the band?"

"Great," Curt said.

"Avery was just talking to me about getting you guys into the Surfin' Spot," the restaurant manager said. "She said that a couple of your guys weren't healthy for that outdoor concert and that I should stop by the Battle of the Bands and check you out again."

Avery gave Curt an encouraging smile, but she knew her boyfriend well enough to realize what he was thinking: that it sounded good. Too good to be true.

"Come on," Avery tugged at Curt's elbow. "Let me grab my bag and we'll go."

She told Anthony she'd see him the next day, got her bag from the coat room, and headed outside and into the dark.

"What was that about?" Curt growled as soon as they were down the beach and out of earshot.

Avery sighed. His jealousy was so predictable. "Exactly what Anthony said. I was trying to get him interested in the band."

"You sure that's all you were trying to get him interested in?" Curt said.

"Oh, Curt, if you only knew," Avery said.

"Knew what?" Curt asked.

Suddenly Avery realized how tired she was of being interrogated and constantly suspected of things she hadn't done. "Forget it, okay?" she said. "It would be nice if you could appreciate me a little more instead of always being so jealous."

"Right," Curt snarled. "The guy's tall, good-looking, the manager of a successful restaurant, and I have nothing to be jealous about."

Avery didn't reply. The image of Lucas appeared in her mind. Yes, perhaps Curt did have something to be jealous about. Only, he was wrong to think it was Anthony.

Thinking about Sabrina was driving Owen crazy. He had never met a girl like her before. One who blew him off after having slept with him. He'd also never met a girl he was so interested in being with. Maybe the two things were related. Or maybe it all went back to his father, whose drunken, cheating ways had pretty much ruined Owen's mother and their family.

The good news was that he'd apologized until he was red in the face about screwing up with Tim and Jamie. To the point where Sabrina seemed to accept the apology and was at least being civil to him. In fact, at that moment he was sitting with her and April on the deck drinking strawberry daiquiris. It was a totally pink girlie drink, but it actually tasted pretty good. The sun was beginning to set, and the thin strips of cloud in the sky were alive with hues of red and purple. It had been a hot day and it was finally starting to cool a little.

"So, April," he said. "I've been to your video store, I've been to Curt's concert, I've seen Lucas at the surf shop, and I've helped Sabrina with the babysitting—"

Sabrina flashed him an annoyed look, as if she may have forgiven him but wasn't ready to start joking about it. Still, Owen pushed on.

"All that's left is to go harass Avery and Polly at their restaurant," Owen said, leveling his gaze at Sabrina. "Who wants to go with me tomorrow? For dinner. Say about sevenish?"

"I'll go," Sabrina said to his amazement and delight.

"Tomorrow? I think I can make that work," April said, clearly not picking up on the whole apparently too-subtle date invitation. Owen sighed. Well, at least it would give him another chance with Sabrina.

Curt strode out on the deck carrying a beer. Suddenly Owen felt a bit embarrassed to be sipping a pink drink.

"Hey, Curt, we're going to go surprise Avery and Polly at the restaurant tomorrow night. Want to come?" April asked.

"Can't. We've got to rehearse for the Battle of the Bands," Curt replied, then focused on Owen. "Dude, if any of your frat friends need a band for one of their parties, you'll put in a good word for us, right?"

"Sure," Owen replied, although any of his "frat friends" who'd heard Curt's band would never go for it. "I'll do what I can, buddy."

Meanwhile, Sabrina shot him the slightest smirk, as if to say, "Who are you kidding?"

"Thanks, man," Curt said, starting to leave. "Nice outfit, Sabrina," he called over his shoulder.

"Thanks."

Owen was puzzled. He'd never heard Curt compliment anyone's clothes before. Now he looked over at Sabrina again. Her bikini top looked new and expensive. It was black and tiny, accentuating her chest. She was wearing designer, low-rider jeans that were also tight in all the right places. Very sexy and also very expensive looking. "Wow, that *is* a nice outfit," he said.

"Thanks for noticing," she said with an amused look as if she, too, knew he hardly ever noticed things like that.

April also seemed to have just noticed the outfit. "How can you afford that on a nanny's salary?" she asked.

"My parents bought it for me," Sabrina said.

"I thought they were in Europe for the summer," April said.

Sabrina shrugged noncommittally. "You never heard of the Internet?" She stood up. "Anyone want to take a walk?"

"Uh, sure," Owen said.

"Want to come?" Sabrina asked April.

"Can't," April said. "Got stuff to do."

"So, listen," Owen said, "maybe I'll ask Lucas if he wants to come to The Seashell tomorrow night, okay? That way it'll be two guys and two girls."

"Okay with me," Sabrina said.

"Me too," said April as she headed off. "Have fun."

The next thing Owen knew, he and Sabrina were walking toward the boardwalk. He couldn't quite believe it had happened so fast. Now he was walking beside this incredibly hot babe. Almost every guy, and girl, who approached them couldn't take their eyes off her.

"So, uh, what do you want to do?" he asked.

"Ferris wheel."

"Excuse me?" he asked, surprised.

"The Ferris wheel," Sabrina said. "I want to go on it. How about you?"

"Sure!" He was ready to do just about anything she wanted.

"I haven't been on it yet and it's on my summer To-Do list," she said.

Owen was tempted to ask if he was on her summer "To-Do list." Or, more appropriately, her "To-Do Again list," but he managed to suppress the comment. Together they strolled down the boardwalk, looking at the lights and different rides and attractions.

Fifteen minutes later they were sitting on a seat on the Ferris wheel as the attendant locked them in. Owen thought briefly about putting his arm around Sabrina, but decided not to push his luck. The Ferris wheel creaked. Their seat started to sway and then rose gracefully into the air. They sailed up into the sky until the ocean, pier, and beach all seemed at their feet. Below them was the crazy swirl of red, blue, and green that beckoned strollers to explore, spend, laugh, and play.

"It's beautiful," Sabrina whispered beside him.

He looked over and thought he saw only sincerity in her eyes. He hadn't seen her in such an unguarded moment since the night they'd spent together, and it made him want to know her better and be with her all the time.

Slowly the chair began its descent. Lights and people came back into sharp focus, and the sounds of music and laughter rushed at them. They reached the bottom and then began to climb upward once more. At the top they came to a gentle stop.

"Thank you," she said, lacing her fingers through his.

Owen wasn't sure what she was thanking him for, and he decided not to ask. He sat still, afraid to move, or even to breathe in case he might break the spell. Above them the moon hung high in the night sky, casting a reflection down onto the water. Only the smells of the ocean reached them as they sat suspended above the chaos of people and music and junk food. He let his breath out when the seat began to move again. At the bottom, the attendant let them out. As they exited the ride, Sabrina kept her hand in his.

They walked along the boardwalk, but despite the noise and colors, Owen seemed to only be aware of the beautiful girl beside him. It was late when the boardwalk began to close down. Where once there had been brilliant signs and lights on the roller-coaster tracks, there were now only shadows and darkness. Nearby, the carousel came to a final stop, and its cheerful timeless music ended. In the gathering dark the moon seemed to become only brighter and the stars filled the sky.

They walked back to the house in silence. Owen thought of stopping and kissing her, but he dared not push it. If this was some kind of test, he was determined to pass it. But when they got inside the house, he could feel a sudden change. They were no longer walking in a fairyland of lights and sensations, but back in reality.

She turned to look at him. "Thank you for a nice evening, Owen." She offered him her hand.

Owen stared at her hand. He'd hoped for more, and felt disappointed. Maybe it had been a test. Or maybe she just wanted someone to go on the Ferris wheel with. He took it and nodded, then let go. Sabrina marched up the stairs and closed herself in her room, leaving him, once again, alone.

Eight

April spent the morning visiting her grandmother while her mother was at work. She loved her granny, but it frightened her when she saw how sick and frail she looked. She always remembered her grandmother as having round, pink cheeks but now they were hollow and pale. *Like a ghost,* April thought, back in her little room. *Like me.*

She had been running away from life for years. She hadn't wanted to be noticed or touched by anything or anyone. Maybe it was time to stop running. She didn't want to be eighty and look back on her life and realize that all she had done was run. She needed to start living.

April had heard The Seashell restaurant where Avery and Polly worked was nice. After going through her closet for half an hour she finally decided that nothing she had could be classified as "nice." She bit her lip and made a decision. A moment later she left her room and knocked on Sabrina's door. Sabrina opened her door, wrapped in a fluffy pink towel, fresh from a shower. *Must be nice to have a private bathroom*, April thought with a stab of jealousy.

Sabrina looked surprised to see her, but opened the door wide to let her in. Sabrina's room was huge, with a king-size bed and its own sitting room. April tried to block out thoughts of the closet-size room she was living in. She knew she had told Curt that the size of the room didn't matter as long as she had her privacy, but the tiny, dark, windowless room had started to depress her.

"What's up?" Sabrina asked.

"I was wondering if I could borrow a dress," April said, hating herself for asking but feeling like she had no choice.

Sabrina gave her a coy look. "Sure. Can you fit into a size two?"

April nodded, hoping the dress wouldn't be too small on her. Sabrina studied her for a moment before crossing to her closet.

"Black or red?" Sabrina asked at last. April took a deep breath. She always wore black, so tonight the answer just had to be, "Red."

Sabrina turned with a smile, holding what appeared to be a designer dress. It was a red halter with a short, full skirt. April took it from her hesitantly. *I don't know if I'm ready to live this much,* she thought. "Thanks," she told Sabrina.

Back in her room, she tried the dress on. It fit surprisingly well. A sudden knock on the door startled her. "Who is it?"

"Sabrina. What size shoe do you wear?"

"Eight why?" April called.

"Open up."

She opened the door, and Sabrina handed her a pair of strappy red heels. "You're going to need some shoes."

"Thanks," April said, taking them.

"You look great, by the way." Sabrina glanced into the room, and her brow wrinkled. "Hey, is this really a room? Or a closet?"

Lucas hadn't anticipated wearing a jacket on his vacation, but now he was glad his mother had snuck one into his suitcase. Owen said they were to dress well for dinner. *Armani should be dressy enough,* Lucas thought. Underneath the jacket he wore a white shirt, unbuttoned at the neck. *No way am I wearing a tie.*

He inspected himself in the mirror and had to admit that even his parents would be pleased with the results.

"You ready?" Owen called, knocking on his door.

Lucas glanced at himself again in the mirror. It had been eons since he'd seen this much forehead. The dreads were gone, sacrificed earlier in the day on impulse. He still wasn't sure why. It just seemed like the time had finally come. He turned and opened the door.

Owen blinked, then grinned. "Sorry, I was looking for a guy with dreadlocks named Lucas."

"Very funny." Lucas grinned.

"Dude, you clean up well," Owen said.

"So do they," Lucas said, pointing toward the stairs. *Snow White and Rose Red,* he thought as he and Owen watched April and Sabrina descend the stairs. April was stunning in a red dress that showed off her long legs. Sabrina wore a white, filmy dress that hugged her curves in a way that had to be making Owen crazy.

He noted with satisfaction that the girls were also staring unabashedly at them. Owen was wearing black flat-front slacks with a blue pin-striped shirt, but it was Lucas they were clearly puzzled by. Then, at the very same moment, it seemed, they both realized who it was.

"Oh, no!" April gasped.

"Oh, yes!" Sabrina cheered.

Everyone laughed. Lucas and Owen joined the girls at the bottom of the stairs. Lucas extended his arm to April. "Shall we dine?" he asked.

April took his arm and Lucas noticed that Sabrina took Owen's. The walk down the boardwalk to The Seashell was pleasant, but amusing. Dressed the way they were they were attracting a lot of attention.

When they entered the restaurant Avery stared at them in shock, especially at Lucas. He, in turn, noticed that she looked gorgeous in her white dress and her hair piled on top of her head. He had never seen her in her work clothes before and found himself enjoying the view.

"Lucas?" Avery said uncertainly.

"The real deal." He gave her a big smile.

Avery smiled back, then turned to the others. "What are all of you doing here?"

"We are here to dine," Owen said.

"But the place is packed. You'd need a—"

"A reservation?" Owen asked, sounding pleased with himself. "Ah, but we have one. Party of four."

Avery glanced down at her papers. "The only party of four I have listed for right now is the Sola party."

"My dear lady," Owen said with feigned formality, "that is us. Sabrina, Owen, Lucas, and April. The SOLA party."

Avery laughed, obviously glad that her friends would be able to enjoy dinner after all. With an impish grin, she led them to their table. "I'll send a certain waitress over right away," she said with a wink.

They settled into their seats. A moment later, Polly hustled over, an armful of menus in one hand and a pitcher of water in the other. "Hi, welcome to The Seashell." She started handing out menus and began her waitress rap. "I'd just like to tell you about tonight's specials. For an appetizer . . ." The words stopped. Lucas looked up. Polly's mouth was hanging open. The pitcher of water in her hands had tilted slightly, and a thin clear stream was pouring onto the floor.

"Watering the carpet?" Owen asked with a grin.

"I don't believe it!" Polly blurted.

• • •

When Avery saw Lucas standing in front of her in his black jacket and short hair, she had thought for a moment that she was going to faint. She had heard the blood rushing in her ears and felt her heart begin to pound like a triphammer. He had looked so good that she had wanted to throw herself in his arms.

Steady, you're going to be okay Remember your boyfriend, Curt? The one you love? Just, don't think about Lucas, she coached herself. *Don't think about him looking gorgeous. Don't think about how he listened to you when you were upset about your mother's death. Don't think about how determined he was to find those two boys, and how gentle he was when he found them. Don't remember the way his arms felt when he was holding you on that surfboard. And, most of all, don't forget to breathe.*

Fortunately, as hostess, her job was over once she delivered the "SOLA" party to their table. Still, she found her eyes drifting their way frequently throughout dinner until Owen caught her staring and waved her over.

When she got there, Polly was serving dessert. Owen raised his glass of water. "I would like to make a toast," he proclaimed. "To two of our hardest-working roommates. Polly, Avery, great job."

"Here, here," Lucas said as he and the others raised their glasses first toward Polly, then toward Avery. Avery caught Lucas's eye and for a long moment neither of them could tear their gazes away. She felt her heart begin to race and knew she was in trouble. This had to stop. It was too complicated and confusing.

As soon as she could, Avery once again retreated to the front of the restaurant. It wasn't long, though, before the group was finished and came her way.

"Restroom?" April asked.

Avery pointed, and April, Sabrina, and Owen headed down the corridor. That left her alone with Lucas. An awkward silence fell in which she could hear her heart start to pound again. "How was dinner?" she asked.

"Great," Lucas replied. "It was cool seeing you and Polly in action. Too bad you couldn't join us. Maybe we can do it again on one of your days off so you can relax and not work."

He's always thinking about making someone else feel good, she thought. *So selfless. And sweet. And handsome.* Before she could stop herself, she stepped forward and gave him a hug. He wrapped his arms around her tightly and for a moment she felt safe against him. Then she realized what she was doing and stepped back, forcing herself to break the contact. *Idiot! Control yourself!*

Of course, it was just then that everyone else returned from the bathrooms. "My turn!" Owen said, swooping in for a hug of his own.

"You're welcome," Avery said, laughing and immensely grateful for Owen at that moment.

Both Sabrina and April stared at her. None of them were

really at the close-enough-to-hug stage. Suddenly, though, April stepped forward and gave Avery a quick hug. Surprised, Avery hugged her back.

"Fine, if everyone's doing it," Sabrina said with a shrug, giving Avery a quick half hug.

Avery glanced again at Lucas. His smile was broad and his eyes were shining. *He knows,* she thought miserably. *Hugging the others was a good cover, but he wasn't fooled.*

Then they were out the door and waving good-bye. As soon as they were out of sight, Avery collapsed against the podium. Life had become unbearably complicated.

Curt was fuming. He was sitting at a table in the Surfin' Spot with the rest of STF, checking out the competition for the upcoming Battle of the Bands. The Naked Mole Rats were steaming. But much more aggravating was what had just happened with Avery. Since the bar was right next door to Avery's restaurant, he had decided to drop in and tell her he was going to be out late.

What he'd seen through the window had set his blood on fire. He had seen Avery hugging some blond guy in a black jacket. He'd been on the verge of busting in on them and confronting her when Bobby grabbed him and hustled him into the bar.

"Don't do it," Bobby said, as if he could read Curt's mind.

"I want to know who she was hugging," he growled.

"Forget it, dude. It's just a friendly hug. Probably some friend of hers."

Curt was about to break free of his grip when Sabrina, April, and Owen came up and hugged Avery as well. Curt relaxed. Okay, it was just friends. He let Bobby lead him back into the Surfin' Spot.

"Why are you so freaked, anyway?" Bobby asked. "It's Avery. You know she's totally into you."

"You never know," Curt grumbled.

"Come on, man, hugs mean nothing to girls. They hug everyone."

Bobby was probably right. Girls *were* always hugging people. Maybe Avery hadn't even initiated the hug. It was probably nothing. He relaxed slightly and began to listen to the Naked Mole Rats again. *They're good, real good,* he thought. He wished STF could play this place. Maybe if they did well at the Battle of the Bands, they would. It was the kind of break they needed.

"Another beer?" the bartender asked.

Curt nodded and as he started on his second beer felt himself begin to relax. *It was just a hug. No big deal. Forget about Avery. I have bigger problems to worry about.*

It was early in the morning when Sabrina slipped into Lucas's room. She knew he was out surfing and it was too early for anyone else to be up. Even in the age of credit and debit cards, everyone still carried cash. *Especially here.* April's employer wasn't the only one who preferred to pay his employees off the books. Sabrina quietly began opening drawers and rifling through them, looking for money. She came up empty. She checked the closet but found nothing. Finally she slid her hands underneath the mattress. Halfway down the right side, her fingers brushed an envelope. She pulled it out and opened it. Inside were bills. She pulled out about forty dollars and then carefully put the envelope back. The important thing was not to take too much at once. People often forgot how much they had. She slipped the envelope back under the mattress and turned around. April was standing in the doorway.

Sabrina froze and felt a horrible sinking sensation in her gut.

"So it's you," April said quietly.

Sabrina's mind raced as she tried to think of a convincing lie, but nothing came to her. Finally she sank down on the bed. Her hands were shaking, and she pressed them together between her knees. "Happy?"

"No way." April's reply surprised her, and she looked up curiously.

"I would have been much happier if it had been some stranger—not someone I'm sharing a house with," April explained.

"How did you know?" Sabrina asked.

"The clothes. They were new, but there was no way you could afford them on a nanny's salary."

Sabrina nodded sadly as she realized her mistake. She'd

been too obvious. "My parents cut me off, just like that," she said, snapping her fingers.

"So?"

"You don't know what it's like," Sabrina said. "I've never had to work for anything, ever. It's hard. And I've never had to go so long without shopping. I just can't do it."

"You're kidding, right?" April asked.

"No, I can't be patient and count my pennies," Sabrina admitted, desperation welling up in her. "Like those jeans. I saw them and just had to have them."

"Uh, hello? Welcome to the real world," April grumbled, not taken in. "That's not how life works, okay? Most of us have to earn what we get. You can't just take it. What do you think the rest of us are doing? My mother works two jobs to care for my grandma, and I help as much as possible. Don't you think there are things we want? You'll just have to wait like the rest of us."

"That's sad, but that's not me," Sabrina replied.

"It is now, at least until you're back in Mommy's and Daddy's good graces. You're just going to have to get used to it. And in the meantime, you're going to give the money back."

The words startled Sabrina. "I can't. I've spent it all."

"Then you'll give them what you earn from now on," April said. "And you have to admit to everyone else what you did."

"No way," Sabrina flared, horrified by the embarrassment she would feel. "I won't do that."

"You will, otherwise, I could report you to the police."

"You wouldn't," Sabrina gasped.

"You don't think so?" April said. "I'll tell you why I will. One, because it's the only way you'll learn not to steal again. And two, because it's the only way I'll know for sure you won't steal from any of us for the rest of the summer. I'm giving you a chance here, Sabrina—don't screw it up."

Sabrina felt her head begin to pound. She had never admitted to anyone that she was wrong before, ever. *How can I do this?*

April backed away from the door.

"You're leaving?" Sabrina gasped.

"You're on your own," April said. "You know what to do."

Twenty minutes later, with her heart in her throat, Sabrina knocked on Owen's door. She'd decided to start with him because she hoped he'd be the easiest. After all, he knew about making mistakes. Sleepy-faced, his hair a mess, he opened it and smiled wide when he saw her. "Hey!"

Sabrina dipped her head so she wouldn't have to look at him. "You know how money's been missing?" Rarely in her life had she spoken such painful words. "I'm sorry."

Owen didn't answer. She glanced up to make sure he'd heard.

"It . . . it was you?" Owen asked, incredulous.

She nodded.

"Why?"

She tried to meet his eyes but couldn't. She tried to speak but had no words that would make sense. Finally she just shook her head.

"Hey, it's okay," he said softly. "Everybody makes a mistake. Look at me, right? I'm the king of mistakes. Anyway, it was really brave of you to admit this. I think it's admirable."

Sabrina felt the tears well up and flood out of her eyes. His kind words were the last things she'd ever expected.

"Thank you, Owen," she said with a sniff, and turned down the hall. *One down, four more to go.*

April opened the door almost immediately after Curt knocked. He swept her with his eyes taking in her green blouse and white skirt. What happened to the black? he wondered. But he didn't mind. It was a change, and it looked good on her. She blinked twice as though surprised to see him standing there.

"Sorry, I thought it was someone else," she said.

"Should I come back later?" Curt asked.

He watched her hesitate for a moment. "No, come in," she said, sitting back down on her bed. She closed her song notebook and tossed it on top of her guitar case.

He closed the door and sat next to her on the bed.

"Sabrina's looking for you," April said. There were circles under her eyes and he guessed she hadn't had much sleep the night before.

"Why?" Curt asked, confused.

"She has something to say."

"Can't you tell me?" he asked.

April shook her head. "Sorry to leave you in mystery, but you'll have to ask her."

"Whatever." He had more immediate things on his mind. The memory of the last time they'd gotten close was in his thoughts. Maybe he should have had more of a sense of humor about the whole thing. Or maybe he just had to hope she wasn't wearing the same bra. "You look good in those clothes."

"Thanks. I'm trying something new—color. How're rehearsals going?" she asked.

"We're working on some new material and I think it's going to be pretty good," Curt said, staring intently at her.

"Oh?" she asked, twisting around to face him.

She's not wearing all that makeup either. She's really pretty without it, he thought. "Yeah. I gotta thank you, too. You have been a real . . . inspiration."

Her lips parted slightly as she stared at him. He smiled back at her. "Inspiration? I don't think I've ever been that before," she said.

"That's hard to believe," he said, letting his eyes run over her body again. "I can't be the only one to find you so . . . inspiring."

"Maybe, but you're the only one to ever say so," she said.

He slid closer to her. "Well, it's true. You've inspired me. Talking to you feels so comfortable, so right."

She nodded in agreement, her head tilting back as she looked up at him.

"It's just made me remember," he said.

"Remember what?" she asked.

"The last time."

She was staring into his eyes, and he knew that he had her.

He moved in and kissed her. Her lips parted in response, and he slid his tongue inside her mouth. She made a little whimpering sound as his hands roamed up under her shirt.

Suddenly she stiffened, clamped her lips shut, and pushed him away. They were both red-faced and panting.

"What's wrong?" he asked.

"I can't," she said, tucking her shirt back in. "This is so wrong."

"Why?" he asked. "It wasn't so wrong last time."

"You have to go," she said.

He didn't move. She was so tempting. He started to reach for her again.

"No!" This time she slapped his hand away. "I didn't know Avery then, but I do now. She doesn't deserve this. Go before we're both sorry."

Curt rose to his feet. He knew April was right. Despite all his suspicions about Avery, he knew she'd basically been faithful. Even with people like that jerk Anthony trying to tempt her. So yeah, hooking up with April would have been wrong. But he was pretty sure he wouldn't have been sorry.

• • •

It had been a strange day and it was shaping up to be a depressing night. Most everyone was out of the house, probably on dates or at parties. Polly curled up on the living room couch with a bowl of popcorn and a chick flick she had rented for the evening. *Sleepless in Seattle* was a classic and very romantic, but it was doing nothing for her mood.

She still couldn't believe Sabrina was the thief. Well, she believed it. What was truly amazing was that she'd gone to each of them and apologized, promising to pay them back as soon as she could.

The front door opened and Curt strolled in. Polly stiffened. He was so moody; she never knew what to expect from him. He headed straight for the couch as though he had been looking for her. She groaned inwardly and curled up into a little ball in the corner of the couch.

"Hey, Polly. How are you doing?"

"Fine. You?"

He sat down on the couch and gazed at the TV. "Can you believe Sabrina?"

"I know, amazing, huh?" Polly relaxed a little. Tonight Curt seemed pretty mellow.

"Guess you never know," Curt said. "You think girls like her just feel so superior they think they can break the rules?"

It was funny, but the same thought had crossed Polly's mind. "I don't know."

They both watched the movie for a while.

"Isn't it amazing how messed up relationships can be?" Curt asked.

"Are we talking about the movie, or everyone we know?" Polly asked, half joking.

"Actually, I'm talking about Avery and me."

Polly frowned at him. This was utterly unexpected. He returned her gaze, and she saw that he was serious.

"I don't know if you know this, but Avery's mom died a few years ago," he said.

"I heard."

"It really tore her up," Curt said. "She was vulnerable for a long time—still is, really. Because of it, she doesn't always think of things the same way other people do."

He paused as though to get her reaction. Polly still had no clue what he wanted from her, so she just nodded.

Apparently that satisfied him, because he continued. "She's very pretty and very smart, but she's also very naive. I'm sure you've noticed that, especially where men are concerned?"

"She never knows when a guy's flirting with her," Polly confirmed.

"Exactly!" Curt said, more enthusiastically. "You're exactly right. And that's part of the problem. When a girl as sweet and pretty as Avery is that naive, guys try to take advantage of her." He paused and eyed Polly for a moment. "You do know what I mean when I say 'take advantage' right?"

"Of course I do," Polly said, her cheeks flaming.

"Good," Curt said. "That's why I really need your help. I need you to help me watch out for her."

Polly stiffened. *Oh, my gosh, he's going to ask me if she likes Lucas!*

"You see, I'm worried—" Curt continued.

What am I going to do?

"about—"

I can't tell him about Lucas!

"Anthony."

Polly blinked. She sat stunned for a second before she repeated, "Anthony?"

"Yes."

"There's nothing going on between Avery and Anthony," Polly said, bewildered.

"I know, I know," Curt said, putting a hand up. "I'm just worried about the guy." His tone and mannerisms were gentle and persuasive, but there was a look in his eye that confused her.

"I really don't think you have anything to worry about," Polly said. "I mean, they talk to each other a lot at work, but not about anything important. And, if you're talking about what happened at that surprise dinner . . ."

"Surprise dinner?" Curt repeated solemnly. Avery hadn't said anything about that. "Thank you, Polly," he said, his voice distant and his eyes far away. "Thank you."

He got up and left, leaving Polly with the queasy feeling that somehow she had said the wrong thing.

The next morning, Polly tried to get Avery alone to tell her about Curt, but things were too crazy. Avery was running late, and Polly finally had to leave for work without her. Avery arrived at the restaurant about five minutes before the doors opened and the customers started streaming in. Before Polly knew it, they were halfway into the lunch rush. Every table was jammed and she was constantly running from table to kitchen and back again. The other waitresses were in a similar rush and narrowly missed a dozen collisions with customers and one another.

When the inevitable collision came, Polly was the one who ended up with chili all over the front of her shirt as the waitress, Terry, swung the kitchen door open and right into Polly's tray of half-empty plates. Polly ran to the bathroom and spent ten minutes trying to get the stain out before she realized that she would have to fix it later. She abandoned the shirt—thankful that she was wearing a plain white tank top underneath—and threw it into her employee locker before heading back into the restaurant. She got there just as Curt exploded through the front door. Polly knew at once that he had been drinking. He was unsteady on his feet, and the scent of alcohol wafted from him.

Avery was standing at the hostess podium talking with

Anthony, and Polly watched in horror as they both turned and saw Curt. Before anyone could say anything, Curt grabbed the front of Anthony's shirt.

"Stay away from my girlfriend!" he shouted, loud enough to get the attention of everyone inside the restaurant. All conversation ceased, and heads turned their way.

"Excuse me?" Anthony asked, keeping his voice low to avoid disrupting the customers.

"Curt! Let go of him." Avery tried to pry Curt's hand from Anthony's shirt.

"I'm going to pound this guy," Curt grumbled, pulling his fist back.

"Why? He hasn't done anything to you!"

"He's done plenty. What about the surprise dinner?" Curt grunted.

Polly groaned. She knew it! He'd only used her to get information the night before. And he'd gotten it all wrong.

"What are you talking about?" Anthony asked.

"The surprise dinner!" Curt said.

Avery stared at Curt, eyes wide. It was a telling look, as if she was thinking, "How did he know about that?" The entire restaurant seemed to be holding its breath, awaiting her response. Polly felt helpless, as though she was rooted to the ground, incapable of movement.

"I don't know what you heard," Avery hissed. "But whatever it was, it was wrong." She was clearly trying to keep her voice down, but by this time everyone in the restaurant was hanging on to her every word.

"Don't lie," Curt said. "I know all about it. Polly told me."

And suddenly, all eyes were on Polly. She wished the floor would open up and swallow her. "It's not true," she protested. Her voice was barely above a whisper, and yet it seemed to echo throughout the room. "He asked me if you talked to Anthony, that's all. I told him that of course you talk to him, you work together. That's all, I swear." Polly felt her eyes filling with tears.

"You women all lie for each other," Curt snarled. It looked like he was going to hit Anthony, but just then a big, muscular cook sprinted from the kitchen and grabbed Curt's raised arm, twisting it behind his back and forcing him down to his knees. During the scuffle, Curt managed to tear the front of Anthony's shirt open. "What about the surprise dinner?" Curt yelled.

"Anthony had nothing to do with it," Avery said. "It was Sabrina, Owen, Lucas, and April."

"What?" Curt asked from his knees. "But I thought—"

Anthony turned on him. "Get out of here before I call the cops!"

"This isn't over," Curt muttered. The cook let go of him, and he staggered to his feet. Avery hurried him out the door.

"It is for you," Anthony said. "You and your lousy band can forget about playing here, ever, and if I catch you in here again, I'm calling the police and pressing charges." Then he rounded on Avery: "And you, you're done too. Get out of here—you're fired."

"Fired?" Avery and Polly gasped at the same time. Avery was trembling from head to toe. Polly couldn't believe it. Avery'd done nothing to deserve being fired. She surged to her friend's defense.

"It wasn't her fault," Polly pleaded. "You can't fire her. She didn't do anything wrong."

Anthony pointed at Curt. "Just knowing that idiot is wrong enough."

No, it was too unfair, Polly thought. "If she goes, I go," she said defiantly.

"Fine, you're both out of here," Anthony answered.

The restaurant went still.

"You fire Red, I'll never eat here again," a man suddenly shouted from the back of the dining room.

"Yeah, leave the girls alone," another man shouted.

"It's disgraceful how you're behaving, young man," an older lady reproached Anthony.

"Red stays, she's the only reason I eat here," another guy piped up.

Polly was stunned. She lifted her hand slowly to touch her red hair. Red, that was her. They didn't want her to go. Tears sprung to her eyes. It was the first time in her life that she had actually felt appreciated.

Anthony was staring slack-jawed at his customers. This

was definitely the kind of bad publicity he could not afford.

"Okay, okay, maybe I was a little hasty," he grumbled. "You can both stay, but I never want to see that jerk around here again." He turned and disappeared into the back room.

Amidst the cheers of the patrons, Polly felt Avery put her arms around her and give her a hug. "Thanks," Avery whispered. "You saved me."

The blazing sun was hot on Avery's skin and even by the ocean the air was still and steamy. She tried her best to relax and enjoy it while she watched Lucas surf. Closer to the boardwalk the beach was so packed that she'd practically had to sit at the water's edge.

It had been a couple of days since she and Curt had had the fight in the restaurant and things still weren't completely smooth between them. Somehow the fact that she hadn't gotten fired only seemed to make him angrier.

She glanced back at her companions sitting just behind her on the beach. Owen was drinking as he sunned himself, his face and chest glistening with sweat. Avery felt bad. Clearly the scare with the little boys had not been enough to get him off drinking for good. Near him, Polly was building a sand castle.

"You should put a moat around it," Avery said.

"What?" Polly asked, wiping a dainty drop of sweat off her nose.

"A moat, so when the tide comes in, it fills the moat instead of washing away the castle," Avery explained.

"It doesn't matter," Polly said. "Some castles aren't worth saving."

"Mine are never worth saving," muttered Owen.

That was when Avery began to suspect that she was the only one actually talking about sand castles. Owen seemed even more despondent than Polly.

"Owen, what's the problem?" Avery asked.

"Problem?" Owen repeated. "You mean, besides the fact that I'm a total screwup. I couldn't even keep an eye on those kids for Sabrina for, what, ten minutes?"

"Owen, that was weeks ago. The kids are okay," Avery said. "Stop beating yourself up over it. And look at Sabrina. She's made some pretty serious mistakes herself."

"Yeah, right, so we're both screwups." Owen said. He stood up unsteadily. "It's too frickin' hot. I'm going for a swim."

"Is that wise?" Avery asked, looking at the collection of empty beer bottles around his chair.

"Who are you, my mother?" he asked, and started into the waves.

Avery followed him for a moment with her eyes. The waves seemed kind of big and rough. Well, you never knew. Maybe the water would sober him up. She glanced out at Lucas. He looked good out there, cutting up and down the faces of the waves. Next, she turned her attention to Polly. "I owe you an apology," she said.

"What for?" Polly asked, sitting up. "Remember I promised to find you a guy?"

"Oh, no thanks," Polly said. "Not after what happened. Besides, that wasn't your job. It was a sweet thought, that's all. I'm the one who should be apologizing, after what happened at the restaurant. I really feel like it's my fault that you and Curt are fighting."

Avery sighed. "We've already been through this, Polly. You were right in the restaurant. It's *not* your fault. You couldn't have known that Curt was going to do that. You didn't tell him anything you shouldn't have. And at the end of the day, you were the hero. You saved my job."

Polly shrugged and rubbed some sand off her hands. Avery could see that she was still down in the dumps.

"Something else bothering you?" Avery asked.

"It's this whole summer. Nothing is turning out like I planned."

Nothing ever does, Avery thought. *I never planned for my mother to die. Never planned to spend most of my summer fighting with the band for Curt's attention.* Her eyes drifted out to the ocean again. *Definitely never planned for Lucas.* At the thought, she felt herself blushing.

"The summer's almost over," Polly continued "Sometimes I feel like everyone in the house can't decide whether to be friends or to hate one another."

Avery shrugged. "Don't you think some of that is pretty

much inevitable? Different personalities, you know? Maybe we should just be grateful no one's slit anyone's throat in the middle of the night."

Polly laughed darkly. "The summer's not over quite yet. It could still happen."

"My money's on Sabrina killing Owen," Avery said with a laugh.

"Or Owen might kill himself over Sabrina," Polly said.

"They've both got a lot of baggage," Avery noted. "A lot of things they've got to overcome if they're ever going to be in a steady relationship with anyone, let alone each other."

"I guess the good news is, maybe they have a shot at it," Polly said.

"Help!" The cry was faint, but it reached Avery and she swiveled her head back to the ocean, feeling panic rise in her. Polly's wide eyes met hers. "Where's it coming from?" she asked, her eyes scanning the water.

"There!" Polly cried, her finger pointing. "Oh, no, it's Owen!"

Avery saw his arms flailing about wildly in the water, but he was being pulled farther and farther away from them. *Must be caught in a riptide!* She quickly looked toward the lifeguard stand. Why was it empty? There was no time to find out. She was stricken by a thought. *I shouldn't have let him go swimming drunk! Now he's going to die and it will be my fault.* Without thinking, she sprinted for the waves and splashed in. The water was surprisingly cold compared to her sun-heated skin, but she forced herself forward and began to swim. She could hear shouts behind her, but not the actual words.

The waves were big and turbulent and current was strong, and she quickly realized it was pulling her more than she was swimming through it. The waves buffeted her about. Twice she ended up with a mouthful of water and was left coughing.

She renewed her efforts and finally saw Owen bobbing and splashing haplessly a dozen yards away. Her arms were beginning to feel weak with exhaustion, but she kept swimming and forced her legs to kick even harder. She was not going to let him drown. Not when she should have stopped him from going in, in the first place. Just as she reached him, his head slipped beneath the waves. She dove down, grabbed his arm, and kicked hard to haul him back up. Eyes closed, his head burst out of the water and he gasped for air.

"Owen!"

Owen's eyes opened with surprise. In desperation he grabbed her arm and held tight as he started to sink again. Avery kicked hard and pulled him to the surface again, but the effort to keep them both afloat was exhausting her. "Owen, I've got you, but you've got to help me! Owen?"

His eyes bulged with panic and he coughed and sputtered. His hands were locked on her arm, and she had to keep kicking and stroking to stop from being pulled under.

"Owen, you've got to help!" she gasped. "Try to swim!"

Instead, he disappeared once again beneath the choppy surface, his hands on her arm like a death grip. Exhausted from battling the waves and his panic, Avery felt herself start to sink.

Nine

Lucas was bummed as he strode up onto the sand. All morning the waves had been getting larger and larger and the surf better and better. He wasn't ready to give up surfing for the day, but the riptide had come out of nowhere and the currents had turned squirrelly and it just wasn't safe to stay out any longer. The red danger flags were up along the beach and lifeguards were busy calling everyone out of the water. He put his board down, shook his head, and pounded water out of his ears.

"Lucas!"

Polly was running down the beach toward him. "Owen is drowning! Avery went in after him!" She pointed out toward the ocean.

Lucas instantly looked for a lifeguard, but they were all a hundred yards down the beach trying to pull a bunch of kids out of the rough surf. He turned in the direction that Polly was pointing and saw heads bobbing in and out of the waves and arms flailing and splashing. Lucas grabbed his board and started to run. He passed Polly and kept running down the beach until he could see Avery swimming directly out from where he was. Then he splashed into the water and started to paddle as hard as he could.

She's crazy! You never try to save a person by yourself. Especially without some kind of flotation device. Every year almost as many people drown trying to save drowning people as those who actually drowned. Now I'll have to save two people instead of one.

His thoughts were angry and chaotic, but his strokes were strong and purposeful and the surfboard surged through the waves. He saw Avery and Owen at the top of a wave, Avery struggling to stay afloat and Owen hanging on to her to keep from going under. *Classic. Frickin' classic!* Lucas's fury only helped him paddle harder to reach them.

He was a dozen yards away when Avery's face broke to the surface and she gasped for air. Owen came up beside her, clawing at her before they both went back down. Lucas dove off the surfboard. Avery and Owen were about three feet under. Lucas grabbed Avery and pulled, scissor-kicking toward the surface. He got her to the surface, where she gasped for air and gave him a startled, panicked look.

Now it was her turn to grab wildly at him.

Smack! It was the only circumstance in which he could ever imagine smacking a woman, but their lives depended on her paying attention.

It worked. Avery gave him a startled look.

"The board!" he shouted, shoving the surfboard at her. "Hold onto it!"

Avery appeared to understand. She was about to reach for the board when Owen burst to the surface behind her and grabbed her around the neck, yanking her head back. Avery let out a garbled shriek. Lucas knew Owen was out of his mind and only trying to save himself, but he couldn't let him take Avery down again. Owen had his left arm wrapped around her neck like a vise, though. Lucas struggled to break his grip.

"Owen, I can save you, but you have to let go!" he shouted.

Owen either didn't hear or didn't understand because he kept thrashing and pulling on Avery.

"I'm sorry about this, man," Lucas shouted, then grabbed Owen by the throat. Owen's natural reaction was to let go of Avery and grab Lucas's arm, which was just what Lucas wanted. Lucas yanked him toward the board.

"Yo!" someone shouted nearby.

Lucas turned his head. A female lifeguard was swimming toward them with a bright orange rescue tube.

"Know what you're doing?" she shouted at Lucas.

"Yeah," he yelled back. "Used to be a lifeguard." He gestured at Avery. "You take this one. I'll bring the other one in."

"Gotcha." The lifeguard slid the rescue tube under Avery's arms and began to swim away, towing her. The trick was to swim parallel to the shore and out of the rip tide before trying to go back in.

With Owen holding on to the surfboard for dear life, Lucas began to follow the lifeguard. He knew he was running out of energy. Rescuing someone when you've been sitting in a lifeguard chair all day and were fresh and strong is one thing. Rescuing someone after hours spent surfing is another.

They got out of the rip current and Lucas stopped swimming for a moment. He knew he had to rest before trying to swim through the breaking surf. A look toward shore showed people gathering to watch. The riptide had been sudden, and there were rescue efforts up and down the beach. One man waded out into the water and helped the lifeguard pull Avery up onto the shore. *At least she's safe.*

"Oh, man." Still clutching the surfboard, Owen groaned beside him.

Lucas turned. "You okay?"

"You kidding? I'm alive, dude. I'm great."

Lucas was relieved that Owen had come back to his senses. It would make what was going to happen next a littler easier. But not much. Anyway, it was time.

"No matter what happens, don't let go of the board!" Lucas yelled. "This is going to get hairy."

Before he had learned to surf, Lucas had learned to bodysurf. Now he waited, treading water, for the right wave. When it was nearly upon him, he began to kick hard. The wave caught him and Owen and carried them toward the shore at a breathtaking pace.

That was the easy part. Now he just had to get ready for—

Crash! The wave broke half a dozen feet before he expected it to. The next thing Lucas knew, he and Owen were tumbling and flailing like rags in a washing machine.

He and Owen were rolled, beaten, and battered in the surf. Lucas's face was slammed painfully into the sandy bottom. His arms were so tired, they were useless—just a couple of rubber bands flopping around.

Two more waves smashed him. He lost Owen. Running low on breath, he couldn't figure out which way was up. The undertow was dragging him backward. Just as Lucas began to think he was going to be sucked back out into the deep, he felt arms lifting him, pulling him.

A few moments later he found himself on the beach, coughing and spitting out seawater. He could feel sand everywhere, scratching his eyes, in his ears, and in his shorts.

"You okay?" someone asked.

"Yeah," Lucas gasped, then coughed up more seawater. "What about the other guy?"

"He's okay."

Lucas sighed with relief and closed his eyes, remembering the feeling of being on the bottom and the undertow pulling him. He would have drowned. He was certain of it. He'd been a few seconds away from the end.

"Lucas!"

He opened his eyes again. The blurry image of Avery loomed

over him. All he could think about was how close they'd all come to dying.

"Don't ever do that again," he muttered, and closed his eyes.

"What?" she asked, faltering.

"You didn't know what you were doing. You could have gotten us all killed. You almost did."

"I was only trying to help," Avery insisted, but Lucas could only think of how close she'd come to drowning. Suddenly he realized he couldn't stand the thought of losing her.

"If there's ever a next time, don't," Lucas said.

Avery's face went tight. She turned and ran off. Lucas knew she didn't understand what he'd meant. But he was too tired to get up and stop her.

April was watching TV when her roommates started to come into the house. Something was wrong. Owen and Avery were soaking wet and shivering even though it was a hot day, water dripping from them in rivulets. Owen looked white, and Sabrina and Polly were hovering close to him as if he might teeter over at any moment. The two boys Sabrina took care of were trailing behind them. Avery's eyes were red, and April could tell that some of the drops on her cheeks were tears, not seawater.

Fred, who had been in the downstairs bathroom double-checking the plumbing, came out to see what was going on.

"What happened?" April asked.

"Owen nearly drowned," Sabrina said.

"Avery went to save him and she nearly drowned," Polly added.

"And Lucas saved both of us," Avery finished. Her face was flushed, and her eyes were puffy. Scratches on her neck oozed little droplets of blood. April had a brief vision of kissing Curt, and with it came some of the most intense guilt she'd ever felt. What had she been thinking?

"I'd be dead meat without those two," Owen said, looking grim and coughing.

"Seriously, I probably would have drowned if Avery hadn't gotten there when she did. And then it would have been both of us if Lucas hadn't shown up. I swear this is it, I'm going to stop drinking."

"You went into the water . . . drunk?" April asked in disbelief.

"You believe it?" Owen chastised himself. "Like it was just waves, right? Who thinks about riptides? I swear, not another drop of liquor will ever touch these lips."

"Owen, please," Sabrina scoffed.

"You'll see," Owen said, and April definitely heard a determination in the words that had not been there before.

The front door opened and Lucas trudged in, looking shaken and pale. Like the others, he, too, was shivering. Without a word he crossed the living room and started to open the door to the downstairs bathroom.

"Lucas?" April had never seen him like that before.

"Sorry, right now I need a hot shower," Lucas muttered,

and closed the door behind him. A second later they heard the shower start to run.

April watched as Avery gazed longingly at the bathroom door. "Can you believe that?" Avery said in a low voice. "He just saved two lives and all he can say is he wants to take a shower."

The memory of coming out of the ladies' room at The Seashell and seeing Avery and Lucas embracing was still fresh in April's mind. *That girl is head over heels,* April thought. *I wonder if she even knows it.*

Sabrina left to take the boys home and the others started to go to their rooms to wash up. April climbed the stairs quietly. She took a shower and changed into fresh clothes. She felt weird. Just now, being in the same room with Avery made her feel awful. She knew she'd done a bad thing with Curt and wished she could ask Avery's forgiveness. Feeling at loose ends, she tried to turn some of her thoughts into poetry in her notebook. But it all came out jumbled, and she finally shut the notebook and headed back downstairs, too antsy to stay cooped up in her little room.

Downstairs the group—except for Avery and Lucas—had reassembled. Everyone was showered and changed into street clothes and, as if to put the earlier events behind them, the conversation was about what to do that night and on the nights to come.

"I still think we should plan to have a big pre-Battle of the Bands dinner on Saturday," Polly said.

"No!" the others shouted in chorus.

"We could have a wake for STF afterward," Owen suggested, apparently feeling like himself again.

There was a knock on the front door and Martin stuck his head in. "Owen, we're heading over to see Gear Shift. You coming?"

Owen glanced at Sabrina, who'd dropped the kids off and returned. He clearly wanted her to give him an excuse to stay, but she turned her head and faked a yawn.

Owen shrugged. "Yeah, let's party," he said, getting up and leaving with his friend.

As soon as the front door closed, Sabrina turned toward April. "See? He'll be drinking again in five minutes."

April thought of the way Owen had earlier looked at Sabrina. "It doesn't have to be that way. Maybe if you went too. I'll go with you. It would be good to get out."

Sabrina mulled it over and slowly rose to her feet. "Oh, might as well go check out the band. But if they suck, we're out of there in five."

April smiled to herself. She was starting to understand Sabrina. The girl would never admit that going had anything to do with Owen, but this time, maybe it did.

Lucas took a long shower and then rested in his room for a little while. Partly because he was really shaken up by what had happened with Avery and Owen, and partly because he wanted to avoid being in the spotlight. By the time he went downstairs, Avery, Polly, and Fred were in the kitchen talking about watching the Friday night fireworks. Polly asked if he'd like to join them. He said he would.

He'd rather be outside, anyway, instead of stuffed into some smoky club. More than that, though, he wanted to talk to Avery, to apologize for snapping at her before. She'd only tried to help. It wasn't her fault.

As the sun set they walked down to the beach with a cooler and sat on the sand drinking and waiting for the show to begin. Despite the warm, calm air, the waves were still big and rough. Now that he was on his second beer, Lucas began to relax. He sat next to Fred, and Polly was next to Avery. So far, Lucas had not been able to catch her eye.

"I wish we could have agreed to have a pre-Battle dinner," Polly said, her voice laced with disappointed. "I just thought it would be fun, especially since the end of summer is almost here. We could have ended with a dinner just like we started with a dinner."

"Sort of neatly bookend it, huh?" Lucas asked.

"Exactly!" she said, seeming pleased that at least someone understood the symmetry she had been going for. "I mean, I really don't see what the big deal is. I'd do most of the legwork."

"I know how you feel, Polly," Fred said. "It's a drag when you're trying to make someone happy and you're not appreciated."

Lucas suspected that Fred wasn't speaking in general terms.

The remark was aimed at Polly. The cool evening breeze began to pick up. It felt good on his skin and he breathed in deeply.

"It's a little chilly," Polly said. "I'm cold, I'm going back to put on something warmer."

"Do you want me to walk you?" Fred asked, his voice hopeful.

Lucas watched as Polly glanced uncertainly at him and Avery. He sensed she would have enjoyed Fred's company, but was afraid what others would think.

"Sounds like a nice offer," Lucas said, to encourage her.

"Well, okay," Polly said.

Fred smiled broadly and jumped up.

With Fred and Polly gone, it was just him and Avery. Her hair was blowing in the moonlight and she'd had the foresight to wear a sweatshirt. Lucas longed to reach out and touch her. She was looking out at the water. Lucas knew it was time to speak. "You know, they actually make a cute couple."

Avery nodded, but didn't say anything. Lucas knew she had other things on her mind.

"I'm sorry I blew up at you before," he apologized.

"No, you had every right to," she said. "I could have died out there. Owen, too. I had no business acting like I knew what I was doing. You were right to be mad."

"No, I wasn't. You were just trying to do the right thing."

Avery grew quiet. "Seems like I'm always trying to do the right thing," she said. "At some point I stopped being a kid and became the 'right thing' young woman."

"About the time your mother died?" he guessed.

She nodded. "I really miss her sometimes. Especially when I realize that I'm sort of stumbling through life with no idea what I'm doing. I used to think I knew. Before this summer, I thought I knew. But something happened here. I know this is going to sound dumb, but this summer the world became a bigger place."

"I understand," he said.

"Did that happen for you too?" she asked.

"Well, not in the same way. For me, the world's been a big place for a while already."

"Because of your famous economist parents?" Avery asked.

Lucas felt a moment of surprise that she knew, then nodded. It wasn't so shocking that she'd figured it out. Just like she'd figured out that he worked for Habitat for Humanity. "When I was younger I got dragged around to a lot of international conferences."

"Must have been exciting," Avery said wistfully.

"Well, in a kid kind of way," Lucas allowed. "Like, who gets madder when you push all the buttons in the elevator, the French or the Germans?"

"And the answer is?"

"Both. It's the Italians who just think it's cute."

Avery laughed, and Lucas moved closer and put his arm around her shoulders. She didn't resist.

"So, have you decided?" she asked.

"Decided what?" he asked.

"If you're going to do what your parents want you to do," she said.

Again, she'd caught him by surprise. "Yes, I . . . I think I owe it to them to give it a shot. Then, if I'm not happy, at least they'll know I tried. What about you? Have you decided?"

She didn't answer. He could feel her uncertainty and confusion and he wished he could do something to ease it. Her life had not been easy, and he wondered what she would have been like had things been different. *Probably the same Avery, but perhaps a little surer of herself. Maybe even sure enough to not feel she needs Curt.*

Several moments passed and neither of them said anything.

"Thanks," she said after a while.

"What for?" he asked.

"Sometimes just sitting quietly is the best thing."

"Oh yeah, I knew that," he said, and winked.

She smiled and seemed to relax more. He didn't know whether she even was thinking of him as anything more than a friend at that moment. He did know that he was going to keep his arm around her as long as she would let him.

From the other side of the pier came a deep boom! Suddenly the sky overhead was filled with light. The initial burst was a cascade of red, white, and blue. More followed, lighting up the night, some with a high-pitched shriek, others fluttering toward the ground like butterflies, and all accompanied by loud booms. Lucas suddenly realized that Polly and Fred hadn't returned.

"Isn't it beautiful?" Avery breathed, looking upward.

"Sure is," Lucas said while staring at her.

Slowly she turned her head and her eyes met his. Lucas felt a wave of emotion rise up inside him. "I'm really sorry I yelled at you. It's just that, you know, I got scared when I thought you might drown."

"Was that why you were so angry?" she asked softly.

He nodded. And with the sky alight above them, he took her face in his hands and kissed her.

After five minutes at the club, Sabrina was glad April had convinced her to come. The band, Gear Shift, was really good and she found herself moving happily to the music. The dance floor was packed and the crowd around the bar was four deep. Half the people in the place were doing Jell-O shots. She wrinkled her nose. That was so high school.

"He's over there," April said, pointing to Owen.

"I wasn't looking for him," Sabrina lied, but once her eyes found Owen, they didn't stray. She knew her feelings about him had changed. It had started when he'd insisted on apologizing for what had happened with the boys. Too many other guys would have tried to come up with excuses, no matter how lame. But Owen had acted like a man, admitting it was his fault and not trying to excuse himself in any way.

And then, when she'd gone to him and admitted she was the one who'd stolen the money, he'd been sincerely forgiving.

She hadn't been nearly as forgiving about the boys, and she knew Owen could have laid into her if he'd wanted. But he'd resisted in a way that only someone who really cared about her would do.

But still, there was the heavy drinking. She couldn't abide by that. It was the last big barrier between them. She wanted to see if he'd keep his word and not drink again. More to the point, she was hoping he would.

One of Owen's friends handed him a Jell-O shot. Before he could down it, though, he turned and caught Sabrina staring at him. She could feel the embarrassment at being caught creep through her, and yet, she returned his gaze for a long moment, almost daring him in her thoughts to put down the Jell-O shot.

April nudged her and whispered in her ear: "He wants you to go over there and tell him not to."

"No," Sabrina replied. "He's a big boy. He should be able to make his own decisions. If he really wants to quit drinking, he'll quit whether I want him to or not."

"Maybe he just needs someone to help him, someone to be on his side."

"And what would happen if I wasn't there?" Sabrina asked. "I can't be with him every time he walks into a bar."

"Maybe not physically, but he'd know you were somewhere thinking about him." April put her hand on Sabrina's shoulder. "Do it. Go to him. I know you care, even if you won't admit it to yourself. Now get your skinny butt over there and help him do the right thing."

"My butt is not skinny," Sabrina said.

"Who are you kidding?" April laughed. "You're going even if I have to kick you over there. Don't think I can't."

Sabrina knew April was only telling her to do what she herself really wanted to do. "Oh, fine."

She walked over to Owen, the shot still in his hand. Finally she was standing in front of him. "Hi," he said.

"Hi."

"So, uh, how can I help you?" he asked. His words may have been slightly mocking, but his eyes were pleading. She knew he wanted something from her.

"April told me to come over," she said coolly.

"April told you, huh? So it's not like *you* actually care whether I drink or not?"

"Do whatever you want," she heard herself say, but she was thinking, *I wish he wouldn't drink. I think I could really care for him, but he has to prove he can deal with his problem.*

He started to lift the cup.

But how will I know what he would choose if I don't let him know there is a choice? she wondered. She watched the cup as he raised it toward his lips, but before it could touch them, she grabbed his arm, overcome by the emotion she was feeling. "I'm not saying I care." She could feel tears well up in her eyes.

"Then what are you saying?"

"I'm saying maybe you shouldn't do this."

He wavered, and even she wasn't sure that she had said

enough. There had to be something she could say, something she could do to let him know. "Come on," she urged. "Let's get out of here."

He stared at her for a moment before placing the cup on the bar. A smile spread through his lips. "Thank you," he whispered.

Curt knew that Avery was royally upset with him. She just didn't understand the pressure he was under. This Battle of the Bands gig was going to decide the fate of Stranger Than Fiction. If his band couldn't beat a bunch of no-talent local shore bands, then what chance would they have in the real world? The pressure was enormous and it distorted everything he thought and felt. Even if he'd been wrong about Anthony, Avery had to understand that he'd just needed to blow off steam.

He found her in their room, sitting on the edge of the bed looking puffy-eyed. He felt a pang of guilt for having caused it. Not that it was the worse thing he had ever done to her—his thoughts immediately went to April—but picking the fight with Anthony was the worst thing that *she knew* he'd done to her. She must have really been taking it hard if she was still crying about it.

"Hey, sweetie," he said.

She looked up, hastily wiping away some tears.

"I got you something," he said, handing her a box.

"You didn't have to," she said, looking up at him with teary eyes.

"Yes, I did." He sat down next to her on the bed. "I'm sorry I've been so preoccupied with the band. And I'm sorry for what I did at the restaurant. That wasn't cool. I'm just so wired. Everything gets distorted."

"It's okay," she said with a sniff.

"If it was okay, why were you crying?" he asked.

Instead of answering, she opened the box and lifted out a heart-shaped shell pendant on a black cord. He helped her put it around her neck.

"I know this summer hasn't been easy, Ave," he said. "I know it hasn't turned out the way you wanted, and I've asked a lot from you. But I really need you now more than ever. The Battle of the Bands is really important to me and it's almost here. I just need you to be here for me, to support me."

She nodded, but once again her eyes began to fill with tears. He wrapped his arms around her and whispered, "I love you."

Avery began to sob.

Avery lay awake listening to the sound of Curt's breathing. It had grown deeper and slower and she knew that he was asleep. She rolled onto her side and stared at the picture of him on her nightstand that was illuminated by the numbers on her alarm clock. The picture was three years old. She had taken it just a month after they started dating, and two months after her mother had died.

Things had been different then. She had been different—fragile and broken. Now she was whole again, and saw their relationship differently. It seemed to her that Curt had actually preferred her broken and needy. He obviously didn't like it when she attempted to be strong and independent, and it was beginning to dawn on her that he'd never really been very good to her. She'd just been too needy in the past to see it.

But just because she no longer needed him the way she used to, was it fair to walk away? Maybe it was no longer a question of her needing him. He'd said he needed her. Things weren't going the way he wanted for his band. STF wasn't that good, and even great bands rarely succeeded in the real world. There was little hope for his. Sooner or later he was probably going to crash and the dream was going to die. He would need her then, maybe more than she'd ever needed him. *I can't let him go through that alone. Not after all he did for me when I was the needy one.*

Carefully and quietly, she got out of bed. She was thirsty and she needed to think about the future and what she needed to do. Like Lucas had said, the world was a lot bigger than she'd ever imagined. There was a lot more out there than her little town and that junior college that was within commuting distance. She slipped on a robe, crept out the door, and went down the stairs. A single reading light was burning in the living room, but she didn't pay attention to it. She headed straight for the kitchen and downed two glasses of water, trying to wash the bad taste from her mouth.

Out of the corner of her eye she saw someone come out of the downstairs bathroom and sit on the couch beside the light. So she wasn't the only person in the house who couldn't sleep tonight. Avery splashed some water on her face and turned to go back upstairs.

She walked into the living room and glanced at the figure reading on the couch. She stopped short when she saw that it was Lucas and he was staring at her. For a moment, neither of them moved.

Then, slowly, Lucas stood up and crossed to her. He took her hand and led her to the front door, then outside and down the sidewalk toward the beach. The night air was cool and damp. Neither of them spoke a word until they were standing on the beach, underneath the moonlight. There in the darkness, with only the light of the moon and the sound of the waves, they were alone, completely and utterly alone. *At last.*

He reached out and slid her robe off her shoulders and she let it fall, exposing the filmy nightgown underneath. He took her in his arms and she breathed in the scent of him. Her mind was telling her one thing, but her heart and her body seemed to be in charge. When they kissed it was because she initiated it.

Avery knew this was where she wanted to be. She wished the moment would last forever, that she would never have to leave Lucas's arms and face the world and Curt. She knew that what she felt for Lucas was real and beautiful and more powerful than anything she had ever felt for Curt.

Too soon, Lucas was pulling away from her. "What do you want, Avery?" he asked.

The question caught her by surprise. "I would have thought that was obvious," she heard herself reply.

"I meant, what do you want tomorrow, next week, next year? We can't just be together tonight, or even for the rest of this summer, and then pretend it never happened. Both of us deserve better than that."

His words hit hard. Suddenly she realized what he meant. She had to choose. Not that he was forcing her to. It was just a fact of life. She started to cry softly. He hugged her again. There was only kindness in his embrace.

"I didn't want this to happen," she whispered through her tears. "I never expected to fall for you. I never thought I'd have feelings for anyone but Curt."

"I know," he said, stroking her hair. "I know. But it's happened, and I need to know what you're going to do about it."

She felt like she was being pulled apart. What was any relationship worth if you turned and ran each time your partner felt low and needed you? She pulled back slightly and stared at him. "I can't leave Curt, not now. He needs me. And I owe it to him. He was there for me when no one else was."

Lucas hung his head. "What about following your heart and being true to yourself?"

"There's more to it," she said. "I owe him so much."

"Did he really do anything more than what a good friend

would have done?" Lucas asked. "Sure, he was there for you, but he had a lot to gain for himself too. Beautiful, smart, kind, giving women are hard to find."

"But what about loyalty and faithfulness?" Avery asked as she wiped the tears away.

"They're really important," Lucas confirmed. "But what about being loyal and faithful to yourself? If he's not the one you really want, then how long are you willing to stay with him?"

She didn't have an answer for that. Her head was swimming with thoughts and feelings. She stared at Lucas for a moment, feeling the warm tears run down her cheeks. She didn't know what to do or say. The only thing she knew was that right now, there were two men in her life and she wasn't being fair to either of them. Or, more importantly, to herself.

"I'm so sorry," she whispered. Then she picked up her robe and fled.

Ten

April was excited as she stood with Owen, Avery, and Polly in the crowd for the Battle of the Bands. More than anything she loved music and more than anything all summer, this was about music. They were in between acts. Up on the stage, guys were busy moving equipment around. Down in the crowd, people were milling about, laughing and talking.

"Too bad Sabrina has to babysit and is missing this," Owen said, obviously wishing she were there.

April understood how he felt, but she also knew how important it was for Sabrina to be working and not out playing. Not only because she still had to pay her housemates back for the money she'd taken, but because she was facing the fact that life wasn't always fun and games with Mommy and Daddy paying the bills.

"She'd be here if she could," April assured him.

Owen nodded and raised a bottle—of Coke—to his lips.

"And now, for our next band, let's give it up for the Naked Mole Rats!" the announcer shouted to the crowd.

April cheered along with everyone else. Naked Mole Rats was the best band she'd heard all summer. Without thinking, she turned to the person beside her and said, "These guys really rock!"

The person beside her was Avery and she was looking really glum. "Yeah, they do."

April felt a pang of regret for having sounded so enthusiastic. *Avery's bummed because she knows there's no way Curt's band can compare. If she only knew about Curt and me, she might not be so bummed for him.* For the hundredth time, April thought about telling her. She hated keeping the secret. *Avery deserves better than a guy who would cheat on her.*

And I deserve better than a guy who would cheat with me on his girlfriend. And with that thought came another pang of regret. If she could take back one thing in her life, it would be kissing Curt.

She shook her head, trying to push away the unpleasant thoughts and just enjoy the music. Naked Mole Rats had a great classic-rock-meets-grunge sound that made them different from most of the other bands. She was thrilled when they played "Honey Girl"—one of her favorites of their songs. "Rockabye Baby" was great too. The set was over too soon. The crowd roared with appreciation as they left the stage to make way for the next group.

The announcer took to the stage. "And now for the last band of the night, Stranger Than Fiction!"

Avery cheered louder than anyone, which wasn't very hard since hardly anyone else was cheering. April watched as Darek, the drummer, came out and sat down at his drum set. The rest of the band came out. The crowd quieted and Curt strummed the first few chords. Avery leaned toward April. "I don't recognize this opening," she said.

"Must be a new song," April said.

"I hope so," Avery said.

Then Austin began to sing. "Our bodies went down . . . the moon went up. Slipping . . . sliding . . . the mating dance has just begun. It's the moon and not the sun. Yeah. It's the moon and not the sun."

April felt her jaw drop. *That's my song!*

Curt and Bobby joined in to sing the chorus. "The moon means romance, the moon means romance. Baby let's dance. The moon means romance."

"Wow! That is way better than anything else they've ever done!" Owen exclaimed. April looked around and saw that the crowd was nodding and bobbing happily to the music. *Unbelievable!*

April was stunned. Onstage, Curt was smiling and eating up the adulation of the crowd. *He thinks everyone loves him and his band,* April thought. *It's the song they love, and it's mine. He stole my song. How could he do that? How could I not see that all he wanted was my music?*

"In the light of day, you can't be mine. Baby, that's just not our sign. He owns your hand, but I have your heart. We love in the moonlight, and then we part," Austin continued singing the next verse.

"Where did they get such a great song?" Avery asked.

April knew she wasn't going to like the answer, but it was time she knew the truth, "You really want to know?"

Avery frowned as if she didn't understand.

"He got that song from me. Your boyfriend stole it," April said.

Avery stared at her with wide eyes. "Stole it?"

"The moon means romance, the moon means romance. Baby let's dance. The moon means romance," the band sang.

April nodded. "Right out of my notebook. I played it for him one day. He kept coming to my room. I thought he liked me, but I guess it was all so that he could steal my songs."

The color drained from Avery's face and for a moment April thought she was going to faint. "Did . . . did anything happen?"

"Not really," April said. "But he tried."

Avery turned and stared at the band. April wondered what was going through her mind. Whatever it was, it couldn't be good.

The song ended, and STF played a second song. By now, April knew better than to be surprised that this was also one of her songs. It was unbelievable, just unbelievable that Curt would take the songs and not tell her.

The band finished and the crowd cheered loudly.

"All right, everyone, give all the bands a hand," the announcer yelled, returning to the stage.

People broke into more applause.

"And now from the judges we have the top three bands of the night/7 the announcer said. "Number three . . . Gear Shift. Number two . . . Stranger Than Fiction."

"All right!" Owen shouted. "Go, roomie!" He and Polly gave each other high fives and turned to April and Avery.

"Curt's band got second place!" Owen cheered.

"And number one . . . Naked Mole Rats!" said the announcer.

The crowd roared its approval. In a way, April felt a slight wave of relief. At least the winning band was the one that really deserved it . . . unless they stole their songs from someone else too.

Owen wasn't sure what was going on, but both April and Avery looked really pissed. Naked Mole Rats had come out for an encore, but the two of them were standing stock-still like major sour pusses. Could they really be that upset that STF came in second? The smoke and spotlights swirling through the crowd gave them an eerie backdrop. *What's gotten into them?* he wondered. *And I thought Sabrina was intense. I wish she was here.*

Just then Curt came through the crowd to cheers all around. "You totally rocked!" Owen slapped him on the back.

"Thanks, dude!" Curt said, jumping with excitement. "Where's—"

He turned, saw April and Avery, and didn't finish the sentence. Owen had received a lot of nasty looks from girls in his life, but he was pretty certain that no girl had ever looked at him with as much anger as April.

"How could you steal my songs?" she asked Curt.

Whoa! Owen thought. *That's where those awesome songs came from? They were April's?*

Curt's eyes shot in Avery's direction. Now Owen understood why both girls were so mad.

"Look, let's face it," Curt said, his smile gone, "you never would have used those songs, anyway. You should be thanking me. At least I put them to good use. Now other bands will probably want them too. I did you a favor."

Interesting way of turning things around, Owen thought. *Nice try, anyway.*

"She told me what you did," Avery said. "You used her to get her songs."

"It didn't mean anything, Avery—" Curt started to say.

And even Owen knew that was the exact wrong thing to say.

Whap! Avery slapped Curt hard across the jaw. Then she and April left, together.

For a second it looked like Curt was going to follow them. Owen assumed he wanted to explain, or apologize, or do something to get Avery back. But then a couple of strangers came up. "That was awesome, dude, you rocked hard," one told him, clapping him on the back.

"I know the judges don't agree, but I thought you crushed the Naked Mole Rats," said the other.

"Really?" Curt asked, beaming.

"For sure." More fans began to materialize, and Owen realized that Curt wasn't going anywhere. He was exactly where he wanted to be.

Martin appeared out of the crowd with a funnel and a hose. "Owen, do a beer bong."

Owen looked at it for a moment, tempted, but fighting the urge. *This is the perfect time and place. Sabrina isn't here, and Avery and April just left. He could do it. Just do one and not more. Just to get a nice little buzz.*

Then he took a deep breath and shook his head. *Are you insane? What are you thinking? That is exactly what my father used to say.* "No thanks, dude."

"Don't be a wuss," Martin urged him.

"Sorry," Owen said, starting to smile. "I'm sober, and planning on staying that way. You should try it some time."

He turned and saw Polly, who still looked stunned by everything that had just happened. Oops! Good thing he hadn't had that beer bong. You never knew who might be watching.

"Do you believe what Curt did?" she asked him.

"Come on, Polly," he said, "let's get back to the house."

They started toward the exit and came face-to-face with Sabrina.

"What are you doing here?" Owen asked, surprised.

"The brats' parents came home early," Sabrina said.

"Well, we're just leaving," Owen said.

"I'll go with you," Sabrina said.

"But you just got here," Owen said. "Don't you want to stay for a while?"

Sabrina smiled. "I've been here for a while."

Owen didn't get it. "Then why didn't you come over sooner?"

"I wanted to see what would happen," Sabrina explained.

"You mean with Curt and Avery?"

"No," Sabrina said and slid her arm through his. "With you and Martin."

Owen suddenly understood and grinned. "I did good, right?"

"Yes." Sabrina stood up on her toes and kissed him. "You did good."

Why did I wait all summer to do this again? Sabrina wondered as she sat on Owen's bed kissing him. It felt so good to be wrapped in his arms and held close. *It's so different from the last time,* she thought, and chuckled to herself. *Both of us are sober this time.*

She pulled back slightly and started to unbutton her shirt. Before she could get very far, Owen's hands closed around hers, stopping her.

She leaned back, her guard instantly up. "What's wrong?"

"Nothing," he said. "I just . . . I don't want it to be like last time. I want to wake up in the morning and see you here and know you're happy about it."

She pulled him close and kissed him long and hard. "I couldn't be happier."

Polly watched the sun come up over the watery horizon. She'd been sitting on the beach for hours, unable to sleep. It was over, summer was gone, and it was time to head home. Back to school, back to her parents' house, back to being boring Polly again.

Nothing went the way I'd hoped, she thought. Tears slid down her cheeks.

There were footsteps on the sand behind her, but she didn't turn around. Probably just some early morning jogger.

"Mind some company?"

She looked up and saw Fred. She shook her head and turned back to the ocean. *Let him see me crying. What does it matter? I'll never see him again. I'll never see any of them again.*

"What's wrong?" he asked, settling down beside her.

"Nothing," she said.

"Hey, come on," he said. "Talk to me."

She had to smile a little. One thing about Fred, he was always attentive. They never made it back to the beach the night they were supposed to watch the fireworks, because Fred had entertained her with his amazing collection of funny magic tricks. It turned out that he was an amateur magician—just the sort of thing that would have invited putdowns from her roommates but that Polly actually found incredibly entertaining.

"Well," she said, "I guess the truth is, it's been a pretty lousy summer."

"You serious?" he asked, sounding surprised.

She wanted to lie, to tell him that it wasn't true. She wanted to make him feel good, and should have kept her secrets to herself.

"You want to talk about it?" he asked.

"I know I shouldn't feel this way," she said. "It's just . . . it wasn't what I'd hoped it would be."

"Why?"

"I just wanted us to all be one big happy family. It didn't work, did it? A happy family doesn't steal from one another and abuse one another and sleep with one another and act like it doesn't mean anything."

"Guess not."

"I came here looking for the time of my life," Polly went on, letting out all the pent-up frustrations of the summer. "I wanted to feel free, and all I felt was trapped. I wanted to make friends and meet a . . ." She let the words trail off, unfinished.

"Polly, I really think you're too hard on yourself," Fred said. "You're a good person and you care about others. You're also a lot of fun when you relax."

He was being nice, but she wasn't in the mood to be consoled. "You want to know what the worst part is?"

"What?"

"I'm still a virgin."

Next to her, Fred was silent. Polly started to bite her lip. Why did she tell him that? Hadn't she already suffered enough humiliations this summer? Why couldn't she just keep her mouth shut for once?

"Well," Fred said with a slight chuckle. "Guess that makes two of us. Think of it, Polly, we must be the only virgins on the whole Jersey Shore."

She felt a smile grow on her face. Once again, he'd made her feel a little better. She turned to him. "You're funny, you know that?"

"Sometimes," he said. "But you know what I think?"

"What?"

"I think maybe people like you and me aren't made for heavy-duty partying and one-night stands and summer flings," Fred said. "Deep down, neither of us really wants that. We have our own way of having fun and we're both looking for someone we can share that with."

For the first time all summer she looked at him, really looked at him. He wasn't a muscle-bound jock and didn't have model looks, but he'd always been decent and real. Why hadn't she taken him more seriously? Just because some of the others made fun of him, did she have to also?

"I'm sorry," she said, regret filling her. "I wasn't really very nice to you all summer."

"It's okay," he said with a knowing smile. "I'm kind of used to that. All my life people have sort of passed me by without taking a second look. But I've always kind of thought of myself as a diamond in the rough."

She smiled back at him and slid her fingers through his. Somehow the summer didn't seem all that bad after all.

"I know the summer's ending, but you don't live that far away," he said. "Think maybe I could come pay a visit one of these days?"

"I'd like that," she said, feeling warmth spread through her. She leaned on his shoulder and smiled. The sun was a little higher now, and she was just beginning to feel its warming rays.

"What are you thinking?" he asked.

"I'm thinking," Polly replied, "that maybe being a virgin isn't so bad."

Avery came down the stairs for the last time. She had come to Wildwood innocently looking for quality time with her boyfriend and now she was leaving older, wiser, and a different person. She hadn't gotten the time with Curt she'd wanted, but now that didn't seem to matter. The house was quiet. Everyone seemed to be feeling moody as they packed up and started saying their goodbyes.

Standing alone in the living room, her eyes strayed to Lucas's door. She hadn't seen him the night before or this morning. She was anxious to talk to him. There was so much she wanted to say.

She had left Curt's stuff outside the room the night before. He must have come over late and gotten it because it was gone when she got up. Unlike Lucas, she had nothing to say to him.

There was a knock on the front door. Avery opened it and found Darek, the drummer for STF.

"Hi," Avery said, puzzled. She couldn't imagine why he was there.

"Hey, Ave, is April around?" he asked.

"I'm not sure. I'll go check." Avery went up the stairs, knocked on April's door, and told her. At first, April didn't want to see him, but Avery urged her to at least hear what he had to say. Together, the girls came downstairs. When April saw Darek, she crossed her arms and pursed her lips with disapproval.

"Listen," Darek said, "I just wanted you to know that what Curt did wasn't right, and the rest of us in the band would never have gone along with it had we known he stole those songs."

"Where'd you think they came from?" April asked.

"Curt told us he wrote them," Darek said, then added sheepishly, "I guess we should have known better."

"That's for sure," said Avery.

"Well, in a way it almost doesn't matter now," he said, his eyes darting to Avery. "As of last night the band's officially broken up. It's been coming for a while, but last night was like the straw that broke the camel's back. I guess Bobby and Austin have had it with this rock thing. Bobby says he's going to college, and Austin wants to get a steady job."

"What about you?" April asked.

"I'm gonna stick with it," Darek said. "Maybe hook up with a group that needs a drummer, or put one together myself. Actually. . ." He trailed off.

"Yes?" April asked.

"I was kind of wondering if maybe you wanted to do something. Like a kind of reverse White Stripes, where the girl's the singer-guitarist-songwriter and the guy's the drummer."

April stared at him for a minute. "You serious?"

"Well yeah, totally."

A smile grew on April's face. "That's a deal. You want to come upstairs for a second? I've got some songs I never showed Curt. I think they're way better."

"Great." Darek followed her up the stairs.

Avery watched them go. It seemed like things had worked out for everyone. Owen and Sabrina had spent the night together, and she'd seen Fred and Polly holding hands on the beach earlier that morning. She was hoping it would work out for her, too. If only Lucas would come out of his room.

Summoning her courage, she knocked on Lucas's door. There was no answer and after a moment she pushed the door open. The room was empty. She was shocked. He was gone. Avery backed out of the room, not knowing what to think.

"Looking for Lucas?"

She turned. Owen had just come in the front door. She nodded.

"I took him to the bus station a couple of hours ago," Owen said.

She stared at him almost uncomprehendingly. "Hours ago?" she repeated numbly.

Owen nodded. "He's gone."

Eleven

Avery had caught glimpses of the Princeton University campus in the movie *A Beautiful Mind.* But the movie gave little hint how beautiful the actual campus was, with its magnificent ivy-covered stone buildings, vast green lawns, archways, and towers. She was awestruck by the place, and slightly amazed that anyone could simply stroll on the grounds. Signs around campus were announcing freshman orientation, and as she walked across the grass she saw groups of new students being led this way and that by older students in bright red T-shirts. Maybe it was her imagination, but everyone she saw seemed to look really smart, or maybe they just appeared smart because their clothes were a little dorky.

The Bendheim Center for Finance was located in the Dial Lodge, a three-story, slate-roofed stone building that looked from the outside like an old mansion. Inside, it was air-conditioned and filled with modern office spaces and computer rooms. M. Lucas Haubenstock, Jr.'s office was on the second floor, and as

Avery nervously climbed the stairs she expected that at any second, campus security would swarm in and escort her away.

Instead, she found herself outside a heavy wooden door that was open just enough that she could see a sandy-haired man with bushy eyebrows inside reading with his feet up on his desk. He was wearing a white-and-red-striped shirt, a blue bowtie, and khaki slacks. A pair of reading glasses was perched low on his nose. Avery paused outside the door, swallowed anxiously, then knocked.

"Yes?" the man looked up. "Come in?"

Avery pushed the door open and stepped in. The office was piled high with textbooks and journals, and odds and ends—an African mask, a model of a Buddhist temple—that appeared to have come from all over the world.

"Can I help you?" the man asked.

"Are . . . you . . ." Avery suddenly hesitated, not sure whether to call him Mr. or Professor or something else entirely.

The man scowled, "Am I . . . ?"

"Uh, Lucas Haubenstock's father?"

The man frowned, then smiled. "Oh, you mean Trey."

"Sorry?" Avery said.

"Trey. That's what we call him. He's the third, so we call him Trey. It's been so long since I've heard anyone call him Lucas that for a second there, I forgot. Yes, I'm his father. How can I help you?"

"I'm a friend of his. From the beach house this summer.

And, well, I lost his address and phone number." This wasn't true. Lucas, or Trey, had never given them to her.

"But you knew that his parents taught here, so you came," M. Lucas Haubenstock, Jr., inferred. "Very smart. And you'd like to find him. Well, you're in luck. I believe he's over at the Firestone Library, probably asleep on a couch." At Avery's frown, he added, "Or wasting his time reading Russian literature."

Then he smiled and winked.

Avery thanked him and found her way across the campus to the library, yet another tall, magnificent stone building with archways and enormous windows. Inside she wandered past the endless computer stations and stacks of books and tables until she spied Lucas lounging on a couch, absorbed in a book, his feet up on the corner of a low table—almost the same position she'd found his father in.

She sat down on the other end of the couch. Lucas looked up. When he saw her, he blinked long and hard. Then slowly he lowered the book to his lap.

"This isn't the way it's supposed to happen," Avery said.

He responded with an almost imperceptible nod.

"I mean, if this were a movie, here's what would happen," she went on. "I would have come in here and found you with another girl. And you'd be whispering or touching or somehow being close in a way that would make me think she was your girlfriend. So I'd burst into tears and run away, but just as I did, you'd look up and see me and you'd run after me and be really glad to see me and I'd say, but who was that other girl, and you'd say, oh, that was just my cousin. And then we'd hug and kiss and the movie would end and we'd live happily ever after."

She hoped he'd smile. But he didn't. Instead, he asked, "What about Curt?"

"It's over," Avery said. "It's been over for a long time. I just had to figure that out."

"Are you sure?" Lucas asked. "Because you weren't so sure last time."

"I'm sure," Avery said.

Lucas scowled thoughtfully and studied her. Avery began to feel anxious and uncomfortable. He didn't look that happy to see her. Had she made a huge mistake?

"If you're wondering how I found you, I went to your father's office. Listen, Lucas, if I've made a mistake. If I shouldn't be here, I—"

Lucas lifted a finger and pressed it to his lips. "Shush."

"Huh?" She scowled.

He gestured around. "It's a library, remember?"

Avery felt a wave of cold dread sweep over her. Was she making a scene? Lucas swung his legs off the table and leaned toward her. "You're at Princeton now, Avery," he whispered somberly. "It's a very important place. A serious place. A place for great learning."

He kept leaning toward her, forcing her to lie back on the couch.

"A place of great minds," he continued, only now she saw the slightest grin on his lips and sparkle in his eye. "You have to be on your best behavior. Because this is serious."

By now, she was lying on her back on the couch and he was pressing down on her. "And I'm seriously glad you're here," he whispered. "Because you're the best and it's great to see you again."

And then he kissed her. Right there in the middle of the library.

Seriously.

LB
(Laguna Beach)

For all the good people who work at John Jermain Memorial Library and Westhampton Free Library—you know who you are

And for Lauren—artist, surfer, friend

One

"Headbanging sex," said Linley Cattrel, thrusting open the door of the dorm room.

Without looking up, Claire Plimouth used the old standard: "Not tonight, I have a headache."

"Again?" said Linley.

"Always," said Claire. "It's how I've maintained my purity." She turned the page of her Intro Psych notes.

Leaning over the desk where Claire was working, Linley splayed her hand across the page. Her golden hair swept forward in a perfect curve across her sun-golden cheeks. Somehow she managed to smell like a good day at the beach, Claire noticed not for the first time, even though they were a continent away from Linley's California home.

I probably smell like libraries and books and long, cold New England winters, thought Claire. *Not sexy.*

Not that she knew what sexy smelled like. Or sex, for that matter. Aloud, she said, "Philosophy exam tomorrow?"

"I act, therefore I am," said Linley. "Descartes."

"I'm not quite sure that's how it goes."

"Can't study anymore. Besides, our first year of college is *over.* We should be partying. Hooking up. Sucking . . ."

"Suck off," said Claire. "I'm studying. It's not over until the final bell rings."

"Suck-up. That's what you are!" said Linley.

"I fail to see how studying for my last final of my last class of my first year of college is sucking up," said Claire. "I like to think of it as the intelligent choice. The way you think of, say, condoms. Or tequila as opposed to gin . . . although I don't entirely agree with that. . . ."

"That's because you're from New England," retorted Linley. "Home of the WASP drink by which you are embalmed alive."

"Don't have martini envy on me *now,*" said Claire. "Go away and play."

"These are extremely worthy parties! One's been going on for at least two days. They need reinforcements."

"Well, may the reinforcements be with you, Luke Skywalker. But I'm not one of them. Now Go. Away." Claire held her notebook up to block Linley from her sight. She'd been seduced into acts of reckless abandon by Linley too often. Not tonight.

"You know, you will die of stubbornness if you're not careful. Stubbornness killed the cat." Linley flopped down on her bed and flung her arms wide.

"Curiosity killed the cat, I'm not a cat, and no one has ever died of stubbornness." Claire was trying not to laugh now.

"Headbanging sex," said Linley again.

"Where? The party?" asked Claire.

"No. The house. The summer . . . the beach . . . *this* summer . . ." Linley's voice trailed away dreamily.

Was she imagining having headbanging sex on the beach? Claire wondered. *Could* a person have headbanging sex on the beach?

Linley cut across the room to her. "The head-banging sex is contemplated for both of us, on another coast, for the summer. Said summer to also include parties; jobs that are not internships, career builders, or network opportunities; and, oh yes, a house on the beach. Laguna Beach, to be exact."

"Beach house? What beach house?" Claire said. She snapped her notebook shut.

Linley grinned. "Uncle Martin came through. He got a stunt gig last minute on a shoot in New Zealand. And when his favorite niece called all sad about her summer plans—i.e., none—he told her—me—that I could have his beach house for the summer."

"Merde," said Claire.

"Merde non," said Linley. "It's big, it's old, it's funky, and it's free, except we have to pay the utilities and make sure it's all nice and tidy when he gets back." She thought for a moment and added, "That's why I'm appointing you house manager."

The Pacific Ocean. Claire had never seen the Pacific. She'd spent her whole life in New England boarding schools, and now a small New England college, making her grades good and her parents proud. Well, making good grades, anyway. Parental pride might be stretching it. When Claire brought home perfect marks, her parents took it in stride. Good grades was just part of what a Plimouth did, like living in Lexington, Mass.

A summer job in her father's Boston bank was also what a Plimouth did. Her sister, Melanie, the investment banker had started that way. So had her brother, Jim, the corporate lawyer. And that was where her mother had met her father, her mother also being "in banking." Claire sometimes wondered if they had a marriage or a corporate merger.

"I can't," said Claire.

Linley jumped to her feet. She put her hands on her hips and somehow made herself look taller.

Towering and glowering now, Linley said, "I'm actually considering murder at this moment." Then she leaned forward and swatted Claire on the back of her head with the palm of her hand.

"OW! What was that for? Did your mother teach you nothing? Hitting is wrong. Bad Linley." Claire leaned back in case Linley decided on a repeat.

"It's a dope slap," said Linley. "I learned about it from listening to public radio."

"You? Public radio? I doubt that," Claire scoffed, still keeping a safe distance.

"*Car Talk*," said Linley. "It's good for bonding with my dad. But that's beside the point. The point is, what *are* you, a Woman or a WASP? After I go to all this trouble to set up a perfect summer, this is what you say?" Linley pitched her voice into whine key. "I can't. Oooh, I'm afraid. Oh no, no, no, no."

Amused and annoyed, Claire said, "Linley, you don't under—"

"No," said Linley. "No words unless they start with 'yes.'"

"But—"

"No. . ."

"My father has—"

"No."

"The bank—"

"No. . ."

"Linley!"

"NO!"

They glared at each other. Claire looked away first. She thought of the cold, respectable corridors of the bank. One day, she would go into one of those vaults just as her sister and brother had, and never come out. But did she have to start now? Right this minute?

This summer?

Did people in banks have headbanging sex?

Not her father. Not her mother. She shuddered at the thought. Best not to think of that at all.

"California," said Claire, almost dreamily.

Linley smiled triumphantly.

Then Claire remembered where California was.

She looked up at Linley, her eyes tragic.

"What?" said Linley. "Claire, what's wrong?"

"I hate flying," said Claire. "I did it once. That was enough."

The two girls stared at each other.

"Some suggest," Linley said slowly, "that fear of flying is actually fear of sexual pleasure."

"It's not *all* about sex. In this case, it's about being in a silver tube with stupid wings that don't even have feathers being driven by someone who maybe is having a bad day and might not see that mountain or, say, the other plane headed—"

"Stop," said Linley. She considered a moment, then brightened. "Okay, drugs. No problem."

"I don't do—"

"One little pill. Trust me. Now, what word are we looking for here?"

Claire looked at Linley. Linley the beautiful, Linley the spoiled, Linley the most fun person Claire had ever known. Life was never dull when Linley was around—dull, as in a summer spent in a bank under her father's eyes.

Claire looked at Linley, into eyes she thought might actually be the color of the Pacific Ocean. She took a deep breath.

What could it hurt, to spend a summer in California? She'd find a way to convince the 'rents.

"One word," Linley prompted.

"Yes," Claire answered.

"You'll like Jodi." Linley had been talking ever since the plane had taxied into takeoff.

So far, Claire had neither shared the contents of her mostly empty stomach with the rest of the passengers nor passed out. In fact, she was pretty sure she'd loosened her grip on the seat arms. Fractionally.

"I've told you about Jodi, remember? We were the Two all through high school." Linley held up two fingers and waggled them to demonstrate.

The plane leveled out. The FASTEN SEAT BELT sign blinked off.

A flight attendant appeared and looked at Linley. Linley looked at her two fingers and grinned. "Vodka and cranberry, rocks," she said.

Suddenly, absurdly, Claire felt like giggling. She raised one hand and fluttered her fingers. "Me, too," she sang. It seemed like a very good idea. The ground was leaving the plane so very, very fast. No, wait—it was the plane leaving the ground.

"I'll need to see some I.D.," said the flight attendant.

"I'm twenty-two," said Linley, smiling her gazillionwatt

smile. "And no one ever believes me." She flipped open her wallet, and the attendant glanced at the fake I.D. and nodded.

"But my friend isn't," Linley went on. "She's only twenty. She'll have cranberry juice and soda."

"What?" said Claire, trying to feel indignant. "I have I.D. I. . ."

Ignoring Claire, the attendant smiled and handed the wallet back to Linley. "Coming right up," the attendant said.

The guy in the aisle seat said to the attendant, "Scotch, rocks, and let me take care of their drinks."

"Thanks," said Linley.

"I want a real drink, too," said Claire.

"No, you don't," said Linley. She lowered her voice. "Not with what you're flying on, you don't. That little pill is plenty all by itself."

Claire giggled again. She couldn't help it.

"First time you've ever flown?" the guy said to Claire. But he only glanced at her. He was really talking to Linley.

"No," said Claire.

"She had a terrible experience as a child," Linley said.

"What?" Claire sputtered.

"Are you from California?" Linley asked him.

He laughed. He had those white square teeth that Claire had always thought weren't real outside of photo ops. "I wish," he said.

The flight attendant returned. He was good-looking, Claire

noticed. Maybe it was the uniform. She wondered if Linley had noticed too.

"Massachusetts," said Claire. "I'm from. . . ."

The guy said to Linley, "I'm a graduate student. Headed for a summer internship in San Diego."

"Nice," said Linley. She leaned closer, sliding a finger down his arm, her voice dropping.

To be a part of this conversation, Claire thought crossly, *I'd have to sit in Linley's lap.*

But then suddenly, she didn't mind. Peering out the window, she discovered that the earth had gone missing. Below were only clouds. Ahead, the sun was setting. Pretty. *Look at me, I'm flying into a postcard,* she thought.

She yawned.

Beside her the voices dropped to a murmur.

She was on her way to California. She, Claire Plimouth. All because of Linley.

Linley was a pain. Linley was insane. Linley was the kind of roommate Claire had avoided all her years in the best boarding schools of New England.

It hadn't been hard, avoiding those girls. They'd barely even known she'd existed.

But she was good with that. She figured someday she'd own the company that they—or their husbands—would work for.

When Linley had burst into her dorm room that first day of

college the previous fall, Claire had winced. Black clothes and pink shoes—what was *that*?

It was, as it turned out, two of Linley's favorite colors. She'd looked at Claire in her khaki and navy and said, "Wow, your eyes are the most amazing color. They're, like, golden!"

"Brown," Claire had corrected. "Light brown."

"No, golden," Linley had corrected back.

And somehow, they'd become friends. Not all at once. Claire had tried to keep her distance. But Linley didn't seem to notice. She'd made Claire join her on what Linley called her "party rounds." She'd dragged Claire shopping and talked her into "colors, for god's sake."

And then made Claire wear the fuzzy cropped sweater Linley said was "Caribbean blue" to a party. Had included Claire in nighttime pizza attacks.

She had a sudden memory of a weekend in Vermont. The snow had been perfect powder. Linley, in electric pink and several other colors unknown in nature, had stared down at the snowboard strapped to her feet. She'd looked up at Claire. "What the hell," she'd said, and taken off.

She hadn't made it. But she almost had. Claire had boarded down to check on her and found her laughing at the bottom of the hill.

"You okay?"

"Oh, better," Linley said. "That was amazing. Awesome. The absolute second best thing in the universe."

"The second best?" said Claire. "And the first?"

She'd expected Linley to say "sex," but Linley had surprised her. "Surfing," she'd said. "And I can tell by the way you board that you're going to love surfing too."

"Right," said Claire, thinking, *Like I'm ever going to get anywhere near a surfboard.*

"You'll see," Linley had promised, scrambling to her feet. "Now, teach me how to get down that hill."

She'd asked Claire to show her—not some cute guy, not some instructor. That, Claire thought, was the day they'd become real friends, because she'd realized she had something to offer Linley in exchange for the excitement and color—literally—that Linley brought to life.

That night, hanging out in the ski lodge, they'd swapped snow and surf wipeout stories. Claire described learning to ski from her mother, who had, as far as Claire could tell, never fallen off her skis.

"Didn't you just want to push her?" Linley had said, and Claire, shocked, had said, "No!" and then, bursting out into laughter, "Yes!"

Linley had talked, a little bit, about growing up in San Francisco and going with friends to the beach and then discovering surfing. Had laughed at how her parents had tried to make her "respectable" and then finally given in and let her buy her first surfboard.

Many nights of many drinks and talks and pizzas and old

movies had cemented their friendship, but that had been the beginning, the real beginning.

And now Claire was on her way to California, where, Linley had promised, she was going to learn to surf.

Friends, thought Claire. *That's a good thing.*

First friends, then a boyfriend. How hard could that be? And then she'd no longer be . . .

Nope. She wouldn't think about that now.

From somewhere, she'd acquired a blanket. She hitched it up over her shoulders and settled back in her seat. *Sleep,* she thought. *That's a good thing, too. And when I wake up, I'll be in California.*

As she fell asleep, she vaguely heard the guy asking for another round of drinks.

When Claire woke up, she wasn't in California. She was in the dark.

Not total darkness, but the hushed darkness of a plane where people were sleeping.

Claire squinted at her watch. Two hours had passed. She felt peculiar.

Her drink was gone, her drink tray folded away. But next to her, Linley's drink sat half-full on the tray. Linley had disappeared.

Claire reached out and took a sip of watery, slightly warm cranberry and vodka.

Her whole stomach did a flip.

Barf bag or bathroom, Claire thought frantically, and staggered to her feet. Barely noticing the startled faces peering up from books held in tiny pools of light, or eyes turned toward her from the personal movie screens, Claire lurched down the aisle, one hand over her mouth, the other grabbing at anything she passed for balance.

A woman emerging from a row of seats took one look and jumped back.

Claire grabbed the bathroom door and fumbled it open. She barely got it closed behind her before she lost it.

She didn't know how long she was sick, but when she was finally able to bathe her face and rinse her mouth, the face she met in the mirror had gone all-American hag. The French braid had started to unravel, and wisps of dark hair stuck damply to her forehead and neck. Sleep marks hashed one cheek.

The only solution was to go back to her seat and pull the blanket over her head. Lurking in the toilet was not helping, anyway. Resolutely, Claire opened the bathroom door and stepped out.

She came face-to-face with Linley.

"Claire?" said Linley. Her face was as flushed as Claire's was pale. And she had what Claire would have called bed head hair at any other time.

"Hi, Linley," Claire said, trying to sound normal.

Glancing back over her shoulder, Linley hastily pulled shut the bathroom door.

She frowned and peered at Claire. "Did you just get sick?"

"No," said Claire. "I'm fine."

"Right," said Linley. She clamped her hand on Claire's arm. "If that's fine, I don't want to see you on a bad day. I'm walking you to your seat."

"I'm fine," Claire insisted, but she was too whipped to argue and she let Linley steer her back down the aisle. She kept her eyes lowered, trying not to look like I-just-barfed girl to the whole plane.

They reached their seats, and Claire half-fell into hers.

"I'll be right back," said Linley. A moment later she sat down by Claire and pulled the blanket around Claire's shoulders. Then the guy in the seat next to Linley was there, handing Linley a plastic glass.

"Thanks," Linley said to him, then to Claire, "Drink this."

"Not thirsty," Claire croaked.

"Seltzer," said Linley soothingly. "That's all. It'll settle your stomach. And take this with it."

"But—"

"Claire," said Linley. "Do it. Or else."

Or else what? thought Claire. "Drug pimp," she said to Linley.

"Whatever," said Linley, and practically shoved the pill down Claire's throat. "Now, count to a hundred," she ordered Claire.

"Bossy drug pimp," muttered Claire.

"One hundred, ninety nine . . . ," Linley said.

"Ninety eight, ninety-seven . . . ," said Claire.

"How bad is she?" the guy whispered.

"Shhh!" ordered Linley. To Claire, she said, "Keep counting."

Claire kept counting. But she was losing track. Whatever Linley had given her was pulling her under. Fast.

She saw the guy reach down and pull something out of his pocket. He leaned into Linley and said softly into her ear, "You forgot something."

Seventy-three, seventy-two . . . Even in the semidarkness of the cabin, Claire recognized the scrap of silk underwear. *California pink,* she thought. Linley's.

Seventy-one, seventy . . . Claire saw Linley glance at her watch, then smile up at her new friend. "Keep them," Linley said. "Maybe I'll get them back later."

He laughed. She laughed.

Sixty-nine, Claire thought, and passed out.

Two

He stood, watching the house. He'd been there before, when he was younger. Much, much younger.

Okay, maybe not that much younger.

It had been a party house. A girlfriend-at-the-beach house. A "getting sex right" house.

Practice had made perfect. Or at least, that's what he'd thought at the time.

She hadn't.

Long time ago. Maybe not in ordinary time, but in his time. She'd been his whole world, although he'd tried to be cool about it. Had he failed? Is that why he felt the way he did now?

Not that he'd been totally faithful. But she couldn't have known. Not about that.

His whole world. Well, he'd seen a lot more of the world since then.

But he wouldn't mind seeing her again. Seeing her. And maybe more.

• • •

She woke up in California with the mother of all hangovers.

The morning light was fierce.

The smell was either delicious or disgusting. Or both.

Coffee and salt air.

Claire sat up cautiously. The room did not swoop or swim. Her stomach remained in place. *Let that be a lesson to you,* she told herself. *Never take unknown substances and fly. With or without an airplane.*

Possibly, she would live. Maybe she'd even drink some coffee. If she could walk that far.

She could. Claire pulled on shorts beneath the T-shirt she'd slept in; ignored the luggage dumped, and apparently Dumpster-dived, on the chair and floor of one corner of the room; located the bathroom across the hall; and then began to follow her nose. The long hall took her to a flight of stairs, which led to another short hall that opened into an enormous room that was the whole front—or was it the rear?—of the house. The room was so big, it had a kitchen across the back; a wall of windows and glass French doors across the front, opening onto a deck that looked out over major sand and sea real estate; a stone fireplace on another wall; and plenty of room to walk around in between.

Two people sat at the counter that divided the kitchen from the rest of the space. One of them was Linley.

"She lives," said Linley.

"Not yet," said Claire and headed for the coffeemaker, something with dials and steamer attachments and who knew what else—a sort of color-coordinated working monument to coffee enthroned on the granite kitchen countertop. And there was coffee in a gleaming carafe. Claire tried not to lunge for it, went heavy on the sugar and milk, then turned around.

There was Linley, all safe and familiar and not looking at all like a girl who'd spent a plane trip having sex in an airplane toilet. And who'd probably partied most of what was left of the night after she'd gotten to California.

And Jodi. Claire barely remembered meeting Jodi at the airport.

She remembered more about how Jodi looked from one of the photos Lindsey had stuck to her dorm room wall.

Today, however, Jodi looked like a small dandelion on acid. Claire hadn't noticed it on the cramped trip from the airport in the battered Subaru. She'd barely been conscious then.

But she couldn't help noticing now. Jodi's hair seemed to explode in bleached-white tips from her head. She had faint golden freckles across her cheeks. Her eyes were almost turquoise and were startlingly framed by pale, spiky lashes.

Little and takes no prisoners, she remembered Linley saying about Jodi. An amazing artist. An unfortunate only child. Why unfortunate? Claire had asked. Well, her mother who had made a bad second marriage. The stepfather from hell . . .

Come to think of it, Linley had told her . . . what else had Linley told her?

Linley interrupted Claire's thoughts by pushing back the

barstool next to her own with a practiced motion. "Have a muffin," she said, indicating the bag on the counter.

"Not now," Claire said. "My stomach has a headache. What are you wearing, Lin? Is that a wet suit?"

"A shorty," Linley explained. "A short wet suit."

"You should rinse it off," Jodi said. "It's gross just to sit around in it."

"We went surfing," Linley explained. "I was trying to sleep and I heard a burglar crashing around in the kitchen. . . ."

"You knew it was me," said Jodi. "You came downstairs dragging your wet suit with you as if it were a dead dog."

"I've never dragged a dead dog. I wouldn't know . . . so I thought, well, Claire's gonna be sleeping it off all day, so I'll catch some waves."

"Surfing," said Claire, finally getting it. "You've been surfing? Weren't you up all night partying?"

"Sure," said Jodi. "You don't surf?"

"New England," said Claire. "Specifically, Lexington, Massachusetts—and not the Cape or the Island, though I summer there."

"She's got some good moves, however," Linley put in. She paused. "On a snowboard."

Jodi studied Claire. "Balance. If you've got balance, you could learn, maybe."

"Maybe," Claire agreed noncommittally. She drank coffee, looked out at the blinding sun. Definitely not New England. She said, "Okay, now that you've got your surfing out of the way for the day. . ."

"For the morning," Linley corrected.

"We should get started on roommates. And jobs."

Jodi raised pale eyebrows.

"Where's the computer? I can make flyers to put up," Claire went on.

"Flyers?" Jodi said.

"For roommates," Claire said.

"Ah, no," said Jodi. "No flyers."

Claire frowned at Jodi. "But . . ."

"We have an excellent house by the beach. And we're not charging outrageous rent. We'll have our choice of roomies. No worries," said Jodi.

Linley said, "Claire, as the official house manager and rent collector, I applaud your, ah, diligence."

"Oh, yeah, and the rent . . . ," Claire began.

She stopped at the warning look Linley gave her. Linley had insisted that they collect rent from everyone except Linley and Claire. And that it be a secret. Linley didn't want anyone to know that she wasn't paying rent.

"Why not?" Claire had asked. "It's no big deal, really, is it? After all, it's your uncle's house, so that makes it your house, technically."

"No," Linley had said firmly.

"What about Jodi? I mean, shouldn't she be in on the deal too . . ."

"No. Just you and me. Our secret. Okay?"

Mystified, Claire had given up. She still didn't get it. But she was willing to go along. Linley's house. Linley's rules—at least in rent.

"Today," Linley went on, "we're just going to take it easy. Relax. Go to the beach. Have a few drinks. Score a little of . . . whatever. And, oh yeah, go to the beach."

"Don't you want to rest?" asked Claire.

"Sure I do. On the beach. In the sun. Get rid of the library tan." Linley stood up. "Okay, we need to stock up on some basics—and then let's hit the sand."

"I'll drive," said Jodi.

"A grocery list?" Claire said. "Don't we need a . . . ?"

But her two roommates were out the door.

Basics, Claire discovered—or maybe she should have known—meant wine, beer, liquor; it also included mixers, a strange collection of organic frozen dinners, a potato field of chips, more coffee, and cases of diet soda.

If it hadn't been for the diet soda and the organic factor, Claire would have sworn they were shopping for a fraternity.

She began to fling vegetables into the grocery cart, but Linley stopped her. "We can get that stuff at the farmers markets," she said.

But she allowed Claire to add milk and even a few boxes of cereal. "For late night munchies," Linley conceded, although Claire had been planning to use them for breakfast.

Jodi topped the cart with a large assortment of energy bars and three varieties of organic tea and headed for the checkout.

So much for grocery lists, thought Claire. *Why am I surprised? I've been roommates with Linley for nine months.*

As house manager, she was going to have her work cut out for her. But today clearly wasn't the day.

Claire was still considering the options—should she volunteer to shop? Cook? Suggest a common fund for basic items, of which she would be in charge?—on the way home when Jodi wrenched the wheel of the car, did a U-turn across a double yellow and in front of an oncoming vehicle of the suburban assault type, and canted the car into a marginally legal parking space.

"Gandhi on a surfboard, Jodi," said Linley, almost shaken into emotion.

Claire knew her mouth was open, but she couldn't make sound come out. She was pretty sure she was trying to say something about surviving a cross-country flight only to die in an illegal U-turn. She'd noticed earlier that Jodi was a fast driver, but this . . .

Still moving fast, Jodi was all ready out of the car and headed for a tiny table outside a tiny coffee bar.

At the table a woman looked up from the bowl-size coffee cup she was cradling and smiled languidly.

"Jodi," said the woman. She spoke in a low voice, but it carried clearly.

"Nice driving," said the guy sitting next to her.

They were an eye-candy couple, especially on the guy side. He leaned back in the chair, studying them, blue eyed and blond and looking good. And looking as if he knew it.

"Poppy," Jodi said, with a glance and a grin for the guy. "I'm glad I saw you. This is great, running into you like this. Linley, Claire, this is Poppy. She was the teaching assistant in my art workshop this past year. I was just thinking about you, Poppy."

"Almost as good as being talked about," said Poppy. Her own hair was dark red and, Claire thought, amazing. It hung loosely, blowing in the faint breeze, stunning against her pale moon-gold skin. Her eyes were cat-colored green, and her lips were vivid red to match the scarlet slip dress she wore and which, Claire thought, might be all she was wearing—unless you counted the worn leather slides that looked as if they'd been made from the braids of whips.

She wasn't even wearing jewelry, Claire realized. And it made her look incredibly . . . naked. In a good way.

Good grief, thought Claire, *what am I, some kind of pervert?*

Did guys see Poppy as naked?

I am a pervert, thought Claire. A WASP virgin . . . pervert.

"Claire? Helloooo?" Jodi had turned, and Claire realized that everyone was looking at her. She hit rewind and said, "Oh! Right. Nice to meet you, Poppy, and, ah . . ."

"Dean," he supplied. "The pleasure is all mine."

At the word "pleasure," Claire lowered her eyes. And made eye-crotch contact.

Package? Unit? Basket? What was the word Linley favored?

She looked up again and met Dean's eyes. "All mine," he repeated, and Claire felt herself turn red, or possibly purple.

And then she heard the words ". . . roommate? And I thought of you."

Poppy said, "Did you?"

"It's just for the summer, but it'll give you time to look around for something more permanent," Jodi said. "Poppy and her roommate weren't such a great match," she told Linley and Claire. "So Poppy's looking for a new apartment."

"Let's just say she needs her space. And I need mine. Stat." Poppy paused, then said thoughtfully, "A summer share. Why not? It could be entertaining."

"What?" said Claire. *"What?"*

"I told you we'd find roommates, no problemo," said Jodi.

"Do all of you come with the house?" asked Dean.

"And in the house," said Linley. She smiled sweetly.

Claire took a step back. *Jesus, Linley,* she thought.

"I could use a cheaper place to hang for the summer. Sublet my place, crash at yours, save a little money," said Dean.

"Really?" said Jodi.

Claire opened her mouth to say, wait a minute, we don't even know this guy.

But Poppy said, "Dean is an old friend. I'll vouch for him. He'll pay what he owes on time."

"And maybe with a little interest," said Dean.

He looked not at Linley, or at Jodi, but at Claire.

"Uh, well," Claire said.

"I'm into pay-as-you-go," Linley said. "That's what keeps me interested."

"You work at the college?" Claire asked Dean.

Dean shrugged. "Grad school," he said.

Oblivious to everything, Jodi was writing on the back of a napkin. She shoved it across to Poppy. "Here's the address. Move in anytime."

"With a deposit," Claire finally managed to croak.

That got everyone's attention.

"A deposit? And after I promised to pay interest?" said Dean.

"Everyone has to pay a deposit," said Claire. "To cover any unexpected bills or expenses."

"Claire's the house manager," said Linley. "She's very anal."

"Anal," said Dean.

"And we obey the house manager," Linley added.

"Anything you want," Dean said instantly.

Claire lifted her chin. "A deposit," she said. "Equal to one month's rent. And the first month's rent. In cash. And *then* you can move in anytime."

"Tomorrow," said Dean.

And Claire wasn't sure if it sounded like a promise—or a threat.

Three

"Cute," said Dean.

"Oh, behave," Poppy said. They both watched the Subaru double-back on its original U-turn and rocket out of sight.

"Not your type?" Dean said.

Poppy didn't answer, and Dean smiled. He reached over and slid one finger along the inside of her wrist. She made a little sound, stood up. Stretched like a cat and began to walk away.

Still smiling, he slid money under a cup and followed.

"So you know Poppy from school?" Claire asked as she trailed Jodi and Linley back to the car.

"Yep. She's an excellent artist. I told you about her, Linley—remember?" Jodi said.

"I seem to remember you mentioning her once or twice," Linley said. She didn't sound entirely pleased, Claire thought. Good.

"You just met Poppy, right, Linley?" Claire asked.

"Correct."

"And Dean. Did anyone know Dean before?" Claire asked.

Jodi shrugged and threw open the car door. "I've probably seen him around."

"Seen him around? Shouldn't we get references. Or something?"

"Poppy's a reference," Jodi said impatiently.

"Linley . . . ," Claire appealed to Linley. But it was useless.

"If Poppy says he's okay, and Jodi says Poppy is okay, it must mean Dean is okay. Math equation, right?"

"Right," Jodi cut in. "I'm very good at math, you know." She'd managed to extricate them from the parking lot without damage and they were headed . . . where?

"Where . . . ," Claire began.

"Look," said Jodi. "Trust me, okay? Poppy's great. They'll be great. And he's cute, right?"

"Cute isn't high on my list of roomie qualifications," Claire said.

"Hey, we're all cute. Therefore, we should have cute roommates," said Jodi. And floored it.

Claire fell back against the seat. After that, she got busy *not* watching where they were going. And, as far as she could tell, so was every driver in California, including Jodi.

And she'd thought drivers in Boston were bad.

So it really could happen. She could die a . . .

"Pretty boy," said Linley. "Pretty girl."

"You sound like a parrot. Or a parakeet. Some kind of pet

shop girl," said Jodi. "Anyway, we've got two roommates. Only four at most to go. See how easy it is, Claire?" she added, glancing back at Claire, who had taken up the cower position on the backseat.

"Watch. The. Road," Claire managed through clenched teeth.

Scenery of a non–New England style bathed in blinding sunlight raced by. Claire wondered why she had ever thought flying was dangerous. Large objects looming in a side window were much, *much* scarier to contemplate than the distant wrinkles of mountain ranges and water far below.

The car lurched, dipped, and spun. With a spray of dirt and gravel it bumped off the road and down a narrow track. Parts had to be falling off the Subaru, Claire thought, but a glance into the miasma of dust they'd left behind showed nothing but the dim outlines of ruts and flattened weeds.

They burst through a scraggle of trees to nothing but bright blue sky. *A cliff.* Claire opened her mouth to scream when Jodi jammed the car to a stop behind a pickup truck.

"We're here," Linley said cheerfully, and jumped out. Rubber-fingered, Claire plucked at her seat belt and managed to Jell-O her way out of the backseat.

They were in a dirt bowl in a small, haphazard circle of beat-to-hell cars and trucks. At the edge of the bowl, a path twisted down to another bowl, this one of sand and water. Pulling surfboards and gear from the car, Jodi said, "Perfect."

"W-was this where you surfed this morning?" Claire asked. Good. Her voice sounded normal. She was pretty sure.

"No. We went closer to the house. More newbies, smaller waves," said Linley. "Sort of a universal-donor spot."

"What place is this?"

"I dunno. Everyone calls it Farmer," said Jodi. She jerked one thumb over her shoulder. "I think that used to be a farmer's field, y'know?"

"Let's go," Linley said impatiently, and led the way down the trail.

The sky was blue. The sand was golden. Waves roared into the curve of land. Dunes, echoing the set of the waves, marched up toward the sky. Claire made a mound of sand, then flattened it with her palm. Out beyond the breaking waves, figures drifted up and down the swells. Two of those figures were Linley and Jodi.

"We could teach you," Jodi had offered halfheartedly after they'd dropped towels, clothes, and a cooler on the sand.

"I'll just surf the beach here," Claire had answered quickly. "I'll pretend this towel is a surfboard."

"Ha," said Linley, stalking past with her board under her arm. "You wait. You'll be begging for it before you know it."

"You're the one who begs for it," retorted Claire.

"Ooooh," said Linley. But her attention was already fixed on the water. She was looking at it the way she sized up a guy for sex. Only now her look didn't have the smug edge to it that said *I always get what I want.*

Claire dragged a hard lemonade out of the cooler and settled back. "Go play in the water," she said. She took a long drink and watched the two of them plunge into the water with the synchronicity of long association.

Drinking slowly, Claire tried to sort out her thoughts. She wasn't too happy with the whole roommate tip, but maybe Dean wasn't an ax murderer. Just a garden variety perv. That, she could handle. Hadn't she been dealing with boarding school teachers all her life?

Anyway, worrying about it wasn't going to change things. Besides, it was probably against the law to worry in California while on a beach.

Or in a car, especially one driven by Jodi.

With a smile, Claire leaned back. She took a long chug of lemonade. She wouldn't worry. Not on the beach. Not in the car. She closed her eyes and turned her face to the sun and chanted aloud to the rhythm of *Green Eggs and Ham.* "I will not do it in the car, I will not do it in the sand, I will not—" She had been going to finish "worry, Sam-I-am," but someone said, "Do what?"

Claire jumped and spilled her drink across her bare stomach "Aww!" she said in disgust. "Hell!"

"Do what?" the voice repeated patiently.

Dabbing at the sticky mess with the sandy corner of her

towel, turning her stomach into hard lemonade sandpaper, Claire said crossly, "What?"

"You said, 'I will not do it in the car, I will not do it in the sand . . .' It seems to me you're eliminating a lot of good possibilities."

Claire looked up into eyes of a gray that was almost silver. They were fringed with the sort of black lashes that guys seem to have and never appreciate.

And he was definitely a guy. From her angle, there was no mistake.

A quick glance up and down the beach revealed that it was still as empty as a few minutes before. So where had he come from?

Then she played his question back in her mind and felt the slow burn up her neck and cheeks. "Worry," she said. "I was talking about *worrying*."

"Disappointing," he said. "Or maybe not."

"So why are you standing here, exactly?" Claire swept her arm out, channeling her mother the banker in no-loans-for-you mode. "Big beach. Plenty of empty sand. And water."

To her indignation, he sat down. Ragged dark hair almost brushed his shoulders. He was wearing jeans bleached of all color and missing quite a few threads. The T-shirt had once, she thought, been red.

He wasn't *that* good to look at, she told herself, and made herself look away. Remembering her sunglasses, she pulled them down. There. Better.

The better to see you with, she thought. And then realized he looked familiar.

Hmm. Minor TV celeb? Relative of same?

"The view," he said. He looked back out at the water. A slight figure with sleek, bleached hair dropped in on a wave and went for a ride.

"Jodi," he said. "Better than ever."

"You know Jodi?" asked Claire.

"Yeah. I know her stuff, too." He motioned at the scatter of possessions across the three beach towels.

Jodi had painted or sewn big scarlet "J's" on all of her gear.

And then something clicked. She'd seen his picture on Linley's mirror. One of a hundred photos of a hundred parties that Linley continually updated with a hundred more pictures of a hundred more parties. But this picture, lower left corner, half-hidden, had never changed. He'd had his arm around her waist; she'd been bending forward laughing, generous cleavage in a half-zipped hoodie sweatshirt, the light of a beach fire behind them in the royal blue darkness. On his other side, arm hooked through his, Jodi stood, swallowed in an enormous man's shirt, staring down at Linley. Linley's head was half-turned toward the guy in the center. He'd been looking out, past the camera, past whoever had been taking the shot, a thousand-yard gaze.

A Linley ex, she thought. Or maybe, Jodi's. But then why had Linley saved the photo? She had a couple of other photos of Jodi and herself that she used as screen savers sometimes.

And Linley liked to throw things away. Traveling light, she called it.

But she hadn't thrown this picture away. It had stayed in the rotation.

Definitely Linley's ex.

Claire looked back out at the water. Jodi and Linley had both just dropped into a wave. They seemed to work together, dancing the boards in tandem over the face, crossing each other without getting in each other's way. They finished gracefully, sinking into the water as the wave played out. Simultaneously, they began to paddle out again.

"The Two," said the guy meditatively.

Still channeling her mother, Claire said, "I'm sorry. I didn't introduce myself. I'm Claire. I go to school with Linley. Jodi and Linley and I are roommates this summer."

She waited for him to say his name, but he was either dim or rude, or possibly both. He said, "I heard Linley was back for the summer. Where are you staying? At her uncle's?"

"Yes."

"Tolerant guy. Always was. But then it's a big house." His eyes had never left the water.

"He's away for the summer," Claire said.

"Nice," said the guy. And that's all he said.

Well, fine, Claire thought. She turned to watch the water, too.

Jodi was standing at the ocean's edge, watching as Linley sank gracefully into the froth as she finished a final ride and headed for shore.

The two were laughing and talking as they ran up the sand. It stopped abruptly as they reached Claire.

The roar of the surf made the cone of silence enveloping the four of them even more intense.

The guy stood up. "Linley, Jodi," he said.

In one unselfconscious motion, Linley stripped off the top of her wet shirt and stood topless. Deliberately she reached down for a towel and began to dry her hair. "Max," she said. Smiled. "Look at you."

"Hi, Max," said Jodi, her voice expressionless. She turned slightly away to pull off the wet suit and drop on her oversize T. Only then did she step out of the wet bottoms and into her shorts.

Linley began to rummage in her gear bag for a dry top. She took her time.

An ex, Claire thought. An ex for more than sex.

Still channeling her mother, this time as social-doyenne-in-difficult-situation mode, Claire pulled the cooler forward. "Anybody want a drink?" she asked brightly.

Holding her shirt in one hand, her eyes still on Max, Linley reached into ice and pulled out a beer. She tilted it up, arching her back.

"Good," she said. She peered at Max over the rim of the bottle. "Want some?"

"I'll get my own, thanks," said Max, and bent to the cooler.

Linley smiled more broadly and finally put her shirt on.

Hardly knowing what she was doing, Claire opened a beer, too, and took a drink. She choked.

She hated beer.

"It's been an almost perfect day, Jodi, don't you think?" Linley asked. She sank down, yoga style, next to Claire.

"Sure," agreed Jodi, who'd remained standing. "Um . . . Max, this is Claire. Claire, Max."

"We've met," said Max. "Just now. Claire was worried." He smiled suddenly at Claire.

Don't do that again, thought Claire. Definitely good for way more than sex, but she'd bet he'd been pretty damn good for sex, too. She could ask Linley. She might ask Linley.

"I wasn't worried," Claire retorted. "I believe that was my point."

"Claire's the official house worrier. Like, you know, the house mom. If she doesn't approve, we all get grounded," Linley said.

"House manager," said Jodi. She scored a beer and settled onto the blanket. To Max, she said, "It's a big house. Join us."

Again with his smile, Claire thought. Then she realized what Jodi had offered.

"A room of my own? That would be nice," Max said. "Well, Claire. May I? Do you approve?"

"She'll get back to you on that," Linley said quickly. Then, reverting to her cat-with-cream purr, she said, "So, Max, what're you doing here?"

Max took a long pull of beer. He turned his smile on Linley. "Well, I *was* looking for a place to live, actually."

This time, his smile was only for Linley.

Four

Linley held up her hand. "How many fingers am I holding up?"

Jodi leaned forward and shouted above the din on the deck around them, "FOUR!"

"One. Two. Three. Four." Pointing at each of them in turn, Linley said, "Four females."

"So?" shouted Claire.

"*FOUR* FEMALES," Linley enunciated loudly and carefully.

"GOT. IT," Jodi said. "ONLY YOU CAN'T COUNT. THERE'RE ONLY THREE OF US." She slammed her glass down and added, "THIRSTY!" Rising, she plunged directly into the melee on the tiny worn area of planking that seemed to be the unofficial dance floor.

The place was called Banger's, and its main recommendation was that it was within walking distance of their house.

Apparently it was convenient to every other house near the beach, too, Claire thought.

The music crashed to a stop as Linley shouted FOUR again. No one even looked in their direction.

"So?" Claire repeated.

"We have four females at the house. And only *two* guys."

"Two?" asked Claire.

"Dean and Max," said Linley.

"I'm not sure I like Dean," said Claire, enunciating way too carefully. "There's something sneaky about him, don't you think? Like he's waiting for something to happen and he wants it to be bad."

"Don't we all," said Linley. "We need Dean. Two guys, four girls. Bad."

Claire gave up. Apparently, she was the only one who got a weird vibe from Dean. And she wasn't sure why. Was it because during that whole conversation, his eyes had never ceased moving? What was he looking for?

"Dean and Max," said Linley again.

"I thought you said you'd let Max know," Claire reminded Linley.

Linley made a face and waved four fingers vaguely. "What am I going to do? Kick him to the curb? He's an old, *dear* friend."

"Uh-huh," said Claire, not bothering to hide her skepticism.

Linley leaned forward. Her eyes were shiny, and Claire knew she'd been doing more than the specialty of the house, Banger Slammers. "You know what you need. More drinks. More drugs. More sex."

"Like you had with Max?" asked Claire, before she could stop herself.

Linley jerked back, actually speechless for a nanosecond. Then she hooted. "Good one, Claire." She leaned forward again and crooked her finger, beckoning Claire closer. "Here's a secret," she said.

Claire leaned forward.

"Max is an old, *dear,* good friend," she explained again, solemnly.

Holding position, Claire said, "As in good in bed."

Leaning forward even more, Linley said, even more solemnly, "He was. All night. Not just quantity, quality. The boy had an appetite, you know?" She ran the pink tip of her tongue along her upper lip.

"Too much information," Claire said, trying to sound bored rather than shocked.

Jodi returned and claimed the chair.

"Dean's here," she reported.

"Everybody's here," said Linley, waving at someone in the crowd. "It's like a big ole reunion. Hey, Kerri Lynn! Hey, Marie! And Micki! Hey, y'all!"

"You are messed up, aren't you?" said Jodi scornfully. "You're going all bad Southern belle accent. And you were born and raised in San Francisco, just like me."

"Southern belle, *y'all,* honey," drawled Linley.

"And he said, *honey,* that they were hiring waiters," Jodi

went on. "Said we should come in tomorrow. He'd put a word in for us."

"And the drinks?" Linley asked.

"Oh. I forgot," Jodi said. She laughed uproariously, then sobered. "I'm not sure I like Dean."

"That's what I was trying to—" Claire began.

A waiter interrupted by settling a round of Slammers on the table.

"On the house," he said, and Claire realized it was Dean. He leaned a little closer. And leered.

Claire burst out laughing.

He smiled, winked, and was gone.

"Nice," said Jodi, eyeing the drinks. "Okay, maybe he's not so bad."

"Cheap," said Linley.

"Easy," retorted Jodi.

"Wait. What if these drinks have, like, date rape drugs in them?" Claire said.

"He's not like that!" Jodi said, shocked.

"He's like something," said Claire. "I'm telling you."

"You're right," said Linley, and quick as a snake, she grabbed Claire's and chugged, then chugged her own.

"Now you're safe," she said.

"Asshole," said Claire. She got up to go in search of another drink. And sober up a little in what she knew would be an endless wait on the bathroom line.

She returned from the bathroom to a sea of people around the table, like shipwreckees clinging to a life raft. Everyone was shouting cheerfully and no one seemed to be listening. Someone bellowed introductions. Claire didn't bother to listen.

"Syllablitis," Claire heard Jodi say suddenly.

"What?" Claire asked.

"Big words, use of, when approaching a state of inebriation. In Linley. A sure marker," said Jodi.

"Indubitably," said Linley, raising her glass.

"Lots of practice drinking together," noted Claire.

"Yes. Friends don't let friends inebriate alone," Jodi said solemnly. She leaned over. "One time, when Linley was grounded, we went and sat in her father's new car, right. In the garage. And we were passing this nasty bottle of cheap wine and we heard something, right?"

"Right," said Claire encouragingly.

"So Linley got scared—"

"Did not!"

"And jumped out of the car and ran around to the trunk and threw the bottle inside and slammed it shut. And locked it."

"It could've happened to anybody," Linley said.

"Did you get caught?"

"Yes. Because Linley had locked the keys in the trunk." Jodi rolled her eyes, and then she and Linley started to laugh.

Laughter bubbled up in Claire, too.

Then the band began on the back of the deck, and Claire was dancing and laughing and leaning against the railing and drinking some more, and once doing a definitely dirty grind with one of the guys from the table who clearly wanted to bump and grind without the interference of clothes, and then she was leaning against Jodi watching Linley and it was much, much later than it had been.

So late, it was early again. Except in Massachusetts, where it was . . . what? Dead. Yes, dead.

Sometime during the night, Jodi had switched to diet Coke. At least, that's what Claire thought it was. She squinted down at her own drink. Was she drinking margaritas?

"I like this place," she said, speaking with great care.

"Yeah," said Jodi. She sighed. "And thank God this year is over."

"Bad?" Claire asked. She decided to use the shortest possible sentences. They seemed easiest.

"Are you kidding? Local college, living at home? I think there's a law against it, somewhere." Jodi sucked on her diet soda. "Hated every minute of it, let me tell you."

"Parents much?" asked Claire. She wasn't sure what she was trying to say.

But Jodi seemed to understand. "Parent. Mother, with stepfather."

"Right. Linley. Told me." Claire tried for sympathetic sounds of one syllable.

"I can't believe she married him . . . he's . . . creepy. . . ." Jodi's voice trailed off. Then she took a deep breath. "Anyway, I'm outta there. I'm going to work two jobs this summer, and I'm up for a full scholarship next year at a real art school and . . . it's going to get better."

"It will," agreed Claire. "It is already. Could've been a bank for the summer. I mean—in a bank."

Jodi made a face. "And living at home?"

"And living at home. Parents. My sister has her own place, and my brother is married and working on the family thing."

"Are they nice?"

"Mm?"

"Your parents. Your family. Nice?" Jodi repeated.

"Uh . . . yeah." Not something Claire had thought much about.

Jodi sighed. "My mom's nice, but she's not what you'd call the independent type." Another sigh.

"So, you and Linley—both only kids," Claire said, swerving slightly off subject. "You think that's one of the reasons you're friends?"

"Maybe." Jodi sounded doubtful.

"And Linley and I . . . hey! Our parents are still married to each other," Claire said. "We have *that* in common."

"I guess." Jodi gave Claire an odd look. "But I think the reason Linley and I got to be friends is she was the only person I met at our stupid high school who was willing to do anything. I mean, she is totally fearless. Without fear. The first time we surfed together, I knew we were solid."

"Right," agreed Claire. She thought a little longer. "And Max. About Max?"

"Max is the ex-love of Linley's life. Old story," Jodi said flatly.

"'s cute," Claire slurred.

"Color me overcautious," Jodi's tone remained flat. "But I wouldn't look in that direction. He may be history, but I've got a feeling he's still not in her past."

"Right," Claire said. "Well. Anyway, thanks to Linley—no bank."

"Thanks to Linley," Jodi said. "Yes. Linley makes things happen. But . . ."

"But ...?"

"But wait for the end of the summer before you thank her for it." Jodi flicked the rest of her soda over the deck railing. "I know some people who'll give us a ride," she announced. "Let's go."

"What about Linley?" Claire asked.

"Linley," said Jodi, "can find her own way home."

Five

"You're twenty-one?" asked the burly guy with the round baby blue eyes behind the counter. He'd introduced himself as Joseph, and Claire was discovering that the ferocious scowl was probably an illusion caused by thick, jutting eyebrows that almost met over the bridge of what looked like a once-broken nose. He wiped the same place in the counter over and over again with a rag that might have also been used for oil changes. Claire couldn't be sure.

"Twenty-two," corrected Claire, following Linley's rule that if you're going to lie, lie big.

He looked at her a moment, his blue eyes blank.

She wondered if the massive hangover from the all-nighter at Banger's made her look older, or just skeezy. She was grateful for the interior gloom. It cut down on the wince factor.

"I.D.?"

It was a phony I.D., but since it was from Massachusetts, she figured he might not spot it. She flipped open her wallet.

His eyes flicked over the license.

"No experience." His eyes flicked across Claire: chest, face, chest. Then he made a pretense of studying the employment application that she had filled in.

"None," said Claire. *In so many ways.*

"Well, you could add some class to the joint. You don't need to be no rocket scientist." That made him laugh. "Start tomorrow."

"Tomorrow's fine," Claire said primly.

"Good," he said. "Be here by ten a.m. You'll start with lunches. We're sandwiches and beer; lunches are our bread and butter." That made him laugh again. He pulled open a drawer, folded the application, and crammed it in. "Jan—she's who you'll be working with most—can show you the ropes." From another drawer he withdrew a T-shirt emblazoned with the name of the place. "Your uniform. Wear it with a skirt. A short skirt."

The shirt looked small. Very small. The words STACKED SNACK SHACK spread across the chest. It did not in any way fit Claire's definition of class, but who was she to argue?

"Great," she said. "Uh, why 'Stacked Snack Shack'?"

"Sandwiches," uttered Joseph, as if this made all things plain.

Claire shook her head.

He elaborated. "What's a sandwich? A stacked item. A piled-up meal. A stacked snack? Get it? I didn't just want to call this the Sandwich Shack. I mean, it says it all, but it doesn't say it memorably, y'know?"

"Oh. Right."

Joseph bared his teeth in a terrifying way that Claire was pretty sure was a friendly smile. "So Stacked Snack Shack. Has an edge, y'see?"

"Definitely. It's . . . it's brilliant."

More of the large, terrifying teeth were exposed. "Yeah, thanks. I'm good with words, y'know?"

"Clearly. Well, see you tomorrow."

"Right," Joseph said.

She had a summer job. And it was most definitely not in her father's bank.

And not, a small voice in her mind pointed out, at Banger's, either. She might have to share a house with Dean, but she didn't have to see him on the job, too.

But she was definitely sharing a house with him. He was the first person she met when she got home, stretched out on a deck chair wearing a banana hammock bathing suit and dark glasses, a forgotten joint in one hand sending up a last curl of sweet dying smoke.

Claire stopped.

"Welcome home," he said.

"You're here," she said.

"All moved in," he agreed.

"So I see," she retorted.

"Please don't tell me you're a drug-free house," he said. "I join the rest of the world in looking down on those who view drugs as more than purely recreational, but you have to admit the right pharmaceutical choice can add so much to the moment."

The ironic flow of words made Claire blink.

He looked around, picked up the joint, toked it back to life, and extended it to Claire. "Care to join me in the moment?"

"No thanks," she said. "And we have a no-smoking-in-the-house rule. From Linley's uncle."

Exhaling lazily, Dean said, "Yes, ma'am. I do like a woman who likes to be on top . . . of things."

"Linley or Jodi around?" asked Claire.

"Out on the job trail," he said. "At this very moment, they are, I believe, talking to the pathetic control freak who runs the business end of Banger's."

"Banger?"

"No, sadly. Darling Banger is the whipped slave of the vile Vickie. He's the sweetness-and-light front man, she's the penny-pinching numbers whore lurking in the caves of avarice—in the back, fortunately for business. And fortunately, after the initial interview, you work mainly with Banger. Except to run a sharp eye over the paycheck, because she *will* short you, even if it's only pennies. She makes cheap look like an all-night spending binge."

"Nice," said Claire, turning to go in the house.

"And Poppy is, of course, at her gallery. Art is life, you know," he said.

"I thought life imitated art," said Claire, in spite of herself.

"Ah, you know Wilde. Good for you," Dean said, flashing a smile. His teeth were just as terrifying as Joseph's, but in a different way. Joseph really was smiling, after all. Dean looked as if he were preparing to take a sample bite.

Then the smile was gone and Dean leaned back, seeming to lose all interest in the conversation—although he didn't quite yawn.

Somehow annoyed at being so rudely dismissed, Claire narrowed her eyes at Dean. She didn't like him any better for the conversation, but now she was . . . intrigued.

Giving herself a mental shake, she pushed open the door.

Dean's voice stopped her again.

"And you. Out looking too?"

"I found a job," said Claire.

"I'm sure you did. You know, though, that you easily could have had a job at Banger's. Banger listens to me."

"Thanks, but . . . but . . ." Claire stopped. But what? I didn't want to owe you one? Spend one extra minute with you? I don't trust you? Like you?

"No, no, don't thank me. Where did you say you're now employed?"

Mute with embarrassment, Claire held up the T-shirt.

"The Stacked!" Dean laughed, but this time the display of

teeth didn't look predatory. "It's an institution. You'll have fun. I congratulate you."

Claire eyed him suspiciously.

"No, really. It's the meeting point for every surf bum in the universe, and has been forever. A perfect welcome-to-California job. And Joseph treats his employees well—apart from the fashion abuse." Dean indicated the T-shirt.

Without meaning to, Claire laughed. "He told me to wear it with a skirt. A *short one*," she added with an attempt at Joseph's accent. "I have a wrap skirt that goes over my bicycle shorts. It'll have to do."

"Wear the shorts, too," Dean advised. He added, "And, of course, you can always pick up some extra shifts, and money, at Banger's."

"Thanks," said Claire, surprised.

He waved his hand, dismissing her again. This time, instead of being annoyed, Claire was amused. Maybe he wouldn't be such a bad house-mate after all. Except for his questionable taste in swimwear.

Dean's voice followed her. "Rent's on the kitchen table. And the deposit. Cash. Naturally."

Jodi studied herself in the mirror of the cramped but relatively clean staff-only bathroom at Banger's. The stall door slammed back, and a thin boy emerged and nodded.

"Busy night," he said.

"Not too bad," she said. Mark? Marcus. That was his name. "Decent tips, anyway."

"You've waited before," he observed, leaning over to inspect his own face in the mirror. "Girl, look at these bags."

"Cucumbers," said Jodi automatically. "Slices, you know. Draws off the puffiness."

"They say," he said cynically. "Sleep would work too. Or at least some horizontal time."

"Truth," agreed Jodi, although she wasn't really tired. But horizontal time, that was different.

It had been a long year and a careful one, living under her stepfather's BB pellet–size eyes. He wasn't a churchgoing man, but he was fond of calling on religion to support him in the rules he made. "My house, my rules," he said, and it was plain he didn't see much difference between himself and the Almighty.

Jodi wanted to point out that the house was only half his, at least in the state of California. The other half belonged to her mother. But her mother, never the strongest force for justice in the universe, would have breathed, "Oh, *no,* Jodi," and Jodi would have been grounded.

In college. With a job. Grounded. Confined to her room when she wasn't at class or at work, just as if she were still in high school.

And he charged her rent.

It was creepy, too. He patrolled the house at night, pushing open her door to look in. She'd caught him at it more than once. Raised her head and said, "Mom, is that you?"

He'd withdrawn swiftly and without speaking, but it hadn't put an end to the nocturnal peeping. She'd learned to lie still, body tense, eyes slitted, waiting for him to go.

He always had.

She was devoutly thankful her mother hadn't married the Steppervert until Jodi was in high school and capable of defending herself, if needed. And that she was an only child and didn't have a younger sister—or brother—to worry about leaving behind in the Steppervert's power.

"See you later," said Marcus, cutting across her fond family memories.

"Same time, same place," agreed Jodi.

Maybe that's why she'd been so shut down. Living in close proximity with the Steppervert was enough to make anyone's sexual instincts hibernate. How her mother stood to let him touch her—ugh.

But the idea of people that age doing the nasty was ugh-worthy any way you looked at it.

Doing it.

It had been a while. A few times around that guy's apartment over Christmas break, but that had been more about staying out of the house than pleasure. And Andrew—Andrew? She was terrible with names—he hadn't wanted to talk about art, except of course his own, which didn't seem to involve the art of sex.

Before that, those times in high school, especially . . . no, she wouldn't think about it. Only two people knew about that, and if you didn't think about it, it would go live and die quietly somewhere in her id, or subconscious, or whatever it was.

But she was restless. Hungry. She needed skin on skin.

Easy enough to find, especially with the setup she had for the summer. Except she needed a second job if she was going to make "Leaving Home and the Steppervert" stick.

The bathroom door slammed back. "Jodi! C'mon. I don't want to be here all night!"

"Coming, Linley."

Jodi sighed and added another layer of lip gloss, even if it was only for the ride home with Linley.

Six

By the second day at Stacked Snack Shack, or the Stacked, as everyone called it, Claire had the routine down. It was a small place and no one seemed too particular, and she and Jan, a classically perky type who said she worked at the Stacked to support her body board habit, quickly developed their own cheerful rhythm.

Joseph worked the counter, the register, and the grill with another short-order cook he called Fry. Fry never spoke, and in spite of the health laws, he could be seen from time to time framed in the pass-through with a cigarette dangling from his lips.

Claire decided that as long as no ash hit the food and no one complained, she wasn't going to think about it. Once, when Fry leaned forward with an order and a particularly gnarly silver cylinder of ash, Claire's and Jan's eyes met.

They both smiled and shrugged. Old pros at work.

He came in at the end of the first week. He strolled in

through the open doors with a medium-size red and white dog that had a tail like a raccoon following on his heels and sat down at the counter.

Given the cigarette situation in the back, Claire figured Joseph wasn't going to say anything about the dog. So instead of saying, "No Dogs by Order of the Health Department except on that rickety stretch of boards we call the deck," she'd asked instead, "What's your dog's name?"

He'd glanced over and smiled, not at her, but at the dog. "Barrel," he said. "His name is Barrel."

The dog waved his tail gently in acknowledgment.

"He's beautiful," she said sincerely. She liked dogs. Her family always had a pile of Labradors lying around, snoring and farting and waiting to go swimming and play fetch or clean plates. She loved them all, and mourned the ones that had died . . . thought of them often still.

A secret sentimental weakness, she told herself.

"Yes, he is," the guy said simply. He looked at her then, with a slight smile that was easy and without hidden meanings. She smiled back and took his order and later saw that one of the two sandwiches was being handed down on the coffee saucer to Barrel.

Barrel was much more polite than the Labs. He waited until the plate was on the floor before inhaling the sandwich.

On the next order, she made a detour through the cooler and swiped a piece of cheese and passed it over to the guy. "For Barrel," she said, and went to pour coffee.

He was still there when her shift ended and she began totaling out her day's checks. Joseph was working the daily paper's crossword puzzle at the end of the bar, and Jan, who was pulling a double shift, was just sitting on a stool, staring out at the passing crowd on the boardwalk.

"From around here?" asked Claire, and laughed inwardly because she sounded like a local.

He shrugged. "I give surfing lessons over at the Belle Azure," he said, referring to one of the upmarket mega hotels farther down the beach.

"Room and board?" she asked, and would later remember that.

"Freelance," he said. He grinned. "I'm good at it." He seemed to find this funny, and added, "My mom always wanted me to be a teacher."

"As a matter of fact," he went on, "Barrel and I are looking for a place for the summer. Living in the van now, but no way is that a long-term plan. But with a dog, y'know . . ." His voice trailed off.

And Claire the careful, Claire the cautious, said, for no other reason than she liked Barrel, "We have a room. We have a house."

"That'd be cool," he said. "Far from here?"

"A short skate away," Claire said, and it was true. She'd hiked a few blocks to the boardwalk with her in-line skates on her shoulder and cruised on down to work that day.

"Well, I can give you wheels home when you're through," he offered.

Claire punched one more button on the register, then wound the receipt around the checks. She stuck that in one of Joseph's many drawers behind the counter. She hung up her apron and retrieved her pack from a cabinet and said, "I'm through for the day."

"Cool enough," he said, and she followed what could have been an ax murderer, for all she knew, out into the sun and into his van.

Only as she left the Stacked did she even think about caution. "Joseph," she said.

Joseph glanced up.

"This, ah, I'm getting a ride home with . . ." She let her voice trail off.

"Finn," the possible ax murderer with the nice dog, said. "Everybody calls me Finn."

"Right," said Joseph, without interest, and went back to his puzzle.

Great, thought Claire. When they came to question Joseph about her missing body and the stranger she'd left the Stacked with, he'd probably give the word for 8 across, 9 letters, meaning "unconscious in winter."

Barrel looked up at her and gave her canine grin, and she thought, *Well, if I do make it home, I've brought another guy to the house.*

Only this one is *not* for Linley.

• • •

But Linley didn't seem that interested in Finn. She was just getting up, and her face above the coffee mug had that dark, thwarted look of an unsuccessful night and a painful morning after.

"Men," she declared bitterly as Claire came back downstairs after giving Finn and Barrel a choice of the last two rooms.

A mental review told Claire that she could have been referring to Max, who had joined the house quietly and then seemed to absent himself from it. Although he had only been there a few days, he'd seldom been around when Linley was.

Or possibly Dean, except that Dean had seemed more than willing to enter into whatever Linley had suggested, which for once had made Linley less interested.

Settling on what she hoped was a neutral topic, Claire said, "Where's Jodi? Does she work tonight?"

"No. Party. Oh yeah, the house is invited." Linley flicked at a piece of notebook paper lying on the counter.

Claire picked it up to read the time and directions. "You going?"

"Working," said Linley.

"You could probably switch with somebody," Claire suggested.

"You have to choose your parties," Linley said cryptically. "Jodi's over at the loft, or gallery or whatever, helping." Linley raised a finger to a nostril and pretended to snort.

"Poppy's having a party?" Claire said, linking gallery with art with Poppy.

"Friend of Poppy's. An artist. Naturally." Linley's tone expressed her opinion of artists.

"You don't like Poppy?" Claire said, surprised.

Linley shrugged. "I don't know Poppy, do I? I just met her when you did. She'll make the rent, and that's what matters."

"You really don't like her," Claire said.

"Whatever," Linley said, sounding annoyed.

"What about Dean?"

"You're the one who doesn't like Dean," Linley pointed out.

"What do we know about him? He works at Banger's, he's a friend of Poppy's, and he moved out of his apartment just like that when he heard about this share."

"He liked the way we looked. He liked the setup. Big deal," said Linley.

"He's sketchy," said Claire.

"Makes him interesting, don't you think?"

Exasperated, Claire said, "Fine. Maybe I'll see if Finn wants to go to this thing. You think that'd be cool?"

Cool? An hour in Finn's company and she was talking like him.

If Linley noticed the Claire conversational aberration, she didn't let on. "Sure," she said. "Max is going. Your boy Dean's probably already there."

"Oh," said Claire. Definite bitterness factor in Linley's voice.

"Max hasn't even come to Banger's to say hi," Linley went on. "Not that I care."

"Well, he does live with you. In the house, I mean."

Linley gave her a look. Then she stood up, went over to the cabinet, extracted a bottle of vodka and a bottle of Kahlúa, and returned to doctor her coffee.

"Better," she said, after generously dosing her cup.

"Yuk," said Claire. The first time she'd ever gotten drunk had involved old school White Russians, and she'd never been the same around Kahlúa since.

Linley, who knew the story, said with the first hint of humor that day, "Weak."

"I prefer to think of it as developing more sophisticated tastes," retorted Claire.

That got her the Linley Look again.

"I thought Max was an ex," said Claire. "So what difference does it make that he hasn't come to see you?"

In answer, Linley picked up her cup and marched across the room and out through the French doors onto the deck. Claire followed. The afternoon sun had begun to cast long shadows with the promise of another fabulous sunset. Below on the sand two joggers sped enthusiastically by, both wearing headphones and both talking, either to each other or singing in time with whatever they were playing inside their heads.

"Maybe I'll take up jogging," said Linley, settling into a deck chair. "I could lose a few pounds."

"Ha, and can you say eating disorder?" Claire shot back. She sat down on the edge of the hammock and began to rock gently. "Max?" she prompted.

"I'm so over him," said Linley crossly.

Claire waited.

And waited.

Finally Linley added, "Well, I am. It's just that . . . the whole age thing isn't that big a deal, but—"

Claire said, "Stop. Story: beginning, middle, end. Unless you're planning on becoming a writer for *The New Yorker.*"

"Okay, then. It was like this. High school. He's two years older, so my parents for once get involved and make 'he's too old for you' sounds, and I ignore them, naturally . . ."

"Naturally," said Claire, who'd never ignored her parents in her life.

"And we start dating. My parents back off and hope that when he graduates, it'll be 'nice knowing you.'"

She stopped and sipped her fuel-injected coffee.

"Which of course it's going to be, no worries. Because I've got to have a social life, right? And he's going to be gone and I don't want to be the little college commuter girlfriend doing the long-slow breakup with e-mails and phone calls, right?"

"Got it," said Claire.

"So I'm going for the great final summer romance. Sex on the beach, surfing, maybe a camping trip . . . and right in the middle of the summer he says he's bagging college and going to travel. See the world. Figure some things out."

Was that a catch in Linley's voice? Claire stared at her. But Linley's face was turned away, studying the progress of yet another jogger, this one pushing a baby jogger that appeared to have snow tires—or was it sand tires—on it. Possibly, Claire thought, it had four-wheel drive. In California, she wouldn't have been surprised.

"And then he's gone, just like that," Linley concluded.

"No explanation?" Claire said. "I mean, apart from 'see the world'?"

"*Nada.* I asked him, was it someone else, was it me . . . and he said he'd always love me, it wasn't me it was him, and—"

"Bye-bye," finished Claire. "Standard exit line." You didn't have to be widely experienced to know that kiss-off from the guys' breakup manual.

"And I just didn't think Max was that kind of guy." Linley's face hardened. "I was young."

"Did you have anything on the side?" Claire asked. She knew Linley.

"Well . . ."

"Linley?"

"Well, he *was* leaving, after all. I mean, I'd done the whole faithful girlfriend bit and all of that for a *whole* year, but life goes on, you know."

"So you'd started seeing someone else. Did Max know?"

"No!" Linley frowned. "No, I'm positive he didn't. He would've told me. I'm sure of it."

"Did you, you know, stay in touch?"

"A few e-mails, and an actual postcard once, from a place in Asia somewhere that I don't think was wired at the time. That was it. I just kinda stopped answering, you know? I mean, what was the point?"

Claire took a deep breath and asked one final question. "Did you think he was back now? I mean, in your life like before?"

"No! I mean, it's been *years* . . . okay, maybe not that many years. . . . But I *have* moved on. It's just that . . . well, he's not even interested," Linley blurted out.

And that was the whole point. Linley didn't like it when people—guys—weren't interested.

Still, Claire thought it was something more. Was Linley telling her the whole truth?

Had Max been telling Linley the whole truth?

Not a guy who liked to talk, she'd noticed. But hot, hot, hot, as the old song said. She couldn't blame Linley for not being able to forget.

Hot.

Seven

It was a gallery in a loft.

And Finn, after a text message from Jodi assuring Claire that "well-behaved dogs were okay," had agreed he'd like to come along.

"Cool," he'd said.

It was for Finn she was wearing her most abbreviated sundress. It was black—not exactly a California basic, but she'd pulled a bright, oversize T-shirt on top and knotted it on one corner. It was a little five minutes ago, but it would do.

Waitressing had given her a new appreciation of shoes without heels, and she'd gone with sequined flip-flops she'd swiped from Linley's room.

Finn, on the other hand, looked almost preppy in cutoff khakis and a faded oversize workshirt. He'd pulled his sun-gold hair back with a leather tie that had a bead on each end. She liked the look, at least on him.

"Good," he said when he saw her, and she decided it was a compliment.

"Darling," said Poppy, when she saw Claire, and then her eyes crinkled in amusement. "And . . . ?"

Claire suddenly realized that Poppy didn't know about Finn. "Our newest share," she said. "Finn, this is Poppy, who also lives at our house."

"Very cool," said Finn, taking Poppy's hand. He gave it a friendly shake and released it. "And this is Barrel."

"Ah, yes. The well-behaved dog *and* another share. I hope Barrel likes parties."

"Barrel's happy anywhere there's food and me," said Finn simply.

"Good dog. Would that all our significant others were so easy. Although I'd prefer the priorities reversed," said Poppy. She gestured. "Meet Miwako—she's one of the gallery's artists. The food is somewhere over there, with drink nearby. As for the rest of the recreational enhancements, you're on your own."

Finn caught Claire's hand and led the way to the food. Having made sure that Barrel wouldn't starve, he heaped a second plate and offered some to Claire.

"Thanks," said Claire, taking a slice of California roll.

"I never say no to free food," Finn explained.

Claire pushed away the thought that this was why he had come to the party.

He cleaned the plate as thoroughly as Barrel and set it down.

He surveyed the room. "Let's dance," he said, adding, "Barrel, stay" as he caught her hand again to lead her into the fray.

She danced until she saw Jodi across the room, deep in conversation with Max, and half-danced over to introduce Finn to most of the rest of the house.

"One big happy family," Max observed. "Drink?"

"Beer," said Finn. "I'll get it. Anyone else?" He took orders, told Barrel, who'd somehow appeared at his side, to "Stay," and made his way back to the bar.

Barrel sat down and looked at them expectantly.

"Good dog," said Jodi, bending to scratch Barrel between the shoulders. He showed his approval by flattening his ears and lolling out his tongue.

"You like dogs, I hope?" Claire asked Max.

"Sure," said Max. "And I can tell Barrel is a nice one. It'll be a better house with a dog in it."

Jodi had squatted down to go nose-to-nose with Barrel. Claire didn't need to ask her if she liked dogs.

"I grew up with bad dogs," Max went on. "Or, really, spoiled. Their idea of a good time was to chew the legs off furniture." He grinned. "Of course, I've been there myself."

Claire laughed, and told him about the Labs.

"Raised by Labs, huh? How are you at fetch?"

"Depends on what you throw," said Claire.

Max looked at her then, and laughed. "You're a surprise," he said.

Taking the drink that Finn had scored for her, Claire took a sip, trying to look demure, yet surprising. Whatever that meant.

"Oh, yo," said Finn suddenly. "It's Curly Dave. And Jean and Lenore. I haven't seen them in, like, forever. C'mon, Barrel. Let's say hi." He was off across the room with Barrel in tow.

Jodi stood, and beamed. "I like that dog," she said.

"Down girl, I think he's taken," Max said.

Jodi froze, her smile slipping, and Max, his own drink halfway to his lips, stopped. He and Jodi stared at each other.

Or had Claire imagined it? It was only for a second, and then Jodi said, "As soon as I have my own place, I'm getting a dog." She took a deep breath and added, "Dogs are faithful and love you always."

"Most of them," observed Max. He paused for a beat, and said, "But Claire grew up with Labs that were yours for the right T-bone."

Another pause, and Jodi laughed and Max gave a lopsided grin, and Claire said, "Oh, they were much cheaper than that," and then Jodi waved at someone and the three-way was absorbed into the party again.

But Claire didn't forget it.

And she wondered if it all seemed as obvious to anyone else as it seemed to her.

Finn didn't kiss her goodnight. He had also given Max and Dean a ride home, leaving Poppy and Jodi and half a dozen *artistes* deep in wine and local art scene conversation amid the litter of the party. Dean, it seemed, was not an artist after all.

Claire had not yet found out exactly what he was.

She'd turned from watching Finn and Barrel go up the stairs to the second floor to find Dean watching her. He'd smiled and winked and given her an almost fatherly pat on the shoulder—if her father had been the type. "Patience," he murmured, and let his fingers trail off her shoulder and down her arm as he headed off to his room.

Okay, not the fatherly type of pat after all.

That had left Max—Max, restless, pulling a beer from the fridge. "I'm going to walk on the beach for a little while," he said. "Want to come?"

"Sure," Claire. She thought a moment and said, "Linley'll be home soon. Want to wait for her?"

"No," said Max, still peering into the refrigerator. "Beer? Drink?"

"A bottle of water," Claire said. "Anything that's in there."

Beyond the light on the deck, at the bottom of the sand, the night was soft and dark. Far down the beach Claire spotted the blaze of a dying bonfire.

They strolled in silence wrapped in the sound of the surf and the sounds of parties still coming from the bars and houses up beyond the dunes.

"You surf?" Claire asked, after a while.

"Sort of. It's never been my thing."

"So I guess it wasn't surfing that brought you and Linley together."

"Me and Linley," he said thoughtfully. "No, not surfing."

"Hot sex, then," Claire suggested, and stopped in horror. She hadn't had that much to drink. Had she?

Max laughed. "Well, you do know Linley," he said. "But it wasn't just that. It was that, plus . . . oh, I don't know, many things. Many fine things."

Much more carefully, Claire said, "She told me a little about it, but not too much. And I'm being nosy. I'm sorry."

"No. No big deal. It is, after all, history."

"Not so much, I think," Claire said.

"Maybe not," he said, and lapsed into silence.

Guys, thought Claire. Getting them to talk was like pulling teeth. Not that she'd ever pulled teeth, exactly, but then, she'd never really gotten guys to talk to her either.

But then it really wasn't any of her business.

After another long, wind-and-water-filled silence, Max said, "Linley and I have some unfinished business. And I've got some decisions to make. About my life. And what I'm deciding is not going to make anybody happy. My father and mother—well, they have barely spoken in years, I don't think they have even seen each other since they split up . . . but if I do what I think I'm going to do, it'll be the one thing they agree on."

"Mmm," said Claire. Now that Max was talking, he wasn't making much sense.

"I was over in India." He stopped. He looked out at the ocean. "This is such a cliché."

"India," Claire prompted.

"I met this rinpoche. This teacher. Studied with him."

"Oh," said Claire.

She waited. But Max had apparently used all of his words for the moment.

Still, she got the distinct impression that he wasn't looking to get back together with Linley. This was not going to make Linley happy.

Claire shuffled through the sand, her thoughts running ahead. She lost track of time and hardly noticed that they'd returned to the steps leading up to the deck and the house.

Max put his arm around her shoulders and gave her a quick squeeze. "You're a peaceful girl, Claire," he said.

"Yes, well, that's always been my problem," she said.

He gave a snort. "Not a problem," he said and, releasing her, gave her a little push up the stairs ahead of him.

Linley was sitting on the sofa, her feet on the table, a joint in her hand. "Welcome back," she said. "Did you have a good time?"

The glitter in her eyes warned Claire that any answer would be wrong—especially saying "No dope in the house."

"Hey, Linley," she said.

"How was the party? Or do I need to ask?" She took a deep drag and held it.

Claire reached over, took the joint, and inhaled. She never smoked—and almost choked, but managed to hold it in. *Saved from answering,* she thought.

Exhaling along with Linley, Claire said, "Gotta go to work in the morning. See you in a few."

"Stay," said Linley. "What difference does it make?"

Claire didn't answer. She'd decided on being a coward and living to see another day. She retreated toward the stairs.

"Claire!" said Linley.

"I've gotta get some sleep too," said Max.

"Why? You don't have to go to work," said Linley.

"Don't I?" His voice sounded teasing and affectionate.

"Max," Linley said, the brittle note gone. She sounded different from anything Linley had ever heard. "Max, don't go."

Claire almost ran to her room, and closed the door firmly behind her.

Eight

Sitting and looking out at the ocean, Linley tried not to cry. She never cried. Crying was for people who didn't get what they wanted, and she always got what she wanted.

She was a very determined person.

You might as well be. You could lose everything in an instant. And die in the next instant. So you might as well get what you wanted as soon as you wanted it, or you might not get it at all. . . .

Damn him, she thought. Why had he come back? Why couldn't he just stay far, far away, in Rangoon or Bhutan or wherever he'd been?

Who needed Max on this side of the planet? Who needed Max in her world?

Her world. Her perfect summer.

It was not going as she'd planned.

She dug her fingers into the arm of the chair and thought *cigarettes*. On that thought she was up and down the hall and in her uncle's study. He was an ex-smoker who still smoked cigarettes now and then.

"Never give anything up completely," he said, "or you'll never be able to give it up at all."

Amazing, her uncle. Since he'd quit smoking when she was ten, she'd seen him have maybe three or four cigarettes, usually at family parties.

She found them in the freezer in the bar refrigerator behind the desk in his study and took the whole pack. All natural cigarettes. She smiled grimly. It figured. Did that mean you'd get organic lung cancer?

She was just coming out of the study when she heard Jodi and Poppy come in.

She stopped and slid back into the shadows, leaving the door almost closed. She didn't want the company. Not now.

Especially not Poppy's company. Poppy saw too much. And not like Dean. Dean was some kind of scam artist, Linley thought. She'd picked that up pretty much instantly. She'd voted him in just to twitch Claire. It was fun to do that, like watching her squirm over the whole paying-no-rent secret.

But Poppy was solid. Smart. And she really looked at people, really listened to them. It made Linley . . . nervous.

And, of course, Jodi thought Poppy was some kind of art goddess. Jodi began entirely too many sentences these days with the words, "Poppy says . . ."

"Well," said Jodi, her voice bright with a little too much of everything. "That was fun."

"It was," agreed Poppy. "Very successful party."

"Successful and fun are not the same," said Jodi.

"True," said Poppy. She was walking around the room, turning off lights, until the only one left was over the bar.

Jodi yawned hugely. "It's funny," she said. "I missed it like crazy, partying with Linley all this past year. We've been best friends forever." She paused, as if thinking that over. "But Linley went to school in Boston, and I had to stay here."

"Did it change things much?"

The clink of ice in a glass. Linley remained rooted in the shadows. Eavesdropping.

"Yes. No. I don't know. Anyway, I wish she would have come to the party tonight, but she didn't. Maybe because of Max . . ."

"Or me," said Poppy.

"You?" said Jodi, sounding surprised.

"Linley doesn't really like me, you know."

"Sure she does," said Jodi. "She can be sort of brusque, but she's great."

"I'm not arguing that."

Linley peered out and saw Poppy settling herself on one of the bar chairs, vivid in the half-light. The long purple dress she wore should have warred with the burning auburn of her hair, but it didn't. Glints of gold flashed from her earlobes and wrists, and she had gold sandals on her feet.

Showstopping, Linley conceded grudgingly. And of course Poppy had figured out that Linley didn't like her. Damn her, too.

Jodi was pacing around the room like a caged animal.

Poppy went on: "Linley is great. She can be great and still not like me." Amusement deepened her voice. "Liking me is not a requirement for greatness."

"Oh, you know what I mean," said Jodi. "Anyway, it was the best party. Thanks, Poppy." Jodi turned to face the vivid figure at the bar.

Poppy finished her drink and stood up. She crossed the room to where Jodi stood by the stairs, her own short hair a halo of white gold. "Don't thank me," she said. "You belonged. That's all there is to it." With that, Poppy put one hand on each shoulder and leaned forward and kissed Jodi lightly on the lips, a feather touch of a kiss, once and then again.

Then she walked past her and went gracefully, unhurriedly, up the stairs. At the top she looked down at the still figure, standing now with one hand clutching the stair railing as if for support, and said, "Don't stay up too late, Jodi. Don't forget you have work tomorrow."

"I . . . know," whispered Jodi.

After Poppy's door had closed, Jodi stayed frozen for a long moment. Then she shook her head a little, like someone breaking the surface of a wave and flinging the water from their eyes. She went up the stairs behind Poppy in a quick rush, and Linley, listening intently, heard Jodi's door close.

Linley went back into the study to her uncle's big leather chair by the window, tapped out a cigarette, and lit it. She took a long, practiced drag and exhaled theatrically. She smoked for a long time, staring out at the night until the thin edge of dawn began to separate sea from sky.

She hated surprises. Surprises implied lack of control.

And she'd just been caught by surprise. No, Max's return had been the first surprise. That, now this.

Maybe that was why Max's exit had stuck with her. Another surprise.

In her way, she'd probably loved him. But Linley knew love didn't last.

The important thing was to be the one who said good-bye. Leave just a little before it was time to go. Leave behind the hint of unfinished business.

She'd planned a different ending with Max—her terms, her rules.

But Max had gotten there first.

She hadn't expected it and she'd never understood it.

Damn him.

Guys were so easy. You didn't even have to like them as long as they got the job done. And they would do anything as long as you promised them a blow job. Linley's mouth curled in the dark. *As if,* she thought. Guys never reciprocated, so why waste the time?

If they complained, she moved on. Simple. Satisfying.

Max. Jodi. Poppy.

Thoughts whirled in her brain.

At last she stubbed out a final cigarette and stood up. "Fuck it," she said.

She'd leave it all alone until the time was right. Jodi would come to her for advice. Max would return, and she'd finish what he'd started.

And then she'd see what happened with a little truth or dare.

Claire looked up from the kitchen counter at the view from the beach house without seeing the spectacular scenery. She looked back down at her coffee and the crossword puzzle from the *Times*. She'd never been big on crosswords until she'd started watching Joseph whip through them at the Stacked. She couldn't figure out how he did it. He wrote in ink and he never seemed to make a mistake. Good with words, he'd said. He hadn't been kidding.

She was still working on the one from the previous Sunday.

Damn Joseph. Not that she didn't like him. He'd turned out to be a decent boss, just as Dean had predicted. And aside from the other perks of the job, she'd met Finn, who . . .

"Hi."

"Hey! Jodi! You're up early."

Claire had barely seen Jodi or Linley for the past few days. Everyone seemed to be pinballing through the house as if they were all on their way to cram for a final in . . . what? Having fun? Having sex?

Were the two things the same, exactly?

". . . a job," Jodi was saying.

"A job," Claire repeated obediently. Rewind. Replay. Beep. "But you already have a job."

"I need another one, and the Vile Vickie says she can't give me any more shifts at Banger's." Jodi sounded tired. She looked tired.

"You look tired," Claire said. "How are you going to do another job? When do you plan on surfing? Or, more importantly, sleeping?"

"Surf first, sleep later. Gotta make the rent, right?" retorted Jodi automatically. She was fiddling with the spaceship/cappuccino maker on the counter. For a girl who could fix anything else in the house, Jodi wasn't very handy in the kitchen.

Not that Claire could motor around the kitchen any better. But then, she stuck with basic coffee making.

"Just don't blow us up," she said aloud. The rent, she thought, and had a moment's pang. She was still keeping the fact that Linley and she were not paying into the rent a secret. And it made her feel guilty.

Why couldn't Linley just tell people? And what did she need the money for, anyway?

"What we make after we pay the bills is ours," Linley had said. "We earned it."

But how had Linley earned it? By being her uncle's niece?

"The rent's not that much, Jodi," Claire said defensively.

Which was true. It wasn't like she and Linley were slumlords making a killing.

"Summer *and* winter. As in, I'm never going home again." Jodi gave something on the machine a thump. "Wait . . . wait . . . I've almost got it figured out here."

"In your dreams," said Poppy, coming through the doors from the deck.

Jodi and Claire both jumped. Claire said, "I didn't know you were out there."

"I went for an early walk on the beach," Poppy said. "It's going to be another luscious day."

Luscious, thought Claire. I guess that means the sun is shining and the surf is good.

Jodi stood motionless, one hand clutching a lever on the espresso maker.

Had she broken something? Claire wondered.

Poppy said, "Jodi, let me do that."

"It's all yours," said Jodi, moving quickly out of the way.

"I thought you preferred tea," said Poppy.

Poppy was right, Claire realized. She flashed on Jodi slam-dunking three different kinds of tea into the shopping cart that very first day.

"Serious caffeine needed," Jodi said. Going around the counter, she commandeered a bar stool. "Can you make me a double shot?"

With graceful efficiency, Poppy pulled a double shot and slid it across the counter. Taking it, Jodi stirred in what looked like a tablespoon of sugar before tossing back the whole thing as if she were doing a shooter. She made a face as she slammed down the espresso cup.

"It's not medicine, you know," observed Poppy.

"Whatever works," Jodi said. "Gotta go." She rummaged in the cupboard, and said unemotionally, "The next person who takes my Clif Bars without replacing them is dead meat," and in hyper speed she yanked the last one from a twelve-pack, crumpled the empty box in the recycling bin, and headed for the door. "Later," she said, and was gone.

Possibly, there was a whoosh of air as she left.

Poppy raised her eyebrows.

"Job search," Claire offered.

"Oh. Coffee?" asked Poppy, motioning toward the machine.

"Sure, if you're making," said Claire. "Cappuccino, if I have a choice. Chin in hand, she watched Poppy make two cappuccinos. She liked watching Poppy work. She did everything with quiet efficiency, a quality Claire admired.

At first she'd been nonplussed by Poppy's air of detachment and faint amusement, but now that she'd gotten used to it, Claire didn't mind. In a house of seven people, Poppy was the ideal roommate. She was low-key, self-sufficient, undemanding—and she cleaned up after herself.

"Jodi has a job at Banger's," said Poppy, sitting down across the table from Claire.

"She wants two," said Claire. "So she won't have to live at home next year."

"I left home when I was sixteen," said Poppy.

"Did you?" Claire couldn't imagine doing that.

My mother, she thought wryly, *would have killed me.* "Why?"

"Things happen," Poppy said with a shrug. She smiled, but for once she didn't look amused. "My family—my father, in particular—strongly encouraged me to leave. 'Get the hell out of my house' were his exact words."

"It . . . ah, must have been some fight," Claire said.

"He strongly objected to my lifestyle," Poppy told her. "Which I couldn't change. My father believed I could—like putting on a different dress. But it just didn't work that way."

"He didn't want you to be an artist?" Claire asked.

"Something like that." Poppy smiled, and this time it was genuine. "And I just had to be me."

She took a sip of coffee. "But it worked out. My mother brought him in line. She's my biggest fan, these days. And my dad, he's getting pretty cool in his cranky old age." She laughed. "They don't live too far from here. I see them two or three times a month now."

"I wish I was really good at something, believed in something like that—like your art," Claire surprised herself by saying. "But I'm not sure I have a talent for anything."

"It takes longer for some people than others. You'll figure it out. And I'd be willing to bet you won't make as many stupid choices as some of us have."

"Really?" Claire felt pleased.

"Yep," said Poppy. She stood up. "I have to go open the gallery."

"And where would the Stacked be without me?" Claire said. "It's a tough life."

"But a good one," Poppy said unexpectedly.

"Yes," said Claire. "Yes, it is." She grinned. "So far."

Nine

"There's no such word," Claire insisted.

"Stands to reason if it's in the puzzle, it's a word," Joseph said.

"But what does it mean?" she said.

"What the clue says," he said.

"'A state of excitement' is 'alt'?" Claire shook her head. "I've never heard of it."

"Doesn't mean it's not a word," said Joseph.

Coming up to where Joseph and Claire were bent over the puzzle, Jan cleared her throat. "I think this one is yours, Claire."

Claire glanced up to look at the customer who had just come in. "Oh!" she said, and felt her face flush. He wasn't hers, but she was working on it. She walked over, trying to look cool, and said, "Hi, Finn. Hi, Barrel."

She actually hadn't seen Finn in a couple of days. She was struggling to avoid being obvious, to not lurk around the house waiting for him. He might keep her in alt, but she wasn't going to show it.

Finn smiled, his eyes crinkling.

"Lunch? We still have some good stuff left," Claire said, motioning toward the specials board.

"No, thanks, not today. Barrel and I got comp'ed for lunch at the hotel," said Finn. "Another satisfied customer. I mean, patron. That's what the hotel calls its guests." He made a goofy face.

Instantly Claire was jealous. "Well, I'm glad you give satisfaction," she said, closing her notepad with a snap. *Good grief, listen to me,* she thought.

But Finn remained oblivious to nuance. "Yeah, me too. This little dude, he might be a good surfer, if he could just stay in California. Or someplace with some surf."

"A . . . little dude . . . took you to lunch?"

"Yeah, on his daddy's expense account. It was funny." Finn nodded. "Stepped right up and ordered, added in the tip, signed the check. I think his dad's some kind of CEO, or something. Come to think of it, maybe the little dude is headed more in that direction."

"Maybe he could do both," suggested Claire.

"Maybe," said Finn, considering. Then he shook his head. "No, you've got to do one or the other. Nothing halfway about the ride." He made a surfing motion with his hand.

"I guess not," said Claire.

"Anyway, I stopped by to see if you wanted a lift home," he said.

"Sure," said Claire.

"By way of a little break I know." He made the surfing motion again with his hand to elaborate. "It's not much. Nice little waves. Thought you'd like a lesson."

"Sure!" said Claire instantly, then tried to slow down. "But I don't have any . . . I don't have my bathing suit with me and I've never actually surfed before."

"No," he said. "But you can swim. I've seen you at the house. I bet you could borrow a shorty from Jodi or Linley, right?"

"Sure," Claire said, and thought, *a four-letter word meaning yes, overused by people named Claire.* "I mean, yes of course I can. Wait here while I close out."

Claire found the house completely empty and had a momentary vision of going back down to the van where Finn waited and saying, "Why don't you come up to my room?"

Then, before she could stop it, her imagination threw in the obscene gesture Linley liked to use— pushing the index finger of one hand back and forth in the circle made by the index finger and thumb of the other hand.

She snorted, knocked on Linley's door just in case, and went in. Linley's room was as usual almost obsessively neat. It didn't take Claire long to confirm as she passed the bedside table that Linley still preferred condoms in every color, relied on a variety of birth control, and was reading erotica in French (or pretending to).

Rifling through the closet and doing a quick check of the attached bathroom with Jacuzzi (Linley had naturally claimed the master suite as her own), she discovered that the wet suit was nowhere to be found. Claire did find a stash of old photographs in a drawer that she'd yanked open randomly, looking for what? Clues that said, "X marks the spot where the wet suit is hidden"?

The photographs were mostly familiar, or of familiar subjects: Linley at parties, looking smashed or laughing insanely; a few of very fashionably and formally dressed people against formal party backgrounds featuring the same couple, which Linley I.D.'d as Linley's metaphorically AWOL parents; a couple of Linley's school pictures—elementary school, from the looks of them—along with a much younger Linley and an older girl on what looked like the deck of a boat, a cousin, Claire guessed, from the resemblance; and a surprising number of Max, including one of just Max and Linley.

Wow, thought Claire. *Linley looks so . . . young.*

Then she remembered Finn, and surfing, and took her search to Jodi's room.

Jodi's room was messier and also wet suit free. There was nothing hanging in the shower. Turning, Claire thought of the tiny back porch of the house, what in New England would have been called a mudroom. Of course. That's where the wet gear was generally left to air out. She was about to go when she spotted the open plastic scrip bottle amid the jumble on Jodi's bathroom counter.

The bottle was old, the label faded into near-invisibility. Inside, Claire found a jewel-colored collection of pills. "Whoa," she said, in early Keanu Reeves. And then, *"Whoa."*

She knew a couple from casual acquaintance— bumps that got you through the all-nighter and into the exam with your faculties more or less intact. She'd seen several more around dorms and parties, the pills ranging from stupid-laughter-inducing and high-speed chatter to one at least that probably should require filing a flight plan before ingesting. A couple of others were unfamiliar, but given the crowd they were hanging with, they were probably speed too. And wedged into the bottom of the bottle was a neat little plastic bag of white dust.

"Wow, Jodi," said Claire aloud. "Who knew?" Then, feeling like Harriet the Spy, she put the bottle back carefully. Not her business, and what was she thinking, anyway?

Besides, Finn was waiting. Grabbing necessary gear, she raced back down the stairs and found both wet suits on the little porch. She took Linley's and, forgetting all about Jodi's pharmaceutical collection, tried to hurry back to the van without looking as if she could hardly wait to get there.

It wasn't much of a beach—a few families, gentle water.

Claire was grateful for that. She didn't feel quite so dumb, standing on a surfboard on the sand, balancing.

Actually, it probably wasn't possible to feel any dumber.

But Finn was a good teacher, calm and patient and willing to explain the reasons for his methods. So she surfed the sand for a long, long time until he was satisfied.

Then they went into the water. "Cold?" he said with his nice smile as he showed her how to get on the board and paddle out. "We're not going far."

"Not so cold," she said, and it was true. Her family's summer place on Cape Cod boasted much colder water in even the warmest months. People surfed, but it never occurred to her to try it. She was glad for the wet suit. For one thing, when she did an endo, she would not be leaving pieces of her bathing suit behind in the waves.

They didn't go out far, although it looked far enough to her. Finn showed her how to look for the right wave, how to paddle into it—at least in theory— and let her try to ride one.

She fell. And fell. And kept falling until at last Finn called it quits.

"You'd be extraordinary if you got any kind of ride at first," he said. "But it's great, isn't it?"

"Great," she agreed, and might have meant it. But great also included being there with Finn. She drifted closer to him. A nice, romantic kiss, one surfer to another, might be interesting. "Finn," she said. "It's been so amazing . . ." She leaned toward him.

And flipped the board.

"Whoa," said Finn, hauling her back up. "You want to keep your balance."

"Right," she said, hoisting herself ungracefully onto the board again. "Balance," she said.

"So let's take it in," he said, and began to paddle for shore.

She glumly followed.

Do I have no pheromones? she thought. *And if not, where can I get some?* Her mind flashed back to that bottle of little pills. Did they make pills for that? Besides the Viagra that old men seemed to need?

Barrel was waiting by the gear, barking in excitement as if they'd just come back from months at sea. The families had cleared off, and yes, it was another glorious sunset.

"Isn't there ever a bad sunset in California?" Claire asked crossly, toweling off and modestly putting on her own clothes beneath the towel.

Finn looked up from his joyful reunion with Barrel and said, "Yeah. Sometimes. Hawaii's got some sunsets that'd put this to shame. You ought to see it."

"Yeah?" She was still cross.

"Sunset Beach," he said. "Big surf. Perfect. It's . . ." His voice trailed off.

"Nirvana? Heaven?" *Get the edge out of your voice, girl.*

"All that and more. But Barrel and I can't make that scene—can we, boy? Hawaii's down on dogs from off island."

"They won't let Barrel in?"

"No. I mean, not without, like, *months* of quarantine. Barrel'd hate that—wouldn't you, boy?" Barrel appeared to agree that he would.

"So maybe for short visits. But it's expensive, Hawaii, any way you go. So Barrel and I, we'll settle for places where we're both welcome."

"It's great that you're so loyal. Not everybody would be, to a dog," said Claire.

"Hey, those that aren't just don't know any better," said Finn.

Claire scratched Barrel's ears, and he sighed in contentment.

"Barrel likes you," said Finn.

"That's good," said Claire. "Because I like Barrel." She paused, took a deep breath, and added, "And I like you, too."

Finn's eyes crinkled. He studied her for a minute. "That's good," he said at last. Then he leaned over and kissed her.

She didn't exactly throw herself at him, but she kissed him back.

It was the best kiss she'd ever had—or given. She didn't know how long it went on, but when she came up for air, she was breathing hard.

Finn was too. He looked down at her and said, "Wow," and she echoed, "Wow," and he looked up and down the beach and then grabbed a towel with one hand and her hand with the other and said, "Come on," and Claire went with him pretty sure she was about to find out about sex on the beach.

Ten

Dean knew.

Coming out onto the deck and into the dusk with Finn behind her, Claire could tell by the way he looked up from the grill, looked back down again.

"Claire, where have you been? We're having a party!" Linley called across the deck.

"I know," said Claire. "We passed Margaritaville on the way in." She was . . . automatically her mind started a list: thirsty, hungry, still a little stoned, her lips felt chapped, she was, well, a little sore, and oh yes, she wasn't a virgin anymore. Couldn't people tell? People besides Dean. But Dean hadn't known she was actually a virgin, had he? He just knew, or strongly suspected, that she and Finn had been doing the deed.

Dean raised an eyebrow. "Get a drink," he advised. "You look as if you could use one."

"I'll get it for you," said Linley, swooping up exuberantly. She disappeared in the direction of the blender noise and returned a minute later with Jodi. Both held drinks. Pressing a drink into Claire's hand, Linley looked up at Finn and smiled. "'Rita?" she asked. "It's strawberry. Very healthy. Strawberries are an aphrodisiac, you know."

"Actually, I think it's the chocolate they're usually dipped in," said Claire.

"Or the champagne you're supposed to drink with them," said Poppy from the shadows, where she was sitting on a rail with someone Claire recognized as An Artist.

"Champagne," said Jodi. "Like when my mom remarried?" She made a face.

"You just haven't had the right champagne," said Poppy.

Jodi turned, took an enormous swallow of her margarita, and said, "You think? Because this margarita is working just fine."

Poppy didn't answer. She turned back to the artist, a handsome woman with kind eyes and short, dark red hair named Pat, Claire now remembered, a woman whose daughter had been pointed out to Claire as a chef.

"Looks like we're all here," Claire said, and immediately felt stupid.

"One big happy," added Dean. He motioned to the grill. "Menu: dogs, burgers, veggie burgers, and organic chicken."

"I wish I'd known," Claire said. "I . . . we could have stopped and gotten something on the way."

"Don't worry. It just sort of happened." Dean smiled. It

wasn't a reassuring smile. Claire had the sensation of being watched—studied, almost. "Things do just sort of happen, don't they?"

Finn said, "I'm not particular. A 'rita would be great. But Barrel here prefers hamburgers. Pretty much fully loaded except for onions."

"Come sit with us, Claire." Linley patted the seat next to her. "Catch up with the party."

Claire glanced at Finn, but he was engrossed in menu negotiations with Dean on behalf of Barrel. Obediently, Claire went over to join Linley.

"This is Nicholas," said Linley, motioning to the guy on the other side of her. "He's a fan of Banger Slammers."

"More of the people who serve them," Nicholas said. He looked smooth and surfer preppy, as if he'd learned to do a lot of things well from expensive lessons. Claire had been in California long enough now to not be surprised at how ubiquitous the East Coast prep boys she'd grown up with really were.

Linley laughed. "Tell me about it," she said.

Jodi slid down on the other side of Claire. "If everybody's here, who's working at Banger's tonight?" asked Claire. *I'm not a virgin anymore and it doesn't even show,* she thought.

"Others who are not us," said Jodi solemnly. "Besides, I found another job today. At an after-hours sort of place. Booze and breakfast . . . Had to celebrate while I had the time. And how was your day?"

Claire felt herself blushing. But it was dark. So that was okay.

"Fine," she said. She was fine, wasn't she? She didn't know. She'd wanted it to happen, but then it had all seemed to happen so fast.

"Claire? Hello?" said Jodi.

"Oh," said Claire. She would *not* look at Finn. "I had a surf lesson. With Finn." Saying his name, she felt herself blush again. She had to stop doing that.

It had been very surprising. Had she done everything right?

"How'd it go?" Jodi asked. "Are you totally hooked?"

"On . . . on surfing? Yes! Well, not totally, but. . ."

"Not totally. Not yet. But give it a few more times. That's the way it is when you're a virgin."

"What?" Claire choked on her drink.

"A surf virgin," said Jodi. She raised her glass. "Here's to Claire, who's not a virgin anymore."

"Who's a virgin?" The word had caught Linley's attention. "Claire? Ha. She's just a . . ."

"Watch it," warned Claire, trying to keep it light.

"'Careful girl,' that's what I was going to say," Linley finished with mock primness.

"I bet you were. Jodi's talking about surfing. I had my first surf lesson today," Claire explained. She took a drink to steady her nerves.

"Ohhh. How did you like the feel of that nice big board

between your legs?" Linley was being impossible. But at least she didn't seem to notice anything different about Claire. She went on: "Jodi, on the other hand, is a switch-hitter, aren't you, Jodi?"

"What?" said Jodi sharply.

"You body board, too," said Linley, her gaze now fixed on Jodi.

Jodi stared back with narrowed eyes. Her spiked hair made her look like a fierce porcupine.

"I would've liked it better beneath my feet. I kept falling off," Claire answered. What was Linley up to? Sometimes she hated Linley. How could she be so, so insensitive?

Get a grip, she told herself. *Linley doesn't know.*

She felt different. She *was* different. Quickly, Claire said, "Good margaritas. Oh! Max is making them."

"He lives here, remember?" said Linley and turned immediately back to Ned. Or Nathan, Claire wondered. Nicholas? Whatever his name was—a generic Linley one-nighter. But then, he probably had the same goal in mind, Claire thought.

She allowed herself a quick Finn-scan. He was talking to Poppy now while Barrel remained on hopeful guard duty at the grill with Dean.

Claire suddenly realized she was hungry. No, ravenous. She jumped up. "Food?" she asked. "Anyone?"

"So not hungry," said Jodi. She'd stepped to the edge of the gathering as if putting a safe distance between herself and Linley. But she kept glancing over her shoulder as if something might be sneaking up on her. Although what could be sneaking up on Jodi from a party full of people, Claire couldn't begin to guess. She heard a shriek from the direction of the hot tub and saw one of Finn's surf buddies, the one called Curly Dave. He appeared to be making waves with two girls Claire vaguely recognized from Banger's.

Jodi almost jumped as Claire brushed past. Claire had a sudden urge to pat her shoulder and tell her it would be all right. She settled for a sympathetic smile and was surprised at the sudden, brilliant smile she got in return.

As Claire joined Dean, he expertly flipped a burger and said, "In a former life, I was a short-order cook."

"What are you now?" Claire couldn't resist asking.

"Many things to many people," he said.

"I can imagine," Claire said dryly. She took another big gulp of margarita. They were nice and strong . . . like Finn's bare back under her hands. Bare back? Wasn't that a brand name for a condom she'd seen courtesy of Linley? It wasn't the brand Finn used. . . . Interesting engineering, condoms and guys . . . *Stop that,* she told herself. *You're drunk.* And she was blushing again.

What had she done? Had she been stupid? But Finn was a good guy. She liked Finn. He liked her.

Or maybe he didn't, now. She'd done everything wrong, she was sure of it. It hadn't been at all what she'd expected. She wasn't sure she got it. Got the reason for the whole idea of doing it.

It couldn't have been what Finn expected either. He'd been

affectionate afterward, but maybe he was just being kind.

Oh god. And now she had to live in the same house with him for the rest of the summer. She was so dumb. Dumb, dumb, dumb. She felt like crying. To stop the feeling, she took another gulp.

"Can you?" Dean said.

"Can I what?" Claire had lost the thread of conversation. Lost virginity; now she was losing words.

"Imagine," Dean reminded her. "You're pretty quiet. And pretty thirsty."

Claire braced herself for some insinuating Dean remark. But after glancing at her, and then at Finn, Dean just said, "He seems nice."

"Poppy likes him," Claire said.

If she hoped to make Dean jealous, she missed her mark. Dean laughed. "Poppy likes most people," he said.

"Don't worry. Finn is safe," Dean added.

"It doesn't matter," Claire said, completely off-balance now. The party, unreal to begin with, was spinning deeper and deeper into the surreal zone for Claire. Another drink would help, she decided.

"I'm going for a refill. Want?" she asked Dean.

"Sure," he said. "I'll have your order ready when you get back. What *was* your order, by the way?"

"Anything," she said.

"I'll keep it in mind," he said.

"You do that," she shot back, recklessly. Dean didn't scare her anymore. Hah!

When she returned, Dean produced a plate, complete with chips, burger, and bun. "I'll watch your drink while you decorate that," he told her, deftly snagging her drink as well as his own.

Finn had settled down next to Poppy and was deep in conversation, making a familiar surfing motion with his hand. Claire heard Jodi's laugh from the shadows and thought it wasn't a happy sound. When Linley joined in, it did not improve the cheer factor.

She wanted to go over to Finn and lean into him and have him smile down at her and put his arm around her. And if she did do that, he probably would—leaving one hand free to make that now familiar surfing motion as he talked intently to Poppy and Pat.

But, perversely, she didn't want anyone to notice if she did. She concentrated on making her burger just right.

Was he her boyfriend now? Were they dating? All very gray area questions. A list of rules would be nice, Claire thought.

The feeling of wanting to cry came back more strongly. She wished she had someone she could talk to, but who? *I'll eat something,* Claire thought. *I'll feel better then.*

Come to think of it, she'd rushed out of the Stacked without the end-of-shift meal Joseph fed everyone.

No wonder she felt strange. That, and, oh yes, sex on the beach.

But after two bites of burger, she wasn't hungry anymore. Just thirsty. Very, very thirsty.

She looked up from the rim of her glass and met Dean's eyes. Quickly, she bent and gave Barrel the rest of her meal. When she straightened up, Dean said, "You know, you shouldn't just give it away."

Claire gulped. "Shouldn't give it away why? Unless I give it to you?"

He looked taken aback for a nanosecond. Good. She pushed on. "Who are you, anyway, Dean? What kind of power trip are you on?"

"Knowledge," he said. "As in 'knowledge is power.'"

"Politician or blackmailer or both?" she shot back.

He grinned. "You know almost as much— although not quite—as I do about what's going on at our dear little home sweet summer home. So much has happened in such a short time! What has it been, four weeks, more or less? And if I was a blackmailer, what could I get for being quiet that I couldn't get, anyway?"

Her head was spinning. She looked down to find her glass was empty once again.

She looked over at Finn. Help, she wanted to say.

Then she thought, *If I hadn't just had sex with him, would I want his help?*

No. Or at least, I wouldn't expect it.

Jodi flitted by. "New batch coming up. I'm thinking peach."

Poppy held out her glass as Jodi passed, but Jodi kept going.

"Guess she's all excited about the new thing in her life," Dean said, raising his voice slightly, looking across at Poppy.

Poppy gave him a level look and stood up. Finn turned all his attention to Pat.

"Me, too. I'll have 'nother drink," said Claire.

Dean rapped her wrist with the grill spatula.

"Hey, watch it!" Claire said.

"Friends don't let friends . . . ," he remarked. "Slurp tonight, urp tomorrow, to put it crudely. It's not your style."

"My style. *My* style. What do you know about my style? What does anybody know about my style?" Claire said. Her nose felt numb. She reached up to check it out and almost jabbed herself in the eye.

"Too late," remarked Dean to no one in particular. He flipped the last burger onto a plate, covered it with another plate, and shut the grill lid. "The dining room is now closed."

Claire wasn't sure afterward, but she thought she heard him add as she charged into the house for another drink, "And the show is about to begin."

Eleven

She woke up slumped sideways in the dark, with her face against something soft. She was thirsty and didn't feel so good. Possibly she was dying.

She squinted. Her room? She was pretty sure it was. Had she slid out of bed, or just not made it up into it?

She closed her eyes again. It didn't help. Even in the dark she could tell that someone was either rolling her over and over or somehow doing the same thing to the room.

Claire. Good. She could remember her name. She didn't feel so sick. And also who was president of the United States. She made a face in the dark and suddenly felt sicker.

I will drink two glasses of water and take two aspirins, she thought, with a dim recollection of what Linley did when she feared hangover retribution.

Step one: Stand up. This took some effort, and Claire felt quite pleased when she succeeded. Maintaining an upright position, however, was much harder. Best to walk only by holding on to the wall . . . yes, that worked. She was doing excellently. Hah.

Claire groped her way into the hall, lit by light from the floor below. What the hell time was it? She could still hear the party going on somewhere. Feeling petulant and left out, she tottered to the top of the landing. A wave of sound from the hot tub area rolled up the stairs.

She made her way back to the bathroom and fumbled in. Putting together water and aspirin took great concentration and required several refills of one of the little paper cups from the cup dispenser.

Claire smiled at the cup dispenser affectionately. She'd added that. Executive decision of the house manager, and see how it had paid off? She was very smart.

She drank several more little paper cups of water.

In the hall she swayed to a stop. Finn. Ah, yes. She was experienced now, and handling it very well. She would not, for example, go knock on the door of his room. She was dignified. Let him come to her. Hah.

Maybe he was down in the hot tub.

Claire heard a shriek and decided to risk the stairs. She edged down, clutching the rail, and found herself in a room full of empty bottles and glasses. Someone she thought was Maryann, wearing an old Rolling Stones T, was passed out in a chair. Someone else was passed out on the sofa. Closer inspection revealed that the sofa surfer was Dean.

Odd. She didn't remember him drinking. She tiptoed past and peered out at the hot tub. Linley and Nicholas-Ned-Nathan were in the hot tub, having a water fight. They dashed sheets of water at each other and shouted and shrieked. Clearly, they had completely abandoned the concept of clothes.

Claire blinked. Then accidentally kicked over a beer bottle that clattered around on the tile floor. Then she said the first thing that came to mind. "Linley! All those stories you told me were true!"

The two of them turned. Linley burst out laughing. "Claire! Come on in. The water is fine!"

"It sure is," Nicholas-Ned-Nathan said.

Claire gave her head one quick shake and spun to stagger back into the house. She amost crashed into the bar as she headed back toward the stairs. She paused, gripping the counter's edge.

Dean hadn't moved at all. Claire was seized by a sudden suspicion that he wasn't even asleep. She reeled over and pressed her hands into the sofa back and stared down at him.

"Wake up," she said.

He didn't answer. She thought of pouring water on him. It would have been an interesting experiment. But if he really was asleep, it would also be rude.

She, Claire, was not a rude person.

Politely, she turned away. She began to make her way back up the stairs.

A door opened. Poppy stepped out into the hall wrapped in a gold silk robe, backlit by the light in her room.

At the same moment, Jodi came out of her room, pulling a towel around her. It was Jodi's own towel, Claire noted. It had the letter J stitched on it.

"Claire?" she said.

"I am," Claire agreed politely.

"You okay?"

"Oh, yes, thank you," Claire said. "And you? Did you have a nice bath?" How nice and clearly she seemed to be speaking. She hardly sounded drunk at all, though she was sure she was.

"Bath?" Jodi looked down at the towel, then said, "Oh. Well. I was in the hot tub and decided I needed to come upstairs for . . . for a minute."

"You're going back down?"

"Sure," said Jodi. "You should come too."

"No!" Claire said. Then, because she didn't want to be rude, she added, "Nothing personal, Jodi." She moved quickly toward her door. Or at least attempted to move quickly. The attempt made her insides swoop, and she thought, *If I don't lie down, I'm going to puke.*

"What about you, Poppy?" she heard Jodi say. "Hot tub?"

Claire opened her door and shut it firmly and reeled to her bed, fearing she would never sleep again.

She went out like a light.

Outside, the shrieks from the hot tub ceased abruptly.

• • •

Jodi stood in the hall staring defiantly at Poppy. Her pill-bottle courage wavered, and in spite of herself, her hands found the towel edges and tightened the towel. Poppy held her own gold robe loosely together with one hand. A long bare leg showed through the slit. Jodi could see the familiar outline of Poppy's nipples beneath the silk. She knew that outline by heart, she realized, and raised her eyes with difficulty to meet Poppy's.

Poppy was regarding her steadily.

Licking her suddenly dry lips, Jodi said, "Why don't you come join us?" She motioned toward the stairs and then grabbed the towel as it slipped.

With deliberate grace, Poppy walked toward Jodi. Jodi took a step back, then stopped and raised her chin.

Poppy stopped very, very close to Jodi. "I have a better idea," she said softly. "Why don't you come join me?"

Linley watched him dress in the early morning light. She was looking her tousled best, she knew, but she didn't feel much like capitalizing on it. She didn't feel much like talking, either. She was glad he was going.

"Too bad your friend bailed on us. We could have had even more fun." He smiled.

She returned the smile. "That's Jodi for you. One big old chicken." She yawned. "Still, it wasn't *too* bad."

"No," he agreed. "Not at all, ma'am."

She rolled over and pulled up the covers. "It was fun. Thanks."

He hesitated, and then said, "It was. See you?"

"See you," she agreed. Maybe she would.

When he'd left, she rolled back over and stared out the window at one side of the room. It was open, and she could hear the waves and smell the clean smell of the ocean pushing through the room.

She yawned again and snuggled under the sheet. She'd had some fine nights in this house that last summer. She'd awakened more than once in Max's arms, she remembered sleepily. Those had been the best mornings—maybe the best mornings of her life, even knowing that they couldn't last.

Maybe that had made them sweeter still.

Not in this room, of course. In the room she'd given Claire. Falling back into sleep, Linley thought dreamily and a little sadly, *I hope my old room brings Claire luck.*

Something was tickling her nose. Claire opened her eyes and gasped. She instinctively yanked at the covers. "Finn! What are you doing in my room?" Then she winced at how loud her voice sounded.

"Sorry. I knocked, but no answer," he said, and smiled, his brown eyes sympathetic. "Rough night for you. Thought you might like some coffee." Claire saw then that Finn was holding a tray—an actual tray with a mug of coffee and the sugar bowl and a milk carton on it. He set it on the table beside her bed and said, "I even remembered a spoon and a napkin."

She sat up, amazed that she was still alive. "Thank you," she said as he handed her the cup.

"Careful. It's hot," he warned. "Milk? And sugar?"

She watched in a daze as he doctored her coffee. "Thank you," she said again, and blurted out, "No one's ever done this for me before."

"Rude and unlucky dudes," Finn pronounced. "Aren't they, Barrel?" And she realized that, of course, Barrel was there, too.

As Claire drank her coffee, Finn leaned across the foot of the bed as if he belonged. Barrel jumped up, too. Without thinking, Claire reached out and smoothed back a strand of Finn's sunstreaked hair. Then she yanked her hand back, blushing.

But Finn caught her hand and patted it, almost the way he patted Barrel.

Claire felt shy and self-conscious and hung over and confused. But she liked it, too. If felt cozy, if not entirely comfortable. Barrel inched up the bed and put his nose on her hip.

"Did I . . . was I bad last night?" she asked at last.

"I think you just drank too much on an empty stomach. Happens." He released her hand and leaned over to give her a quick kiss. "When you finish your coffee, gear up and we'll go look for a break. Best hangover cure I know."

Full-body immersion in cold water—she wasn't sure she was

ready for it. She couldn't tell Finn that, of course. "I have to work," she said instead.

"Me, too. It's way early enough. Surf first, work later, be happy." He patted her on the shoulder and loped out of the room. Barrel scrambled off the bed to follow.

She stared after him, hands still cradling the cup. *Well,* she thought. *Domestic bliss.*

Jodi woke suddenly and completely from the best and worst night of her life. She turned her head and saw the long spray of red hair fanned out on the pillow next to her.

What had she done? Couldn't she do anything right? She had probably ruined another good friendship forever. . . .

No, wait, she hadn't ruined her friendship with Linley. Because Linley didn't know what she had done . . . what a miserable, sneaky, disloyal friend she'd been. No way Linley could know.

And Linley wasn't going to know about this, either.

Sliding hastily and silently out of bed, Jodi groped for something to put on. Then she remembered she'd been wearing only her towel, the one with the big red J on it.

She groaned inwardly, grabbed the towel, and wrapped it into place. As she opened the door, she thought she heard Poppy move in the bed behind her. Without looking back, Jodi darted into the hall.

"Jodi, hi! You're up early, too." Claire smiled at Jodi—beamed, actually. "Good. May I borrow your shorty?"

"Sure . . . You're going to the beach?" Jodi managed to ask.

"Surfing!" Claire sang. "Isn't it a great day?"

How could she be so cheerful—wasn't she totally hungover? The last time Jodi had seen Claire, Claire had been knee-walking smashed.

No, not the last time. The last time she'd seen Claire was in the hall when Claire had run into her own room, leaving Jodi and Poppy to . . .

No. She wouldn't think about it now. "May the surf be with you," Jodi croaked, grateful that Claire hadn't noticed that this is exactly how she had seen her the night before—in the same hall wearing the same towel. As Claire let out a peal of laughter, Jodi made it to the safety of her own room.

Only later did Claire realize that it looked as if Jodi had been coming not out of her own room but Poppy's and in what looked like the same towel as she'd been wearing the night before.

But Claire didn't want to think about that whole hot tub scene, and anyway, she'd probably been mistaken.

The beach Finn chose for the morning lesson was closer to everything, but it was early enough that there wasn't too much of a scene. With Claire in tow, Finn approached two people standing in the sand surveying the water.

"Sloppy," one of them said.

"Lot of chop," agreed another, and then, "Hey Barrel, hey Finn."

"Hey," said Finn. "Rita, Axel, this is Claire."

They were a startlingly similar pair, except for the gender difference. Fuzzy, sun-bleached short hair twigged into two tight tails, one behind each ear, dark blue Excel wet suits, and the same patient stance in the sand. They were even much the same height. Different boards, though, Claire noted.

Rita gave Claire a nod, but she wasn't really interested. Axel smiled and said, "Hey. Not much to work with today. The wind keeps shifting offshore. We're gonna go up the beach and look for a better break. Want to come?"

Finn said, "Thanks, brah, but we're not doing much of a session, so we'll stick. Work."

"Too bad," said Rita sympathetically. "No patrons for me until this afternoon."

"Dude, later," said Axel and the two headed back to the parking area.

"She works with you? Rita?"

"Axel, too, except he's one hotel over."

"Are Rita and Axel . . ."

"Twins," said Finn. "Cool, huh?"

I'm not jealous of Rita, Claire thought, and decided to concentrate on the lesson.

She actually got up once. Not for long, only a couple of seconds—just long enough to feel the energy coming up from the water through the board and into the soles of her feet.

"That was *awesome*," she gasped, breaking the surface and

in that moment falling in love with more than Finn. She also gained a whole new respect for the surfer vocabulary—in its place, she assured herself.

This time, when she was back on deck, Finn leaned over and hugged her. "Excellent," he said.

After the lesson as the three of them made their way back to the van, Claire could still feel the tingle of energy. In fact, between Finn and the ocean, she was on all-over tingle. *Luscious,* she thought.

"You can change in the van, if you want," Finn said.

"Thanks," Claire said, relieved. Having sex with Finn was one thing, but she wasn't ready to go full-body naked with him while she struggled into her work clothes—even if the parking lot was empty.

He grinned. "Me, I'm already pretty much rigged for my day. He unzipped the top of the shorty and pulled it down and went around to give Barrel a bowl of water.

At the Stacked, Claire said, "I hope I didn't, you know, mess up your surfing for today."

"Oh, no," said Finn cheerfully. "I'll catch some waves this afternoon on the way home from work."

He didn't ask her to join him. On the other hand, he'd called the house "home." He leaned over to kiss her, a nice slow burn of a kiss and, pulling back, grinned happily and said, "See you later, Mermaid Claire."

Mermaid Claire, she thought. Silly . . . but she liked it.

• • •

Max was thinking about his life. It was pretty much what he'd been doing for the last three years except when he was working on not thinking about his life.

You reached a point when you had to move on. But somehow he couldn't. So here he was, back where he'd staπrted from. This time, however, he had his own room down the hall and someone new was up in that old room where he and Linley had spent so much time getting it right.

They'd had some very good nights in that room.

Not nights like the one before, he thought, and he knew that in some ways he had moved on, had left that whole party hearty scene behind. There were, after all, bodily limitations to how messed up you could get, and no matter what you mixed or dared, morning always came.

Max laughed at himself and shook his head. *Keep going,* he told himself, *and you're going to sound like your father.*

Still, he'd hated that whole scene the previous night. Because the people acting out the little anti-morality play were people he liked. Friends. Old friends. Lovers.

Twelve

The battered Subaru almost took Claire out as she was Blading home from work that day. Staggering and clutching a street sign, she took a few to register that the assault vehicle was Jodi's and that Linley was leaning out the passenger window.

"Good, we found you," Linley said, oblivious to the fact that she and Jodi had almost turned Claire into roadkill.

"Yeah, but you missed me," Claire retorted. She released her death grip on the street sign and added, "Nyah, nyah, nyah."

"And here I thought all that sex, ah, I mean surfing, would mellow you," Linley said. She grinned wickedly.

Claire felt her cheeks turn red. How did Linley know? Did Linley know?

Pleased, Linley said, "Anyway, Jodi and I feel that now that you've started surfing, it's time for another important event in your life."

Claire skated over to the car. "Thanks, but I'm not into

sharing hot tubs." She was pleased at how calm she sounded in spite of her stupid blush.

"Jodi's not either," Linley said unexpectedly. "She bailed on me too."

"Another time," said Jodi in a slightly strangled voice, and Claire thought, *Hah. I'm not so uptight after all.*

Rolling her eyes, Linley went on. "Anyway, this doesn't involve water sports of any kind."

"What does it involve, exactly?" asked Claire.

"No trust," said Jodi. "That's your problem."

"Strong survival instincts, you mean."

Jodi drummed the steering wheel with all ten of her fingers. "Come on, trust us, you'll love it."

Claire gave up and got into the back of the Subaru. She'd managed to avoid what she'd secretly dubbed Jodi's Taxi of Death all summer, but at least now she would not die a virgin.

"So did you have fun last night?" Claire had decided on attack as the best defense.

"Tons," said Linley. "Jodi *so* wishes she hadn't gone to her room and passed out—don't you, Jodi?"

The car speeded up suddenly and whipped around a corner, and Claire was pretty sure she felt two wheels leave the ground. "Slow down!" she shrieked. She focused on taking off her skates to avoid looking out the window.

Jodi said, "The speed limit is for thousand-year-old people in Buicks. Gives them a sense of security, y'know? Plus, they get to wave their tiny little fists at us as we go by, and talk about how awful we are. So really we're providing exercise *and* conversation, too."

"And how do you think they get to be a thousand?" snapped Claire.

"Who wants to be a thousand?" Jodi shot back.

"Who wants to be old?" Linley said at the same time.

"Drive a thousand, don't be a thousand," Jodi sang, and somehow managed to go faster still.

Fortunately, the trip wasn't a long one. Jodi swerved into a turn lane, actually put on her signal, then accelerated into the sort of shopping strip that had never seen better times.

Deciding to get out of the car first and ask questions later, Claire jumped for safety, taking her skates with her in case she needed to make a quick escape in the near future. She surveyed the shops. "We're here why, exactly?" she asked.

Linley laughed exuberantly. "Okay," she said. "Take your choice: bikini wax, tattoo, or piercing."

Sure enough, one place offered bikini waxes and manicures, which sort of boggled Claire's mind, and another tiny storefront promised "Big, Bold, Beautiful Tattoos" and "Practically Painless Piercings."

"What? No! No way. I am so *not* that kind of girl."

"Come on. It'll be fun. A nice Brazilian wax," Linley coaxed.

Jodi gave a snort of laughter. "Nice? *Nice?*"

"Have you ever had one?" Claire asked. As Linley's roommate for a year, she knew the answer.

"Well, no," Linley admitted. "But I will if you will."

Linley, Jodi, and Claire looked at each other. Jodi sort of danced in place, her eyes darting back and forth between the shops, more like a dandelion on acid—and speed—than ever. Linley stood, one hand on her hip, looking like a gunslinger in California girl drag, her lips curled in her familiar *shoot first, ask questions later* smile, her gold hair falling in its perfect cut across one cheek.

Claire did not trust that smile. She smoothed her now-frazzled waitress French braid and silently shook her head.

"I don't know," said Jodi at last. "Hot wax all over"—she made a gesture—"and then everything ripped out at once . . ."

"No," said Claire, regaining her voice. "No, no, and hell no. Also, no."

With a sigh of long-suffering, Linley said, "Well, that leaves tattoos, or piercings. And at the moment, I personally don't want to get anything else pierced."

"What? No nipple rings?" Jodi feigned shock.

"Claire could get a navel ring, though. It'd look good on her now that's she's got a tan," Linley said.

Claire cut in. "I appreciate the thought and I'll think about a piercing. Or even a tattoo. But not today."

"Coward," said Linley.

Since this was true, Claire saw no point in arguing. She decided on diversionary tactics. "I'm willing to shop, though. In fact, I *need* to shop."

"Shopping is good," said Jodi. "We like shopping."

"And since I can't keep borrowing your shorties, I think it's time I got one of my own."

"It's a plan. I like it. Good plan," said Jodi, staccato style. "Let's do it, let's get to it."

Losing the gunslinger smile, Linley said, "Well, okay. Tattoos later, wet suits now."

Much, much later, thought Claire with an inward sigh of relief.

"Now this is shopping," declared Linley. She was draping surf items and anything else that caught her fancy across Claire's arms with reckless abandon.

The shop was the sort to break a bank account and a surfer's heart—or at least a surfer dilettante's, Claire thought. Racks of gear as far as the eye could see, from skins to surf socks to surfboards.

But Claire already knew that most surfers didn't buy their boards off the rack—or the wall. They had them shaped to specifications, and every surfer had an opinion about the best shape and an idea on who was the best shaper.

She wasn't looking for a surfboard, however. At the moment, she was going for fashion. If she was going to spend the rest of the summer falling off a surfboard, she wanted to look good while she did it.

Funny how she'd never thought much about things like that before.

"Look at this. I love this color blue," said Linley. She held up a skin, the lightweight, quick-drying surfer's version of a tight T-shirt. It protected surfers from board rash in warmer water.

Jodi said cynically, "Because it matches your eyes."

"You're going to need at least one skin before the summer is over," said Linley.

"Okay." Claire was examining wet suits. They looked so—tiny. Snug. Impossible. Yet she knew that she could fit into one because she'd been wearing Jodi's and Linley's.

"I like this one," Claire held up a shorty, a 2.1-mil, one-piece wet suit with short sleeves and legs that stopped at the knees. It had a short zipper with a long zipper pull-cord on the back.

"That company makes designs especially for women. They look great," Jodi said. "But I like men's gear when I can wear it. I think they're made stronger."

"Wouldn't surprise me—they probably are," Claire agreed. "But I'm trying this on, anyway."

Dozens of suits and skins later, Claire piled a dark ocean-green shorty, two skins in what Linley disdainfully called conservative colors, and a pair of sunglasses on the counter, and prepared for credit card meltdown.

"Sex wax," said Linley and plopped a final item on the pile.

"What?" Claire felt her face go red.

Big-eyed innocence, Linley said, "For Finn. I'm sure he needs it."

"Needs it? Needs"—involuntarily, Claire's voice dropped—"sex wax?" Good grief, the things your mother never told you—not that her mother had ever told her anything.

"You can never put too many coats on your ride," the girl at the checkout assured Claire solemnly. Her name tag said "Carrie."

Claire looked wildly from Linley to Jodi to the clerk. Did they all know that she and Finn had been up in the dunes together?

Then Jodi started laughing madly. "Your board. Your surfboard. It protects it and you."

"Surfboard wax," said Claire.

"Will that be all?" asked the Carrie-the-clerk, beginning to ring up the purchases.

"Yes," said Claire.

"And you want the sex wax?" She indicated the little container on top.

"Yes," said Claire.

Linley leaned over and patted Claire's arm and whispered loudly, "Finn will be *so* pleased."

"Yes," said Claire, and gave Linley and Jodi a big smile.

They cleared the parking lot and Jodi slammed on some music. Shouting above it, she said, "Let's give your gear a workout, Claire."

"You mean, now?"

"Sure. Surf report!"

Linley flipped open her phone and punched in digits.

Claire said, "Surf? But—"

"Wait! We need boards! We need our stuff!" Jodi burst out laughing, and the car careened wildly as she banked off a driveway to turn around.

"That's my baby," said Jodi, patting the car's dash. She cranked the music, and Linley laughed.

"Don't you have to work tonight, both of you?" asked Claire.

"All night," said Jodi cheerfully, but I don't start until eight."

"I'm just eight-to-two tonight," said Linley.

"Remember sleep? Naps?" Claire tried again.

"Naps—babies; sleep—when I'm dead," Jodi declared, and accelerated as if to emphasize her point.

They were in and out of the beach house in record speed. Claire yearned to go knock on Finn's door and see if he was there, even though she was pretty sure he wasn't. But how uncool was that? She compromised by calling as loudly as she could, "Hey, Linley, what beach did you say we were going to surf at this afternoon?"

If Finn was there and that didn't wake him or buy him a clue, then Claire could do nothing more.

She put on her bathing suit and paused to admire herself in her new short suit. Did it look too new? Did she look too newbie?

Well, she'd practice. Surprise Finn.

A short time later, she surprised herself by hooking an actual ride. Okay, it was on a baby wave, what Linley called a beach-break, and her exit from the board was just this side of a face plant, but she couldn't complain.

After that, she gently floated for a while, savoring her victory. Through half-closed eyes she stared at the shining, irregular crescent of beach, felt the warm sun through her new wet suit. Time seemed to slow down.

But this was not the slow march of time while she watched a clock in a bank. This was time spread out around her like the ocean. Her friends drifted and surfed and laughed and talked. *She had friends.*

Farther along this same beach, Finn was probably teaching someone to surf while Barrel waited patiently in a nearby patch of shade. *She had a boyfriend.*

High overhead, a bird wheeled and Claire felt as free as that bird.

I could live like this, Claire thought. *I could die right now and I'd die happy.*

And ten yards away, a triangular fin broke the water.

Thirteen

Claire jerked her feet up instinctively and almost tipped her board. She grabbed hold and somehow righted herself and croaked, “Shark.”

The fin slid down leaving no mark in the water. Fin, and then no fin. Shark, and then no shark.

Her voice had come out the whisper of a whisper, lost in the sound of water and wind.

Claire tried again. “Linley. Jodi.”

Louder. Good. Much louder. But not a scream of panic.

Not yet.

Linley glanced over and straightened. “Claire. Are you okay?”

Raising a shaking hand, Claire pointed. “P-porpoise?” she said hopefully, although she knew better. As if Claire had conjured it, the fin appeared again. It was farther away this time, but not nearly far enough. Was that just the tip of it? Was that an enormous shadow she saw below it, the hulk of the beast itself?

In a deadly quiet voice, Linley said, "Paddle slowly toward shore. Don't splash or thrash, do you hear me?"

Claire nodded.

"And whatever you do, don't fall off your board."

As if I needed anyone to tell me that, Claire thought.

They began to move. Time slowed even more. No, time stood still.

From some far distant place, Claire heard Linley's calm, conversational voice. "Dusk and dawn is when they usually come out the most. That's why it's good never to surf alone, especially early morning or at sunset."

"Yeah, and it's probably not a white, or anything like that." Jodi's voice was quick and breathless with excitement. "Those are the ones that use surfboards for toothpicks."

"Better the board than me," Claire heard herself say. Her voice sounded far away. Would they never reach the shore? She was afraid to look back, afraid of tipping, afraid of what she'd see. She dug into the water with her hands, but not too deeply. Every minute she expected to feel the thump of shark against board, for her to be turned over into a shark soup. Would it hurt? Would she scream?

". . . spearfishing," Linley was saying. "You want to avoid that, believe me. That's why you want to paddle without thrashing. Thrashing is shark language for injured fish. Or, in a single word, dinner."

As if it were a fishing line reeling her toward shore, Linley's calm voice pulled Claire along.

"Don't look back," Jodi advised in a staccato whisper, as if the shark might attack at the sound of her voice. "Just wastes time."

No time to waste, that was for sure. Claire paddled in long, slow, shallow strokes.

Something brushed her hand, and she jerked it up with a strangled cry. The board rocked.

"Claire!" Lindsey's voice, taut, low.

Looking down, Claire saw not a bloody stump but a strand of seaweed. "Seaweed," she croaked. "Sorry."

"Just keep paddling, nice and easy," Linley said. "We'll be there soon, no worries. I remember one time, I was out on this break . . ."

Her voice rippled along, and Claire concentrated not on the words but on the calm tone of them, concentrated, too, on paddling through the bright sun that suddenly reminded Claire of the heat lamps above the food at the restaurant. She was the food, the ocean was the plate, and . . .

And then they'd reached the froth of water's edge, and Linley and Jodi had flicked off their quick releases and stood up to grab their boards. With single-minded efficiency, Linley reached over and flicked Claire free and somehow Claire didn't run out of the water, but walked as calmly as if she'd done this every day of her life, walked out of the ocean and away from a shark.

Then Claire saw that some of the other surfers who had been nearby had come in, too, although she hadn't even noticed them paddling toward shore. No one had screamed, no one had shouted. Everyone had just removed board and body from the water, and now those boards and bodies stood in a rough line in the sand, facing the water. Farther down the beach, other surfers still floated and rode.

"What about them?" Claire said.

"Someone'll pass the word," Linley said. Now that they were out of the water, her voice had gotten thinner. She headed for their spot on the beach without looking back. When she reached it, Linley didn't shinny out of her wet suit this time. She sat down and pulled a towel over her hair to rough it dry.

Jodi dove for the cooler, and Claire sank bonelessly onto the blanket next to Linley.

"It was a shark," she said, just to be sure. Her voice didn't sound like her own.

"Yep," said Jodi, drinking off half the hard lemonade she'd pulled out. "After all, we're swimming where they eat. It's only natural." Her words were casual, but her voice sounded funny, too.

"Attacks happen, but not that often," Linley said. She dropped the towel and leaned back and turned her face to the sun. She was, Claire thought, a little pale.

"Didn't it . . . weren't you scared?" Claire asked. She could still feel her heart trying to escape from her chest. She pulled out a hard iced tea and practically drained it.

"Yes," said Linley.

"You didn't sound scared," Claire said.

"We've been here before," Jodi said. "Water, surfboard, shark."

"If you hadn't been so calm, I don't know what I would have done," Claire said. "You might have saved my life, maybe."

"Nah," said Linley, looking faintly embarrassed. "You stayed calm. You didn't panic. Panic is what'll get you killed."

"Hey, it was totally panic-worthy," Jodi said. "Big. Huge!"

"Big enough," said Linley. "Don't freak, Claire. I mean, you didn't freak in the water. Don't do it now."

She could have been talking to herself as much as to Claire.

Claire nodded and realized somewhere in the back of her mind that Linley feared losing control maybe more than she feared a shark.

She herself was no longer scared. Just . . . shaken. "It's so weird," she said aloud. "I had just been thinking how cool it all was, how if I'd died right that moment, I'd die happy and—"

"The shark of tempted fate came swimming along," said Linley almost harshly. "First rule of happiness: Don't kiss it hello, because it'll kiss you good-bye."

Frowning, Claire stared at Linley, who went on, her face almost angry. "It'll die right in front of your eyes and there's nothing you can do about it."

Was she talking about Max? It seemed extreme, even for a broken heart.

"Better chance of getting struck by lightning than being shark chum," said Jodi, who was apparently bobbing along in her head, pursuing her own thoughts. She'd toweled her hair into the usual spiky points, and her eyes glowed with excitement. They seemed huge in her pointed face, and Claire thought she looked thinner, if possible. "Hey, better chance of buying it out on the freeway than dying on your surfboard. . . ."

"When you're driving," Claire said, before she thought.

Jodi straightened at that. "What?"

"You're an insane driver," said Claire. Her near-shark experience had unhinged her inhibitions, unleashed her tongue.

"I am not," Jodi said indignantly. "I've never even had a single teeny-tiny accident. Not one. Never. *Nada.* Zero."

"Well, that's good, because for you, it's only going to take one," Claire retorted recklessly. "You and whoever you're driving won't live for the second one." She finished her drink of whatever it was. And burped.

Linley stared. "Claire? You just burped."

"Get used to it," said Claire.

"I'm not a bad driver," said Jodi, sticking to her subject. She began to rummage for another beer. "God, I am so thirsty."

Leaning forward, Claire put her hand on Jodi's shoulder. "Insane. The word I used was insane."

Glaring at Claire, Jodi wrenched another bottle from the cooler and drank.

Claire refused to look away.

"Assertive, Claire, very assertive," murmured Linley.

Suddenly Jodi started to laugh. "Buy the girl a wet suit and she's all that," she said.

"Hey, I swim with the sharks," Claire shot back.

And then they were all laughing helplessly.

So she blamed it on the shark.

That was how she ended up a few nights later working the midnight-to-four a.m. shift at the no-name, marginally legal after-hours club where Jodi had her second job. She and Jodi had somehow bonded. Jodi seemed almost to seek Claire out, almost as if she didn't want to be alone. And she'd gone from Monosyllable Me to Motormouth. She talked. She talked to Claire while Claire did laundry, made grocery lists, sat in the sun. She talked so much that Claire began to wonder what it was she wasn't talking about. . . .

Jodi talked to other people in the house, too, but somehow, Claire had become the designated listener. It was during one of these conversational rambles, watching Claire make a list of things that she needed to get done that day, that Jodi came full halt, paused thoughtfully, and then pronounced, "Party."

"Yeah?" said Claire without looking up. "Where and when?"

"Here."

"Okay. When?"

"End of summer. Last night blowout."

Claire crossed an item off the list with some regret. "Uh-huh."

"And *you* should plan it."

That got Claire's attention. "What?"

"You should plan it." Jodi motioned at the list. "You're so organized."

"What's to plan? As far as I can tell, parties happen," Claire said. Or spontaneously combusted, she added silently, at least in this house.

"No, a real party. You know—with, like, real food and ah, ah, someone in charge of drinks and stuff like that."

"Real food."

"Yeah. Like, not chips and dip, you know?"

Claire couldn't help but grin. "I see. Fruit, maybe? Smoked salmon with dill cream cheese on little slices of rye?"

"Smoked salmon? No!" Jodi made a face. Clearly she was not a fan of salmon in any form. "But we could have . . . shrimp! And . . . and decorations. You know. Like at your prom there's always a big sign that says 'Class of Whatever' and streamers and balloons. . . ."

Claire was laughing now. "Are you serious?"

"As a shark," said Jodi solemnly.

At that moment, Finn came in, and Claire, who had been waiting for him without trying to seem as if she was waiting for him, said, "Finn."

He said, "Mermaid Claire," and then they smiled at each other for a second.

Jodi glanced between the two of them, but she wasn't about to be distracted from the more important topic at hand. "What do you think, Finn? An end-of-summer party. A nice party, and

Claire could plan it. We'd all chip in and help, but Claire could do it. She's so organized. It'd be awesome."

"Awesome, totally," agreed Finn. "Claire could do it, no question."

And that was that.

Now Jodi and Claire had something else in common besides the shark. A shark and a party. And now, a second job.

But Claire blamed the shark.

Linley wouldn't take the shift because she wanted to "have some fun." Fun, as far as Claire could tell, had something to do with reality TV, beer, and Max—mainly, she suspected, Max.

So Jodi called her because they were shorthanded at the club. Called her, Claire, as if Claire were an old buddy she could count on. And Claire—who'd been hanging out with Max and Finn and Linley and enjoying the surprisingly mellow atmosphere and wondering, in a beginning-to-be-sleepy sort of way, if she and Finn would continue the night, or maybe she meant finish it, in her bed or maybe his—had cursed herself for answering her phone. At first she said, "I don't know, Jodi, I'm totally wiped," and then it was, "Well . . . ," and then she was drinking double espresso shots and hoping she could stay awake.

"I'll give you a ride over," Finn said, smiling. "That's cool, helping Jodi, so I'll help, too."

Max had said, "Let's all go, check it out."

Linley had looked annoyed. "Let's stay here," she said.

"We can come back," said Max.

"Or we could stay," said Linley.

But Max reached down and grabbed Linley's hand. She resisted for a moment, her eyes darkening. Then she said, "So, a road trip, then."

The dark seemed darker on the small almost-alley, where the club lived by night and slept by day. Unkempt, anonymous storefronts fronted the street on either side of the club, and a warehouse loomed at one end. Cars filled a pitted parking lot on the side. A bored bouncer with flat eyes, silver hair, and the hulk of a Super Bowl linebacker thumbed them through, on Jodi's name, to the interior murk, stamping all their hands first. "You go out, you don't come back in tonight," he said.

Jodi seemed to fly out from the gloom, and Claire jumped as Jodi seized her arm. "Thanks Bob," she said to the bouncer, and to Claire, "Good, you're here."

The sign outside, faded neon the color of dried blood, said BAR. Inside, another sign agreed: BAR. The room was long and narrow and dark and smoky. A scarred wooden bar edged by an uneven line of stools lined one wall. Or maybe the stools weren't uneven—maybe it was the people on them. They all seemed enormous. Some drank alone. Some talked, heads and voices lowered, eyes watchful. Claire tried not to stare as she followed Jodi, but she couldn't help noticing unimagined dimensions in tattoo art.

Halfway down the bar was a door on the opposite wall. It looked as if it had been made with a sledgehammer or possibly a truck, and led to a parallel universe featuring a row of pool tables. In a far back corner there was a poker machine and what looked like an ancient pinball machine.

People, mostly more guys with more serious tattoos and hair, although a couple of women fit the description, too, worked the pool tables. A lone guy hung over the pins, working the controls with body language that went beyond manic.

The music was loud but not deafening, and Claire was pretty sure she wasn't imagining the undertone of quiet potential menace. She blinked, her eyes watering from the smoke.

"This is Claire," Jodi shouted, and Claire turned back toward the bar. The guy behind the counter looked as if he might be six and a half feet tall. A black beard covered most of his face. He was wearing gold loop earrings in each ear and when he smiled, he looked exactly like a pirate. "Claire, this is Eric. It's his bar."

Eric nodded, running quick, appraising eyes over Claire. He nodded. "Thanks for coming," he said.

"Oh, anything for a friend," Claire said. The sarcasm was wasted.

"Come *on*," said Jodi and dragged Claire through a swinging door. In a narrow room that seemed to consist mostly of kegs and boxes, she fitted Claire with a tiny apron with two pockets, one for an order pad and pencil stub, one for tips.

"Okay," said Jodi. "This is the deal. Beer, liquor, chips. Water is the only mixer. Keep an eye on things. Don't expect trouble, but be ready for it."

"What things," said Claire. The apron was the same length as her skirt. She'd gone with a plain white V-necked T-shirt, but she was thinking that something in Kevlar might have been more appropriate. Jodi's shirt, drawn up and knotted, said, "Wish you were there."

Whatever that meant.

"You know, trouble."

"Trouble," said Claire.

"Three kinds of beer, all one size, all one price. All liquor, with or without water, one price. Chips, one price. I made you a cheat sheet."

Claire pocketed the price list. "What kind of trouble?" she repeated.

"We take turns, front room, back room."

"Back room," said Claire.

"Not that kind of back room, just the room with the pool tables. So I'll take the back room until you get the drill down. It's easy. Just keep the drinks coming and the tables more or less wiped and you've got it."

"And the trouble part?"

"What's illegal outside isn't necessarily illegal in here. Bodies, dead, bad. Bodies putting things into bodies for fun and with full consent, good."

"What?" Claire said.

"And if Eric shouts 'CLEAR' that means get out the back door. There are two, this one"—Jodi pointed to a massive metal fire door at the end of the storage area—"and one at the end of the hall where the bathroom is, back by the machines in the other room. Both have alarms on them, emergency use only."

"I hope the tips are worth it," Claire managed to say.

Jodi's lips curled. "You bet they are," she said as she pushed back out into the bar.

Somehow, it seemed even murkier and smokier and more crowded and noisy.

Max, Finn, and Linley were at the bar. They did not exactly blend. But no one seemed to mind.

Glass shattered in the back room. Not a single person looked around except Claire and Jodi. The pin jockey was staring down at the busted beer bottle on the floor. "Damn! Damn! Damn!" he said, his voice getting thinner and higher each time he said it.

Trouble, thought Claire, looking wildly around.

A hand clamped her arm for the second time that night. Claire leaped what felt like several feet in the air. The hand belonged to a beer barrel of a man with a walrus mustache, a shaved head, and dark glasses. He didn't seem to notice Claire's reaction. Flipping her hand over, he pressed something into it. "Buy the boy a beer before he loses his shit completely," he growled. "Keep the change for your trouble."

Claire looked down. She was holding a twenty.

Mustache headed for a pool table.

"No trouble," Claire said, and went to work.

By two a.m., Claire had a pocket full of money, a headache from the smoke, and a desperate need for coffee. Finn found her in the narrow back storage room, slamming open cabinet doors. She'd just discovered some coffee that was roasted the color of blacktop and was pouring it into the filter of the surprisingly clean coffeemaker. Hearing the door swing, Claire said automatically without looking, "Off limits. I'll be out in just a minute."

"Hey, hey, it's me," Finn said, and Claire looked up, feeling her face grow a ridiculously pleased smile.

He came over and put his arm around her and gave her a quick kiss. She leaned into him, and her headache went away a little. "You're really handling it, you know?"

"You think?" She smiled into his shoulder. Beneath the cigarette smoke, she could smell the ocean. She looked up. "I'd rather be surfing. With you."

"That's my girl," he said easily. "We'll do it tomorrow, after work. But I've gotta bail. Early lesson. And Barrel will be worrying about me."

They'd left Barrel, indignant but resigned, sitting by the back door of the house. According to Finn, Barrel didn't like bars.

"The others are going to stay and ride home with Jodi," Finn added, pulling her to him for another kiss.

"Save it for later," advised Jodi, flinging open the door.

Shit, Claire thought, caught, guilty.

But Jodi barely seemed to notice. She sniffed. "Coffee. Hah. Coffee is for amateurs." But she poured herself a cup.

"Tomorrow," Finn said with a smile. He touched the tip of Claire's nose and slid away.

Claire watched him go. *Not tonight, then,* she thought. No tangled sheets and sliding bodies and . . . oh, well.

She turned as Jodi poured sugar into the coffee at warp speed. "Leave some for me," Claire said. "Looks like I need the energy more than you do."

"Energy? Oh, I've got energy to burn," Jodi said smugly. She slugged back the coffee.

Claire took a cup and filled it and drank it straight, hoping the bitter taste would help. It wasn't bad. Okay, it wasn't good, but she'd had worse.

"LADIES," bellowed Eric. That's what he called his waitresses.

Jodi rolled her eyes. "COMING, MOM," she called back. To Claire, she said, "Give me another minute, would'ja?"

"Sure." Claire downed the last of her coffee and pushed back out into the bar.

Eric squinted at her. "I don't care what you ladies are doing back there, but don't take so damn long," he growled. He began setting beers on a tray. "Table three in the—" he began.

But he didn't get to finish.

The door slammed open, and a man burst in, his shirt torn and a fresh cut open above one eye. The bouncer was right behind him, holding a strip of cloth. The doorway behind the bouncer filled with what seemed like a mob of people screaming and shouting and pushing to get past.

Bob the bouncer turned and gave the nearest person a mighty shove, and the whole group reeled back out of sight.

Seizing his chance, the bloody man ran like a rabbit past Claire and into the room where Jodi was finishing her coffee.

"Help me," he cried. "They're trying to kill me."

Fourteen

The entrance door slammed open again. Three men crashed through on top of the bouncer. Everyone in the bar seized this moment to leave. The room cleared as tables and bar stools went over. Claire would remember later how quickly and quietly it emptied. One minute it was a smoky bar full of smoky people, and the next minute she was practically all alone as the three enraged men rolled over the bouncer. One of them went down with a howl as the bouncer got to his feet.

Claire heard Jodi shout something behind her.

Eric cleared the bar in a single bound, a baseball bat like a toothpick in one massive hand.

Glass broke, wood hit concrete as more tables went over.

Bob the bouncer was—bouncing. He'd gotten hold of one man, a guy wearing a red bandanna twisted around his head, and was doing his job very thoroughly.

It was nothing like the movies.

Then the exit alarm in the door behind Claire sounded,

and the men wheeled toward the noise. It put Eric off his stroke, and the bat he raised came down on a chair back, splintering it.

The five men fell apart. Then the bouncer seized the nearest one and hurled his catch past Claire and into the wall.

Claire caught a glimpse of sideburns and pitted skin, and then the man half-stood, bloody but still full of fight. He got one foot up and into Eric's middle as Eric charged. Eric thudded backward into the bouncer.

They went down again, and the man rolled under the swinging doors as he scrambled to his feet.

Eric came behind them like a freight train.

"The first guy went out the back," Jodi shrieked. "He knocked the coffee cup right out my hand!"

"Oh no, you don't," said Eric and closed one baseball mitt hand around one of the red-bandanna guy's shoulders as he dove for the exit.

The guy jerked up and back as if he were attached to a rope and harness.

Sideburns, still in pursuit or possibly running for his own life, crashed through the exit door and out into the night.

Shaking the guy who struggled in his grip as if he weighed no more than a sack of potatoes, Eric growled, "What the hell."

"Let me go," the man said. "It's private."

"When you bring it to my bar, it's not private anymore." Eric continued to shake the man as he talked.

The bouncer came up, dragging the third guy, who was definitely sagging. The fight had gone out of him.

"Don't I pay you to keep this out of my bar?" Eric turned on the bouncer.

"Three against one," said Bob, unmoved. "Four, if you count the rabbit."

"Don't call the cops," said the bouncer's prize.

"Cops!" Eric snorted. He took two giant steps to the back door and hurled the man into the night. Claire heard a crash and a howl.

A smell of rotten garbage blasted through the door.

"Two points. You got the Dumpster," said Jodi wrinkling her nose. But she was smiling as if she was enjoying some huge private joke.

"Turn off the alarm. It's disturbing me," said Eric and went back out into his bar.

Bob stepped past them, preparing to hurl his victim into the Dumpster, too. But on the upswing, the guy flew free of his jacket, fell, and rolled. He scrambled to his feet, and they heard him lurch away, kicking bottles and cans.

Jodi rushed forward and slammed the door against the smell. "Nice work, Bob," she offered the bouncer.

Bob shrugged, turned off the alarm, and left without answering.

Eric shouted, "Ladies all right?"

"Fine," shouted Jodi.

"Then get up here and help us. Drinks on the house."

Claire looked out the door. Bob was turning tables and righting chairs, and Eric was lining up a long row of drinks. The people who had melted away had magically reappeared. She noted that Linley and Max were among them.

Linley looked thrilled, Claire thought. She would.

Except for the trashed front of the bar, it was as if the whole thing had never happened.

She turned to Jodi. "He didn't say, 'Clear,'" she said. Now her voice sounded shaky.

"Nah. Guess he didn't think it was worth it," said Jodi. She bent over and knocked on the cabinet door, then opened it.

The rabbit—the guy the other three had been chasing—unfolded himself and stood up. His Bob-fisted eye seemed to grow more purple as he stood there, swaying slightly.

"Thanks," he said.

"I didn't do anything—forget my name and you're on your own now," Jodi advised him.

"Yeah," he said. "I think I'll go have a drink. Since they're on the house."

"Do that," said Jodi.

As he walked by, he tucked something into Jodi's apron pocket. "Thanks again."

Jodi pulled out a hundred-dollar bill wrapped around a small glassine envelope.

"Anytime," she said.

"Whoa," said Claire, doing early, middle, *and* late Keanu.

Holding up the hundred, Jodi said, "I'm going to save this." She tucked it away. Then she held up the tiny envelope. "This," she said. "I'm going to spend. You want?"

"What is it?" Claire asked.

"Given the source, I'd say something to speed me through the night. And pretty unstepped on, by the look of it. Sweet, *sweet* boy."

"He's a drug dealer," Claire said.

"Low end of the merchandise chain. Not to worry," said Jodi. She began tapping out perfect white lines on the countertop. With a grin, she rolled the hundred-dollar bill into a tube. "I've always wanted to use a hundred-dollar bill this way."

"LADIES!" Eric thundered.

"Coming," Jodi sang, and snorted up two lines. She offered the bill to Claire.

Virginity, thought Claire. *My first guy, my first surf ride, my first shark* . . . Aloud, she said, "Okay. But tomorrow, I'm just going to say no."

"Do that," said Jodi. "It's gonna give you a wicked nose-burn rush."

"Okay," said Claire, deciding not to tell Jodi that the most she'd ever done was a few tokes on occasion, which hadn't done anything for her. Boring, really, perhaps explaining why perpetually stoned people were so frequently boring.

She inhaled. Once.

Her head felt as if the top were going to come off. Passages inside her head she didn't know she had cleared. Her eyes watered and she began to cough. The room reeled.

"LADIES, DON'T MAKE ME COME BACK THERE."

Jodi grinned, folded the bill into her pocket, tucked the glassine envelope into another, hidden pocket, and hurtled through the door.

The room righted itself. Color blossomed along the edges of every object in the dingy, cramped space. She could see everything so clearly. She could *do* anything.

Claire pushed back the swinging door like a gunslinger stepping into a saloon in an Old West movie, raised her order pad, took aim, and stepped into the fray.

Fifteen

"If I were a rich girl," Claire sang in the back of the car. She leaned over and pounded on the dash. "Faster. *Faster.*"

"You *are* a rich girl," Jodi retorted, and jammed her foot down on the pedal.

That seemed so funny to Claire. She fell back as the car accelerated, laughing hard.

"Ha. Ha." Linley, who had managed to get in the back with Max. She sounded annoyed. "Did I miss something?"

In answer, Jodi jammed on the brakes.

"A yellow light. You stopped for a yellow light!" Claire burst out laughing again as she was thrown back against the seat. Jodi laughed too. They looked at each other and Claire said, "Dumpster," and they laughed harder.

Claire was in the death seat. With Jodi driving. She had a pocketful of money and a head full of white powder, and everything was *so* funny.

And thirst-making. Claire twisted, reached over the seat,

and grabbed the go cup Max held. She took a long swallow and gasped. "It's ginger ale!"

"You're welcome," said Max mildly.

"I thought it was at least beer," said Claire.

"You hate beer," said Linley. "What's going on?" She sounded suspicious, almost peevish.

Claire noticed how close Linley was sitting to Max, one hand on his thigh. But Max didn't seem to be sitting close to Linley, somehow.

"Max! Do you like Linley?" Claire blurted out.

"Claire . . . ," Linley began in a low, threatening voice that would have been a warning growl if she had been a dog.

"Yes," said Max, simply.

Linley jerked around to look at Max.

"Max likes Lin-ley, Max likes Lin-ley," sang Jodi and the light must have changed, because they were flying again.

"Are you sleeping with Linley?" Claire asked. "You know, having sex?"

Linley came out of the backseat like a great white shark and grabbed Claire's arm. "Shut up! I've had it. What're you on?"

"I'm guessing some kind of flight powder," said Max.

Linley's grip tightened. She gave Claire's arm a shake. "Tell me what's going on."

"Because I am," Claire went on. "Having sex. With Finn. I wanted to keep it a big secret, but now I'm wondering why? It's no big deal, right?"

"Secret sex lives in the big house by the ocean," intoned Jodi, sounding like a talking head. "Details at eleven."

"No secret," Claire repeated stubbornly. "I'm a girl, he's a boy, it's natural. We had sex."

"Where'd you get it?" asked Max.

"From Finn. The boy," Claire explained patiently. "Boy. Girl. Sex."

"The speed," said Max patiently. "Jodi. Where?"

"Tip," said Jodi, who'd suddenly gone from garrulous to word miser.

"For outstanding life-saving service," added Claire and laughed.

"Whatever," said Jodi. She didn't laugh.

"What?" said Claire. "What did I say? I'm not supposed to talk about sex? When you and Linley talk about it, like, all the time? Where's the rule written, huh, Jodi? Claire can't talk about sex, Claire can't have sex? Well, it's a free country and I can have sex with any guy I want—"

"Or girl," Jodi interjected, almost sulkily.

"Please. I'm not *that* kind of girl," chortled Claire.

"I want some," demanded Linley.

"Sex?" asked Claire. "But maybe Linley is that kind of girl, Jodi." She was brilliant. Witty. Funny.

"Why don't you let them finish their trip alone," said Max.

"Why? What's in it for me?" Linley turned to Max.

"We're here," said Jodi, and slid out of the car. She slammed the door and headed for the house.

Claire frowned. Moody Jodi.

"Jodi, wait," Linley called.

"Come on, Linley," said Max softly.

Finn, thought Claire. Or maybe she said it aloud. But Finn had said he had to get up early. He wouldn't be as happy to see her as she would to see him.

Linley had stopped and turned to face Max as he got out of the car. He put one hand on each arm. They faced each other in the half-light from the house. Max's face looked serious.

And Linley, thought Claire, looked like one of those pictures of the goddesses from the art history books: cold and still and very beautiful.

Her smile made her more beautiful still as she slid her hands up Max's arms.

"Yes, Max, what can I do for you?" she said, and Claire wondered why she had thought Linley looked cold.

"We could talk," said Max, catching Linley's hands and holding them.

"Talk?" she said, and Claire, thought, no, not cold. Frozen.

Claire must have made some sound, because Linley's head turned.

"Claire," she said, as if she'd forgotten about Claire. "There's Claire. There's always Claire. Always there. Always there Claire."

Claire took a step back at the sudden venom in Linley's voice. She'd clearly stayed too long at this party.

"Claire likes to listen, don't you Claire? It's so much safer than living, isn't it Claire? Wait! I know! You don't need me! Why don't you just talk to Claire—"

"Linley," interrupted Max. "It's you I want to talk to. We need to talk."

"Talk!" Linley spat. "What about? Talk to Claire. She'll say, 'Oh, poor Max. Oh that awful Linley. You had to leave her. You had to treat her like leftover meat. Poor, *poor* Max.'"

"You don't really believe that," he said.

Her face hot, her mind whirling, Claire turned to go. She had to get away. Linley's voice was so full of anger, of contempt. What had she done to make Linley hate her so much?

Linley's voice followed her. "Claire the good, Claire the perfect, slumming in California for the summer. Ask her to listen to you. She'll say the right thing. She'll do the right thing. She always does, don't you, Claire? Everybody loves Claire, don't they, Claire?

Claire whirled around. "Stop it, Linley. You don't know what you're saying!"

But Linley wouldn't stop. "Helping Jodi out, Jodi's new best friend, planning biiiig parties, moving into my life and my house . . ."

"You asked me! You talked me into it!" Claire gasped.

"Linley, you don't want to do this," Max said.

"And now Max. You want Max, too, don't you!"

"No . . ."

"You'd think Finn would be enough for Miss Good and Perfect. I let you have Finn . . ."

"Oh!" Claire gasped. "You let me? You *let* me? You think Finn wants you?"

"Given the choice between me and you?" Linley laughed angrily.

"He might want to get lucky with you," said Claire, "although from what I've seen, it doesn't take much luck or anything else to have it off with you. But he knows he can do a lot better than you. Hell, anybody can."

"Is that what you think?" Linley screamed. "Like you'd know."

"It's what Max thinks," said Claire, coldly and cruelly. "That's probably why he left you the way he did. And probably why he doesn't want you now."

Linley lunged toward Claire and if Max hadn't been holding her, they might have been at each other like a bad movie. But he held on tight and before Linley could say anything else, Claire turned and ran into the house.

She was shaking. She'd never been so angry in her life, so coldly, clearly angry.

Behind her, she heard Linley shouting something. She heard Max's voice, loud and stern. Moving like a cartoon robot, she went up the stairs.

She passed Jodi's room and stopped. Claire wanted to talk to somebody, she needed to talk to somebody.

But although the door was open and the light was on, Jodi wasn't inside.

Claire kept going, past her own room and all the way to Finn's door. She knocked.

After a moment, he said, "Hello?"

"It's me," said Claire, pushing open the door.

She'd learned a lot about herself that summer, and that night in the bar, and now she learned one more thing. A guy was almost always glad to see you get into his bed.

Claire was glad to know that, too. Because it meant that Max saying no all summer to Linley had to hurt even worse.

And Claire wanted Linley to hurt.

Sixteen

"Want to go surfing?" Claire asked Jodi one morning. She'd found her standing in the middle of the deck, staring at nothing.

Jodi blinked, found Claire's name, and said, "Claire."

"Yes, that's me. Going surfing." Claire found herself making the wave motion that was Finn's description of everything from surfing to the living is easy. Jodi went from moody to spacey to just plain literally absent these days. And she'd taken to locking the door of her room, which Claire had discovered by accident earlier when she'd tried to go in to leave change from the grocery money. She'd ended up taping it to the door in an envelope.

Not that she was going to mention the locked-door thing, because it wasn't any of her business. She would respect Jodi's privacy, unless of course Jodi was locking her door because she was keeping a truly frightening amount of stash in her room, in which case Claire *was* going to mention it.

She just hadn't figured out how. Now wasn't the time. Now she was going surfing.

"I don't know . . . ," Jodi said.

"We could make more end-of-summer party plans," Claire offered. She was going ahead with the party plans in spite of the deep and icy distance that had opened between her and Linley.

"You're going alone? You should never surf alone."

"I'm not going alone if you're coming with me. And if you do come with me, you have to show me a new set. I've been going over to the hotel beach every day after work, so technically, I'm not surfing alone."

"Finn's beach," said Jodi, her mood changing. She sing-songed, "Finn and Claire, sitting in the sea, k-i-s-s-i-n-g."

"Good to know your IQ matches your age," said Claire. "Are you coming, or not?"

"Coming," said Jodi, reverting to her normal hyper mode. "Give me five."

An hour later, as Claire completed a ride and paddled back out with Jodi, Jodi said, "You're becoming decent."

"Practice," said Claire.

"And love," added Jodi slyly.

"Finn, you mean?" Claire thought about Finn and couldn't help smiling.

"So it's been Finn and the surfboard these last few weeks," Jodi went on.

"Can't have one without the other," Claire said lightly. She knew he had a private lesson that afternoon. With the same girl who'd been buying his time for the past two weeks. She tried not to be jealous, but it was hard.

Of course, Finn wasn't interested. He loved her, even if he'd never said the words. Not exactly.

They coasted up a swell and down again. "I mean, you haven't been around much," Jodi went on.

Claire was surprised Jodi had noticed. She wondered what else Jodi had picked up on. Had she noticed the cool distance Linley and Claire were keeping from each other?

The first time Claire had seen Linley after that fight, passing Linley on her way out to work, Claire had thought Linley looked as if she wanted to speak.

But Claire had felt her face go stiff with anger and hurt feelings and, raising her chin, she had sailed by.

Since then, they'd circled each other with chilly politeness.

Claire was surprised she didn't miss Linley's company more. But her increasing involvement with Finn had made it easy to avoid Linley. And in the general mill of the ongoing house party, Claire had been careful to include Linley in offers to get drinks or plates of food or even general invites to surf the beach or bars. She'd also consulted her about the end-of-summer party plans, to be met with Linley's freezing, "Whatever."

"I know," said Claire. "I can't believe the summer is so close to over. I mean, it feels as if it just started."

"Tell me about it," said Jodi. "But we'll end it with a party that will go down in time."

"California time," Claire said wryly. She paused, then said, "You haven't been around much either. With two jobs and all."

"I know." Jodi sighed.

"Poor Jodi. All work and no summer romance," said Claire.

Jodi sighed again without answering. They drifted peacefully. Then suddenly she said, "Have you ever known any, like, gay people?"

Claire thought of all her years in boarding school and grinned. "Hey, I come from some of the finest L-word incubators on the East Coast." She didn't add that some of her best friends were lesbians, because it wasn't true. Until Linley, she hadn't really had a best friend.

"Have you ever, you know, thought about it? I mean, how someone knows that they're, whatever?"

"No," said Claire slowly. She hesitated, then said, "I thought about sex a lot. Because it seemed like everybody was doing it—except me."

She felt Jodi's gaze, but she didn't look up. She surfed her hand through the water. And added, "Until this summer. When I met Finn."

"Whoa," Jodi breathed. "Get out. He's your *first*? Does he know it?"

"I don't think he does. We were on the beach and we were

both sort of stoned and, uh, it went pretty well," Claire said. *Could I sound any more stupid?* she thought.

"You're lucky," said Jodi. "My first time with a guy was at some dumb party. It was at this McMansion that had its own putting green. We did some . . . putting." Jodi grinned slyly. "I walked away thinking, *Good grief. Is that all there is? People are insane.*"

"People *are* insane," Claire felt compelled to point out. "And it wasn't perfect the first time, but we're practicing. And I think Finn's pretty good. No, very good."

"Definitely not the putting green," said Jodi. "Get it in, get it out. Even a bad wave usually gives a better ride."

Thinking of Finn and some of the things he did with her and the way it made her feel, Claire grinned and said, "Definitely not true with Finn."

"And not true . . ." But Jodi didn't finish because a perfect set came and kept them busy until it was time to book.

They were walking back across the beach to the car when Jodi said, "It's been putting green quality for me ever since then, until this summer."

It took Claire a moment to figure out what Jodi was talking about. Hoisting the board into place on the roof of the car and strapping it down, Claire said, "Oh!" Then, "Oh, I thought you hadn't had time for . . . for anything . . . this summer?"

"Well, uh, not exactly." Jodi made elaborate work out of

adjusting her board and checking the roof rack straps. "There's this, uh, girl, you know."

Again, Claire was slow.

"Girl," she said stupidly.

"Yeah," said Jodi. She cinched the last strap and turned to face Claire. "Poppy."

"Poppy."

"And me," explained Jodi.

"Poppy and you . . . oh!" Claire went from slow to totally uncool in a nanosecond. "You and *Poppy*?"

Jodi's chin came up. "Yes. You got a problem with that?"

"No!" said Claire, which was true. She just couldn't believe how slow she was to catch on. "I just can't believe . . . I mean . . . when? Am I the last to know?"

She figured the answer had to be yes. But to her complete amazement, Jodi said, "No. The first. Besides me and Poppy, I mean. Although I'm pretty sure Dean got it all Googled by now."

"Whoa. Wow. Good grief," said Claire.

A short silence fell. Jodi stared at Claire almost defiantly. Claire stared at Jodi, really looked at her. For once, Jodi wasn't dancing in place. She returned Claire's gaze seriously. "You," she said, "have hidden depths, Jodi."

Jodi looked surprised, then pleased. "You think?"

"Well, yeah."

"So . . . what happened?" Claire said.

Jodi leaned over, fished in the backseat, and came up with some coolers. She handed one to Claire, opened the other for herself, and jumped up on the hood of the car. Claire slid up beside her.

"You know, one of the nice things about surfing is that wherever you go to do it, the view is fabulous," Claire said.

"True," said Jodi.

"So," Claire said, because she wanted to know and because she thought Jodi wanted her to ask, "tell me."

"Well," said Jodi. "I'd been vibing Poppy for a while, pretty much ever since I saw her in art studio at school." And she went on to tell Claire all about it.

So she wouldn't have been human if she hadn't felt a little smug about Jodi's true confession. Jodi had told her, Claire, instead of Linley.

Why?

Claire thought about this as she drank her coffee a few mornings later. The house was warm and sunny and quiet. Unless the party went on all night before, Claire often had the mornings to herself.

Until Max appeared, which was another thing that happened as often as not—except that Max usually arrived by way of the beach, in a uniform of ragged cutoffs and faded-to-no-color shirt.

He got coffee and returned to settle wordlessly by her on one of the chairs on the deck. He never spoke unless she spoke first. It was a peaceful way to begin the day.

This morning, she felt like talking. She said, to her own surprise, "Linley's still angry with me."

"I know," said Max, not surprised at all. He was so calm, calm in a different way from Finn.

"I don't get it," she said. "I thought she was my friend." How little kid on the playground was that? She wanted to grab the words back.

But Max didn't seem to notice. He said simply, "She is."

So Claire said, keeping it just as simple, "Why?" And wondered if Max had always been like this and if so, how he and Linley had ever gotten together.

Max didn't answer right away. He seemed to be considering the question. He said at last, "Linley's had some hard times. Bad times."

In spite of herself, Claire gave a little snort of disbelief. "As Linley herself would tell you, she always gets what she wants."

"She always gets what she says she wants," Max corrected. "Big difference."

"How difficult could her life have been. No worries about money, no worries about looks, no worries about smarts. In short, no worries," Claire said.

"She's not the way she seems. I can't tell you any more than that, because it's not mine to tell. But I can tell you she's angry with me, and she can't go there, not yet."

Claire said again, "Why?"

He sighed this time, ran his hand through his salt-curled hair. "For so many reasons. Because I'm not who she wants me to be. Because I never was, or will be."

"Vague," said Claire.

He smiled at that. "I know. I'm still sorting it out in my own head. But I know this: I shouldn't have run away the way I did. And I did run, you know. I loved Linley and I ran away from that."

Claire didn't say anything this time.

After a long silence, he added, quietly, "And now I'm back. But not the way Linley wants me to be."

The silence lengthened again.

And then the world joined them. Or rather, Linley did. "How cozy," she said, coming out onto the deck. "Lose Finn, Claire?"

Claire saw a fleeting expression of what looked like tiredness cross Max's face. Linley was like a child, Claire thought. An unhappy child. Me. Now. Tantrum.

No tantrums for me, thought Claire. "Finn had an early lesson," Claire said, as pleasantly as she could, and went into the house for more coffee.

She found Dean lounging at the counter, his eyes on the scene on the deck.

Why am I not surprised? thought Claire. Dean was like an eternally circling shark that never moved in for the kill.

"You remind me of that shark we saw," Claire said.

Dean switched his attention to her. "So we're talking about that shark again?" he said, unperturbed.

"That's not a compliment," Claire said.

Dean's gaze went back to the deck. Linley was leaning toward Max, smiling. Max was smiling back.

Tantrum averted, Claire thought.

Dean said, "Now me, I would have said Linley was the shark in our little tidal pool."

"Really," said Claire.

Dean waited, but Claire didn't go on. She didn't want to talk about Linley to Dean.

"Ah," said Dean after a minute. He smiled. "So many secrets. So little time."

Before she could ask Dean what he meant—or even think about if she wanted to know—feet pounded on the stairs. Jodi darted to the coffee, poured out two cups and doctored them, and turned to hand one to Poppy as she made a more leisurely entrance to the kitchen. Settling on the stool, Poppy took a long drink, said, "Perfect," and then to Jodi, "Thanks."

Then Poppy smiled at Claire and said, "Good morning Claire," and Claire knew by the way she said it that Poppy knew Claire knew.

"Hey," she said.

"About this party," Jodi said.

"Ah," said Dean. "I thought we'd get to the party soon."

"It's important," insisted Jodi.

"It'll be a good party," Poppy said unexpectedly. "With Claire in charge."

"Thanks," said Claire, pleased. She added, "And now that the last month's rent is all in, I'm collecting for said party."

"What do you want money now for, rent girl?" It was Linley. She couldn't have looked more beautiful in the morning light. Her gaze followed Max as he went for more coffee. Then Linley glanced at Poppy and Jodi, a thoughtful, considering look. She didn't acknowledge Dean at all. She returned her attention to Claire.

"Money. For the party," said Jodi.

"I don't understand why you're making such a big deal of this," Linley said. "I mean, dial up the drinks and party favors and you're there."

"Would you rather handle it? You can, if you want," Claire said, trying to keep her voice even.

"Oh, no," said Linley. "It'll keep you busy and a busy Claire is a happy Claire, right?"

"True," said Claire agreeably, because it was.

"I've got my share right here," said Dean suddenly, and for once, Claire had the feeling that he was trying to put out a fire rather than stoke it. "Cash, right?"

"Me too," said Jodi.

"Get to work, rent girl," Linley said, and laughed.

Claire whirled. "Right," she said. "And when will you pay

your share, Linley? It shouldn't be too hard, especially since you didn't pay any rent all summer!"

"What?" said Jodi.

"Big secret," said Claire. "Linley decided she could use the extra cash."

Poppy said, "Well, it is her uncle's house."

"You thought you'd need the extra cash?" Jodi said, staring at Linley.

"It's my house!" Linley cried.

"You know how strapped I am, you know how badly I need to get away from my . . . from home, and you decide to make a little extra cash on my back?" Jodi's voice went up.

"Claire didn't pay rent either," said Linley.

"We're not talking about Claire. We're talking about you and me," Jodi said.

"It's not that much money," Linley said.

"Big mistake," Dean said under his breath. At the same moment, Max said, softly, "Linley . . ."

Jodi went pale. "Not that much money," she repeated.

Poppy reached out and patted Jodi's arm.

Linley narrowed her eyes.

Jodi let out a long breath. She shook her head as if to clear it. "You're too much, Linley, you know that? But Poppy's right—it is your house."

No one spoke. Then Linley laughed. "I'm so glad you see it my way. But to be fair, I'll donate the extra money to the party fund."

"Now you're talking," said Max.

"Good," said Claire briskly. She stood up. She wanted out of there. "Well, I have to go. See ya."

"Later," agreed Linley, and Claire wondered: Was that a promise, or a threat?

Seventeen

Claire opened her eyes to find warm brown eyes staring into hers. "Barrel," she said softly, and Barrel's mouth opened in a panting dog grin. She rolled over to look at the clock. It was very early.

Quietly she slipped out of bed and headed downstairs to let Barrel out for his morning loop around the house. She made coffee, working the formerly fearsome cappuccino maker almost automatically. She let Barrel back in, gave him a biscuit, and poured up and doctored two mugs of coffee.

They went back up the stairs, Barrel leading the way and looking over his shoulder as if to make sure she could manage the stairs on her own. She smiled. "Good boy," she whispered.

Barrel. Two more days and she'd be gone and she'd miss Barrel.

Finn slept like a child, on his back with his arms spread. Asleep, with his sunstreaked brown hair spread across the pillow, he didn't look much older than a child.

She set the cups on the bedside table and sat next to Finn. Barrel jumped back on the bed and settled down with a sigh.

Claire laid her hand on Finn's bare chest. He opened his eyes and peered up at her and smiled his familiar smile. "Hey," he said.

"Hey," she said. "I brought you coffee."

It was a ritual they had now. The first one up brought coffee.

Finn sat up. "Excellent," he said. He patted the bed next to him. "It's still pretty early. Come back to bed for a while."

Instead, she leaned forward, her head against his shoulder. He put down the coffee cup and put his arms around her. She listened to the thump of his heart.

"Two more days," she said.

"Yeah," he said, and began to stroke her hair. "I'm going to miss you, Mermaid Claire. Barrel and I are going to miss you."

"I'm going to miss you both too." She heard the thickness of her voice and thought, *I will not cry.* She pulled back and sat up. "You know," she said, "I've got a ton of stuff to do for the party tonight. And today's my last day at the Stacked. I'd better get going."

Finn regarded her for a long moment, and then nodded slowly. "Okay," he said. "Maybe later. We've still got time."

No, we don't, Claire thought, and made her escape as the first tears spilled down her cheeks.

By the time she'd changed into her "uniform," she'd gotten

control of herself. She banged on Jodi's door, then banged again, louder. "What?" said Jodi, crossly.

"We have shopping to do," she said.

"Go away," said Jodi.

Claire looked down at her list. "Nope. Farmers market, grocery store, and I need your help. If you're not downstairs in ten minutes, I'm coming up to get you."

She left, ignoring the creative use of swear words she could hear on the other side of the door.

Jodi made it in fifteen, looking rumpled and cross and not at all speedy hyper. Claire thrust a travel mug at her, took the keys from her hands, and said, "You're giving directions. I'm driving."

"Who died and left you queen of the world," Jodi grumbled.

"It's too early for near-death auto experiences, thank you very much," Claire said briskly.

"How did I get dawn patrol, anyway?"

"You're working this afternoon, remember?" Claire said.

"I hate you," said Jodi unemotionally, and followed Claire out to the car.

But coffee and morning air brought her back to life, and a few sessions of sharp bargaining in the farmers market made her human. They staggered to the car with an amazing array of fruits and vegetables and several melons that Jodi declared, with a professional air, were "perfect spikeables."

Their haul from the grocery store filled up the rest of the car, and Claire commandeered Max and Poppy for unloading.

She consulted her list. "Max, you and Dean are the kegs. They're paid for, and here's what we ordered and a copy of the receipt. Don't lose it."

"Yes, ma'am," said Max.

"Poppy . . ." Poppy held up her hand. "I know, I know. The booze. The bar. I have the list. And the receipt. You gave them to me yesterday, remember?"

"Just checking," said Claire. "Don't forget to . . ."

"Spike the melons," said Jodi. "We won't forget."

"And ice when you pick up the beer . . ."

"On it," said Max.

Claire looked at her watch. "I'll be back after work. Start on the fruits and vegetables, and the ones you cut up, cover before you refrigerate. You—"

"Claire," said Poppy firmly. "Go. I know how to handle fruits and vegetables."

Which for some reason made Jodi crack up. Claire left Jodi laughing hysterically and Poppy shaking her head at her, and Bladed off to work, not at all sure that she was going to be able to pull off the kind of end-of-summer party she'd so carefully planned.

But as the sun began to set that evening and Claire flew through the last-minute details, she began to think she might succeed after all. Beer kegs on ice waited on the porch, where Dean and Max had lovingly placed them. Party tubs filled with ice and drinks, some tubs designated non-alcoholic, the rest brimming with every kind of bottled goodie Claire could think of, were scattered across the deck. She'd even remembered garbage cans and had labeled them: CANS AND BOTTLES ONLY and TRASH.

As Poppy sliced the last of the fruits and vegetables, Claire, in the spirit of party irony, was making little sandwiches of cucumbers and cream cheese.

Linley wandered into the kitchen as Claire finished cutting the crusts off the last of the silly sandwiches.

"What's this?" Linley demanded, peering down at the dainty-looking triangles.

"Try one," Poppy advised.

Claire barked, "Max, napkins!" and had the satisfaction of actually being obeyed.

Power. She could get used to it. She could go all Martha Stewart in a heartbeat.

Except for the totally bogus jail thing Martha had gotten, of course . . .

"Cucumber sandwiches?" Linley chewed with an expression of incredulity.

"Good, huh?" said Max. "I'd have never believed it."

He scooped one up, and Claire slapped his hand and said, "Hey! Wait till the par-tay."

He grabbed another and crammed it into his mouth, ducking out of reach.

"Little sandwiches?" said Linley. "Finger sandwiches?"

"Strictly vegetarian," Claire assured her. "No fingers, just cucumbers."

Staring as Poppy settled a bowl of dip in a tray of fruit, Linley shook her head. "It's just a *party*, Claire. Don't you think you've gone, well, a little overboard?"

"Looks good to me," said Dean.

"Who asked you?" Linley said.

"Ooh, a private conversation," commented Dean.

"Did you put the plates out yet?" Claire asked him.

"As always, your wish is my command," said Dean.

Claire handed a plate of vegetables and dip off to Poppy as she returned to the kitchen.

"Plates?" Linley shook her head. "Why not just something simple? Like, oh, I don't know, napkins?"

"Aren't you in charge of something?" Claire said. She was only half-listening to Linley. "Like, spiking the watermelons and putting them on ice?"

"Spiked, iced," said Linley.

"Good for you," Claire said, almost absently, running her finger down one of the lists she'd magnet-spackled to the refrigerator.

"I'm surprised you'll allow spiked watermelons in the same house with finger sandwiches," said Linley.

"My radically liberal upbringing," said Claire. Forks? No, right, she'd decided against forks. The only weapons of food destruction being put out were toothpicks for the spiked melon. Everything else was strictly fingers. . . .

"Your banker-in-a-box family?" Linley said. "Hardly radical. Fashionable liberal, maybe. It *is* fashionable to be rich and liberal in Boston, right?"

Claire frowned. Clearly she needed to give Linley something to do.

The door banged open. "Ta-dah!" cried Jodi. "I'm here."

"And we cheer," said Dean, who, with Max's help, had begun to unroll streamers across the rafters of the house.

"And I brought the strawberries," Jodi went on.

"Strawberries?" said Linley. "For margaritas?"

"For chocolate-dipped strawberries," Jodi corrected. "Except they're all dipped. We did them at work. I made everybody at Banger's help."

Dean said, "What about the Vile Vickie?"

Jodi giggled. "Her sister is having a baby and she had to help."

"Poor baby," commented Dean.

"So since Vickie wasn't there and things were slow, Banger said go ahead. And guess what? He might even try to stop by the party!"

"You invited *Banger*?" said Linley.

"Why not? Claire invited the guys at the Stacked—anyway, it was a slow day, so we got the guys in the kitchen to help. And they sort of threw in some other fruit, so a lot of stuff got dipped."

"Jodi, that is excellent," said Claire.

Jodi beamed. "Thanks," she said. "And thanks to Mynor and Leslie and Allison and Emily and Tina and, let's see, Malinda and Terri and—"

"Everyone at Banger's," interrupted Linley. "Well, since they're all apparently going to be at the party, we'll be sure and thank each and every one of them. Maybe Claire can write them all thank-you notes."

The tone as much as the words at last got Jodi's attention. It got everyone's attention. Jodi frowned. "What's your problem?" she asked.

"I don't have a problem. But chocolate-dipped strawberries? Cucumber sandwiches? Party streamers, for god's sake?" Linley gestured scornfully. "This party has gotten a little out of hand, don't you think?"

"What? Since when have you ever thought *that* about any party?" Jodi said. She laughed. "This is me, Jodi—remember? I know you."

"You know me? Maybe you once did, when we were friends," said Linley.

"What?" Jodi sounded both startled and annoyed.

Ignoring her, Linley went on. "But whatever you think you know about me, this doesn't look at all like my kind of party. It's . . . I mean, Claire, sweetie, we put you in charge to make sure we had enough beer. And tequila. Not to . . . to make such a big deal out of it."

"Unfair, Linley," said Max.

Linley said, "I appreciate that you've worked so hard and tried to make it special, but really, Claire. And it's nice that you like being so busy busy and have all these nice new friends to play with and that everybody is humoring you, but admit it, this is just ridiculous. And it's not going to impress Finn, trust me."

Claire gasped. Because it hurt. It actually physically hurt, hearing those words. It was as if Linley's words were rocks hitting Claire.

Looking down to hide her shock, Claire noticed that the napkin she'd somehow started folding and refolding was now shredded paper, and noticed, too, that her hands were shaking. She threw the napkin away and put her hands flat on the counter.

I've tried to make it a good party, Claire thought numbly. *I thought everyone else wanted it that way, too.*

I thought they were my friends. And yes, she'd been showing off a little for Finn, even if he didn't notice. . . .

She looked around at everyone now—Max, Dean, Poppy, Jodi. And Linley.

Linley was watching Claire like a cat at a mouse-hole.

No one else spoke. Did they agree with Linley? Did they all think she was being ridiculous? Were they just humoring her?

"Is that what you think?" Claire said slowly, to everyone as much as to Linley. She felt as if she might cry.

"Isn't it obvious?" Linley said.

And then Dean said, his eyes bright and watchful, "Sounds

as if you've got a problem with what a great party Claire's put together here, Linley."

"A problem?" repeated Linley.

"Maybe you're a little jealous," he added conversationally.

Don't, Claire thought automatically, and saw Jodi's hands go out as if to stop the words. Even Poppy looked taken aback.

But it was too late.

"Me? Jealous? Of Claire? *Claire*?"

"I don't know," Dean said, smiling with deeply fake innocence. "Just a thought."

Claire said, "I . . . you . . . we should . . ." At least they didn't *all* think her party plans were stupid. She looked around. The party, she told herself. We have to finish putting it together. Inside, she wanted to cry. She wanted to curl up in a ball in the corner. She wanted never to have come to California, never to have met Linley.

But then she wouldn't have met Finn. She wouldn't have learned to surf.

Or to wait tables, she thought, and in spite of herself, smiled a little.

Linley saw the smile.

"Are you laughing at *me*?" she snapped.

And then, a new Claire thought, a dark, angry Claire thought: *I'll murder Linley later.*

And put it on her mental list: Linley. Later. Murder.

Claire's silence, the silence of the whole room, was too much for Linley. Claire would think—later— that it was the silence of a whole summer exploding, a whole lifetime, maybe.

"Don't you dare laugh at me, Claire Plimouth!"

And Claire heard herself say, in the old Claire's voice, calm and unemotional, but using words only the new Claire would have used: "Why, Linley? Because you can dish it out, but you can't take it?"

And then Linley was almost up in Claire's face, shouting, "I have a list for you, Claire! You like lists, right? Here's a list. One: party: overkill, way over the top. Two: I'm not jealous of you, not now, not ever, not possible. So not possible—"

"Linley!" said Max. He moved toward her as if to step between her words and everyone else.

Claire didn't move. She stared at Linley, the Claire of thousands of boarding school days and thousands of more Plimouth family rules. Lists and lists of Plimouth family rules, now that she thought about it. All at war inside her with the Claire of the long shining days of this summer—the feel of the water beneath the board, things little and big, people new and amazing and not so different in so many ways after all, and yes Finn.

Finn.

And Claire said, politely, really, "Oh, get over it, Linley. We have a party starting and we just don't have time for a tantrum."

Eighteen

"Whoaaaa," Dean breathed, stepping back.

Linley's golden tan went maroon with rage. For one moment, Claire thought Linley was going to go for her.

Max must have, too. He put his hand on Linley's arm, and when she tried to shake it off, he wrapped his fingers around her list. Claire realized that she was breathing heavily, as if she'd carved a ride on her biggest wave yet.

And maybe she was right.

"You . . . ," Linley said in a low, furious voice and paused, her own breathing out of control. "You . . ."

She looked around and said, clearly and slowly, "You can all go to hell. Fuck each and every one of you. And especially you, Claire."

"Linley," said Max.

She jerked, but he held on. She swung with her free hand, and Max would have gotten not a slap but an eye full of fist if he hadn't caught her other arm in time. She yanked that arm free, but didn't try to hit him again. Instead, she twisted around.

Jodi said, "Get a grip, will you?"

"Oh, that's good. Me get a grip. I'm not the one that's speeding her brains out night and day. Jodi the junkie, that's what you are. Up your nose, in your mouth, popping it between your toes so no one will know—"

"I do not . . . I would never . . . I—"

"Can quit anytime. Hah!"

"You've got no right!" Jodi said furiously.

"Oh. I'm sorry. Did I hurt your feelings? But I'm just being your friend. Telling you the truth. Which is more than you've done with me!" Linley said.

"I'm not the one who went and lied about paying rent," Jodie managed to choke out.

"No. No, you lied about fucking Poppy, that's what you lied about," Linley said.

Jodi went red, then white.

Now Poppy put her hand on Jodi's arm. "That wasn't yours to tell, Linley," she said evenly. But Claire had the impression that Poppy was really angry.

"Ohh, Poppy, I'm scared," Linley said. "For your information, Jodi's my oldest friend. My *best* friend. You'd think she'd tell me something like that. Especially since it's been going on all summer."

"I was going to tell you," Jodi said. She glanced at Claire.

Linley caught it, figured it out. "You've told Claire," she said. *"You told Claire, but you didn't tell me."*

"You didn't like Poppy," Jodi said. "You made that pretty clear."

"We'd all pretty much figured it out, anyway," Max said.

Was he talking to Linley or Jodi?

"You told Claire," repeated Linley. "And Claire was *sooo* understanding, weren't you, Claire? So fucking grateful Jodi shared your stupid little I'm-a-dyke confession with her—"

"Stop it," Poppy said. "Watch your language."

"Sorry, Poppy. Did I offend you?" Linley said.

"Try every day this summer," Poppy shot back. "Why would Jodi tell you anything? You've pushed her away. You treated everyone in this house like shit. And you've done nothing but throw your own little pity party pretty much every single moment this summer."

Max almost lost his grip when Linley lunged this time. "Bitch!" she screamed.

"Oh, please," said Poppy.

"Stop it!" Claire said. "Stop it. We've got a party—"

"And you," said Linley. "Until I came along you didn't have a life. You were a mouse. A virgin WASP mouse."

Linley had known, Claire thought. She'd known Claire was a virgin. Why hadn't she said anything? "And if it hadn't been for me, you'd be sitting in your daddy's bank right now, still being a boring little mouse. Boring Claire. Right next to the definition of the word, there's your picture. . . ."

This time, Claire's eyes filled with tears. She backed away.

"I'm not . . . ," she tried to say. But not what? A mouse. Boring?

She wanted Finn. She wanted him now.

Jodi had Poppy. Dean was watching them all, his eyes bright. Max had caught Linley by the other arm and was trying to pull her to him, talking softly as if to a crazed animal.

Claire reached the door. Her hand found the handle.

She heard Linley shouting at Max, "Liar. Liar! I hate you. I hate you . . ."

And then Claire was outside in the last of the daylight.

Finn.

She could go to Finn. He'd had a late surf lesson that afternoon at the hotel.

Claire would go see Finn.

What about the party? A little voice inside her asked.

And Claire said aloud, "Fuck the party," and kept going.

Finn saw her coming across the beach and knew something was wrong. He finished the lesson, then turned and said, "What's happened?"

Claire walked into his arms, leaned her head against his chest, and silently began to cry.

Later, late enough so it was full-on dark, Finn took Claire back to the party.

A pirate ship, thought Claire. That's what the house looked like to her as she and Finn drove up to the driveway entrance. A big, strange pirate ship, lit from within and sailing into the new night.

And maybe I'll have to walk the plank before the night is over, she thought.

Finn slowed. Claire was pleased to see someone had remembered to put out the sign. "'Danger,'" Finn read aloud. "'Drive Under Construction. Do Not Enter.'"

He glanced over at her. She laughed. "If it just said 'Keep Out,' no one would." She jumped out of the van and ran to open the gate to let Finn in to park.

The house was jammed. Claire and Finn came in to a sea of people. Music pumped, but no one was dancing yet. They were still drinking, climbing higher, getting hooked up.

Claire caught Finn's hand as much for comfort as to keep close to him in the crowd. Who were all these people? She didn't see anyone she knew—not even her roommates.

She turned to Finn. "I'm going to go change into my party clothes," she said.

"What?"

She pulled out the front of her damp sweatshirt and pointed up the stairs.

Finn nodded. He pointed to Barrel and also pointed up the stairs.

Claire nodded back. She knew what Finn was saying: too many people, too much loud noise for Barrel. She reached down to catch Barrel's collar.

"I'll get drinks," Finn offered. Or at least Claire thought that was what he said.

With a quick glance back to make sure it was okay, Barrel followed Claire obediently.

Upstairs, the noise was less. Claire led Barrel into Finn's room and settled him in, making sure he had plenty of water and his favorite chew toy. She even made a sign that said BE CAREFUL OF DOG INSIDE and taped it on the door, as much to protect Barrel from the party as to make sure she and Finn had the room all to themselves at party's end.

Finn had fed Barrel at the beach when they'd finished surfing. And before they'd gone horizontal. Claire smiled and felt a twinge of sadness. Sex on the beach. Would it be the last time?

The flight back east was at the crack of dawn day after tomorrow. Tomorrow would probably be dedicated to party recovery and cleanup.

And considering all the people who weren't speaking to each other, it wasn't going to be a pleasant day.

But she'd think about tomorrow, well, tomorrow. With a final pat for Barrel, Claire headed for her own room. When she was party ready, she surveyed herself in the mirror. The girl who looked back was almost as golden as Linley. She had brown hair streaked with sunlight. She looked strong and capable and, Claire thought, turning to admire her legs in the very short skirt, damn good.

Sexy. No, smart *and* sexy. When she got back to school, she was going to buy a lot more things in a lot more colors—particularly red.

Confidently, maybe even swaggering a little, Claire headed for the party. As she passed Dean's door, she noticed it was half-open. She gave it a push and called, "Hey, come join the party."

No one answered. Claire peered inside. She'd never really looked in Dean's room. He was the only person in the house who kept his door closed at all times. She didn't know what she expected to see. Fanatic neatness? Wild disorder?

It was as bland as a hotel room. A laptop glowed on a table in the corner. Next to it was a half-eaten chocolate doughnut and a half-full beer bottle. Claire wrinkled her nose at the combo.

Then she saw her name on the screen. She frowned and stepped closer.

Yes. It was definitely her name. And Finn's. And Linley's. And even Barrel's.

She read, "So we have a pretty good idea of what happens when good girls go bad. But what happens when bad girls go off the deep end. A summer of sex and drugs and now what can only be called a bitchslap-fest of epic proportions, with über-bad girl Linley at—"

"What are you doing in my room?" Dean's voice was neither lazy nor mocking.

Claire blinked and tore her eyes from the screen. "What is this?" she asked.

"What it is, is none of your business," Dean said.

"Oh, I think it might be," said Claire. And she didn't step back when Dean stepped closer.

"Why don't you just go to the party and forget it," Dean said.

"Why don't you tell me what is going on?" she answered, glancing again at the screen, at the story on the screen. Then, finally, she got it. "You—you're some kind of wannabe writer, aren't you?"

Dean grimaced. "Ouch," he said. "Little Claire grows up."

"You're writing stories about *us*."

"Well, yes. And actually, I have a contract. For a piece for a magazine. So, technically, I'm not a wannabe."

Claire thought of Dean, always watching, never getting involved—except those times he'd said things that seemed to escalate matters, make situations crazier or more out of control.

"You used us," Claire said.

"Everybody uses everybody," said Dean.

"No, they don't," Claire said.

They regarded each other.

Claire said, suddenly, "Does Poppy know?"

"Poppy's an old friend. She knows I'm a writer, that I'm working on something, that I'm this close to the break I need. But not even Poppy knows everything," Dean said.

"So you used your old friend Poppy, too," Claire said.

Dean looked away, then, not quite meeting her eyes.

"You're a scum," said Claire, simply, and walked past him. She stopped in the hall and leaned back in the door. "Dean. Don't think you're leaving. You're staying and helping with cleanup tomorrow. Meanwhile, feel free to join the party and take all the notes you want. I'll be sure to let everybody know so you'll have their full cooperation." She smiled and knew her smile was a threat.

Power. It was good to be queen, she thought and, walking like a queen, went back to Finn and the last party of the summer.

People had started dancing. Unsurprised, Claire saw Linley in the middle, working it dirty with someone Claire had never seen before.

Finn appeared at her side as if he'd be watching for her. Maybe he had, or maybe it was just part of the Finn mojo. He handed her a drink. It had a plastic surfer riding the frozen crest on one side, and a tiny parasol on the other.

Claire had to laugh.

Finn laughed too. "Excellent decorations," he said. "Jodi tells me you planned it all. Amazing girl, Mermaid Claire."

He had noticed. Screw Linley. Claire took a sip of the frozen drink and thought, *Thanks, Jodi.* Jodi was her friend, after all. "Excellent piña colada," she answered. She saw Jodi, then, dancing with Poppy.

She looked . . . happy.

"Yo, look!" Finn waved. Claire recognized Rita and Axel and NOLA and Suzie and some of the other surfers from the hotel. She waved too. Finn peeled away and went to talk to them as a burly figure loomed above Claire.

"Joseph?" said Claire, hardly believing her eyes. She checked the impulse to make certain her hair was pulled back in a Health Department–approved waitress tail.

"Hey," Joseph rumbled. "Didn't think I'd take you up on your invite, didja?" His eyes roamed the room and stopped. "Sweet," he said.

Claire followed his gaze to Linley doing something Claire thought might be called the grind with the guy she remembered as Nicholas or Ned or Nathan from the Jacuzzi.

"I wouldn't share a crossword puzzle with her," Claire said flatly.

Joseph rumbled, this time laughing. "Darlin', that wasn't what I had in mind." His mittlike hand came down on her shoulder in a reassuring pat that would have buckled her knees had she not known Joseph and been prepared. "But she's too young for me, anyway. That one, now, she looks more my style."

"Poppy," said Claire. "Forget it. She bats for the other team."

"Damn," said Joseph. "What a shame."

"Not for whoever she's batting with," Claire retorted.

Her now ex-boss regarded Claire with expressionless eyes for a moment, then went from a rumble to a roar of laughter. His hand descended again to her shoulder, and Claire winced and thought, *bruises*.

"You know, kid, you're all right. I thought you might be a little too East Coast preppie and uptight when I met you, but you're all right. You're gonna do just fine."

"Thanks," said Claire, and meant it. This was high praise,

indeed. She smiled at Joseph, suddenly realizing she would miss him. "You're my favorite boss, now and forever."

"Thatta girl," Joseph said. "You ever need a job, you come back to me." His eyes were sampling the room again, and Claire hid a smile. "Come on," she said, "Poppy's got plenty of friends who play for your team," and led Joseph over to help him hook up. Poppy would know who to put him next to.

Actually, she probably could have done it herself, she realized. She knew plenty of people. People from surfing and people from waiting tables and people from other parties. She knew lots of people, had all kinds of friends. There were Susan and Kerri Lynn, peering into the punch bowl. Carol and Jill, Frankie and Jolene over by the bookshelves, pulling books off and making a book meltdown mess. There were Kathy and Paula from the bookstore, talking to Sari, who ran the only health food store in the world that specialized in doughnuts. And Emily Tech, the computer whiz. And Jan, of course, with some new guy who was . . . wow, very nice on the eyes. A shout from the hot tub told her where Bonnie and Elaine and Jane had chosen to take the first swim of the night. There was Valerie, dancing, and Per and Ben and Maggie and Leah and . . .

And a whole party full of friends, a whole party that she had organized. She, Claire Plimouth.

"Want to dance?" Finn said in her ear, and Claire took another drink of her piña colada and set it down.

"You bet I do," she said, and went to the party.

Nineteen

Claire danced until her feet hurt, and then she danced some more. She talked and laughed and made plans to see people again next summer. She didn't know if they meant it, but she was beginning to think that she did.

She didn't drink much because she wanted to end this party in remembering, not forgetting. She had plenty of time for the other kinds of parties—or maybe she was already starting to get over them.

She danced with Max. She danced with Poppy and then with Jodi. She cut in on Lauren, who'd hooked up with Jospeh. It wasn't what she'd expected—Lauren was an intellectual type who worked at the coffee shop, but who knew? She mentioned, casually, "Dean's little project."

The information that cut both ways. The members of the household suddenly seemed to find any part of the room with Dean in it where they didn't want to be. But others made a point of seeking him out.

Sometime later, very early in the morning, she pulled Finn after her up the stairs and they went to bed. And Claire was glad she'd had a chance to figure out that while there was more to life than sex— much, much more—sex definitely added more to life.

Especially when you did it right, with the right guy. No, person, she corrected herself, smiling in the half-dark of early morning and thinking of Jodi.

She snuggled closer to Finn, happy and sad at the same time. "Finn."

"Mmm," he said.

"You never talk about the future, do you?" Claire asked.

"The future?" he sounded sleepily confused.

"You know, like what you plan to do . . . where you think you'll be in, oh, I don't know, ten years."

"Ten years! Ten years is a long time," said Finn. "I'm happy now. That's good enough."

Suddenly Claire realized that it was. And that Finn didn't talk about the future because he was living it, right now.

"I love you, Finn," she said. "I always will."

Finn took it the way she meant it. He understood. He tightened his arm around her and said, "I love you, too, Mermaid Claire," and she smiled again, with sadness and joy, and fell asleep.

Going domestic on Finn a couple of hours later, Claire slipped out of the bed to find coffee and water, leaving Finn and Barrel still asleep. She was relieved to see the upstairs hall unscathed and drunken body free. She resolved not to think about what the downstairs looked like until she'd had many more cups of coffee and hours of sleep.

She was almost to the stairs when she smelled the smoke. Claire narrowed her eyes. It wasn't stale smoke from last night's party. Actually, now that she thought about it, people had been pretty good about taking their smokes outside.

But someone, here, now, wasn't.

Dean, she thought, torn between anger and exasperation. She went to his door and pushed it open without knocking.

But it wasn't Dean. Dean was gone. The room was empty, computer and Dean free.

"Coward," she muttered, and then, thinking about the massive cleanup ahead, "Shithead."

She left the door open.

Sniffed. Not Poppy or Jodi. Poppy didn't smoke, and Jodi was a random smoker, and was, from the empty appearance of her room, sleeping in Poppy's room.

Not Finn, not me, Claire thought and groaned inwardly. Linley.

Linley's house, Linley's rules, Claire told herself. It didn't matter now. She'd be gone tomorrow. She'd get a new roommate next year, or better yet, share a house. She didn't need Linley, and she definitely didn't feel like dealing with Linley right now.

But she looked in, anyway, as she passed Linley's room.

The door was ajar a crack, and she pushed it slightly wider and looked in.

Linley sat in the big rocking chair by the window, rocking. A saucer heaped with cigarette butts sat on the nearby table. But Linley wasn't smoking. She was just rocking, slowly rocking, back and forth, back and forth.

It gave Claire the creeps. She swallowed. "Linley?" she said softly.

At first, Linley didn't answer. Then she said, "Have you ever had sex in a rocking chair? I have. Or tried to, with Max. In this rocking chair. Of course, it wasn't in here at the time, it was downstairs. It didn't work out very well, but that didn't matter because Max and I . . . Max and I . . . Max . . ." Her voice broke.

To her horror and dismay, Claire saw Linley was crying. Claire ran across the room and put her hands on the arm of the chair to stop the rocking. "Linley," she said. "Oh, Linley."

Linley was really crying now. No, not crying, bawling. Howling. She doubled over like an animal and wailed. Claire tried to put her arms around Linley, but Linley knocked them away.

"Don't!" she gasped. "Don't touch me!"

"I'm sorry, Linley," Claire said. "I . . ." Linley was still mad at her. Fair enough. Claire had been pretty awful to Linley.

Linley said, "No one can touch me. I won't . . . I can't . . ." And she cried, if possible, harder. Claire gripped the arm of the chair, trying to think.

A sound in the doorway made her look up. Jodi stood there, her eyes wide, her face pale. "Close the door," Claire ordered, and Jodi obeyed automatically. Then she came to kneel on the other side of the chair.

"G-go awaaay," Linley wailed.

"No," said Jodi. Her eyes met Claire's over Linley's bowed head. She mouthed, looking almost panic-stricken, *I've never seen her cry before.*

Aloud, Jodi said, "Linley, stop."

But Linley kept crying, heartbreaking sounds that hurt to hear.

Claire looked around for a tissue, went to the bathroom, and came back with a roll of toilet paper and a damp towel and tried to wipe Linley's face.

Again, Linley struck Claire's hand away. "You'll make yourself sick," Claire whispered. She looked around, feeling helpless, wishing she could figure out what to do.

"I'm sorry, Linley," Jodi was saying. "Okay? I'm sorry."

That was when Claire saw the pictures. They'd tipped off the little table by the chair and had spilled across the floor. She picked them up and began, mechanically, to put them in some sort of order. Linley pictures. Linley's parents' pictures. Linley and Max pictures.

And her hand stopped over the odd picture out, the picture of schoolgirl Linley with the older girl who looked like her.

"Jodi," said Claire. "Who is this?"

Jodi gave the photo a perfunctory glance and said, "Don't know . . . Linley. Linley! You've got to stop."

Claire turned the picture over. Childish handwriting declared, "Caro and Me."

"Linley," said Claire, looking up. "Who's this? Who's Caro?"

Linley stopped crying on a sharp intake of breath. She didn't move. Claire could hear her breathing, harsh, raspy breaths. In a low voice, she finally said, "My sister."

"What?" Jodi rocked back on her heels. "Your sister? You don't have a sister. You . . . never told me about a sister. You said you were an only child."

"My parents just had me, and me they didn't see," said Linley.

"Right," Jodi said, and Claire remembered Linley tossing the line off, too. Laughing. She could get away with anything because her parents were so busy being social citizens. Fund-raisers and society photo-ops kept them off Linley's case.

"You have a sister," Claire said, to make sure.

Linley finally looked up. Her face was swollen, her eyes red. Tears still ran, silently now, down her face. She made no effort to wipe them away. "Had," she said. "Had a sister. She drowned when our boat went over in the bay. A freak squall. I held on to the bottom of the sailboat, but the current took her away."

"You had a sister?" Jodi seemed stunned.

Claire reached out and tentatively patted Linley's arm. This time, Linley didn't even seem to notice. "It was my fault," she said. "I wanted to go sailing. For my birthday. I was nine. Just Caro and me. She was seventeen, and I thought she could do anything."

"Oh, Linley," whispered Jodi.

"We went over and I grabbed on and she was gone. Just like that. I called and called. But she never came back. Another boat came and found me and they looked too. Everybody looked. But she was gone."

Linley looked at Jodi, then at Claire. "I keep thinking maybe she's still alive somewhere. That she just hit her head and one day I'll look down the beach and there she'll be. She liked to sail, not to surf . . . but she might be a surfer now. She could be. She always . . . liked the water."

"It wasn't your fault," Claire blurted out. "Oh Linley."

Linley's face twisted. "Oh, I know that. Everyone said so. Even my parents. But after Caro . . . after it happened, it was like I didn't exist. I was so good. I was the best kid ever. I got great grades and cleaned my room . . . I spent more time with the housekeepers than with them after that. They started this scholarship fund in Caro's memory and then got this whole party life and they'd kiss me good-bye every night before they left and then I wouldn't see them again until the next night."

Words spilled from Linley. She was hiccupping and crying and she couldn't seem to stop. "So I gave up. I decided I could do anything I wanted, what the hell. It freaked them out, but they didn't really care. Our family died when Caro died, and it wasn't my fault, but what difference did that make?"

She stopped. Full stop. "I can't do this," she said.

Jodi grabbed the towel and wiped Linley's face, almost roughly. "Do what?" she said.

"Live," said Linley.

"Linley, I've never met anybody more alive than you are!" said Claire. "You make everyone around you alive, too."

"Truth," agreed Jodi. She put down the towel and unspooled some toilet tissue and held it to Linley's nose. "Blow."

"Everyone you love leaves you," Linley said dully, as if she was talking to herself. "No matter what. I thought Max . . . I loved Max. I thought he would stay. That it would be okay, maybe, then. But . . ."

"Max knew. About your sister?" Jodi asked.

"I told him," Linley said. And then, randomly, "He came back, but not really. He's going to be a monk. Did you know that? A monk!"

"A monk?" Jodi said, sounding horrified.

Claire remembered that first real conversation with Max on the beach. India. A rinpoche . . .

"A Buddhist monk," she said. "That's what he's been doing. Studying Buddhism."

"Why? *Why?*" Linley said, and then, "I've been a shitty friend. I'm sorry. Jodi, Claire, I'm sorry. I . . ."

She started to cry again.

"Get Max," Claire said to Jodi.

Jodi got Max. When he came, awake, as Claire had known he would be, she said, "You and Linley need to talk."

And then, because she was Claire and liked to organize things so no one made any mistakes, she shook Linley's shoulder and said, "Linley, talk to Max."

She followed Jodi out of the room, closing the door quietly behind them.

After the scene in Linley's room, the chaos downstairs didn't seem so bad. What were a few bodies on chairs and sofas, a sea of plates and bottles and party debris?

Picking through the wreckage, Claire and Jodi managed coffee and then went back upstairs, each balancing two cups. Linley's door was still closed. It was quiet.

Jodi said, "You think she'll be all right?"

Claire said, "I don't know. Maybe someday."

And then they went back into their private lives.

They cleaned all day, Claire and Finn, Poppy and Jodi. Max came down and waded in not long after they started. Linley, quiet and subdued, came down much later.

She cleaned without talking. But no one was talking much. No one mentioned Dean, although Jodi did tape a sign on the Dumpster that said DEAN in big letters.

Finally Finn heaved a last bag of garbage out, turned, and said, "Surf?"

"Surf," said Linley, almost the first word she'd said all day.

So they went surfing, all of them together, one last time.

Poppy and Max and Barrel sat on the beach. Finn and Claire and Jodi and Linley mostly floated in the fat waves, catching random rides that didn't really amount to much.

Linley and Jodi drifted down the current a ways, and Claire saw that they were talking. She surfed her hand through the water and smiled up at Finn. "I'll be back," she said suddenly, and knew it was true.

His eyes crinkled. "You think?"

"I think." She paused, then said, "I don't think I'm cut out to be a banker after all. My folks have my sister and my brother. That's plenty."

"What do you think you'll do?" Finn asked.

"I don't know yet. Finish school, probably. Think about it. About this. About life." She laughed because it sounded so corny, and Finn laughed, too.

"Whatever you do, you'll be good at it. Look how you caught on to surfing."

"Oh, I'll keep surfing. You can count on that." Claire took a deep breath. "Finn."

"Here."

"If you decide you need to get to Hawaii, I'll take care of Barrel for you. Call me and I'll come get him, or you can bring him to me. I think of myself as, well, I don't know. His mom. His parents may not be together, but they've got this great kid, and they could share him. . . ."

Super stupid, Claire, she thought.

But Finn was grinning. "Barrel's mom," he said. He nodded. "I like it."

"So you'll think about it?" she asked.

"I think I'll do it. Someday. Soon."

"Someday," Claire agreed.

"We're going to be late," said Claire.

"With me driving? Never," Jodi said.

"Okay, we're going to be dead," Claire gasped as Jodi crossed three lanes and a truck to make the exit ramp to the airport.

"Not an option," said Jodi.

When they slammed into the short-term parking, Linley said, "You did say, Jodi, that Poppy had addressed your speed problem?"

"One speed issue at a time," Jodi retorted. She tapped her watch. "Tick, tick, tick."

Claire looked across the roof of the car at Jodi. Jodi sighed. "Yes, I have a problem. Yes, I'm going to address it. Am addressing it. Have quit. Will have my work cut out for me. . . ."

"Okay," said Claire.

Linley was hauling luggage and ass toward the terminal.

"Listen, keep in touch, okay?" Jodi said.

"I will," Claire promised. "And I won't be gone that long."

"You did mention that," Jodi said. She grabbed another suitcase, and she and Claire hustled after Linley.

Finn appeared, seemingly out of nowhere, almost mowing several people down with the large, carefully-wrapped-toairline-requirements object he'd just pulled from his illegally parked van, where Barrel was barking from the window.

"Mermaid Claire," he said. "Good, I caught you."

"Finn?" Claire said.

"Here," he said. And thrust the object at her. Claire saw Linley and Jodi laughing. "It's a surfboard," he explained. "For you. I picked it out and it was just ready this morning."

"Finn. Oh, Finn," Claire cried, and hugged him hard.

They kissed one last time. Then Finn said, "I have a lesson. Got to go. See you on the next wave."

"See you," Claire said, hugging the surfboard now and laughing and crying at the same time.

"Tick, tick!" shouted Jodi, and Claire, with one last look at the disappearing van, went to catch her plane.

The surfboard slowed them down, but Claire still made it. Outside the security gates, she felt herself wanting to cry again.

"Don't get mushy," Linley ordered. "It's just the end of one summer, not the end of all things."

"No," said Claire. "Besides, I'll see you back at school."

"And we'll find a house."

"And continue the party," said Jodi.

Linley pressed something into Claire's hand. "For when you get up in the air," she said.

And then Claire had gone through the scanners and was boarding the plane, waving one last time at Jodi and Linley.

The plane banked and climbed. Claire unclenched her fist

and looked down. It was what Linley had called a "no-fear-of-flying" pill.

Linley was staying on a few more days at the house with Max and Finn and Jodi and Poppy. Then she'd be back east for school and she and Claire would look for an off-campus house and some new roommates. Max would be heading back to India to study to become a monk.

Linley would be okay. Never happy with losing Max, but who was happy all the time? She'd deal with her sister being gone probably all her life. But now she'd deal.

Jodi and Poppy were going to live together, a summer romance that had legs after all. Finn would stay in the old house on the beach until Linley's uncle got back later in the fall. Then he and Barrel would move on.

The land fell away.

Claire looked down at the pill. It seemed like only yesterday that she'd been so terrified and stoned stupid as they'd flown into the sunset.

She tipped her hand, and the pill fell out and rolled away under a seat. Gone.

Claire leaned back and waited to place her drink order. It had been quite a summer. She wasn't the same girl who had been on that first plane. She wasn't sure who she was, but she wasn't that girl.

One thing I do know for sure, though, Claire thought, and smiled.

I'm not afraid of flying anymore.

ABOUT THE AUTHORS

Todd Strasser is the author of more than 130 books for teens and middle graders including *The Diving Bell* and the Help! I'm Trapped In . . . series, as well as numerous award-winning YA novels including *The Accident, The Wave, Give A Boy A Gun, Boot Camp,* and *If I Grow Up.* His books have been translated into more than a dozen languages, and several have been adapted into feature films. He has also written for television, newspapers, and magazines such as the *New Yorker, Esquire,* and the *New York Times.* His most recent novel is the YA thriller, *Wish You Were Dead.*

Nola Thacker is the author of nearly one hundred books for middle graders and teens, including the thrillers *Secret Santa, The Ripper, Sister Dearest, Mirror, Mirror,* and *The Bride* (all written under her pseudonym, D. E. Athkins).

Need a distraction?

Lauren Strasnick

Serena Robar

Amy Reed

Christine Johnson

Deb Caletti

Lisa Schroeder

Eileen Cook

Charity Tahmaseb & Darcy Vance

Go Ahead, Ask Me.
Nico Medina & Billy Merrell

TEEN.SimonandSchuster.com
From Simon Pulse | Published by Simon & Schuster

LOOKING FOR THE PERFECT BEACH READ?

FROM SIMON PULSE
PUBLISHED BY SIMON & SCHUSTER